By Larry McMurtry

Lonesome Dove
The Desert Rose
Cadillac Jack
Somebody's Darling
Terms of Endearment
All My Friends Are Going to Be Strangers
Moving On
The Last Picture Show
In a Narrow Grave: Essays on Texas
Leaving Cheyenne
Horseman, Pass By

Cadillac Jack

a novel by ——

Larry McMurtry

WITH A NEW PREFACE

A TOUCHSTONE BOOK
Published by *SIMON & SCHUSTER, Inc.*
NEW YORK

First Touchstone Edition, 1985

Published by Simon & Schuster, Inc.
Simon & Schuster Building
Rockefeller Center
1230 Avenue of the Americas
New York, New York 10020

TOUCHSTONE and colophon are registered trademarks of Simon & Schuster, Inc.

Designed by Irving Perkins Associates

Manufactured in the United States of America

10 9 8 7 6 5 4 3 2 1

10 9 8 7 6 5 4 3 2 1 Pbk.

Library of Congress Cataloging in Publication Data

McMurtry, Larry.
Cadillac Jack.

I. Title.
PS3563.A319C3   1982   813'.54   82-5962
                                           AACR2

ISBN 0-671-45445-5
ISBN 0-671-55541-3 Pbk.

For Diane Keaton
Queen of the Swap-Meets

Cadillac Jack

PREFACE

Perhaps the most severe drawback to a long career in writing is that one is forced to read the same author every day for a great many years.

The author, of course, is oneself.

Great scholars may spend a lifetime in daily investigation of Shakespeare or Dante, but few novelists are much like great scholars, and even fewer are Shakespeare or Dante.

To read oneself every morning and afternoon for more than a quarter of a century, as I have now done, is at best a strange chore. As thousands, then hundreds of thousands, then millions of one's own sentences cross the page in front of one, they seem, each year, to move more predictably. They may plod, or they may rush, but whatever pleasure one may once have taken in their lilting rhythms or their little graces has long since vanished.

At least, mine has. I rather enjoyed the daily tramp of my sentences up until about the time that I wrote *Terms of Endearment*. Midway through that book the endless parade of these sentences began to lose its fascination for me; it was as if they were parading in a circle. I began to have the distinct impression that sentences which ought to have been embedded in earlier books had somehow wiggled free and were circling around again.

And not just sentences, either: paragraphs, characters, relationships and motifs all seemed deadeningly familiar.

I have always had a horror of self-repetition, the quicksand that swallows so many middle-aged novelists, and was not cheered to find it swallowing me. I had no interest in recycling my own *oeuvre* a few sentences at a time. And yet it seemed to me that that was more or less what I was doing.

Cadillac Jack is a response to this dilemma. The book's

beginning was simple. I was standing on a street corner in Washington, D.C., one day, waiting for the light to change. A black man was waiting, too. Just as the light changed a Cadillac drew up in front of us, and a jolly gentleman waved at the black man, who immediately brightened. "Ho, ho, Cadillac Jack," he said, waving. The car passed on, and I crossed the street a happier man. Life had just handed me a title; all I had to do was find a book for it.

I decided to seek it in the world of the swap meets, flea markets, junk dealers and small-time auctions, which I had haunted for many years as a bookscout—it had always seemed to me an interesting and somewhat neglected sub-culture. Maybe it could be made to yield some fresh-seeming sentences, at least.

In the event, my sentences didn't hasten to reform, but I wrote the book anyway, determined to hang in there, if only because I really had no place else to hang.

The book that resulted seems a little odd. A friend remarked that it reminded her of certain Diane Arbus photographs of people with their love objects, which were sometimes, but not always, other people. The friend thought the novel particularly resembled an Arbus photo-graph of a woman who had dressed her monkey in a snow suit.

I am easily convinced by almost any description of one of my books, and immediately began to think of *Cadillac Jack* as the sort of book in which someone would dress a monkey in a snowsuit. Early in the narrative someone does put two pugs on a dinner table, which is just as bizarre.

I rarely think of my own books, once I finish them, and don't welcome the opportunity, much less the necessity, of thinking about them. The moving finger writes, and keeps moving; thinking about them while I'm writing them is often hard enough. Writing a book that holds one's own interest until it can be finished is, for the middle-aged and reasonably prolific novelist, a heavier challenge than many would like to admit. I wrote two drafts of this one, bur-dened the whole way by a sense that something was lacking. I remain uncertain whether the lack was in the tale, or merely in the main character, Cadillac Jack.

What's certain is that Jack is a very detached man. I might have called the book *Portrait of the Artist as a Detached Man*, except that Jack isn't an artist. He's a scout—a man who finds things, not a man who makes things. Yet the character of mine he most reminds me of is Danny Deck, a young writer who raced across the lawn of my imagination some twelve years ago, in a book called *All My Friends Are Going to Be Strangers*. Both men are constantly being reminded that they aren't normal, usually by women they're in bed with. Danny Deck becomes convinced that his detachment is a by-product of the artistic vocation; he comes to resent that vocation because it seems to him it deprives him of any hope of a settled domestic life.

Jack doesn't resent *his* vocation—antique scouting—and doesn't rage at his exile from the hearth and the bassinet, as Danny does. The latter was a bruised optimist, convinced that he could love one woman forever if he could just rid himself of the alienating demands of art. Jack isn't so sanguine. When he yearns, he yearns for individuals, not for a home. He recognizes that he is most at home when he is in motion, roaming the country in his search for exceptional antiques.

As an antique scout, Jack is a student, and a fairly acute one, of the way in which people relate to their objects. He would like to hope, at first, that people are better at loving other people than they are at loving objects, but his bleak conclusion is that human love is unstable, whether directed at another human or at a Sung vase. The people he meets are as fickle in regard to their *objets* as they are with one another; they cling to a fine thing for years and then get rid of it in an hour, much as they might a fine person. They become indifferent alike to hall clocks and spouses. In Jack's world, only obsession seems to generate tenacity; moderate love, whether between people and people or people and things, seldom seems to last very long.

These dark pessimistic meats are stuffed in a light pastry

of social satire, most of it directed at the ways of Washington, D.C. I had been reading Pope and Waugh in the year I wrote the book; I had also been pondering my twelve years in Washington. The city, as the old nest collector observed, is a graveyard of styles. It is also a city of museums, and its defining attitudes are curatorial. Indeed, its ponderous social life is not unlike a museum exhibit, in which a good many of the major canvases have long needed dusting. The book became a kind of exhibit of capitol portraits, done, in so far as I was able, as Alexander Pope might have done them.

To the portraits in my capitol exhibit I added a parallel sequence of Jack's women, done with perhaps a bit more charity.

The textures of the book are sometimes appealing, but what of the aftertaste? Is detachment of the sort Jack manifests a workable subject for fiction? Boringness, for example, is not a workable subject; it only leaves the reader bored. Will Jack's detachment frustrate the reader as much as Jack himself frustrates the various women he escapes? Do readers, many of whom are women, resent detachment as much as women do?

Having raised that question, the teller is happy to take refuge behind the tale.

—Larry McMurtry
October, 1984

Book I

Chapter I _____

Boog warned me about Washington, but until I saw the rich lady set her pugs on the dinner table, I didn't take him seriously. A staple of my relationship with Boog is that he warns and I ignore.

"It's because you're self-made that you're so reckless," he said. "I wisht I was self-made."

Actually, to look at Boog, you would hardly think he was made at all, not so much because he's fat and ugly as because of his shiny suits and slicked-down hair. His ties always have silver in them, augmented by colors like yellow, or puke green, a style acquired during the twenty years he spent being a Congressional aide to a cheap politician from East Houston.

It was during those years that he learned his way around Washington well enough to be able to warn me about it, though probably he would have warned me even if he hadn't known what he was talking about. Boog freely admits that it's easier to give advice than it is to lead an interesting life.

"D.C.'s diffrunt from Waxahachie," he maintained. "It's filt up with them stump-suckin' women."

One of Boog's problems is that he insists on speaking in terms that can be understood by the common citizens of Winkler County, Texas, the county his family happened to own. His brothers and sisters had all finally killed themselves off in adulteries and small-plane crashes and other popular forms of risk-taking, leaving him sole heir to Winkler County and the fifteen million barrels of oil that were said to flow beneath it. He's not reluctant to spend his money, either. The day I met him I sold him a narwhal tusk for $3,000 and I've been selling to him regularly ever since.

What I am is a scout. My trade name—Cadillac Jack—

derives from the fact that nowadays I do the bulk of my traveling in a pearl-colored Cadillac with peach velour interior, a comfortable vehicle in which to roam America.

I roam it a lot, too, continually crossing and recrossing the continent in pursuit of objects of every description. I've sold Italian lace and Lalique glass, French snuffboxes and pre-World War II Coke bottles, English silver and Chinese porcelain, Purdey shotguns and Colt revolvers, Apache basketry and Turkish ceramics, Greek cheese-boards, Coptic pottery, Depression glass, Peruvian mummy-wrappings, kilims, Aubussons, icons, Tibetan textiles, camel-pads, *netsuke*, scarabs, jewels, rare tools, early cameras and typewriters, barometers, Sèvres, miniatures, lacquer, screens, tapestries, classic cars, railroadiana, Disneyana, Eskimo carvings, Belgian firearms, musical instruments, autographs, Swiss music boxes, Maori war clubs, and so on.

If you happen to want a World War I parachute—and a lot of people seem to—or a fly-catching machine—never patented but produced in some quantity by a German immigrant in Flatonia, Texas, in the 1890s—I'll try to come up with one. Those fly-catching machines are really wonderful: the flies stick themselves to a little honey-covered roller and are then scraped off into a pan to be fed to the chickens, sort of like crackerjacks.

Most scouts specialize, but not me. I'm too curious, too restless, too much in love with the treasure hunt. I keep on the move constantly, covering as much as I can of the vast grid of dealers, collectors, accumulators, pack rats, antique shops, thrift shops, junk shops, estate sales, country auctions, bankruptcy sales, antique shows, flea markets, and garage sales that covers America like a screen. Nobody can check every square on the grid—I once spent a profitable three weeks hitting nothing but garage sales in the Chicago area alone—but I pride myself on covering more of it regularly than any other scout. I buy and sell as I go, seldom keeping anything more than a week or two. My kind of buying is like my kind of falling in love: a matter of immediate eye appeal. I fall in love with objects, each in its turn, my only problem being that as I get older I also get pickier. First-rate objects don't excite me anymore: I want exceptional objects, and those can take a lot of looking for.

I wouldn't be driving the pearl-colored Cadillac had it not been for an extraordinary Sung vase that happened to be in Mom and Pop Cullen's junk barn in De Queen, Arkansas. It was priced at $20 and surrounded by sets of reproduction fireplace equipment priced at $150 the set. The vase was so obviously an exceptional thing that I had one of my rare attacks of conscience.

"I don't know," I said. "That vase looks to me like it could be worth two or three hundred dollars. I wouldn't feel right paying you less than a hundred for it."

In saying as much I was breaking the first law of scouting, which is that you never implant in the mind of an owner the notion that something he or she has for sale might be worth more than its stated price. It's not simply that the owners are then likely to raise the price: it's that they may freeze altogether and decide not to sell the object until they can figure out what it's really worth—something they usually never get around to doing.

But I knew the Cullens—they just sold junk because it was easier than farming, and they weren't obsessed with prices. I had bought a good Parker shotgun and some nice Tennessee butter crocks from them on my last visit and all I had in mind was to cheat them $80 less.

Momma Cullen was practically insulted, as I had known she would be. She didn't suspect me of mere foolishness—she suspected me of offering charity, since I had prospered sufficiently by that time to be sporting a new Buick Estate Wagon while she and Old Man Cullen still had the same worn-out Dodge pickup and the same dusty, run-down junk barn. Momma Cullen was a large woman who seldom got up from the big Sears and Roebuck chair she installed herself in every morning. The chair had once been covered in blue imitation velvet, but had worn so white in places that it reminded me of the whiskers on an old dog's muzzle.

"Aw, that thang," Momma Cullen said, squinting at the

vase through her bifocals. "Why that dern thang won't even hold flowers. Where'd that thang come from, Poppa?"

Old Man Cullen looked at the vase for about five minutes, scratching his leathery neck and trying to get his thoughts together.

"Momma, I guess it come from that Yankee schoolteacher," he said. "That one that gassed herself. I don't know where else we would have got it."

I gave them the $20 and drank a Delaware Punch with them, to help smooth over the insult. De Queen seemed to be the only place left in America where Delaware Punches still came out of the pop machines, all of which were so old themselves that I could have sold them for big money in Houston or L.A.

"Now, Jack, don't you drive too fast," Momma Cullen said, as I was leaving. "You ought to get married and raise a family, but if you don't, look out for some of that Depression glass. I'll pay for that stuff."

Old Man Cullen just stood and looked. I don't think he had entirely satisfied himself about the origins of the vase, and was still slowly working back in his memory, from one junk buy to the next, hoping to come to the one that had contained the vase. Even unobsessed dealers like to remember where their wares came from.

I wrapped the vase well and put it in a small, brass-bound nineteenth-century traveling trunk I kept for just such a purpose. Naturally I realized that I had just become rich—or at least rich enough to buy the car of my dreams, which at that time belonged to a Cadillac collector in Ypsilanti—but I didn't feel elated, or even happy. I knew perfectly well that I had just shot up and over a peak, and could expect to work the down side of the hill for several months or years. I might live to find objects as great as the vase, but not for $20. The discrepancy between quality and price that made the find almost miraculous was a once-or-twice-in-a-lifetime thing. I could wander through thousands of flea markets and scale an Everest of junk without a combination such as that one coming up again, and I knew it.

Five months later the vase auctioned at Sotheby's for $106,000, to a discreet Swiss collector who had probably never happened through De Queen.

Of course, Boog was right not to credit me with much sophistication. In my rodeo days I had seen a lot of America, but mostly only its filling stations and rodeo arenas. Once I became a scout I tended to spend a lot of time in the parking lots of the same arenas, since that's where a lot of America's flea markets are held.

All in all, I had not exactly lived a high-rent life, except for one week I spent in the Beverly Wilshire hotel in Los Angeles, as a guest of Universal Studios. The reason I was their guest was because they were contemplating a film about my career as a world champion bulldogger.

During my stay at the hotel I rode in the elevator with Muhammad Ali and thought I saw Steve McQueen in the coffee shop. But soon the week was up and nothing came of the movie.

I might have mastered the freeway system in every major American city, but the truth was I spent most of my time with people like Mom and Pop Cullen, who would have considered Waxahachie a frightening metropolis. Stardom on the flea-market circuit, as Boog well knew, does not necessarily equip one to dine with the power elite.

Which brings me to the second part of Boog's admonition: the part about the stump-sucking women.

Chapter II _____

Some horses are called stump-suckers because they have a penchant for chewing wood. Once they get the taste they'll gnaw on stumps, fence posts, boards, and the corners of feed sheds. This neurotic habit is more apt to manifest itself in highly strung, overbred animals than in your common plugs.

Cowboys universally distrust the stump-sucking horse as being a beast with a mental disorder that renders them unfit for the long-term, trust-laden relationships they like to maintain with their mounts.

Boog seemed to hold the women of Washington in much the same distrust.

I have never learned to distrust women. For some reason the motion involved is foreign to me. However, I am quick to notice when I've wandered into a game whose rules are totally unfamiliar to me, as was the case with my first Georgetown dinner party.

The party was at the home of a senator named Penrose, and I was taken there by Cindy Sanders—a California princess I had met and become infatuated with only a few hours earlier. Cindy would not have been loath to instruct me in the niceties of social behavior, but unfortunately she was seated several yards away, across a good seventeenth-century table covered with equally good nineteenth-century damask. She had been placed there to entertain an aged statesman named Dunscombe Cotswinkle, an old man with a jaw like a Carolina mule.

It was obvious even to someone as naive as myself that Cindy had been assigned Cotswinkle because she was the most beautiful woman there, whereas he was the most important man. Unfortunately, the appropriateness of the match-up was lost on Cotswinkle—his mind was elsewhere, or at least I judged it to be, since he kept looking down the table and shouting "Is that you, Winston?" at a nervous little French journalist whose name was not Winston.

I was seated between two well-dressed ladies, neither of whom gave the slightest indication that they knew I was there. They were not young, but both were too modishly done up to be described as old. Evidently they were somewhat testy about their placement at the table, and it was hard to blame them, since each had an ugly congressman on the side not occupied by me.

It was not lost on my dinner partners that the younger and prettier women had been distributed among such senators and minor press lords who happened to be there.

"Pencil will never learn," one whispered to the other, across my *coq au vin*.

Pencil Penrose was our hostess, an ostensibly giddy blonde whose real name was Penserilla.

"It doesn't matter," the other lady said. "There's no one here anyway except Jake and Dunny, and I don't want to talk to them. Dunny's deaf as a brass pig, and Jake wouldn't even talk to me when I was married to him."

Dunny was obviously old Cotswinkle, whereas Jake was the eminent columnist John C. V. Ponsonby, who was seated directly across from me, so deeply bored by the deficiencies of the company that he had lapsed into what appeared to be a coma. He ate no food, but retained enough motor reflex to empty his wine glass into his mouth from time to time.

Ponsonby, by no means unimportant, had his hostess on his left and Lilah Landry on his right. Lilah was the beautiful if somewhat gangly widow of a former Secretary of State. Her tumbling red hair, dizzy smile, and trend-setting wardrobe could be seen daily on the local talk show she hostessed.

Luckily, I had seen it that very morning, while breakfasting at Boog's. The show was called *Win a Country* and matched a panel of columnists, ex-Cabinet members, and socially prominent diplomats against a computer called Big Hank. In order to win the country in question the panelists had to make instant choices between bribery, trade benefits, military aid, covert infiltration, saturation bombing and the like, though all Lilah had to do was exhibit her hair, wardrobe, and cleavage, and occasionally employ her abundant deep Georgia gift of gab to get some taciturn diplomat to talk.

If either of the ladies beside me had turned and suddenly required speech of some kind, I guess I would have dropped Boog's name, for despite his vulgar talk and silver ties Boog's was a name to conjure with, in Washington. His big Victorian house in Cleveland Park was constantly filled to the gills with politicians, lobbyists, aides of all species, committee persons, agency persons, journalists, and lawyers. Some of them were there because Boog had a special faucet in his kitchen that ran Jack Daniel's, while others came because they lusted after Boss, Boog's famous wife; but whatever their individual compulsions, they all liked and respected Boog, the professional's professional when it came to Hill politics.

Of course, the minute I had stepped into the Penrose mansion that night I began to canvas the *objets*, a habit I can't control. A scout scouts, even when purchase seems hopeless. It was hard to concentrate on Pencil Penrose when she happened to be standing next to the magnificent Belgian hall clock in her front foyer.

It's not that I dislike people, or that I'm incurious about them, either. I want to look at the people, but their objects keep jumping in front of them, demanding my attention. Sometimes I tell myself that the best way to get to know people is to first study the objects among which they place themselves, but for all I know that may be pure bullshit. It may simply be that I've been subsumed by my vocation. Until I've sized up a place and separated the good pieces from the fillers I just can't seem to concentrate on the people.

Cindy Sanders was long of limb, but short of patience. Her approach to life was emphatic, an approach she shared with my two former wives.

After ten minutes of watching me eye the ormolu, Cindy expressed herself by coming over and giving me an elbow in the ribs that would have done credit to an NBA guard. In fact, she had once been involved with an NBA guard.

"Stop looking at the furniture," she said. "You'll never own any of it."

"That's okay," I said. "I don't deal in French furniture much."

She gave me a smile that would have sold about a million tubes of any toothpaste.

"Stop yukking around and talk to these people," she said. "You said you knew Big John. They'd love some fresh poop on Big John."

"Is that the only reason you brought me?" I asked. "Because I know Big John?"

The question seemed to interest her. She tilted her head to one side for a moment, a gesture I took to be introspective. A moment was enough. Her purse might be a jumble, but not her soul.

"Naw," she said. "It wasn't decisive, which doesn't mean you can just stand around. I expect a little social support when I ask a man out."

"I see," I said. "If I turn out to be a dud people will think you're slipping, right?"

Cindy laughed, a loud California laugh that boomed right out into the room, startling a number of pale people who were sipping drinks and having muted conversations nearby. I loved it. It was such a healthy laugh that it even affected my scrotum, which immediately tightened. Her laugh reminded me of the absolutely confident way she had ripped a check out of her checkbook that afternoon, when she paid me for a carful of cowboy artifacts.

"I'm not slipping," she said, faintly amused by the thought that anyone could suppose she might be.

Then she turned on her heel and marched off to start a conversation with our hostess, Pencil Penrose.

Chapter III _____

One of my recurrent dreams is of driving backward down the highway of my life.

When the dream begins I will usually just be drifting gently backward in the pearly Cadillac over some broad, beautiful stretch of Interstate—perhaps the wonderful stretch of I–90 between Buffalo and Sheridan, Wyoming, with the Big Horn Mountains off to the north.

But as the dream progresses the cuts get faster and I regress through ten years of cars, back at least to the GMC pickup I used during my first year on the rodeo circuit. The roads get worse, too—often I find myself zooming backward over the gritty wastes near Monahans, Texas, before the little psychic balance bar that keeps me from becoming an insane person tilts me back toward wakefulness.

Once in a while one of my wives is with me, in the dream —always Coffee, my first wife, the more pliable of the two. Everyone called her Coffee because she drank so much of it. From dawn to midnight, if Coffee was awake, she was never without a cup with a swallow or two left in it. Her kisses tasted of mountain-grown Folger, and I could never make love to her without the absurd conviction that Mrs. Olson—the Swedish lady in the Folger commercial—was apt to pop in on us while we were fucking, in order to compliment us on our choice of brands.

Coffee allowed me to drag her around America for nearly a year before she bailed out and went back to Austin to work in one of Boss Miller's real estate offices.

Kate, my second wife, also worked for Boss, but in the Houston office. Boss also had offices in Dallas, Georgetown, and Middleburg, and was waiting impatiently for several young Texas cities to get rich enough to be worth her time. Kate was hard at work when I walked in one day with a suit of samurai armor I hoped to fob off on Boog. During the two years we were married most of our sex took place on the vast couch in Boss's seldom-used office, in hectic moments late in the day when Kate was giving a client time to get a little snockered before showing him a three-million-dollar property.

Kate was a true saleswoman, in the way that I am a true scout. The thought of all that money brought a flush to her face, and if I happened to be around, the flush would often spread downward and engulf us. There was never time to undress, or lay around enjoying the afterglow. Kate would be off down Memorial Drive in her Pontiac convertible, a beer in the hand whose wrist was crooked over the steering wheel. The other hand would be holding her long dark blond hair on top of her head, in an effort to cool her neck and face so she wouldn't look as if she had been doing what in fact she had just been doing.

"I don't care, I like to fuck on the fly. It's better," Kate said, when I teased her about it. In that respect she was the opposite of Coffee, who would drift around and drink a gallon of coffee, listen to several albums, and watch five or six TV shows, ignoring or simply failing to notice gestures from me that other women would have interpreted as passes—only to discover while she was brushing her teeth that she felt a little passionate. Sex was not among the things that Coffee was emphatic about.

There was never any question about my dragging Kate around America. She might have been to Dallas once or twice, but that was it. For Kate, Houston was a sufficient universe, a fact even my dream mechanism seemed to respect.

Boog would have given his eyeteeth to fuck her, but his eyeteeth were in no danger.

About Coffee I'm not so sure. The mistake I made with Coffee was to assume that because we both liked to spend all our time buying things we would naturally have a happy marriage.

The element of miscalculation in that judgment was small but crucial. I liked to buy old things, whereas Coffee liked to buy new things. I bought Sung vases, but Coffee bought Halstons and Steuben glass. She never went anyplace where she might wear a Halston, but that was not the point. Buying the thing was the point.

The problem was never one of money: the problem was that I had become an object-snob. Coffee had reasonably good taste, but mine was better. She loved modern furniture and was constantly buying chairs and lamps, but they were always a cut below the really classic modern chairs and lamps. She bought strange angular chairs, and beanbags you were supposed to sit on. She even bought a custom-made leather chair in the shape of a hippo. It didn't look like a chair, but it could be sat in, if you were willing.

The lamps were apt to be made from ostrich eggs or kettledrums. She even bought one made from a small Chinese boat—not an easy lamp to describe, much less to read by. Pretty soon our modest home in Houston contained more chairs than there would ever be guests, and more lamps than there were sockets to plug them in.

When it came down to it, I loved Coffee but couldn't tolerate her objects. She had been reluctant to leave Austin in the first place and of course went right back. What she really liked to do was talk on the phone when nothing was happening around the real estate office—when she discovered that she could do that without having to put up with my antiques she was delighted. I had traded a phone freak in Milwaukee out of some very sophisticated mobile equipment, and in time ate up thousands of American miles while chatting with Coffee, who had not left Austin since her return.

One of the things she was most emphatic about was that buying old things was an unhealthy habit. In her view the suggestion that old things were often better than new things was an affront to life. She had managed to get through the University of Texas while remaining totally unaware of the existence of people on the order of Mao Tse-tung, and I even discovered one day to my shock that she thought World War II had occurred in the nineteenth century, although her own father had fought in it.

"Oh well, Daddy was real young at the time," she said, not really interested in the question.

Her determined rejection of history fascinated Boog, who was better read historically than anyone I knew. On nights when he wasn't too drunk to hold a book, he read himself to sleep with Thucydides, Livy, Suetonius, Gibbon, and Napier. Every ugly suit he owned had a raggedy Penguin paperback in the inside pocket, always history. Naturally he found Coffee's attitude perverse and charming. Coffee couldn't be bought outright, with money, but who was to say she couldn't be swept into romance by the right kind of presents?

Boog would find the right kind, too: things so new that ads for them hadn't even appeared in *The New Yorker*. He had contacts with all manner of manufacturers, foreign and domestic, and probably swamped Coffee with ponchos and belts —two of her particular loves—or chairs and lamps so esoteric that they might not even be recognizable as chairs and lamps.

Before going further I might quote the well-known Coke bottle scout Zack Jenks, who found a near-mint 1924 Coke bottle beside I–85 near Gaffney, South Carolina, in the summer of 1979.

"Anything can be anywhere," Zack said, a statement that is to scouting what $E = MC^2$ is to physics.

As we were breaking up, Coffee and I had many long talks, in none of which did we quite locate the nipple of the problem, to use one of her favorite phrases. Her view was simple: all my character flaws resulted from the fact that I had grown up in a trailer-house.

"You didn't have a lawn," she said, as if that was all there was to it.

Chapter IV _____

The trailer-house sat in Solino, Texas, and for most of my childhood it had two sad turd-hounds chained underneath it. The dogs were named Lion and Tiger. When they were puppies they liked to chew fiercely on my father's dirty socks, but once grown they lost their warlike attributes. My father kept them chained under the trailer-house anyway, in the hope that their ferocity would return if someone tried to rob us. Nobody did, so all Lion and Tiger had to do was lie in the dirt and scratch.

I grew up in the trailer-house. When I was four my mother was killed in a car wreck, a few blocks away, a fact I don't record in order to gain sympathy. In fact, I had an abnormally happy childhood, running with a lively and sexually precocious gang of Mexican kids, in the warm sun of the Rio Grande valley.

My father, Gene McGriff, took little part in my life, and not much of a part in his own. His only affliction was a lifelong apathy, which he passed on to the dogs but not to me. Clerking in the local hardware store was good enough for him, and still is.

By the time I entered my teens I was already twice as tall as my Mexican companions, and knew that basketball was going to be my game, and it was a basketball scholarship that took me to college, though I was tired of the sport even before I got there. My real passion was gymnastics: I loved the clarity, the precision, and the utter loneliness of it. But of course it was a hopeless passion, since I was six feet five inches. One day I was watching an amateur rodeo when it occurred to me that bulldogging was just a form of applied gymnastics. You jump, you grip, you swing, and you twist, and if the timing of the four actions is precise the running animal will throw himself with his own weight, rolling right across your body and whopping himself into the ground with a satisfying thump.

When I started dogging I was looking for a passion. My world was the Texas valley, where there were no objects of the quality of a Sung vase, or women as beautiful as Cindy Sanders. As yet unaware of the stimulus of beauty, I made do with the stimulus of sport, and rapidly became a crackerjack bulldogger. I qualified for the National finals my very first year on the circuit, and soon fixed upon four seconds as a pure limit, a goal to aim for. To chase and throw a steer within four seconds would equal perfection, the best that concentration and technique could hope to achieve.

Fortunately I had an experienced hazer, an old steer-roper named Goat Goslin. I also had a powerful little dogging horse named Dandy, with a start like a cannon shot. For two years I burned up the circuit, consistently turning in times around 5 seconds. I had a 4.8 in Salinas, a 4.6 in Miles City, and a 4.3 at the Pendleton Roundup. For two or three peak months I felt I was closing in on perfection.

At that point Goat Goslin began to worry about me, though forty years of rodeo had not exactly taught him caution. He had only one ear, the other having been butted off in Tucumcari in 1946, and his left hand consisted of a thumb and first finger, the rest of it lost to a roping accident in Grand Island, Nebraska.

In his day Goat had tried his hand at every event, an eclecticism that had left him with pins in both legs, an artificial hip joint, and a little steel plate behind his left temple that he would sometimes reach up and strike a match on. A person unfamiliar with rodeo, looking him in the face for the first time, would have had a hard time accounting for the sight. A cowboy from Wolf, Wyoming, probably put it best.

"That hairy old son of a bitch looks like he dove off a three-story building into a waffle iron," he said.

And yet Goat was actually worried about *me*. We were chugging along in the GMC pickup, down the east side of Oregon, the day after I posted my 4.3. It was a cold morning and we could neither get the heater to work nor the right window to roll up all the way. Goat was blowing on what was left of his crusty old hands.

"I'm worrit about you, Jack," he said, out of a clear blue eastern Oregon sky.

"Me?" I asked. "Why worry about me? Don't I look healthy?"

"Yeah, you do. You shore do, Jack," Goat said, pulling at a tuft of hair that curled out of one side of his nose, as white as the covering of Momma Cullen's worn-out chair.

He was silent for a few minutes, obviously a little embarrassed by the conversation he seemed to want to initiate.

"Jack, all you thank about is bulldoggin'," he blurted out, awkwardly picking up a pair of wire-pinchers and looking at them as if they might contain the secret of existence.

"I guess you're right, Goat," I said. "I guess it is about all I think about."

"I tolt you," he said. "It's all you thank about."

"But what am I supposed to think about?"

My question stumped Goat completely. He lapsed into an aggrieved silence, staring out the window at the gray sage. I could tell he thought it unsporting of me to turn the question around and point it in his direction.

"Why hell, Jack, I don't even thank you *like* rodeoin'!" he exclaimed, some thirty miles later.

It was true. I didn't, particularly, although I had not got around to admitting this to myself. I was honestly fascinated by bulldogging, but apart from that what I really liked about the life was the opportunity it gave me to drive across vast, lonely American spaces.

Still, there was no way I could dispute Goat's main point.

The world of the arenas was a tawdry one—pridefully crude, complacently violent. I had already started to escape it by spending what spare time I had in junk shops and low-grade antique stores.

The day before, at a little store outside Pendleton called Babe's Antiques and Plaster, filled mostly with hideous plaster lawn ornaments, I had bought what I later discovered was a Tlingit copper-and-bone dagger. I gave Babe $30 for it, just because it was pretty.

But my passion for objects was still latent, and I had not consciously considered Goat's point.

"Well, what do *you* like about it, Goat?" I asked.

Goat could hardly believe I would be gauche enough to ask him two questions in the same day. On the whole he was not a talkative companion, though once in a while he could be induced to talk about some of his more impressive accidents, which he called storms.

"Got in a storm down in Laramie," he would say. "Hung myself to a dern bull and that sucker jerked my arm too far out of the socket, they had to fly me to Dallas, to a socket doctor. Missed two rodeos because of that storm."

My question put him into a sulk, but it's a long way from Pendleton to Sedalia, Missouri, where we were going. By the time we were fifty or sixty miles into Idaho, Goat had looked into his soul and found the truth.

"Why hell, what I like about it is all that over-age pussy," he said. "All them drunk grandmothers. I'd be lucky to get any other kind, bunged up as I am."

It was true that an awful lot of middling to old ladies used rodeos as an excuse to get lit, not to mention laid.

"Some of them was my fans," Goat added, respectfully, meaning that they had been hopeful young women when, as a young cowhand fresh out of Guthrie, Oklahoma, he had made rodeo history at the Fort Worth Fat Stock Show by riding a bull called Sudden Death—a monster black Brahma, sort of the Moby Dick of bulls, killer of two, crippler of several, and never ridden for a full regulation 8 seconds until Goat came along.

Goat was not particularly moved by his observation, but I was. Rodeo people of a certain age, staring out into the arenas around which they have spent painful and mostly disappointing lives, still talk reverently about the night Goat Goslin rode Sudden Death. It was a bittersweet thought that all over the west there were old ladies eager or at least willing to grapple with Goat, in a pickup seat or miserable motel room, because of a brief, dust-cloaked ride thirty-five years back down the highway, that most of them had not even been there to see.

But whether they had seen it or not it was the diamond in the popcorn of their lives—an event that only lasted 8 seconds.

A month later, at the National Finals Rodeo, I nearly hit perfection, throwing a steer in 4.1 seconds. It won me a championship saddle and a belt buckle that would have stopped a bazooka bullet. When I let the steer up I felt sad—the same sadness I felt driving out of De Queen with the Sung vase. I was looking downward from a peak, and my descent was swift. A month later I was taking 10 and 12 seconds to throw steers I should have thrown in 5 or 6. But I lacked even a vague notion of what I might want to do next, and kept on desultorily dogging steers.

In early February the Fort Worth Fat Stock Show rolled around. On the first night, Goat was sitting on the fence by the bucking chutes, smoking and watching, as he had done for thousands of nights.

Tex Ritter—Goat's favorite singer—was there that night. During one of the breaks in the action he sang "Hillbilly Heaven"—it was not long before he departed for it himself. The crowd burst into tears, overcome by the memory of immortals like Patsy Cline and Cowboy Copas. Tex didn't sing his well-known rodeo classic, "Bad Brahma Bull," fearing, perhaps, that it would be an augury.

Twenty minutes after he sang, a very bad and very black Brahma bull smashed through the chute gate, threw his rider, narrowly missed killing a clown, then whirled and leaped the arena fence right where Goat was sitting. The fence, like the gate, smashed as if it were plywood. The bull came down with Goat right underneath him, the bull's front feet hitting Goat in the chest—his cigarette was still in his mouth and still lit when he died, by which time the bull had trotted back to the bullpen, as placid as a milk-pen calf.

So died Goat Goslin, a small legend in his own time. Everyone agreed that the spirit of Sudden Death had finally come back to claim him. Some went so far as to allow that it was fitting.

But a lot of hard-drinking, fast-fucking grandmothers had lost their hero.

I sold Dandy, my wonderful dogging horse, that night. The next day I accompanied Goat home to Guthrie and paid for his funeral. The minute it ended I left for Houston, with a station wagon half full of what Boog Miller called Indian doodads, sure of nothing except that I had gained an exit, and lost a friend.

Chapter V _____

The peculiar thing about my first date with Cindy Sanders was that the whole thing was arranged more or less directly under the anguished gaze of her fiancé, Harris Fullinwider Harisse.

I say more or less directly because the first thing I noticed about Harris was that it was hard for him to fix his gaze directly on anything—up to and including a woman as easy to look at as Cindy. His gaze wandered nervously from place to place, object to object, and person to person, darting away like a hummingbird if it seemed likely that other eyes were about to make direct contact with his own.

When I mentioned this to Cindy, in bed the next morning, she sighed, up to then the first evidence I had that she was capable of even momentary discouragement.

"He looks that way because he can't decide whether to come in or go out," she said.

It was early morning—my brain hadn't started its day.

"Come in or go out what?" I asked.

"The door, of course," Cindy said. "Doors confuse him. He gets one leg through and then he can't decide whether to put the other leg through. So he stands there looking that way."

It was true that Harris had neither come in nor gone out during the hour I was in Cindy's shop. But, apart from noting his anguished gaze, I had been so entranced with Cindy that I hadn't paid him much attention.

"That's a strange problem to have," I said, for so it struck me. I had known confused people in my day, but none so confused they stopped in doorways.

"Not at all," Cindy said. "It's a perfectly well-bred indecision. Choice for Harris is like poetry for poets. It's so filled with nuance that he usually just stops. You have to respect it."

Maybe you did, but it was hard for me to imagine Cindy Sanders waiting sweetly while Harris worked out the nuances of every doorway they came to, as if it were a sonnet.

Cindy got up and tromped off to her kitchen. She returned in a minute, clutching a knife, an expensive Italian salami, a big slab of Brie, and a half-gallon of apple juice. Then she sat cross-legged on the bed and ate heartily, occasionally whacking me off a hunk of salami or swiping up a glob of Brie and offering it to me on her finger.

I was at a loss to understand how a man so indecisive had managed to become engaged to Cindy, a girl who expected immediate contact, eye, mouth, and genital. She liked direct looks and direct kissing.

"Tell the truth," I said. "You're not really engaged to Harris."

Cindy had her mouth full of salami and couldn't talk, but she shook her head vigorously and looked slightly outraged.

"I certainly am engaged to him," she said indignantly, as soon as the salami was on its downward path, somewhere between her breasts.

"Who are you to question it?" she asked, with the open defiance I seem to inspire in emphatic women.

29

What was I supposed to say to that? I was nobody to question it. I wasn't particularly ill-disposed toward Harris, just curious as to how such an arrangement had come about.

After all, Cindy had made the moves, where I was concerned. When I drove up and parked in front of her shops—she had three, all in one elegant nineteenth-century building on O Street—all I had meant to do was sell a carful of cowboyana. The only reason I was in Washington was because Boog insisted that the East had gone cowboy crazy.

"The twain's done met," he said. "Cowboy boots is sellin' quicker than two-dollar pussy, even up in New York, where two-dollar pussy don't have to stand on the street corner very long."

"Not if you're in town, you pot-gut," Boss said. She was making biscuits in her big airy kitchen and Boog just happened to wander past, drinking what he called his breakfast toddy, a mixture of vodka, gin, tequila, and orange juice. Boss turned around and plastered him right in the face with a big wad of biscuit dough, laughed heartily, and immediately set about mixing some more dough.

Boog's uncontrollable lust for cheap women, unabated through three decades of marriage, had inadvertently contributed to Boss's own fame, since she had long since chosen to fight fire with fire.

"What I told the old fatty," she confided one day, "was that I'd fuck six famous Yankees for every little pot he stuck his dipstick in."

Boss had implemented her threat with vigor, if legend was to be believed. She was a tall woman, with raven hair and looks that still stopped people in their tracks, though she was fifty-two and had been married to Boog over thirty years, an experience that would have marked most women deeply.

Since most of those years had been spent in Washington, Boss had not lacked opportunity. Writers were her over-all favorites, though she excluded most journalists and all sportswriters from contention.

"Why would I want a sportswriter when I've already got six kids to raise?" she asked, when the subject came up.

30

Scarcely a poet or novelist of consequence had escaped her, in her time. It was not uncommon to find her latest, a tiny Jewish poet named Micah Leviticus, sobbing quietly in her motherly lap, or else perched on the cabinet watching television, depending on his mood. Micah lived upstairs, sharing a room with Tommy, the Millers' youngest child.

About politicians Boss was more discreet. There were gossips who felt they knew which of the major figures she had accepted, but Boss herself was inscrutable when the great names were reeled off. She spoke of Jack or Adlai or Lyndon as of any other friend, though once in a while a special light would come into her restless gray eyes at the mention of Estes Kefauver.

The light was not lost on Boog, who sometimes dropped Kefauver's name just to see it come on.

"Ain't women sumpin'?" he would say. "Remember Estes Kefauver? Why that big gawky son of a bitch could get pussy Jack Kennedy wouldn't have got the merest whiff of."

When Boss mentioned her threat about the famous Yankees she was sitting at her kitchen table, drinking coffee.

"I learned a harsh truth as a result of that remark," she said.

"Which is?"

"Which is that there's more cheap women than famous Yankees," she said, opening *The Wall Street Journal* to the real estate ads. Boss had a pilot's license and would fly off in her Cessna to any part of America where there was a good property to buy. Her local operations she ran mostly by phone from her spacious bedroom, leaving the legwork to competent young women such as Kate, Coffee, or Tanya Todd—another old girl friend of mine, who ran her Dallas office. I sometimes called Tanya Roger the Dodger, since over the years she had proved about as hard to sack as Roger Staubach. Once in a while she could be blindsided, if one felt up to a sexual blitz, but that was the only method likely to prove effective.

Though neither famous nor a Yankee, I was crazy about Boss and was always shooting her looks of love. I shot her a few while she read the *Journal*, but she looked up and disposed of my candidacy with a vivid smile.

"Get up and go buy some doodads," she said. "I class you with the sportswriters."

"In my view that's very unfair," I said.

Boss ran her fingers through her long black hair, idly testing its texture as she smiled at me.

"Yeah, but your view don't count," she said, and turned the page.

Before I could get her to look at me again, Micah Leviticus came dragging into the kitchen, wearing gym trunks and an old C.C.N.Y. T-shirt. He was carrying a tiny TV, which he plugged into an outlet near the sink before climbing up in Boss's lap. A *Roadrunner and the Coyote* cartoon happened to be playing. Micah watched it raptly, as Boss read the *Journal*. The minute a commercial came on he looked up into her beautiful face.

"I dreamed about Rilke again last night, Boss," he said. "Why is it always Rilke? I don't even like Rilke."

"You sweet thing," Boss said, and gave him a couple of not-so-motherly kisses. Then she favored me with another of her cheerful and vivid smiles.

I wondered sometimes if her cells weren't just better than other people's—more ripe with the lifestuff, or something. It was one way to account for the fact that she seemed twice as alive as the rest of us.

Micah Leviticus was exactly five feet one inch—sixteen inches shorter than myself. That fact alone blew the one solid theory I had about women, which is that even the best of them are suckers for tall men.

Chapter VI _____

Meanwhile—back in bed—the defiance had not entirely faded from Cindy Sanders' face. She swallowed a big glob of Brie and washed it down with three big gulps of apple juice, watching me closely to see if I was going to mount a serious campaign against her engagement.

I kept quiet. Every single time I've gone one-on-one with female defiance, I've ended up face down on the floor, twitching weakly. One thing I've learned to do without is the myth of male dominance. Possibly there had actually been male dominance in other eras, but constant exposure to women on the order of Boss Miller and Tanya Todd convinced me it had gone the way of the dodo and the great auk.

"I want to get something straight," Cindy said. "Did you really know Big John Connolly, or were you just conning me?"

"Sure I know him," I said. "Why would you doubt it?"

"Let's put it this way," she said. "Why would you doubt that I'm engaged to Harris? Do you have some notion that you're better than he is?

"Not better," I said. "Maybe just a little more practical. What if you start the wedding and Harris can only decide to put one leg through the door of the church?

"Of course you could marry him in the park," I added. "No doors."

For some reason her mood lightened.

"In L.A., maybe," she said. "If I wanted some freako L.A. wedding, I'd marry the head of Fox and get the Dalai Lama to preside. Members of Harris' family do not get married in parks."

"I guess he did look pretty proper," I said, trying to remember Harris. All I could remember was that he was tall, aristocratically thin, wore a suit, and had an anguished gaze.

"Changes clothes three times a day," Cindy said, tapping me gently on the chest with the handle of the knife. "I didn't have to make *him* buy a dinner jacket the first time I took him out."

"My gosh," I said. "I'm just a scout. It's not every day I meet a girl like you."

"I'd like to hear more about your wives," she said. "They don't seem to have taught you much."

"They weren't teachers, just wives," I said. "They both work for Boss."

Frankly I was beginning to be sorry I had popped off about her engagement, since the remark had set in motion an interrogation whose purpose was more or less a mystery to me. Cindy was now gathering historical data of a sort all women feel they have an automatic right to. Even Coffee had suspended her antihistorical bias long enough to secure a thorough account of my prior relationships, when we first met.

"I know a flea-marketer's daughter who doesn't work for Boss," I said, to change the subject.

"Where does she live?"

"Zanesville, Ohio," I said, a direct lie. For some reason I wasn't ready to come clean about the flea-marketer's daughter, who actually lives near Augusta, West Virginia, not much more than a two-hour drive from Washington.

"Yeah," Cindy said, looking at me closely. She had probably activated her truth radar, an instinctive lie-detecting mechanism I'm convinced all women have. It is an enormously sophisticated mechanism which frequently enables women to skip quickly over the fact of the lie and zero in on the motive behind it.

I've often been stunned to discover that women can discern with great precision the true motive behind lies I had thought I had merely wandered into casually, as I might wander into a junk shop.

There's really no winning against equipment so finely calibrated, but there are certain evasionary tactics that will sometimes delay the inevitable reckoning. I decided to try and camouflage the lie with a sprig of truth.

"I have a confession to make," I said. "I wasn't conning you yesterday. I do know Big John Connolly. But the Big John I was actually referring to was Big John Flint."

34

Big John Flint is a phenomenal trader whose antique barn just outside Zanesville, Ohio—where I had just fallaciously located Beth Gibbon, the flea-marketer's daughter—was a mecca for scouts of all descriptions. Since the business that had brought me to Cindy was antiques, I assumed she would assume I meant Big John Flint when I uttered the phrase "Big John."

The fact that she thought I meant Big John Connolly was probably what prompted her to ask me to the dinner party.

Cindy owned three trend-setting businesses, two downstairs and one upstairs in the large building on O Street.

One of them was an antique shop called Schlock, my reason for being in D.C. in the first place. Next door was her dress shop, Fancy Folk, and upstairs, over both shops, was her very avant-garde gallery, which was called Sensibility.

At the time of my arrival Sensibility was filled with the bread sculpture of an émigré Latvian peasant woman. Many of the sculptures evidently represented the eternal feminine, being a mixture of lumps and indentations. "Women are the bread of life, in Latvian folklore," Cindy explained.

Before I went to see Cindy for the first time, Boog advised me to dress as vulgarly as possible, reasoning that what had worked for him might work for me.

"A tasteful Texan ain't gonna play," he said. "It'll just confuse the natives, what few they is."

I decided to ignore this advice. I put on a beautiful white doeskin jacket I had bought from a Blood Indian in Montana, and got my Stetson out of its hatbox in the rear of the Cadillac. The Stetson was a brown 100–X beaver, with a hatband made from the skin of an albino diamondback. It had been the Sunday hat of a famous Texas Ranger captain and had probably not been out of its box six times when I bought it from a spur-scout in the Rio Grande valley.

I put on my yellow armadillo boots and a thin silver concho belt that had belonged to a Zicarilla medicine man.

After some thought, I decided to put my Valentino hubcaps on the Cadillac.

Valentino hubcaps were in the form of silver cobras, very

graceful. Anyone who flea-markets much will have seen one or two such hubcaps, all of them purporting to be off Valentino's own cars.

In fact, almost all the hubcaps now being traded are the work of a well-known hubcap forger from Torrance, California. He was finally exposed in the sixties, but not before he had salted the market with several hundred cobra hubcaps. The one detail he neglected, or was too cheap, to duplicate, was the eyes. Valentino's cobras had real rubies for eyes. And of the many cars he owned, only four—all Hispano-Suizas—were equipped with the silver-plated, ruby-eyed cobra hubcaps.

I had one of the four true sets, bought from Valentino's secretary, an aged, contentious, dipsomaniacal woman named Beulah Mahony, who ended her days in a dingy apartment on De Longpre Street, in West Hollywood.

I almost didn't buy the hubcaps from her, not because I doubted their authenticity but because I hated to think of Beaulah without them, knowing, as I did, that they were her last link with youth and glory.

Also, the hubcaps were her last means of securing herself a little company.

Many aged, lonely people own a treasure or two and quickly learn to use them as a tease. By letting it be known that they might—just might—sell the treasure, they can entice collectors and scouts to visit them again and again, if only for long enough to share a cup of coffee or watch a soap opera with them. If the object in question is desirable enough, the old person can sometimes scratch out a marginal social life on the strength of it.

The true test of the honor and discipline of a scout lies in his treatment of the old man or old woman with only one treasure left. When they finally give in and sell it, it means they're done: tired of the small indignities of the tease.

When they sell it, people stop coming to see them and they die.

My claims to virtue are modest, but at least I never went to L.A. without checking on Beulah Mahony—not that she was invariably grateful for my loyalty.

Beulah was a querulous old orange-haired woman, frenzied one day and apathetic the next. She was so incurably addicted to holding garage sales that the last time I saw her she had even sold her cheap formica table and had made a crude replacement out of forty or fifty phone books she had managed to gather up around her apartment building. She just piled them up in a block and ate off them. For drinks she mixed gin and Kool-Aid, probably because Kool-Aid was the only mixer she could afford.

Beulah's attitude was not unlike Momma Cullen's. Any form of charity, even a buddy check, was an insult, but somehow she had figured out that I really liked her, an affection she rightly judged to be a weakness on my part. Consequently —in common with all the other women in my life—she saw no reason to refrain from harsh judgment.

We sat at the phone book table, drinking the revolting drink from two pink glasses Beulah had managed to withhold from her last garage sale. Outside the window, a ditch-digging machine was eating its way down De Longpre Street, belching and roaring as it crunched through the asphalt.

"Jack, I don't know what to do about you," Beulah said, occasionally pulling out a sprig of her orange hair and tossing it on the phone books.

"It's a selfish life, driving around buying things," she added. Being Valentino's secretary had not blurred her sense of values, those having been inculcated long ago in her hometown, Topeka, Kansas.

"A man your age needs responsibilities," she said. "Kids, in other words."

It was a common theme. Both of my ex-wives had hinted darkly that our marriage would probably have worked out if we'd only had children, though, so far as I could see, they were both as frightened of the prospect as I was.

"If you don't want none of your own you could always marry a divorcée," Beulah suggested. "Plenty of them around, and most of them got kids they don't know what to do with."

"I don't think I'd know what to do with them, either," I said, honestly.

Beulah snorted. "Raise 'em to be solid citizens," she said. "Decent citizens."

She had a profound belief in the decency of American citizens in general, though the mostly seedy citizens of her own decrepit neighborhood had often let her down.

"You want to know something, Jack?" she said. "I stole them hubcaps. The one criminal thing I done in my life, besides taking off my income tax, once in a while."

"My goodness," I said. "Why?"

"Justice," she said. "I figured they was my due. I worked for the man eleven years. Some queer would have got them if I hadn't, so I stole 'em in the confusion. And you finally bought 'em off me, after all this time. Life's funny."

And she laughed at it cheerfully, the laugh of a decent old lady from Topeka who had managed to go only slightly batty.

"It's a good thing L.A. is a big town, with fat phone books," she said. "Otherwise I'd be eatin' off the floor."

Six months later, when I checked in again, Beulah was dead, buried, and forgotten, except by me. A family of nine Vietnamese lived in her apartment. They hadn't met Beulah, but they remembered her final table.

"Many phone books," the father said, and the whole small, neat family smiled.

Chapter VII _____

What I supposed, when I finally set off for Georgetown, was that even a lady who owned three trendy stores might derive a faint buzz from the combination of doeskin jacket, yellow boots, albino-diamondback hatband, and Valentino hubcaps, not to mention six feet five of me.

In the event, Cindy hardly gave the combination a glance.

"It was a little over-studied," she said later, with characteristic candor.

When I wheeled the pearly Cadillac into a parking place right in front of Schlock, Cindy was standing on the sidewalk, studying her window display, and Harris was standing in her doorway, looking this way and that.

What really impressed Cindy was that I drove straight to the parking place as if I'd known it would be there waiting for me, although it was Saturday afternoon and the rest of Georgetown was a maelstrom of frustrated parking-place seekers.

"We must be meant for one another or you wouldn't have got that parking place," she said, without irony, when I introduced myself.

The fact that someone meant for her had driven up in a Cadillac filled with steer horns, antelope skulls, Hopi basketry, and Mexican spurs didn't seem to surprise her.

"What's your sign, Tex?" she asked. Then she stepped right over and linked her arm in mine, studying our reflections in the window of her antique shop. It was as if she had decided to try out the concept—or at least the image—of us as a couple, right off the bat.

Then she led me into her store, right past Harris, who, I now realize, was engrossed in his own dilemma. An hour later, when she had dragged me off to buy a dinner jacket from a grumpy old Russian tailor, she casually informed me that the man in the doorway was her fiancé.

Cindy was one of those near-perfect physical specimens that sprout, unblemished as tulips, in certain California suburbs—Montecito, in her case. Words like "gorgeous" and "knockout" applied to her precisely. I was unprepared for such looks in an antique dealer—I guess I had expected to find one of the humorless, overeducated young ladies who populate the antiquities departments of museums and major auction houses. Antiquities seldom attract your giggling ninnies.

My first thought, on seeing Cindy, was that she was probably into mountaineering—a deduction partly based on her glowing health and partly on the fact that she had several antique alpenstocks in her window.

In fact, Cindy *was* into mountaineering, only the ascent she had in mind involved the sheer, ice-coated face of American society—a peak I had never so much as glimpsed, in all my driving.

For the moment she was concentrating on ascending what might be called the East Face, but there was no doubt but that hers was the large view. There was an East Face and a West Face, a crumbling pinnacle or two in the South and a few rockspurs in the southwest, but it was essentially one mountain, broad at the bottom and narrow at the top.

All this was fascinating to me: I had never met a beautiful girl social climber before. Cindy was not reticent about her ambition, either. Reticence was right up there with patience on the list of things she didn't have.

Looking back, I can see that it was a measure of my naiveté that I could suppose mention of Big John Flint, the trader from Ohio, would prompt a beautiful social climber to invite me to a Georgetown dinner party, even though he was, in my view, more remarkable by far than Big John Connolly, to whom I had sold a couple of Rainey oils. Among Big John Flint's many triumphs was the discovery, in a warehouse in Poughkeepsie, of more than 100,000 pre-1925 Boy Scout knives.

I had only dropped his name because it was obvious at a glance that four-fifths of the antiques in Cindy's store came from him. She went in heavily for overpolished American furniture, nineteenth-century tin boxes, churns, weather vanes, early tools, duck decoys, salt-glazed crocks, dining car china, and inkwells, all items Big John dispensed by the thousands.

I found out later that she bought most of her stuff from a scout in Pittsburgh, who obviously trucked it right in from Zanesville. She had never heard of Big John, and what's more, she wasn't particularly interested when I told her about him, the next morning in bed. Cindy was more interested in having her fill of salami and Brie.

"Why are you telling me this?" she asked, whacking me on the sternum with the handle of the knife.

"Because it could save you money," I said.

She shrugged her beautiful, lightly freckled shoulders. If anything was wrong with Cindy's body, only X-rays could have discovered what. I even liked her feet, big though they were. They looked like feet that had trod a lot of beaches and worn out numerous pairs of tennis shoes.

"How much did you pay for those duck decoys?" I asked.

"Twenty-five apiece," she said, her boredom deepening.

"Big John sells them for eight."

Now that the point was made, Cindy ignored it.

"If you're just out to get Harris, you better be careful," she said. "I'm very protective of Harris."

This intermittent conversation forced me to acknowledge what I already knew, which is that relations with women are never simple.

The reason the conversation was intermittent was because Cindy took time out to eat the lion's share of the salami and most of the Brie. The fact was she didn't feed me very much, and while I was lying there watching her eat the mental me reasserted itself over the physical me. I should have got up, scrambled myself some eggs, and met the day on the level of the basic appetites, as Cindy had.

I do *have* the basic appetites, but unfortunately the mental me is the one with the real staying power. It will only stand aside for the basic appetites so long, and the minute it returns the trouble starts.

Chapter VIII _____

Cindy was a supremely beautiful woman, and she sat not three inches from me, having just reduced a large salami to a pile of scrapings.

My heart should have soared at the mere sight of her, but instead my heart sank like a lead turtle. I felt like I had ingested the lead turtle while Cindy was ingesting salami.

What did it was her indifference to Big John Flint. How could I be falling in love with an antique dealer who didn't want to hear the story about Big John? Most of the antique dealers in America sat in their stores all day, gasping like fish out of water for want of the latest news about Big John.

In fact, I *had* the latest news, which was that he had bought a small town in north Georgia and was dismantling it house by house, mainly to get the antebellum fireplace moldings. His passion for duck decoys was as nothing to his passion for antebellum fireplaces. There had only been twenty-seven people left in the town and all of them were tired of it, so they sold it to Big John.

So far as I know, Big John Connolly has never done anything as interesting as buying a town in order to get fifty or sixty fireplace moldings.

I don't mean to suggest that the general public should be expected to judge the two men accurately. The general public knows nothing of Big John Flint, a quasi-mythical figure even in Zanesville.

But Cindy wasn't the general public. She was an antique dealer, whose stock, though predictable, was far from hopeless. She had had an ivory-tipped elephant goad, for example. I bought it instantly and sold it to Boog two days later.

In certain moods Boog could be persuaded to buy almost anything. Objects and people constantly vie for space in his houses.

"Hell, I got a daughter who's an elephant," he said, handing me $400 and waving the goad playfully in the direction of Linda Miller, a sweet teenager who happened to be going through a pudgy phase.

"Get fucked, Daddy!" Linda said, whacking at him with a razor strop I had sold him a few days earlier. It had not yet made its way off the kitchen table.

The Miller kids were scrappers. Linda's whack caused Boog to spill most of his breakfast toddy on a suit that was the color of fresh slime.

Micah Leviticus was sitting next to Boss, eating a bowl of Cheerios and watching an early morning Mary Tyler Moore rerun on his tiny TV. I glanced at it just in time to watch Mary fling her cap up to be freeze-framed. The sight seemed to cheer Micah immensely. His tiny face lit up.

"Look," he said. "It's Mary."

We all looked. It was Mary, sure enough.

"Don't you love her perky smile?" Micah said.

Boss reached over and ruffled Micah's hair.

"It's because of you I'm fat—it's your genes," Linda said, still whacking her father. "I wish I didn't love you!"

Boss laughed, a loud immediate peal of delight that filled the kitchen. It startled Micah so much that he blinked and looked up from his milk-logged Cheerios, looking almost as out of it as had the Congressman from Michigan, when Pencil Penrose's two black pugs trotted across the seventeenth-century table and began to eat his *coq au vin*.

Chapter IX _____

If Perkins, the Penroses' extraordinary manservant, had had his way, the Congressman's *coq au vin* would not have been there for the pugs to eat.

That goes without saying, of course. Perkins was easily the most impressive person at the party, if not the most impressive person anywhere, now that Lord Mountbatten is dead. In fact, Perkins looked so much like Lord Mountbatten that I faltered badly when I first walked in with Cindy. Perkins is as tall as I am, and several times more dignified. I assumed he must be our host, at the very least, so I attempted to shake his hand.

Perkins graciously ignored this gaucherie, but Cindy didn't.

"If he wasn't the butler, he wouldn't be opening the door," she pointed out.

Seconds later I was being introduced to Senator Penrose, our real host, a little fellow I might have missed entirely if left to my own devices. He had the constitution of a whippet and a complexion not unlike that of a rag that has hung in the sun for several weeks. Splotchy and bleached, in other words.

At dinner I spent most of my time stealing glances at Perkins, trying to anticipate his next move. Seldom have I felt so intimidated by a man. Fortunately the two ladies bracketing me were experienced diners, who knew when to pick up a fork or surrender a plate—by watching them I got through the meal without serious embarrassment.

The congressman from Michigan could have done the same, but he didn't. He didn't look dumb, just sort of weakly self-satisfied. He was also compulsively voluble on the subject of Michigan, perhaps the only subject he felt he had mastered.

The person in the unfortunate position of having to listen to him was Cunard Cotswinkle, old Dunscombe's wife, a honey blonde about Boss's age who had managed to marry and outlive three of the world's ten richest men. Her nickname was Cunny and her charm was said to be fatal—evidently a hyperbole, since if it had been, the congressman from Michigan would have been dead before we reached the salad course.

At any rate, the congressman made a simple mistake: he talked when he should have been eating. Consequently, while the rest of us were eating salad his *coq au vin* still sat in front of him, untouched.

Across from me, John C. V. Ponsonby showed signs of being about to come to life. His chin, long since sunk on his bony chest, lifted a degree or two, and one hand began to fumble with his bow tie. The ladies beside me stared at him balefully: clearly he was not a favorite of theirs.

"If Jake starts talking about Egypt I'm leaving," one whispered to the other, across my salad.

"I know what you mean," the other said. "It's bad enough to have to read his columns."

"Oh, I don't *read* him," the first lady said, looking reflective for a moment.

"If it came to that, I'd rather fuck him than read him," she said. "I feel the same way about Max Lerner, for what that's worth."

It was at this point that we all heard the hideous scratching of eight little paws, all of them trying to gain a purchase on the highly polished floor.

Here came the pugs, old, fat, and black, making awful little mewling sounds as they tried to scratch their way across the floor, their wet red tongues hanging over their underbites. Twice they lost their purchase and sprawled on their stomachs on the slick floor, mewling more horribly than ever.

The second time this happened Perkins picked them up by their scruffs and carried them around the table to their mistress. That he managed to perform this chore without losing one whit of his dignity says all that need be said for the man's presence.

Pencil Penrose received the dogs cheerfully and they immediately began to compete with one another to scramble over her bosom and lick her face.

"Wog-ers!" she exclaimed. "Gog-ers!" as the little black dogs flung themselves at her overhanging bosom like salmon at a waterfall.

The immediate effect of her exclamation was to bring John C. V. Ponsonby to full wakefulness for the first time in hours. He blinked slowly, like the old frog he more or less resembled, and watched impassively as Wog-ers and Gog-ers attempted to scramble up or around Pencil's bosom.

Despite her fondness for them, Pencil soon tired of their sharp little claws and wet little tongues, so she without further ado simply sat them on the dinner table.

Chapter X _____

I was frankly shocked. I had eaten at a number of tables where it was customary to set the plates under the table for the dogs, but never at one where the dogs were put on the table and given a go at the plates.

In view of the reaction of the ladies beside me, I'm inclined to think it's not a common thing, even in Georgetown. They snapped to attention and looked around them happily, as if they had received an unexpected benediction.

"Now *that* is an upper-class thing!" one whispered to the other.

Both of them sighed, in a refreshed way. Apparently the burden of years of middle-classness, if not worse, had suddenly been lifted.

The dogs were so delighted to be on the table that they frolicked for a moment, rolling around, mewling, and even briefly simulating copulation.

Fortunately for everyone's digestion, Wog-ers and Gog-ers were long past consummating anything. After a brief hump they shook themselves and stared myopically around the table. Then they trotted across the table as confidently as two black imps.

Just as the congressman from Michigan belatedly reached for his knife and fork, Wog-ers and Gog-ers spotted his chicken and made a beeline for it. The congressman happened to glance down, to see what he was eating, and saw a sight that would have unnerved Douglas MacArthur.

Wog-ers and Gog-ers were by this time ripping their way through a cold but toothsome chicken breast. Thanks to certain genetic drawbacks, such as blunt noses and tiny teeth, they were making a sloppy job of it. Both of them had their front teeth in the congressman's plate and were slinging drippings this way and that as they tried to tear a few filaments of chicken loose from the bone.

When I described the scene to Boog, the next day, he

rolled on the floor and laughed until froth came out of his mouth.

"That gutless little piss-ant," he said. "I hope he swallert his tongue. He can talk more and say less than any man I ever met, unless it was Everett Dirksen."

Jake Ponsonby was making an effort to keep himself awake. He was doodling what appeared to be Latin hexameters on his shirt cuff.

Old Cotswinkle, meanwhile, had suddenly discovered that there was a girl sitting next to him—namely Cindy—and he was staring fixedly at her bosom.

Lilah Landry was employing her Georgia gift of gab for the benefit of an elderly Britisher who seemed to have recently unplugged his life support system. He was either dead or pretending to be, a fact that made no difference to Lilah. She continued to talk rapidly and smile dizzily in his direction.

For perhaps a minute the party seemed to lose what little motion it had. Few conversed, no one got up, the servants held themselves in abeyance, and the water in the finger bowls slowly grew cold. At the head of the table Senator Penrose was talking quietly about Mr. Jefferson—to hear him one would have thought that Mr. Jefferson had been to dinner the night before.

The congressman from Michigan recognized at once that his food was a lost cause, and attempted to put a dignified face on the matter.

Unfortunately, the congressman didn't have a dignified face. He had a weak, selfish face, on which the only thing writ large was self-esteem. Though bug-eyed with embarrassment, he *had* survived fourteen terms in the House, so when Cunny Cotswinkle glanced over to see if the pugs had finished picking his chicken breast he actually smiled—a shit-eating grin to end all shit-eating grins.

"I love dawgs," he said.

Chapter XI ⸻

When the pugs finished mangling the chicken breast they trotted back down the table and had another little frolic, this one directly in front of me. Also directly in front of me were two very fine Charles II casters. I had been admiring them all evening.

The pugs got up, snuffling from their exertions, and one of them started to lift a leg on the nearest caster.

No one was paying the slightest attention either to the pugs or me, so I reached over and jabbed the dog in the ass with my fork. Then, for good measure, I jabbed the other one too.

The reaction was wonderful. The first pug squeaked like a sick bat and darted straight across the table. In his myopia he mistook Lilah Landry for his mistress and leaped straight for her bosom.

Lilah was wearing an attractive burgundy gown, easily loose enough at the bust to accommodate a small slick dog. Since she was still treating the moribund Englishman to a display of southern dizziness she didn't see the dog coming. He hit her just above the breastbone and immediately slid down between her breasts.

The second pug had more voice. She squealed like a shoat trying to get at some slop and raced straight down the table toward Senator Penrose.

The Senator saw the dog coming just in time to swallow whatever he had been about to say about Mr. Jefferson, and ducked. The pug bounced off his chair, hit the floor, and fetched up in a corner, squealing horribly.

"Oh, Gog-ers," Pencil said, giving her a pettish glance. "Bad creature! No table manners."

If it was Gog-ers on the floor, it could only be Wog-ers neatly nestling between Lilah Landry's breasts.

By the time Lilah managed to check the flow of gab all that could be seen of Wog-ers was a little whimpering black snout, directly between her impressive breasts.

The sight was sufficiently novel to cause Jake Ponsonby to stop doodling hexameters. He blinked twice, put aside his pen, and slowly brought his froglike gaze to focus on Lilah's bosom.

At this point Pencil looked around and saw Wog-ers, too, had misbehaved.

"Uh-oh," she said.

Ponsonby was more eloquent. He lowered his head until the prominent vein in his nose was only an inch or two from the more delicate veins in Lilah's breasts.

"Lilah, my dear," he said, "is it your intention to suckle that pug?"

Ponsonby's voice was perfectly adapted to his favored role as Tory panjandrum and parliamentarian of Georgetown. In it one heard not so distant echoes of the Raj.

Lilah looked down at the pug for a second and gave the company her best smile.

"Why puppydawg," she said, "how'd you get in there?"

Ponsonby blinked again. "Perhaps pedantically," he said, "I am put in mind of Livy, the first book. Do you expect to found a city?"

"If I do I hope it ain't nothin' like Macon," Lilah said, addressing herself gingerly to the problem of extracting a pug from her bosom. By this time she had the undivided attention of everyone except old Cotswinkle, who, having found one nice bosom to stare at, saw no reason to play the field.

Lilah reached down as delicately as possible and tried to get Wog-ers by the neck, an action he didn't appreciate. Instead of coming out he wiggled deeper into the pleasant valley.

This brought his sharp little hind-toenails into contact with Lilah's tummy.

"Oh, puppy, don't tickle," she said, jumping up. "I can't stand tickles."

Jumping up was a big mistake. As Wog-ers scrambled for a purchase the law of gravity brought him into contact with yet more ticklish regions—so ticklish, in fact, that Lilah dashed wildly around the table, screeching hysterically and clutching the pug to her stomach as tightly as she could, another act that was counterproductive. Wog-ers concluded that he was being suffocated, a not unreasonable fear, and scrambled all the harder.

By this time Lilah's screeches were so earsplitting that only Dunscombe Cotswinkle, deaf as a brass pig, was unaffected by them.

"Perkins!" Pencil said.

A nod from Perkins was all it took. Two alert Guatemalans grabbed Lilah, arresting her wild flight. Her bosom was heaving, but Wog-ers wasn't heaving with it. He yipped hopelessly from somewhere near her midriff.

"Here, get him," Lilah said, bending over. One of the Guatemalans thrust in a hand and got him, but a snag developed. Evidently one of his hind feet had hooked itself inextricably in Lilah's pantyhose.

At this point the two Guatemalans began to shake Lilah vigorously. Short of cutting Wog-ers' foot off, it seemed the only method likely to work, and it did work. Wog-ers promptly thumped onto the floor. Perkins picked him up and then went over in the corner and collected Gog-ers. Both were handed to a maid.

The company then all stood up. Lilah Landry had quickly shaken herself back into a state of world-class fashionability. The women, well trained as bees, made a beeline for the hallway and went up some stairs.

I started to follow, but came hard up against Perkins, who stood in the door.

"Brandy will be served in the study," he said.

Chapter XII _____

The minute we got in the study most of the men sank into big shiny red chairs and waited listlessly for their brandy.

The only person who had actually seen me stick the pugs was the Englishman I had too hastily taken for dead. His name was Sir Cripps Crisp. Both his name and his powers of observation belied his manner.

"If you'd tried that with my Schnauzers they'd have had your arm off at the elbow," he said, as we walked in together.

A small Philippine manservant was soon distributing brandy, under the watchful eye of Perkins. Senator Penrose trotted around with a box of cigars, looking nervous.

His nervousness was evidently prompted by Jake Ponsonby, who had settled himself in the largest, shiniest, and most centrally located red chair. Then he carefully placed the tips of his fingers against one another, and waited.

Most of the men seemed to know why he was waiting, and made haste to snip the ends of their cigars and get themselves ready. Only Sir Cripps Crisp seemed indifferent to hurry. He deliberated so long over the choice of a cigar that I thought the Senator was going to cram one in his mouth and light it for him. Alone among the company, Sir Cripps seemed unaffected by the fact that Jake Ponsonby had placed his fingertips together.

For his part, Ponsonby seemed equally unaffected by Sir Cripps's prognostications over the cigars, though now and then he made a little rippling motion movement with his fingertips, as a pianist might loosen up a bit before addressing the keys.

Eventually Sir Cripps located a cigar that met with his standards, allowed Perkins to cut and light it for him, and went off to the most remote of the red chairs, where he resumed his impersonation of a dead man.

The moment Sir Cripps's ass touched leather John C. V. Ponsonby cleared his throat.

"Let us begin with the Yemen," he said. "I speak, of course, of North Yemen. South Yemen is—or has been until very recently—ours. Whether the present administration has the skill—not to mention the will—to maintain that highly desirable state of affairs is perhaps open to question, but for now let us pass that question and consider the more vulnerable—and, I need hardly add—the more vital north."

He then proceeded to consider North Yemen and the regions adjacent to it in a speech of some twenty minutes duration, fetching up, finally, in the vicinity of the Sudan. As he spoke he tapped his fingertips ever so gently against one another, as if he were pecking out the sentences on an internal typewriter.

Each sentence came out perfect, edited as it emerged, and ready to go straight into one of his columns. In fact, a day or two later, glancing at one of his columns, I recognized a sentence or two, though the column they appeared in happened to be about Korea, rather than North Yemen.

If my initial respect for the sentences was high, it was certainly no higher than that of the gentlemen who listened with me. Ponsonby's stately periods must have been as familiar to them as their wives' menstrual rhythms, but—with the exception of Sir Cripps—their attentiveness fell just short of worship. He was the orator, they were the chorus, and they greeted his statements with big puffs of cigar smoke and thoughtful nods of the head.

Occasionally some member of the chorus would blurt out two or three sentences of response—"But Jake, there's the factor of Sadat" was popular—during which unwanted interruption Ponsonby would purse his lips as carefully as he placed his fingertips. When the interrupter paused for breath Ponsonby went serenely on with his discourse.

When he reached the Sudan a rumble was heard from Sir Cripps, who stood up and stuffed his cigar in the pocket of his dinner jacket. Fortunately it had long since gone out.

"The Crown lost the Sudan, and now we have lost the women," he said. "Personally, I would rather have the women, if they can be found."

At that moment, as if released by some celestial timer, the women began to pour through the door.

Chapter XIII _____

Whatever the women had been doing upstairs had evidently refreshed them, because they were all in high, if not raucous, good spirits when they returned.

The fuss they made upon entering would have wakened the dead, but at that it was barely sufficient to awaken their menfolk. Ponsonby's Augustan sonorities had done much to dissipate whatever tensions the company entertained—so much, indeed, that about half the company was sound asleep. Perkins had adroitly extracted half-spent cigars from a number of gently snoring mouths, preventing them from either being swallowed or falling out and burning holes in perfectly good cummerbunds.

Waking the gang was clearly thought to be women's work, and the women set about it with a vengeance, emitting shrill, drill-like peals of laughter and administering pinches, jabs, and an occasional well-aimed kick, as the occasion required.

One by one the men awoke, several of them exhibiting traces of surliness at the sight of their mates. Most of them simply sat and blinked, trying to get their bearings.

While I was watching them blink, Cindy came and stood at my elbow. She looked pleased, but it was hard to know what she was thinking. Her healthy smell held few clues.

"I can't imagine why I brought you to a respectable party," she said. "We could have just fucked."

We both looked at Cunny Cotswinkle, who was going at her husband with such a vengeance that it was hard to tell whether her intent was to wake him up or beat him to death.

Cotswinkle had fallen into a deep sleep—probably dreaming peacefully of Yalta, or the Treaty of Versailles, something appropriate to his years and eminence; but his wife was not disposed to let him dream in peace. To put it brutally, she was slapping the shit out of him, as John C. V. Ponsonby looked on with what was possibly meant to be a smile.

"Jake's waiting for him to die," Cindy explained.

"Why?"

"Jake's writing his autobiography," she said. "It's called 'The Last Professional.' Actually, it's finished, but he can't publish it while Dunny's alive, because Dunny's a professional, too. I hope I'm around when he finally publishes it."

"Eager to read it, huh?" I said.

"Are you kidding?" Cindy said. "I just wanta go to the parties. All the right people will give him parties. They do anyway, but these will be better parties. People from London and Paris will have to fly over."

"Why is Mrs. Cotswinkle beating her husband?" I asked.

"That's plain as a peanut," Cindy said. "She just found out he's fucking Oblivia Brown."

Chapter XIV _____

To Jake Ponsonby's evident disappointment, Dunscombe Cotswinkle was not dead.

For that matter, he was not even subdued. As the next-to-last professional, he did not take kindly to being slapped around. When he finally got the sleep out of his eyes anger took its place. I twice saw him try to backhand his wife, but both times Perkins caught his arm and pretended to be stuffing it into a coat.

Within his limited domain, Perkins' professionalism was equal to either Cotswinkle's or Ponsonby's.

If anything, Ponsonby was harder to handle. The evening seemed to have taken a good deal out of him. He began to wobble, as if his legs were made of rubber, and wandered off down the hall in search of Lilah Landry.

Unfortunately, Lilah had just left with Eviste Labouchere, the small French journalist. This fact surprised no one but me.

"Lilah's a star-fucker," Cindy said. "Only she can't figure out who the stars are. On the whole I find her vague."

"I think she's got Eviste mixed up with Bernard Henri Lévy," Cindy added. "Can you imagine?"

I couldn't, since I had never heard of Bernard Henri Lévy. Naturally I didn't admit it.

At that point Ponsonby wobbled back in. Seeing a tall woman, he assumed he'd found Lilah.

"My dear, they said you'd gone," he bleated, staring upward toward Cindy's bosom.

Cindy just laughed her vigorous laugh.

"You got the wrong lady, Jake," she said. "Lilah went home."

The news struck Ponsonby to the heart. "It isn't time to leave. *I* haven't left."

"Premature, so premature," he added. "The silly girl."

With that he turned abruptly and wobbled off in search of a lower bosom. He promptly found one, too—it belonged to the Guatemalan who was gathering up the brandy snifters. The maid was swifter of foot than he was, but he trailed forlornly after her for a while, until she lost him completely by reversing her field and darting off toward the kitchen.

"It's my impression that this means the end of Western civilization as we know it," he said, as he came back by.

"Gee," I said, once he was out of earshot. "Maybe Lilah should have stuck around."

Cindy wasn't worried about Western civilization. "Let's split," she said.

The Penrose mansion was on N Street, while Cindy's house was on Q, down the alphabet but up the hill.

It was a brisk night and we walked along briskly, in tandem with it. Cindy seemed indignant, a state that comes naturally to her.

"Pencil's had it," she said, after half a block.

"Why?"

"She's always using me to entertain her B–list," Cindy said. "That's why."

We continued along briskly until we were up the steps and in the doorway of her house. Cindy flung her coat on a nice French bench, not unlike the one in the Penrose hallway.

She had a tastefully appointed if slightly predictable bedroom, in which only one thing really caught my eye: a white football helmet covered with sparkles, of the sort commonly awarded homecoming queens just as they are about to be crowned. This one sat on a walnut bureau near Cindy's windows.

"Gosh," I said. "Were you a homecoming queen?"

She had already shucked her dress. Before answering she glanced at her watch and took it off, as she walked over to me.

"Of course," she said. "Santa Barbara High."

For a daydream believer like myself it was the acme of something: the boy from the little cowtown in the West, the homecoming queen from the far Pacific shore.

But for Cindy it was no big deal.

"Come on," she said. "Let's go to bed. I gotta have my sleep."

Book II

Chapter I _____

"*Ho, ho, Cadillac Jack*," Boog chortled, when I walked into his Cleveland Park house the next day. He was lying on one end of a huge leather couch, looking deeply hungover, although it was four o'clock in the afternoon.

"Lookit him," he added. "Pussy-whipped, weak in the knee joints, and deprived of his common sense."

"What common sense?" Boss said. She was sitting on the other end of the couch, wearing a red caftan. The couch was littered with newspapers, as was much of the floor.

Linda Miller and Micah Leviticus sat on the floor, playing electronic tennis on the TV set.

A tall, surly-looking man in green fatigues stood over them, observing their every stroke and occasionally offering advice. When Boog mentioned my name he strode over and shook my hand vigorously.

"Moorcock Malone," he said. "Glad to meet you, fellah. That was a fine thing you did."

"What thing?" I asked, trying to remember some fine action I might have taken. I knew, of course, that Moorcock Malone was practically the most famous journalist in America, and that he was probably very well informed. Still, it was unsettling to think he knew more about me than I did.

Meanwhile, he was still shaking my hand and beaming his approval out of big serious brown eyes, though even while he was beaming he tried to keep one eye on the tennis game.

"Down, down!" he said, after Linda had just zipped two aces under the little bar of light that constituted Micah's racquet.

Micah cast an anxious eye at Boss.

"Boss, I'm getting behind again," he said.

"What fine thing?" I repeated.

"Why stabbing those pugs," Moorcock said. "A fine thing. Of course, drowning them in the finger bowls would have been even better. *That* would have been an excellent thing."

"There wasn't much water," I said.

"Oh, there's a way to do it," he said. "I saw it done once, near Vals-les-Bains."

"Like shit you did," Boss said.

Moorcock Malone looked hurt by Boss's disbelief. He stood without comment as Linda zipped another ace past Micah.

Then he suddenly furrowed his large brow, in an effort to better remember the pug drowning. I got the sense that Moorcock furrowed his brow as normal mortals might fiddle with the little knobs on a TV set: in order to sharpen the picture, bring out the living detail.

"Nineteen sixty-two," he said. "I was AP then, of course. European desk. Had been in Berlin, covering the Wall. Seems hard to believe now, but the Wall was a big story then. Jack Kennedy came over. The Wall was always worth a trip."

Micah Leviticus, down two sets, was darting anxious glances at Boss.

"Of course, the Wall got old," Moorcock said. "The Wall got very old. Went to Vals-les-Bains to interview General LaRoche-Jacquelin. Played a hunch. You could do that then.

"LaRoche–Jacquelin had a chateau near the Vals-les Bains. It was a little messy."

"Them chateaus is hard to keep clean," Boog allowed. "All the hired help run off and became movie directors."

"Oh no," Moorcock said, looking surprised. "The chateau was impeccable. It was the *situation* that was messy. The General's aide-de-camp was his mistress' brother."

"Shit, I wisht I had an aide-de-camp," Boog said. "First thing I'd have him do is go around and whip my kids for me. Bunch of little smartasses give me a haid ache."

"The General was tired of his mistress, and the aide-de-camp was tired of the General," Moorcock went on. "Can't blame him for that. LaRoche-Jacquelin was a mean fucker."

Boss got down behind Micah and began to rub his neck.

One reason Micah was so far behind was because of his obsession with trying to put topspin on the little electronic ball. Electronic topspin was beyond his manual skills, a fact Linda coolly took advantage of.

"To make a long story short," Moorcock concluded, "the aide-de-camp drowned the pug while the General was reciting his favorite passage from the 'Chanson de Roland.' "

Boss looked up for a moment. "For your information, Bobby," she said, "you don't make long stories short. You make short stories long."

Despite this criticism, Moorcock seemed satisfied with his account. He poured himself a drink from a pitcher of cocktails sitting on the coffee table.

Micah stubbornly continued his quest for topspin.

"I'd hate like shit to have to listen to a French general recite poetry," Boog said.

"Why, when you recite it to every little hooker who will take your money?" Boss asked.

"Hail, I recite Thomas Hardy," Boog said. "A man of wisdom. A man who understood the human condition, which is more than can be said for any French general."

"Match point," Micah said, hopelessly.

Chapter II _____

Linda Miller had the killer instinct. She seemed to be the Tracy Austin of TV tennis. Instantly she rammed home a final ace and switched the game off. Micah turned to Boss for comfort, while Linda ran and jumped on Boog's stomach, catching him by surprise.

"I heard you call me a smartass," she said. "You asked for it and now you're gonna get it."

Everyone at the Millers' seemed to be in a strange, Sunday

afternoon mood, not easy to put one's finger on. Micah was the first to articulate it.

"What we all need is Mary Tyler Moore," he said. "I hate days when there are no reruns. I miss her perky smile."

Moorcock Malone was glugging cocktails, a little frustrated at not being allowed to finish his story.

"The aide-de-camp got cashiered," he went on quickly. "Not for drowning the pug, for marrying a Greek woman. Then LaRoche-Jacquelin got cashiered, for talking back to De Gaulle. That leaves the mistress, who also got cashiered."

Boog sighed. "The French are a nation of cashiers," he said.

"The mistress sold art," Malone said. "She bought back art the Krauts had stolen from the French, only when she got it back to France she refused to cough it up. LaRoche-Jacquelin denounced her. Finally the CIA got her out, along with the art, in return for services rendered. She lives in Nashville now."

"My God," I said. "Mrs. Chalcocondylas! I know her."

Moorcock swallowed an ice cube, so surprised was he that a cowboy-looking person would have heard of someone he knew from his days with the AP.

Actually Mrs. Chalcocondylas was quite a jolly old lady, well known to every scout who had ever gambled a hundred bucks on a worthless copy of some Old Master. She cheerfully bought them all, cleaned them up, and fobbed them off for a few thousand dollars apiece on hillbilly record producers who felt the need for cultural legitimacy.

I had sold her twenty or thirty myself. She lived in a big corny Southern mansion, filled with real Seurats and equally real Vuillards.

"Jack, you darlink," she would exclaim, when I pulled five or six crappy paintings out of the Cadillac.

In every possible way she modeled herself on Marlene Dietrich, and since she was short and fat the accent was the only possible way.

"École de Titian," she would say, scraping at a painting with a long red fingernail. "École de Raphael."

École de Joplin, Missouri, would have been more like it.

Somehow I could never get across Missouri without buying several worthless paintings.

Micah switched the electronic tennis back on and we all sat watching the little speck of light bouncing monotonously back and forth across the silent set.

While we were amusing ourselves in that fashion, Moorcock left abruptly, to catch the shuttle. Linda Miller could not believe it.

"But he left his girl friend," she said. "He just left her. He didn't even go up to say goodbye."

"A blessing in disguise," Boog assured her.

But Linda was outraged. "How could he do that?" she asked, thumping her father a time or two for emphasis.

About that time the girl herself wandered in. She was a tall skinny redhead in her early twenties, dressed in a green satin running suit. I thought I detected a resemblance to Lilah Landry and I did. Her name was Andrea, but everybody called her Andy. Andy Landry, Lilah's daughter.

When informed that her lover had left, Andy expressed only mild dismay.

"Why that big ole asshole," she said. "We were gonna run."

Then she spread her long legs and began to do stretching exercises. When those were finished she began to jog in place, looking thoughtful.

"Actually, I'd rather run by myself," she said. "Bobby's always stopping to comb his hair."

And she jogged softly out.

"If a man did that to me I'd whack him," Linda said, looking pointedly at her father.

About a year later I was leafing through *The New Yorker*, trying to satisfy my long-standing obsession with Boog and Coffee.

Everytime I see a *New Yorker* I grab it and leaf through the ads, trying to anticipate what Boog might give her next. It's not exactly that I expect to control Coffee for the rest of her life, and of course I know she's not organized enough to set a price on herself, even subconsciously.

I think I'm just curious about what might cause the little

locket of her heart to spring open. A dozen Czechoslovakian Easter eggs? An Icelandic poncho? A Celtic cross from West Wales? Or a four-foot-long white aviator's scarf, a dashing reminder of the early days of flight?

I don't know, and I may never know, but while I was trying to figure it out I came across a poem by Micah Leviticus. The poem was called "Ode to Billy Jean." I don't know much about poetry or tennis but it was clear to me that Mary Tyler Moore had at least one rival for Micah's affections. It was a long poem and only the first stanza or two called back that strange afternoon at the Millers':

> Linda, implacable . . . aces
> Like Tracy's,
> Seven of them on a windy afternoon.
> The tall man did no running.
>
> He was not Pancho Gonzales,
> Far too tall to be Pancho Segura . . . no
> Topspin, despair, a scatter of papers.
> All three cashiered, mistress,
> General, aide-de-camp, and the pug
> Dead under the table
> At Vals-les-Bains.
> Billy Jean,
> Teen queen of San Diego, sees
> Wimbledon rising . . .

Chapter III ————————

The reason Moorcock Malone knew about my violence toward the pugs was because Cindy had spread the word while I was out buying her the Sunday papers.

She had forced me out of bed about noon, at which time it became imperative that she have the papers. For an A-list person like herself, the *Post* and the *Times* were moral imperatives. By the time I staggered back with my load of morally imperative newsprint she had finished her telephoning and was ready to get to work.

Some people approach Sunday papers in the spirit of an orgy—Cindy approached hers in the spirit of a seminar. Her discipline was little short of daunting. She didn't go for the comics, or the gossip columnists, as most people would have, but simply read the papers straight through, from the front page of the *Times* to the last page of the *Post*. She even read the *Times Magazine*. I wouldn't have believed it if I hadn't been lying on her fine sheets, watching her.

Out of shame, rather than interest, I made her let me have the want ads, so I could at least make a pretense of professionalism myself.

Actually I do read want ads professionally, most of the time. One develops an instinct for them—a sense of which garage sales might be worth hunting up, or which auctions might yield a few sleepers.

While Cindy read she brushed her hair, which was as filled with nice lights as good maple syrup. Once in a while she would glance up long enough to pick a few hairs out of the brush, and once or twice she glanced at me thoughtfully, as if considering whether on the whole I had been a good idea.

I kept quiet, halfheartedly drawing circles around a few garage sales, though I knew perfectly well that if there were any scouts at all in the D.C. area the sales would long since have been picked clean of everything but *Reader's Digest* books and cheap glassware, the two great staples of garage sales everywhere.

"What does your father do?" I asked Cindy.

"He owns two thousand apartment buildings," she said, turning a page.

Then she gave me a look.

"You know what I think?" I said.

Cindy looked up, with a touch of impatience.

"I think you ought to get rid of that bread sculpture," I said.

Actually I was nursing a modest inspiration. I already had

a clear sense that I ought to try to get Cindy away from Washington for a few days, onto something resembling my own turf. If I were going to cement our promising relationship I would have to do it somewhere far from butlers, where she wouldn't be distracted by the touching sight of Harris Fullinwider Harisse, stuck in a doorway.

"I think you ought to do a boot show," I said. "At least consider it."

She gave me a big grin. "Giving you the boot is what I'm considering," she said. "If I'm not careful you could fuck up my life."

For a moment my heart leaped up, thinking she must be afraid of falling in love with me, but that giddy sensation didn't last more than a few seconds.

What she meant, of course, was that I was not the most likely partner with which to ascend the social mountain.

"I thought you were always careful," I said.

"Naw," she said. "Sometimes I'm reckless. I've made mistakes before."

"What did the last one do?" I asked, out of morbid curiosity.

"He was an NBA guard," she said. "The point is, it wasn't enough. If he'd been an NFL quarterback it might have been enough, but an NBA guard just doesn't really count."

I kept quiet, trying to figure out where that left me.

A moment later Cindy told me, with a candor that hardly anyone except Tanya Todd and my two wives could have surpassed.

"You see my predicament," she said, pulling a few hairs out of the brush. "Here I am fucking down again. At least Maurice was a sports hero, but you're a complete nobody."

"Oh well," I said—stung slightly—"I was NRA bulldogging champion two years running."

Cindy laughed. "Tell that to Oblivia," she said. "Oblivia thinks a bulldog is something that sits on its ass and wheezes."

"Who *is* Oblivia Brown?" I asked.

"The hostess with the mostest," Cindy said. "We're going to her house Wednesday night, if you last that long."

It obviously didn't matter to her that my name struck terror into the hearts of auctioneers and antique dealers from Maine to Tacoma. She didn't understand that I was the superstar of the flea-market world, the man who found a hundred-thousand-dollar vase in De Queen, Arkansas. And if she had understood it might not have made any difference.

"Hey," I said. "Let's assume I survive a week or two."

Cindy looked up. "Okay," she said. "Let's assume you do."

"I think you should do an exhibition of boots," I said. "It's the perfect time. Cowboy fashions are sweeping the land. Cowboy art sells at ridiculous prices. Get rid of those Latvian breadcrumbs and fill the gallery with spectacular boots. Emerald-encrusted boots. Historic boots. Call your show 'The Cowboy Boot Its History and Aesthetics.' Do a major opening—massive media coverage. Who knows? The right people might come."

"Where would I get emerald-encrusted boots?" she asked.

"Be serious," I said. "Texas is full of emerald-encrusted boots. Also diamond-, ruby-, and sapphire-encrusted. I know an Amarillo millionaire with fifty pair. Every major hillbilly singer has them, not to mention Bum Phillips."

I was making an impression. Cindy looked almost curious.

"Historic boots might be harder, but they're there," I said. "The boots of Wild Bill Hickock, for example. Maybe Pancho Villa's boots."

"Who else?" she said.

"Oh well," I said. "I can't promise, but there's a chance I could get you the boots of Billy the Kid."

"The boots of Billy the Kid?" she said, looking at me with real interest for the first time in a couple of hours.

"Yep," I said. "His last pair. The boots he died in."

Chapter IV ─────────────

No question of it: the Kid's name was magic still.

Cindy's bright eyes, which had yet to cloud even momentarily with love of me, almost clouded at the thought of the media coverage she could get if she exhibited the boots of Billy the Kid at her gallery in Georgetown.

"Yeah," she said, approvingly. Apart from "naw," it was her sexiest word. There was something kind of All-American about the way she said those words. I couldn't begin to resist it—not that I'm known for my powers of resistance.

Then she looked at me closely.

"Are you kidding me?" she asked.

"Not at all," I said. "I know the precise location of the boots of Billy the Kid."

Of course I neglected to mention that every other boot-and-spur scout in the West also knew their precise location: a bank vault in Clovis, New Mexico.

"Finding the boots is no problem," I said.

"Then what's the problem?" she said. "Let's go get 'em."

I was so delighted I practically jumped out of bed. It was just what I had hoped she would say. In my eagerness to get started I was ready to overlook the actual problem, which was that the boots were the property of Uncle Ike Spettle, possibly the oldest and certainly one of the orneriest men in America.

By his own admission Uncle Ike was one of those lucky people who just happened to be in the right place at the right time, which in this case meant being in the backyard of Pete Maxwell's ranch house in eastern New Mexico on a July evening in 1881. He was nine years old at the time.

It was in that backyard that Pat Garrett shot Billy the Kid.

Fortunately for Uncle Ike, it was dark, and Pat Garrett was not immediately sure he had killed the right man. Not wanting to expose himself rashly, he retreated and waited awhile before going back to count coup.

During that interval, Uncle Ike saw his chance and grabbed the boots. As outlaw buffs all know, Billy the Kid was found barefooted, a circumstance usually explained by the fact that he had been lolling around in bed with his sweetheart and had just gone out to the waterbucket to refresh himself when Garrett happened on him.

However, it only takes a nodding acquaintance with the backyards of eastern New Mexico—the haunt of sandburs and scorpions, rattlesnakes and black widows—to convince one that a cagey man like Bill Bonney would have known better than to step into one of them barefooted.

Uncle Ike, meanwhile, had devoted almost a century to hanging onto those boots—in themselves just a scruffy pair of black boots, somewhat run down at the heels.

Long since superannuated as a cowboy, he had been for almost forty years a professional Old-Timer, driving buckboards in rodeo parades and cheerfully telling lies on small-town talk shows all over the West.

I had visited him several times, plied him with steak dinners, and left a standing offer of $20,000 on the boots—modest when one considers that Bat Masterson's Colt recently brought $52,000 at auction—and he hadn't even really been an outlaw.

In Uncle Ike's case, more than money was needed. After all, he had hung onto the boots for 99 years. What was needed was a grasp of the subtleties of possession, and that I had. The fact that Uncle Ike had kept the boots for 99 years didn't mean he would want to keep them for 103, assuming he lived.

Love affairs with objects sometimes end as abruptly as love affairs with people. Beulah Mahony had the Valentino hubcaps for 40 years, but she sold them to me without the slightest flicker of regret. One day they simply lost their magic, after which it was just a matter of seeing that they were passed on to a worthy successor.

In any case, a dash to Fort Sumner, New Mexico, to see Uncle Ike would accomplish my main purpose, which was to get Cindy out of town for a while. Once there, if the old bastard balked I could still run over to Amarillo and fill the car with emerald-encrusted substitutes.

"I gotta get going," Cindy said, stretching. "It's Sunday afternoon. On Sunday afternoon I have tea with Harris and his mother."

"Tea?" I said.

Cindy looked defiant.

"Ordinary tea?" I asked.

"Of course," she said. "High tea would be a little ostentatious."

"Why do you have to do it?" I asked, too surprised to dissemble.

"Mrs. Harisse is testing me," Cindy said. "After all, I am Harris' fiancée. She wants to see if my manners are adequate."

"Why should you have to be tested?"

"Because I come from southern California and have a father who owns two thousand apartment buildings," she said, reaching out to get her watch off the breakfast table. Within two minutes she had arranged her shining hair into a surprisingly demure bun.

Then she went to her closet and emerged with an equally demure tea dress, complete with a prim white collar.

Before my very eyes the unconstrained woman of the California beaches transformed herself into Emily Dickinson. She even put on hose and sensible black shoes. The disciplines of social climbing were apparently unrelenting.

"Hey," I said. "How long do you have to be tested?"

"Probably about another year," she said.

"Haven't you fucked up yet at all?" I asked.

"Nope," she said with a grin. "So far I've been impeccably well mannered. I've never helped myself to the sugar cubes and I never eat more than two cucumber sandwiches. That's the hard part. I love cucumber sandwiches. I could eat about fifty, if I turned myself loose."

"What if you lose control and snarf up eight or ten?" I said. "Is the engagement off?"

"Sure," she said. "Mrs. Harisse would be horrified if I did that. But I won't."

She scratched her armpit thoughtfully for a moment, before slipping on the tea dress. Then she came over and bit my earlobe. We nuzzled around a bit. Maybe Cindy was just making up for the restraint she would have to practice when the cucumber sandwiches were trucked in.

Chapter V _____

Although she lived several blocks from Harris and his mother, she firmly refused to let me give her a ride. It was obvious the engagement would be off in a second if Mrs. Harisse should happen to see her disembarking from a car like mine.

Actually I felt a little better about my chances already. If Mrs. Harisse was worth her salt—and why wouldn't she be? —it would only be a matter of time before she penetrated Cindy's disguise. Even demurely dressed she didn't look much like a New England virgin.

Precisely an hour and a half later I met her at her shop and we spent a pleasant afternoon pricing her newly acquired cowboyana. Then we went to a Chinese restaurant and Cindy put away an amazing amount of shrimp fried rice. I tried to get her interested in scouting by telling her stories about Zack Jenks, the world's greatest Coke-bottle scout, one of the simplest and most amusing men I knew, but it didn't work. Cindy wasn't interested in scouting. She was interested in eating a lot of rice, having a normal amount of sex, and getting her sleep, which is exactly the order in which things occurred.

When I woke up for the second time in her bed she was already up and dressed, ready to bop off for the day to New York to buy some dresses for her dress shop. She looked beautifully organized and also beautiful.

Once she was ready, she came over to the bed and scrutinized me thoughtfully, in the way that she had. She had a newspaper tucked under her arm and an elegant little Fendi briefcase in her lap, all ready to go.

"What are you gonna do all day?" she asked.

"Scout," I said.

"Okay," she said, "but don't go too far away. Just buy things around here. I'll be back on the four o'clock shuttle."

I've always been a little intimidated by women who wake up early. It may have been why I got along so well with Coffee. Not only did she not wake up early: it could truthfully be said that she was seldom fully awake.

Cindy Sanders was fully awake. "Did you hear me?" she asked.

"Okay," I said, willing to agree to anything. "I heard you."

"There's a party at the Iranian embassy tonight," she said. "We might go. Check in with me at the shop about five-thirty."

The minute she went out the door I felt the need to be immersed in my own element again, my element being objects.

Thirty minutes later I was downtown, in the thick of an auction, arriving just in time to buy the best quadripartite icon I had ever seen.

Chapter VI _____

When I say the thick of an auction I mean it literally: nothing short of an execution will pack a crowd tighter than the chance to buy something.

When I walked in the crowd was balled up around the auctioneer like Italians at a meat counter.

As usual—though it was just a normal junky auction, of the sort held regularly in the estate-clearance rooms of big city auction houses—every conceivable kind of person was represented in the crowd. Perhaps there were no *grandes dames* of the ilk of Harris' mother, but excepting the crustiest of the upper crust, all America was there: ghetto mothers, hoping to get a wobbly table or a secondhand coat for a buck or two; lawyers in pinstripes, tired of lawyering; and bankers in camel's hair coats, bored with their banks; junk dealers; antique dealers; scouts and hustlers of every description; pimps and whores, killing a little time before hitting the streets; young stockbrokers hoping to find a good sporting print to go over their fireplaces; old ladies in raggedy furs, with their eye on a demitasse service or a nice footstool covered in needlepoint; finally, wives—wives of all ages, weights, and shades of chic, from suburban mothers in down vests and parkas, looking for a serviceable baby bed or a set of Swedish carving knives, on up to elegant matrons from Georgetown or Chevy Chase, each of them hoping to find something decent to spend their husband's money on.

Mixed in with the wives was the usual heavy concentration of doctors, the world's most persistent bargain hunters, restlessly pawing through the junk in the hopes of finding something worth a hundred times what it would cost them.

As a regular of such gatherings, I might detest the doctors, but the group I feared was the wives. The doctors, however rich, seldom had the courage of their instincts when the bidding got hot; but the wives, however dumb, bid with the absolute courage that accompanies absolute boredom. Wives are the bane of every scout: they welcome challenge and will pay any price for something they have decided they want.

Actually, they just like the thrill of bidding. The crush and competition of the auction turned them on: all that greed is sexy. Their eyes would glow with passionate lights when they triumphantly secured, for five or six hundred dollars, some object any competent dealer would have sold them for two twenty-five.

If there was anything about this particular crowd that bespoke Washington it was all the pasty-looking civil servants, wandering around like newly risen zombies. They wore beige trench coats and cheap little woolen hats, and there were dozens of them, GS–5s to however high GSs go, men so circumscribed in their styles as to seem neither dead nor alive. They stared at the assembled junk without interest, lacking the fever of the doctors or the passion of the wives. So far as I could tell they were only there because they had to go *somewhere* on their coffee breaks or lunch hours.

Possibly one or two of them collected something exotic: the chess sets made from Ecuadorian Twaia beans, for example, but if so, whatever they were turned on by wasn't there and they mostly just stood around in front of the worn-out armchairs or the indifferent chinaware, watching the bidding dully, as if it were a sporting event whose rules and purpose eluded them.

Somewhat to my surprise, Brisling Bowker, the owner of the auction house, was doing his own auctioneering when I walked in.

Brisling Bowker was a huge man, with a permanently pained demeanor not unlike Jackie Gleason's.

I nodded hello to Tuck Tucker, Bowker's amazing floor manager. Tuck was certainly one of the most formidable talents on the popcorn auction scene. When I walked in he was at the pay phone, taking one bid in his left ear while an old lady in a mink coat whispered another into his right ear. In the course of an all-day sale he would take and execute hundreds of bids, on everything from lawn mowers to verdure tapestries, gliding through the crush of the auction like a surfer who's just caught a wave.

His job was to cover the floor, making sure the various hustlers and auction rats didn't stuff a camera or an ivory or some other valuable object into a two-buck box of junky bric-a-brac. He flicked his bids with the éclat of a world-class Ping-Pong player, bidding with a wink, a whistle, a snap of his fingers, the lift of an eyebrow—and he always hit his lot, whether it happened to be a cracked tea service some little old lady had decided to go to $20 on, or a diamond bracelet a lobbyist thought might impress his girl friend.

Boog, who played auctions like some people play horses, reposed more trust in Tuck than he did in the President, the Chief Justice, and the leaders of both houses of Congress.

Over the years Tuck had bought him everything from Amberina punch cups to Owo masks.

I would have dallied an hour or two in Bowker's auction just to watch Tuck, but as it happened I had no immediate chance to do that. The icon came under the hammer just as I walked in.

The sight of it affected me like a big squirt of adrenalin. Brisling Bowker had just finished selling a couple of rusty push mowers and a barrelful of rakes and shovels to two hillbilly junk dealers who were probably planning to take them back to West Virginia and parlay them into a fortune.

Their lot sold for $4, and the lovely quadripartite icon was sitting there next to it, propped up between a worn-out washing machine and a pile of snow tires.

I would have liked a moment or two in which to try and figure out if it could be a fake, but I wasn't going to get one.

"All right, now we have your icon," Brisling intoned, in a voice replete with boredom.

Part of the boredom was real—selling push mowers and snow tires is not inspiring work—but most of it was calculated. Brisling looked ponderous, but he knew his work. He had been moving the junk along steadily, at the rate of three or four lots a minute, and it was plain he hoped to dispose of the icon without missing a beat.

"Do I hear forty dollars for your icon, now?" he asked, just as he happened to glance my way.

"Forty dollars," I said loudly, tipping my hat.

Chapter VII _____

Quadripartite icons, I should point out, are extremely rare. The few that turn up are normally auctioned at Sotheby's or Christie's, on a stand covered in velvet, to a crowd that will include most of the great dealers and collectors in America and western Europe.

Seldom indeed will one be lotted between a barrel of rakes and a pile of snow tires. Moreover, it was early in the morning, when most of the serious antique dealers weren't even there yet.

Obviously Brisling was hoping nobody would notice the icon.

My arrival spoiled that little game, but Brisling, who had been an auctioneer for forty years and seen his share of icons come and go, didn't so much as blink.

"Forty dollars I have," he said. "Forty-five dollars for the icon here."

Thirty seconds later it was knocked down to me for $1,300. The game had had no chance anyway: somebody else was onto the icon, if not several somebodies.

The figure stunned the crowd, most of whom had not noticed the icon and were caught flat-footed when the bidding took off.

The GS–12s looked slightly less blank, the sound of money being spent bringing a tinge of life to their pallid cheeks. Many of the wives looked puzzled and a little troubled, and several doctors looked mad enough to bite themselves, at the thought that some treasure had escaped their attention.

Naturally they assumed that if a cowboy would pay $1,300 for the icon it must be worth $50,000.

I would have liked to try to get a fix on the competition, but the bidding went from $40 to $1,300 in thirty seconds, bids darting in so rapidly that I didn't dare take my eye off Brisling Bowker, who then calmly proceeded to sell the snow tires, bringing the hillbilly junk dealers to life again.

I walked over to pick up my icon. Before I had gone two steps with it a doctor in a green overcoat was at my elbow, squinting at it.

"It could be Byelorussian," he said. "I'll give you two thousand for it, right here."

"Sorry, got a customer," I said, although I didn't. So far as I could remember, Boog didn't have any icons, although he could have been bidding on this one, through Tuck. I had no reason to think so, other than the fact that Boog is usually to be found, in person or in proxy, when the best things are being sold.

Then I noticed someone who took the bloom right off the morning: Schoeffer Schedel was leaning against the Coke machine, wearing his usual malign grin.

Schoeffer, known as the Baltimore Blinker, or simply Blink —after his manner of bidding—was the acknowledged king of American auction rats. He was small, bald, and bullet-headed, seemed to subsist on cigar stubs, and was always dressed in a dirty green suit, a white belt, multicolored shoes, and a blue tie whose knot was as big as an apple.

Blink was not noted for his amiability. He favored everyone with the same malign grin. You felt he was only grinning because he knew you were about to be run over by a truck.

This was indeed always a possibility, since the mysterious interests Blink represented owned a fleet of trucks. The trucks raced all over America, carrying the antiques Blink bought to mysterious warehouses in north Jersey. He seldom bothered with single items, but whenever possible bought estates or whole stores. I had encountered him as far afield as Tallahassee and Seattle, not to mention Harbor City, just south of L.A., where the single largest commercial flea market in the country operates practically full-time, like the casinos of Las Vegas.

So far in our careers Blink and I had not exchanged a single word, but it was well known, to ourselves and others, that we were arch rivals. Why this was so I don't know, since our methods were diametrically opposed. One icon, for example, would not have titillated him, but if he could have found a collection of five or six hundred he would have whipped out a grimy checkbook and scribbled in as many thousands of dollars as were required, after which the trucks would arrive to whisk the icons away to north Jersey. There they apparently would go into vast warehouses, to be fed back onto the antiques market through a complex system of veins and capillaries.

Who the interests were that supplied Blink with the loot to write his smudged but perfectly cashable checks no one knew.

All that was known about him was that he lived in a one-room apartment over a cathouse on Charles Street, in Baltimore. According to reliable witnesses, the oldest thing in the apartment was a television set dating from the late sixties.

At the moment he had every reason to hate me, since I had just bought the centerpiece from a collection of *façon-de-Venise* goblets owned by a retired general in Hilton Head.

Taking one piece out of a collection doesn't bother me. Collections are as numerous as clouds, and like clouds they form, break up, disappear, and form again. Blink immediately breaks the collections he buys, and in any case, nothing needs to stay in Hilton Head forever.

While I was casing the bric-a-brac in the front window I happened to notice a young woman standing with Tuck. She had her hands shoved deep in the pockets of a puffy blue down-filled jacket, and she was staring at me hotly. Either she was very angry in general, or she was very angry with me. If the latter, it could only be because of the icon tucked under my arm. The heat of her disapproval was so unmistakable that I looked away and spent more time inspecting a pewter beaker than was really necessary.

But when I looked her way again, she was still glaring at me, just as hotly. Tuck had his arm around her and seemed to be using all his considerable charm to get her out of her pet. For once, his considerable charm seemed to have no effect.

She was short and rather pretty, in a workaday way. So far as I could remember, a woman had never got mad at me over an icon, and I was curious. Perhaps her family had owned it and she had hoped to buy it back, in which case a deal could probably be struck.

I put on a mild look and strolled over to chat with Tuck.

"Howdy," I said, smiling at the young woman as I shook his hand.

Before either of us could say another word, she blushed, stopped looking angry, and merely looked disappointed, hopeless, and confused. Then she burst into tears, gulped a time or two, and ran out the door of the auction house, almost bowling over two astonished GS–12s, who had been standing there staring solemnly at a couch.

Tuck nodded in a bid on a rusty exercycle. He was evidently relieved that the storm had broken.

"You just bought the only thing she wanted," he said. "I got news for you, too. The fat man ain't gonna buy it."

Boog likes to think he is as smooth and sinister as Sydney Greenstreet, a fantasy Tuck and I went along with, to a certain extent.

"The fat man has changed his mind before," I reminded him. "Who was that girl?"

"A new dealer," he said. "Her name is Jean Arber. She's got a little store, out in Wheaton.

"My, my," he added, in tones of admiration. "That girl *wants* it when she wants it!"

I had the unhappy sense that I had just managed to bruise a kindred spirit.

Probably the young lady was just like me. When I see something like the icon, I *want* it. Sometimes the mere sight of such an object causes me to hyperventilate, out of fear that it will somehow slip out of reach.

I left the icon in the keeping of one of the floormen and stepped quickly outside, hoping to find the woman and make amends.

Sure enough, she was leaning against the window of a carry-out sandwich shop, heaving deep sighs and attempting to dry her cheeks. Her puffy blue coat rose and fell like a balloon, just from the sighs she was heaving.

When she saw me step out of the door she quickly turned away, but I didn't let that stop me.

"Miss Arber," I said, "could I talk to you for a minute?"

"Mrs.," she said, turning her face but not her body. It was an intelligent face, but dwarfed by the ridiculous puffy coat.

"Mrs. Arber," she added, "although I'm taking my own name back as soon as the divorce goes through."

"What's the name you're taking back?" I asked.

She looked at me solemnly. What makes my name any of your business, the look said.

I tried a smile. "Never be afraid to ask," I said. "It's a rule I try to live by."

Actually I was afraid to look at her for fear she'd start crying again, overcome by the memory of the icon. But I did look, that being another rule I try to live by. Women may get annoyed with you for looking at them, but they distrust you if you don't.

"Tooley," she said, with a last snuffle. "Jean Tooley."

"Jack McGriff," I said, holding out my hand.

She looked at the hand as if she'd never seen one, but after a moment she shook it.

Chapter VIII _____

After the handshake there was an awkward pause, made slightly more awkward by the fact that the carry-out place whose window Jean Arber née Tooley was leaning against was full of GS–12s, many of whom were staring at us as solemnly and dispassionately as if we had been a couch.

Like the ones in the auction, these GS–12s also wore beige trench coats and funny little woolen hats. Unlike the ones in the auction they had hot dogs or pastrami sandwiches in their hands, eating them dispassionately even as they directed the same dispassion at us.

"I hate those GS–12s," I said. "Would you like to take a walk?"

I don't think Jean Arber had noticed that her distress had provided fifty or sixty civil servants with something to look at during their lunch hour.

When she looked around and saw them she blushed and ducked down inside her puffy blue coat. I must say it made an effective shield. She was a small woman and when she chose to pop out of sight all that remained visible were her hands and her feet. The effect was so turtlelike that I laughed.

Then I impulsively grabbed the coat by the arm and hustled it a few doors down the street.

This effrontery caused her head to come back up. It rested on a very nice neck.

Unfortunately, Jean still looked miserable. So far my cheerfulness had had no effect. After all, I could afford to be cheerful. I had the icon.

"I hate it when I do things like this!" she said. "There's no excuse, you understand. I knew all along I wouldn't get it."

"Why not?" I asked. "After all, I might not have walked in just when I did. If I'd caught one more red light it would have made the difference."

"No, I wasn't even the under-bidder," she said. "I only have seven hundred dollars to my name and I certainly shouldn't blow it on something like an icon."

"Why not?" I asked, having often spent my last seven hundred dollars on objects like icons.

Jean Arber looked guilty. "Because I've got two kids," she said. "*Little* kids. And Jimmy is not exactly regular with his child support."

"Oh," I said. I could see that kids put things in a different light.

"How high did you go?" I asked.

I still had hold of her arm and had begun to ease us down the street. Without her noticing it, we had begun to take a walk.

"Seven hundred!" she said, spilling a new freshet of tears onto the slick down coat. "I would have blown every cent of it! My kids could have been starving by next week!"

I was feeling better and better. At long last I had found a woman who was just like me. Kids or no kids, I would have done exactly the same thing.

As we were passing an office supply store Jean suddenly stopped and looked at herself in the window.

"I see a bad mother," she said glumly. "A very bad mother."

"Now, now," I said. "If your kids were really starving you could pawn your coat. It's too big for you anyway."

She glanced at her image again. "What's wrong with this coat?" she asked, remorse over her deficiencies as a mother being replaced by a note of defiance.

"I don't think it's too big," she said, still looking. "It's down-filled."

"Right," I said, "and it fits you like a duck blind. All I can see is the top of your head."

She stopped looking at herself and looked at me.

"Well," she said, "you are unusually tall. Most of the people in my life are short."

Then she shrugged, and we continued our unacknowledged walk.

"Of course at the moment the only people in my life are my kids, which explains why all the people in my life are short," she said thoughtfully, as if she had just succeeded in explaining something that had been puzzling her slightly.

"I should have been firm with myself," she added, ducking her head inside her coat for a moment.

"Can you make yourself stop wanting something just by being firm?" I asked. "That's real self-discipline."

"It would be if I had it," she said, ruefully. "I don't have it. Instead of being firm I make up scenarios."

"What happens in the scenarios?"

She smiled, colored, became lovely. "I get whatever it is I want," she said. "Like the icon. All the people with more money than me get the flu and stay home, or else they get stuck in horrible traffic jams on Connecticut Avenue and don't arrive in time to bid against me."

We were walking past a large restaurant. Instead of being full of GS–12s it seemed to be full of high school kids from Wisconsin, come to see their nation's capital. The tour bus that brought them was waiting outside the restaurant, waiting to take them back to Wisconsin.

"Have breakfast with me," I said. "It's your duty as a mother."

"Pardon me?" she said, indicating that the logic of the statement eluded her.

"I know your kind," I said. "In fact, I *am* your kind."

"Now you're telling me you're a mother?" she asked, looking amused.

"No, a buyer," I said. "Like you. Therefore I know perfectly well what you'll do if I turn you loose."

She waited curiously for me to tell her what she'd do.

"You'll run right back into that auction and buy something you don't really want, to make up for losing the icon."

It was not a particularly discerning remark, since that is what any auction-prone person would do, but Jean looked at me as if I were Sigmund Freud.

While she was looking I hustled her into the restaurant, which may well have contained every teenager in the state of Wisconsin.

Jean stared at me from the depths of her coat. She ordered coffee and Danish. I ordered a huge breakfast.

Now that we were alone and hidden from the world by several thousand teenagers, we both seemed to feel a little shy.

I put my hat on the table and Jean nervously reached out a finger and touched the albino diamondback hatband.

"That's beautiful," she said. "Is that from a rattlesnake?"

Then, even more nervously, she felt the sleeve of my doe-skin jacket.

"Gosh," she said. "That's beautiful, too."

The feel of my sleeve seemed to cause the down-filled jacket to lose a few points. She unzipped it, but it still surrounded her, more or less like a duck blind.

"What would you have bought if I hadn't forced you in here?" I asked.

"I'd have bought a few trunks," she said. "They're really my favorite thing. Wooden trunks."

I should have guessed it. She had the look of a trunk person: delicate, wistful, a little withdrawn. I've known many trunk people and I'm convinced they accumulate trunks in order to have places in which to hide themselves away when the world becomes too much—as sooner or later it will.

However, I wasn't about to offer Jean Arber that analysis. Far better to offer her a trunk. It was clear she would be offended if I tried to give her the icon, so if I was going to ply her with anything it had better be trunks.

"Hey, I've got a wonderful trunk in my car," I said, thinking of my brass-bound traveling trunk. It was one of my favorite possessions, but then again it was hardly the only brass-bound traveling trunk in the world. Every rich Englishman of the nineteenth century had one, not to mention all the Continental nobility.

I could easily get another, and possibly a better, traveling trunk, but there was no guarantee I could get Jean Arber at all. She was looking at me with the quiet wariness that is characteristic of trunk people.

Nonetheless, thirty minutes later I sold her my little trunk for only two hundred of her precious dollars. Fortunately her wariness was not as strong as her need for beautiful things.

"Oh, gee!" she said, when she saw that trunk. It was a lovely trunk, but then it caused Jean to smile her lovely smile.

By happy coincidence her beat-up old camper—a relic of her marriage, as she said—was parked right behind my Cadillac, in front of a row of gay burlesques, porn theaters, and cut-rate liquor stores. A number of black dudes in pimp clothes were eyeing my car respectfully.

I had of course taken the precaution of removing the Valentino hubcaps, and also a graceful little Brancusi hood ornament I had acquired in Scottsdale. Brancusi had made it for a rich and titled Lesbian who had had the eventual misfortune to die in Phoenix.

Jean was too delighted with her trunk to pay much attention to my car. She continued to smile while we put the trunk in her camper, but, as her pen was poised to write the check, the smile was briefly replaced by a look of mild suspicion.

"Are you just doing this because I got so upset about the icon?" she asked.

"Which would you rather have if you had to choose?" I asked. "The icon or the trunk?"

The pen remained poised. "I *am* normal in some respects," she said. "I'd rather not have to choose."

She smiled a slightly more subdued smile.

"I'd rather be able to buy everything I want, like you do," she said. "You're pretty lucky, you know. Not everyone can indulge themselves that way."

"When can I come see your shop?"

She frowned. "Do you really want to?" she said. "I don't think I have anything that's in your class."

Naturally I really wanted to, in order to see more of her. Selling her the trunk had been a way of forging a small link.

"I was thinking of coming this afternoon," I said.

She peered at me from the blue depths of her coat for a moment.

"O. Kay," she said slowly, making it into two words. Then she wrote the check.

"You don't believe in letting any grass grow, do you?" she asked.

I just smiled.

"Okay," she said, more briskly. "The address is on the check. But if you come after three you better be prepared to deal with a couple of real kids."

Then she climbed into the camper and eased away, driving very cautiously, with both hands on the wheel.

While I was watching her, a pimp in a pearl-white suit came up and tried to buy my Cadillac.

"Oh, come on, man!" he said, when I demurred. "Don't you see? It matches my threads."

Chapter IX _____

Impressed as I was with Jean Arber, making her acquaintance had not left me entirely bereft of professional instincts. Blink Schedel was in Washington, and it was not likely he had come solely for the pleasure of leaning on the Coke machine. If he was there, it meant he was onto something, and I wanted to know what.

Besides, my other set of instincts—those that guided me, so to speak, through the swap-meets of love—suggested that it would not do to crowd Jean too hard. Better to let her have a few hours to herself, to contemplate all the beautiful things I might have, not to mention the extraordinary trunks I could procure.

I make my share of mistakes, but one I never make is to underestimate the power of *things*. People imbued from childhood with the myth of the primacy of feeling seldom like to admit they really want *things* as much as they might want love, but my career has convinced me that plenty of them do. And some want things a lot worse than they want love.

By good luck, when I returned to the auction the first person I encountered was Brisling Bowker himself. He had finished his stint as auctioneer and was standing at the front of the auction room, lord of all he surveyed.

Specifically, what he was surveying was one of his minions attempting to auction the fixtures from a bankrupt pet store. The pet fixtures consisted mostly of cages for rabbits and hamsters, whose smell lingered after them. The rabbits and hamsters might have gone on to happy homes, but their cages stank like shit, which is perhaps why the minion had so far only been able to raise a bid of $16 for the fifty or sixty cages, plus several packs of unused kitty litter.

Brisling watched the proceedings impassively, out of frosty gray eyes, outwardly unmoved when his minion ceased prodding the unresponsive crowd and sold what was left of a pet store for $16.

Some auctioneers are mesmerized by the ebb and flow of their own junk, and will watch it for hours, as beach goers watch waves, but Brisling was not so easily mesmerized. His frosty eyes restlessly scanned the crowd, keeping tabs on the suckers, the thieves, and the scroungers. Some of the latter were perfectly capable of discreetly chipping a teapot or tearing the fabric on an armchair in the hopes of getting the object a little cheaper.

"I thought Texas was a big state," he said, glancing at me. "How come you can't stay in it?"

"Not enough icons down there," I said.

He looked distant and uninterested. For him the icon had become as remote as World War I, although it had been propped up ten feet from us less than an hour before.

"I've been told it's Byelorussian," I said.

He looked at me as if I were a complete idiot.

"Armenian," he said.

In truth, I wasn't very interested in the icon myself, anymore. Something more interesting, namely Jean Arber, had popped into view. I can be fickle, but not so fickle as to forget Blink Schedel.

"I guess the Smithsonian must be for sale," I said. "Otherwise Blink wouldn't be up this early."

Brisling, normally as stolid as a sleeping walrus, looked as if he'd just been harpooned.

"How'd you know?" he said, too shaken to be able to hold his tongue.

"How'd I know what?" I asked.

It was difficult for Brisling Bowker to look perplexed. Years of selling every imaginable species of object to every conceivable species of buyer had prepared him for just about everything. The secret lusts of the human heart were no secret to him. Nonetheless, I had clearly perplexed him, a reaction so unexpected that for a moment I couldn't remember what I had just said.

I looked at him and he looked at me: then I remembered. I had said the Smithsonian must be for sale.

Naturally, I had been joking. The Smithsonian would never be for sale. Even Blink Schedel, with his mysterious fleet of trucks, couldn't handle a deal that big.

Besides, who could sell it? The Smithsonian belonged to America, or at least so I had assumed.

On the other hand, it is usually a mistake to assume that something can't be sold. France sold Louisiana, and most of the West. Russia sold Alaska. London sold its bridge. MGM sold its back lot. So probably America could sell the Smithsonian, if the right offer came along.

I was so stunned by the thought that I didn't say another

word. Neither did Brisling Bowker, but he did look at me with something like respect for the first time since I'd known him.

All of a sudden Brisling's workaday auction room took on a new ambiance: the ambiance of a spy novel. For all I knew one of the GS–12s, in their humble woolen hats, might be a liaison man. The transaction of the century might even then be taking place, somewhere in the vicinity of Brisling's Coke machine.

Blink was no longer actually leaning on the Coke machine, but he was still holding his position, poking absently in a table full of old books that were piled nearby.

To buy time, which is what one must do in a spy novel, I pretended to be interested in the contents of a row of rusty filing cabinets that were about to come up. Oddly enough, the contents of the filing cabinets actually *were* interesting. Their files were still in them, in the form of thousands of copies of a pamphlet on the kangaroo rat. The pamphlet had been written by a retired admiral whose sideline was mammalogy. Evidently the pamphlet had not sold at all well.

Any other time I would have bought the cabinets just to get the pamphlets, since I knew a pamphlet collector in Mobile who would have bought them in an instant. His name was Beaufort Kiff, and he was one of the most out-of-control collectors I knew. Once at an auction in Pensacola I saw Beaufort buy 4,000 copies of a pamphlet on *terza rima*, the last effort of an Italian diplomat who had, of course, written it in Italian, a language Beaufort couldn't have told from Finnish.

Several thousand copies of a pamphlet on the kangaroo rat would have made him deliriously happy, but for once I was derelict in my duty. If the Smithsonian was indeed for sale, how could I afford to take time to mail thousands of pamphlets to Mobile?

The filing cabinets, with their valuable hoard of pamphlets, were sold to a couple of junk dealers, while I stood around in a quandary, unable to decide what to do.

I was tempted to go back over to Brisling and just ask him point-blank what was going on, but when I looked, Brisling had vanished. Like many large animals, he could move with stealth when the need arose.

Blink, meanwhile, had gone nowhere and spoken to no one, though he was standing next to a dumpy little old woman who was apathetically wrapping string around a few of the secondhand books.

In spy novels, of course, it is just such dumpy little women who manage to throw experienced spies off the scent.

Tuck stood nearby. One of the more timid of the suburban wives had just given him a bid on some Swedish carving knives.

"Who's that little woman?" I asked, nodding at her as discreetly as possible.

Tuck grinned. "Mrs. Lump?" he said. "You're telling me you don't know Mrs. Lump?"

I was beginning to feel like an amateur, a feeling I hate. Like all professionals, I like to feel professional, which in my case involves knowing, at least by reputation, every important dealer, scout, or collector in the country. Admittedly it's a big complex country, but not everyone in it is an antique scout, either. It was chastening to have to think that I had failed to take note of a woman important enough to be able to sell the Smithsonian to Blink Schedel.

I always keep a neatly folded $100 bill in my watch pocket, for just such situations. On the flea-market circuit a hundred dollars will usually buy a lot of information.

But unfortunately Tuck wasn't a flea-marketer. He was a professional, too, with dozens of his own games going. When I showed him the bill he shook his head.

"Keep it," he said. "I don't know that much about the deal."

"I've got to start somewhere," I said.

"Start by asking the fat man," he said. "If God knows more than the fat man I ain't noticed it."

Chapter X _____

Tuck was right, of course. Boog would know about the Smithsonian, or if he didn't know he would find out. Boog had more sources than the *Post* and the *Times* put together, which is why large segments of the staffs of those papers were apt to be found in his kitchen at any given moment.

Since it was plain to me that I wasn't going to learn anything by watching Blink Schedel and Mrs. Lump, I left and headed for Boog's office as fast as I could go. When I passed the National Portrait Gallery, which I knew to be a part of the Smithsonian, I half expected to see Blink's minions loading the national portraits into the fleet of trucks. The fact that it wasn't happening gave me heart.

Boog's office was in a sinister-looking black building on First Street, not far from Union Station. I didn't expect to find him in it, and I didn't. Since he had left politics to become an all-purpose consultant he had felt free to use his time inventively.

His lobby was filled with lobbyists, all of them wearing expensive suits and hopeless expressions. The hopeless expressions probably meant that they knew in their heart of hearts that Boog wasn't going to show up and tell them what they needed to know.

Boog's secretary was a grizzled old girl from Winkler County named Bobbie Proctor. She was smoking as fast as she could smoke, and reading the *National Enquirer* when I came in. So far all my efforts to get on her good side had failed. It was entirely possible that Bobbie didn't have a good side.

"Morning," I said.

"Yeah, it is," Bobbie said, glancing at her watch.

"I just need to see Boog a minute," I said.

"I don't know why you come here, then," she said. "This is just where he keeps his telephones."

"Got any notions about where he might be?"

Bobbie sighed, not happy to have her reading interrupted.

"I got a notion he's off gettin' his rocks hauled," she said.

Beyond that she refused to contribute a syllable of information, though even that was enough to inflame the lobbyists' hopes. When I went out, five or six of them were strung out down the line of pay phones in the foyer, calling various madams and massage parlors, in the hope of stumbling on Boog.

After some thought, I picked up my car phone and called Boss. Micah Leviticus answered.

"Hi, Micah," I said. "Can I speak to Boss for a moment? I need to find Boog."

"Isn't he at the Little Bomber's?" Micah asked.

"The what?"

"The Little Bomber's Lounge," Micah said, impatiently. Then he began to giggle.

"What's the matter?" I asked.

"Oh, nothing," he said. "Boss is just tickling me with her hair."

"Where's the Little Bomber's Lounge?"

"It's in Arlington," he said. "If you find Boog tell him not to forget to buy the new *TV Guide*. The ones they put in the Sunday papers don't have much depth."

"I'll tell him," I said. "Sorry if I called at a bad time."

"It's not a bad time," Micah said. "Bob Newhart doesn't come on for half an hour."

I zipped right across in front of the Capitol, which was looking very white in the bright fall air. Then the next thing I knew I was in the south parking lot of the Pentagon—no real surprise, but something I had been sort of hoping to avoid.

When I claimed mastery of every freeway system in the country I should have excepted the bewildering vortex that innocent travelers get sucked into when they cross the Potomac going south.

Instead of being filled with soldiers, the south parking lot is usually filled with bewildered old couples in Buicks and Winnebagos, from places like Minnesota and Nebraska, who stand around scratching their heads and wondering what their chances are of escaping the parking lot and getting back home. The freeways near there don't seem to quite connect with one another, so that if the old couples did find their way out of the parking lot they were probably doomed to swirl around in a vast concrete roller-rink for an hour or so before they could get pointed toward Nebraska. Seeing them always made me slightly melancholy, since I knew that the Buicks and Winnebagos were filled with ashtrays with the Capitol stamped on them, or else with hideous little embroideries showing the pandas in the National Zoo.

Eventually I found the Little Bomber's Lounge, squeezed in between a 7-Eleven and a TV repair shop.

There was no doubt that Boog was somewhere near, since a muddy black Lincoln with his name on the license plate sat directly in front of the Little Bomber's Lounge.

Even if the car hadn't looked like it had just come out of a swamp I would have known it was Boog's by the back seat, which was piled with whiskey bottles, Penguin paperbacks, Xeroxes of bills Boog had an interest in, and piles and piles of brochures on every imaginable product, from antitank weapons to racquet-ball paddles—all of which one of the lobbyists waiting hopelessly in his office probably hoped Boog would persuade some contact in the procurement division of the Pentagon to buy in vast quantities and disperse to army bases around the world.

When I stepped into the lounge I immediately met a couple of little bombers, both in the process of getting bombed. They were both as plump as ducks and as cheerful as they could be. At most they were in their early twenties and a happier two girls would have been hard to find. Between giggles they drank rum Cokes and watched the same Bob Newhart rerun that Micah was probably watching across the river in Boss's bedroom.

"Lookit them yell-ah boots," one said, in a voice I would have said belonged to South Carolina, possibly the vicinity of Myrtle Beach. In fact the girl, whose name was Lolly, hailed from Nashua, New Hampshire.

"Hi, girls," I said. "Do you know a man named Boog?"

The girls laughed heartily. They were so cheerful I felt like laughing myself, though up to that point I had been feeling rather tense.

"I guess we should know him," Lolly said. "He's putting us through secretarial school."

"Yeah, only I'm fixin' to quit," the other one said. "I don't see why ah need it."

"Well, if you quit I'm quittin'," Lolly said. "I ain't goin' all the way to Thirteenth Street by myself, I can tell you that."

"I don't mind the typin'," the would-be drop-out said. "Shoot, I don't even mind the niggers. What I hate is that shorthand."

"All right, Janie Lee," Lolly said. "You know good an' well Boog ain't gonna let us be his executive secretaries unless we can take shorthand."

The notion that the two plump blondes were being groomed to succeed the redoubtable Bobbie Proctor struck *me* as funny. It also afforded me a rare glimpse into Boog's working methods. Probably half the secretarial schools in the D.C. area were filled with chubby teenagers whose tuition Boog was paying.

"Well, you know what," Janie Lee said defiantly, "I'd rather stay over here in Arlington and suck people off in whirlpool baths than to learn shorthand. I don't mind suckin' people off in whirlpool baths. Sometimes it's kinda fun, 'specially if you drink a bottle or two of champagne first."

"I know," Lolly said agreeably, "but it still ain't glamorous, like bein' an 'xecutive secretary."

"Besides," Lolly added, tapping Janie Lee on the wrist, "Boog said once we get our diplomas he'd introduce us to Teddy Kennedy."

Janie Lee looked sulky for a moment. Obviously a chance to meet the Senator was not to be taken lightly—on the other hand, her dislike of shorthand was great.

Nobody was in the lounge except myself, the two girls, and a small Mexican with a mop. The small Mexican had become engrossed in the Bob Newhart show and was leaning on his mop, watching it. The question of whether fellatio was a better way to make a living than typing and shorthand did not appear to interest him.

In fact, it had even ceased to interest the girls. They were giving my outfit the once-over.

"I seen somebody like you in Las Vegas," Janie Lee said. "Only he had red boots instead of yell-ah."

"We both been to Las Vegas," Lolly said. "We won the Happy Hooker contest."

"Who organized that?" I asked, though I could have guessed.

"Why, Boog," Janie Lee said. "He's real generous. It was an all-expenses-paid weekend."

"The only bad thing about the weekend was the plane ride made my ears ring," Lolly said.

"Where is Boog?" I asked.

"Up at the Bubble Bath, two doors up the street," Lolly said. "We'll take you. We gotta get to work anyway."

"Hey," Janie Lee said. "We could offer him the Double Bubble Brunch. It ain't but ten-fifteen."

The suggestion seemed to dispel all thoughts of secretarial school. I was being looked at significantly by two happy little professionals, their faces slightly pinked by early-morning rum Cokes.

Though well aware that I was already in enough woman trouble, I couldn't claim to feel 100 percent resistant, even with the Smithsonian hanging in the balance.

"What's involved in a Double Bubble Brunch?" I asked.

Lolly ticked off the essentials on her fat little fingers.

"Well, the double part means me an' Janie Lee," she said—"I mean both of us in the bath with you at the same time. The bubble part is just a bubble bath, of course."

"He can get a color of his choice," Janie Lee reminded her. "We got purple an' all kinds of colors."

"Yeah, color of your choice," Lolly said, ticking off a finger. "An' naturally it's a whirlpool bath and you get a bottle of champagne and a massage first, if you want one, and it's only a hundred dollars up to eleven A.M."

"We used to run it till noon and it was real popular," Janie Lee said. "The Congressmen used to just pour in here about eleven-fifteen, hopin' to squeeze it all in between votin' or whatever they do."

"It got too popular," Lolly said. "Nobody wanted to pay the afternoon rates, so now it's only good till 'leven."

The thought of lolling around drinking champagne in a purple whirlpool bubble bath with two chubby girls was pretty diverting, though it was the last thing I would have expected to find myself doing when I left Cindy's apartment that morning.

I probably would have given Lolly and Janie Lee the hundred bucks and had a nice bubbly time with them had we not happened to meet Boog Miller just as he was coming out the door of their aptly named establishment, the Bubble Bath.

Chapter XI _____

"*Aw, no,*" *Boog said* when he saw us. "Cornert again."

He had an orange tie in his hand and looked content enough to have just completed a Double Bubble Brunch.

Full of fun though they were, the girls seemed a little ticked at Boog. Lolly went over and tried to kick him in the shins, while Janie Lee moved in from the other side.

Boog backed up against his Lincoln and made his tie into a garrote, daring the girls to come and get him, an invitation they declined.

"It's just 'cause he spent the whole morning with Ginger when he could have spent it with us," Lolly explained. "Just 'cause she's from Texas don't mean she knows everything."

They looked at me significantly again, but the spell of the totally unexpected had already been broken.

"I guess I'll have to miss the special," I said. "I gotta see Boog for a minute."

"Well, there's six days in a week," Lolly said. "You just come anytime."

"Ain't they sweet?" Boog said, once they had gone into the Bubble Bath. "I love 'em like daughters."

"Let me ask you something," I said. "Is the Smithsonian for sale?"

"Yeah, they're tryin' to sell it, but the deal ain't set," Boog said. "Let's go find a barbecue palace."

We got in my car and drove on out Wilson Boulevard, a street so seedy it gave me *déjà vu*. I kept thinking I was back on Little York Road, in Houston. It was at a flea market on Little York Road that I first met Boog, seconds after I beat him to a narwhal tusk. Shortly after that, I sold it to him and we became friends.

Boog tied his orange tie and put on some wraparound sunglasses, which he immediately took off in order to examine the fine Armenian icon propped in the back seat.

"I meant to buy that thang and hang it in the Winkler County courthouse," he said. "It'd give some of them old dirt farmers a pretty good scare."

Then he took out a little inhaler and squirted an antihistaminic substance up his nose, a noisy process that sounded like somebody trying to start a worn-out car.

"If you was to offer me a fair deal on that icon I'd tell you about the Smithsonian," he said.

"I might," I said. "I'll let you know in a day or two."

Boog looked at me closely. He was a hard man to fool.

"There must be a new woman in the picture," he said. "One with the hots for icons."

"It's a hard life," he sighed. "I was thanking your passion for Cindy would last till at least nine-forty-five. If it had you wouldn't have got there in time to bid. You're a fucking lost generation. Can't even fuck till nine-forty-five."

Soon we left Arlington behind and were in Falls Church, not that it was easy to tell them apart. Falls Church had fewer massage parlors and more TV repair shops, but that was the only appreciable difference.

The barbecue palace Boog had in mind was called The

Cover-Up, and was about as covertly located as any barbecue palace in the land. It was in a little warren of run-down shops behind a construction site in a more than normally depressed part of Falls Church.

Nonetheless, it was packed with men, most of them with their security clearances hanging around their necks or clipped to their shirt pockets. A couple of sullen Pakistanis were slicing barbecue as fast as they could slice, and a grinning Chinaman who was built not unlike Boog slapped it onto plates, splashed a little sauce over it, and handed it to whoever was at the head of the line.

"Wall-to-wall spooks," Boog said. "Only place in town where it's safe to talk. See that Chinaman? Best spy in town."

"Who does he spy for?" I asked.

"The Israelis," Boog said. The line was moving virtually at a trot.

"Hello, Freddy," Boog said, when we got to the counter. "Hit us with a little of that goat."

"Booger-man," Freddy said, in an accent that might have been Princetonian. His eyes scanned me from head to foot, like a radar beam. Then he handed us our barbecue, which in fact *was* goat.

"Yeah, all these spooks eat goat," Boog said. "They get used to it while they're overseas in the Third World, performing covert acts."

"What's Freddy's last name?"

"Fu," Boog said.

"There was a woman at the auction named Mrs. Lump," I said. "Ever heard of her?"

"Bessie Lump," Boog said. "Sure. Only she ain't the one you're saving that icon for. Too old for you.

"These booths must have been meant for midgets to fuck in," he commented, trying to arrange a napkin so as to protect his orange tie. Then he nodded at the eagle-eyed Freddy Fu and a moment later a Pakistani teenager appeared with two bottles of Tasmanian beer.

"I allus drink Tasmanian beer when I eat goat," Boog explained.

"Bessie Lump is Cyrus Folmsbee's girl friend," he added, swabbing up a puddle of sauce with a bit of goat. "Cyrus happens to be the richest man between Upperville, Virginia, and Riyadh, Sau-ou-dee Arabia. His family started up the Smithsonian to begin with. The Folmsbees own just about everythang in America that's worth havin' except Winkler County."

"How can he own the Smithsonian?" I asked.

"Well, he don't, exactly," Boog said. "But ownership might just be a state of mind. I thank it's safe to say Cyrus has the mind of an owner. I thank he thanks his family just kind of lent it to the nation."

"What does Mrs. Lump have to do with it?" I asked.

The second I said it Boog kicked me in the shins. I looked up, he nodded at the carry-out line, and there was Bessie Lump herself, quietly waiting to get some barbecued goat.

Chapter XII _____

The sight of her almost caused me to drip barbecue sauce on my doeskin jacket. She was just a dumpy little woman in an old blue coat, but the fact that she had somehow turned up in a CIA barbecue joint in Falls Church, Virginia, struck me as unnerving.

Boog immediately popped out of the booth and went over to talk to her. Bessie Lump didn't greet him warmly, but on the other hand she didn't seem to mind that he had come over to talk to her. She shuffled up the line and received a modest brown bag, presumably full of barbecued goat.

To my surprise, Boog brought her over and introduced us. "Isn't he tall?" she said, when I stood up. Her eyes were disconcertingly colorless, like Levis that have been washed too many times.

"She followed me," I said, when she was gone.

Boog just laughed. "She never follert you," he said. "Old Cyrus used to run the CIA, back when it was a respectable organization. He picked up a taste for goat, that's all."

"She doesn't seem very friendly," I said, not reassured.

"Well, the Folmsbees ain't exactly just folks," Boog said. "The Shiptons neither. Bessie's a Shipton."

"What's a Shipton?" I asked.

Boog looked amused. "Yore ignorance is so appalling I can't thank where to start," he said, between munchings. "Bessie married beneath her. Husband's name is Northrup Lump. Of course, she would have had to marry beneath her, if she married at all, since the Shiptons got here back in the days of the primordial slime. The Shiptons even beat the Folmsbees, but the Folmsbees hung onto their money and the Shiptons didn't. The Shiptons was shabby genteel."

That I could follow. The shabby genteel are familiar ground to me. I had bought many a second-rate heirloom from meek, shabby genteel ladies in decorous apartments about the land. I could always get the heirlooms for reasonable prices, since the meek ladies could seldom bring themselves to discuss money at all. They would take whatever I offered, and in turn give me tea. If they had lives, it was not apparent.

"Anyway," Boog went on, "having married a Lump the only way Bessie could redeem herself was by shacking up with a Folmsbee. It's been going on for forty years."

"What happened to Mr. Lump?" I asked.

"Why nothin'," Boog said. "I thank he spends his time playin' checkers with the butler."

"It's hard to believe the Smithsonian is really for sale," I said.

"You got the Waxahachie outlook," Boog said. "Thank of it. Seventeen museums in the Smithsonian, not to mention all them warehouses they got strung around in places like Anacostia and Silver Spring. For fifty, sixty years we been sucking stuff out of every country in the world and cramming it into warehouses an' museums—seventy-eight million items, they say.

"Hail, we got more African masks than you could find in Africa, and more Persian doodads than the pore old Shah."

"But that stuff is worth billions and billions," I said. "Who's gonna buy it?"

"That's the fun part," Boog said. "Emergent nations is gonna buy it. What them pore bastards in the Third World don't realize yet is that we bought up most of their heritage years ago, before they even started thanking about emerging. We got it right here. Now, what's the first thang an emergent nation needs when it emerges?"

"Schools and hospitals?" I ventured. "Tractors. Freeways."

Boog shook his head. "What they need is fancy new museums, filt with the native crafts that are their heritage," he said. "Something to remind them of how it was before they shook off their colonial shackles."

"Oh," I said.

Boog grinned. "Cy's got a little brother named Peck, short for Peckham. The Folmsbees kind of look down on Peck because he actually went in business. What he does is build museums. Right this minute he's off building national museums in twenty or thirty little new countries. Naturally the countries ain't got nothing to put in the new museums, since we carted off all their goodies long ago."

"So we'll sell it all back to them," I said.

"Bingo," Boog said, with a grin.

Chapter XIII _____

"*But they can't sell* the stuff that's on view in the Smithsonian," I said. "Those are famous pieces. People would miss them."

Boog was silent, but he grinned at me in a way that suggested Waxahachie was my destiny.

"What if they was replaced by first-rate repros?" he said,

finally. "How long do you reckon it'd take the public to notice?"

I was speechless. The notion that all the superb objects in seventeen museums were being quietly replaced with high-class forgeries was . . . well, mind-boggling. It meant that somewhere in America an army of forgers was working away, making museum-quality forgeries of an almost infinite variety of objects.

"Hodges," Boog said, when I looked at him in bewilderment. "Hodges, South Carolina. That's where they're making the repros."

That made sense. The Carolinas are full of furniture factories, some of which turn out nothing but reproduction furniture. And, of course, forgery itself was hardly a new thing.

"But who gets the real pieces?" I asked. "They're world famous. If they start turning up in museums in Zaire or Bangladesh someone's gonna notice."

Boog dismissed this notion.

"The world ain't really filt with art historians," he said. "Most people ain't scouts. Half the people in museums all over the world are in a bad humor because they've been made to go against their wills. They ain't gonna give a shit if some statue that used to be in the National Gallery turns up in Islamabad."

"What does Mrs. Lump have to do with it?" I asked. "Is she a spy?"

"Ain't we all spies?" he asked, turning suddenly metaphysical. "The way I figger it, to spy is human."

Then he began to talk about Spinoza and Descartes and was still talking about them when I delivered him back to his muddy Lincoln, in front of the Bubble Bath.

"Spinoza was a great man," he said. "Greater than Sam Rayburn or Felix Frankfurter either."

Then he got in his Lincoln and roared off toward Washington.

I sat in my car for a few minutes, staring at the flaking purple front of the Bubble Bath and wondering what Spinoza would have thought about a Double Bubble Brunch.

Suddenly I felt very pressured, not from anything people were doing to me, but from things I was doing to myself.

To put it simply, I was in a phase of wanting too much. I wanted Cindy, but I also wanted Jean, I wanted Boss Miller, and I certainly would not have spurned Lolly and Janie Lee, whose very cheerfulness made them attractive. Of course I still wanted Coffee and Kate and Tanya Todd, and I had a strong fondness for Beth Gibbon—the flea-marketer's daughter, only a scant two hours away, in Augusta, West Virginia.

My capacity for wanting, which had always been great, seemed to have expanded dangerously since I arrived in Washington. I not only wanted several women now, I also wanted a great many things, and I wanted both the women and the things keenly. My ongoing fantasies about Boss Miller were as dark, intense, and adulterous as ever, but at the moment they were overlaid with half-innocent fantasies about Jean, and light cheerful fantasies about Lolly and Janie Lee, and somehow all these fantasies arrived at a time when, thanks to Cindy, I should have been feeling sexually content.

In short, I was just a stew of wants, none of them really significant, but none of them easily dismissible, either.

In such moods, I usually hit the road. If I'm in Maine I head for Oregon, if in Chicago or Detroit for Miami or New Orleans, trusting that the long roads and blue skies of America will restore me to lucidity and a simple sense of purpose: to find the best things to be found along the roads and beneath the skies.

And the last resort, always, when the buzz of wants becomes intolerable, is to head for Harbor City, California, and its great flea market, stuck there between L.A. and the ocean, the *souk* of *souks*, the ultimate American marketplace.

A trip to Harbor City, from anywhere in the eastern half of America, offered the best of both worlds: the ascetic loneliness of the long drive across gray plains and beige deserts, and then millions of goods one could fling oneself into in pure debauch, like Scrooge McDuck into his money bin.

It's not that I ever find much in Harbor City, perhaps the most intelligently scouted flea market in the world, with hustlers of every variety circling like pariah dogs, waiting for someone to give up and drop a price significantly.

What's important is that Harbor City is always there, a river of trash and treasure flowing unwearied through its stalls. If you want to buy a vintage Wurlitzer jukebox or sell a complete set of Little Orphan Annie Radio Club decoders —six in all—you can, almost any time you arrive.

To simple people, content with themselves, the need for such a place must seem degraded. But I love it, and anyway have never been content with myself.

I guess I buy and sell in hope of style—or maybe as a style of hope, and Harbor City is kind of the capital of my nation, where there are always others as restless as myself, who constantly buy and sell, too, for their own reasons.

Chapter XIV _____

I actually sat in front of the Bubble Bath for about ten minutes, in a fretful mood, trying to convince myself to be sensible and stop wanting so many women and so many things.

Wanting even one woman intensely was dangerous enough: wanting several at the same time meant erecting a structure of need and desire which would eventually collapse like a South American bleacher, burying me in angry women.

But after ten minutes I hit the Capital Beltway, in a mood to ply the wistful Jean Arber with icons, or trunks, or whatever it might take.

Main drag Wheaton is so seedy it almost makes Arlington look classy.

Jean's shop was in a little decayed shopping center that looked like it had been built in Cleveland and then rolled end over end from there to Wheaton.

Put another way, it looked like it had been set down whole by some huge crane capable of lowering whole cinderblock shopping centers into place: only in the case of this shopping center the crane operator had nodded for a moment and dropped it into place from a height of about ten feet.

All the buildings in the shopping center were slightly cracked, and the asphalt parking lot had begun to roil and bubble. In fact the parking area looked a little like the surface of the moon, in which big chunks of dusty asphalt were interspersed with sizable craters.

I worked my way through the craters and parked right in front of Jean's shop, which was between an adult bookstore and a pet shop. The door of the adult bookstore was framed with multicolored lightbulbs, which when flashing might have been expected to attract adults, or at least teenagers.

The pet shop was even more depressing. Its window contained nothing but comatose hamsters and a cage full of hyperactive gerbils.

The cracks in the several buildings were large enough that small shrubs or spreading vines could have been planted in them, but instead of shrubs and vines most of them seemed to be full of empty red-and-white boxes, of the sort Colonel Sanders' fried chicken comes in.

The sources of all the red-and-white boxes was not far to seek. A fried chicken outlet was right across the street, sandwiched between a Long John Silver's and a spanking new Taco Belle. Even as I watched, a patron of Colonel Sanders casually tossed an empty fried chicken box out of his rusty station wagon.

I got out and looked in the window of Jean Arber's antique shop. The window had a modest wooden sign on it which said "Jean's Antiques." Inside I could see a number of trunks and what looked like some rather nice blue crockery, but I couldn't get in. The door was locked and a note stuck to it which read:

> Dear Jimmy:
>   Gone to the babysitters. Back at 3:15. Did you really tell them you'd take them to Baskin-Robbins?
>
> XXX
Jean

Although the note was short and not intended for me, I was intrigued by it.

Particularly, I was intrigued by the three Xs, just above the signature. Tanya Todd was always writing me notes and ending them with Xs and I could never quite puzzle out what the Xs were supposed to tell me. Were the Xs meant as a warning, or did they conceal an affection that the woman making the Xs didn't feel like being too specific about?

Since Jean's letter was addressed to the husband from whom she was not quite divorced, I suspected the latter. She might not be quite sure that she still loved him, so she hit him with a few Xs, to warn him to take things slow.

While I sat in the car, reflecting, one of the oldest Volvos I had ever seen drove up and parked beside me. It had once been dark blue but now it was just dark. I knew a good many Volvo collectors, mostly in California—they tend to be a finicky lot, but any one of them would have jumped at the chance to buy such an ancient specimen. It was much smaller than the Volvos of our day—in fact, it resembled those small vehicles, half pickup and half dogcart, that big city milkmen used to deliver milk in.

Instead of containing milk bottles, this Volvo contained a short energetic man in bib overalls. It didn't even contain *him* long, because he immediately got out and headed for Jean's antique shop. He was evidently so accustomed to marching right in that he didn't notice the note until he crashed into the door.

Once that happened he was forced to take cognizance of the note. He was rather likable looking, bushy-haired, bushy-bearded, blue-eyed, and puzzled. He squinted at the note for a moment and then went over and stood in front of the window of the pet shop, looking almost as morose as the hamsters. In fact, he looked not unlike a human hamster, except that his hair was longer.

I had a feeling he was Jimmy. So far he had not noticed me at all, which in itself says something about the state he was in. A pearl Cadillac can't be an everyday sight in such a shopping center.

I had been thinking of Jean's husband as a potential rival,

but the more I studied Jimmy the less like a rival I felt. Who could take pride at beating a human hamster in a contest for the hamster's own wife? Jimmy looked like all he wanted to do was find some nice litter and curl up in it. He had little sprigs of straw in his hair, so perhaps he had already curled up in some.

Before I could reflect further on Jimmy or the Xs Jean's van drove up and parked on the other side of me. I looked around and saw two wonderful little faces peering at me out of the right window of the van. *Those* faces certainly didn't ignore white Cadillacs and cowboys. They were the faces of little girls, maybe about three and five years old, respectively. They looked as intelligent as raccoons, and their faces were surrounded by great puffs of fleecy curls, as if both of them were wearing Harpo Marx wigs.

I smiled at them, an unexpected development that caused them to exchange quick glances. Like their mother, they wore puffy coats, only theirs were red instead of blue.

After a moment of shy hesitation they decided they were charmed by my smile and gave me two smiles in return.

In the few moments that it took me to establish contact with the girls, a marital or perhaps post-marital storm gathered and broke on the other side of Jean's van.

Jimmy stopped being a human hamster and became an outraged ex-husband. He immediately rushed around to Jean's side of the van, and as he did I rolled my window down a little, out of a shameless desire to eavesdrop.

Eavesdropping was no problem, since Jimmy's pent-up feelings burst out of him at the top of his voice. At the mere sound of his voice both little girls gritted their teeth, made faces, and put their fingers in their ears.

"Where did you *go?*" Jimmy yelled.

Whatever reply Jean made was totally inaudible.

"But I drove all the way *in!*" Jimmy yelled. "I thought we were going to get *burgers!*"

At the mention of burgers the little girls whipped around. They still had their fingers in their ears, or at least in their curls, but the burger part got through. They immediately deserted me and began to pat their mother's back. It was obvious even to me, a neophyte with children, that so far as their father was concerned they were willing to let bygones be bygones if he was in the mood to provide burgers.

I felt thoroughly awkward. My visit could not have been more ill-timed. For half a day I had been building interesting fantasies around Jean Arber, but none of my fantasies had located her in the midst of such a charming family. The little girls were absolute darlings, and even Jimmy was something of a darling. A man who wore bib overalls, drove an incunabular Volvo, had straw in his hair, and wanted to buy his ex-wife a cheeseburger couldn't be all bad, or even half bad.

It is hard to sustain adulterous fantasies when faced with such a scene.

For a moment my impulse was to slip away. I had come at the wrong time. Probably I should just go to New Mexico with Cindy. Now that I knew where Jean's antique shop was I could always return.

But it's hard just to slip away when you drive up in a car like mine, and before I could reach any decision the little girls turned their attention back to me. They rapped on their window to get my attention.

I smiled again.

Encouraged, they began to roll down their window. This was not easy, but they persisted. The one who was doing most of the rolling gritted her teeth, and made a face, to indicate how hard it was.

As soon as the window was down they both popped their elbows out. Giggling at their own daring, they leaned way out and looked at the ground. The window was full of red parkas and reddish-blond curls. It seemed for a moment that they might both topple out into the crater that separated the two cars, but of course they were relying on the marvelous balance of children. They didn't topple out. When they'd seen enough of the ground they easily righted themselves, looked at me, and settled down for some frank conversation.

"I'm the oldest," the older said.

The younger girl ignored this flagrant claim.

"What's *your* name?" she asked.

Chapter XV ──────────

"I'm Jack," I said.

The girls giggled, exchanging glances again.

At this point Jean got out of her side of the van. Then she and Jimmy walked right in front of the van and my car and on down the sidewalk, past the pet store. They didn't notice that their daughters were leaning out the window of the van having a conversation with me. In fact, they didn't notice me, my car, the sluggish hamsters, or anything. They were deeply awash in their marriage, intent on desires and resentments known only to them, and apparently too swollen with difficult feelings to be able to say a word. They just walked off, in a silent dialogue, down the sidewalk through the seedy shopping center.

The girls and I watched them go with dispassion. If anything, the girls' dispassion was greater than my own.

"Where are *they* going?" I asked, feeling some reference should be made to this somber departure.

The little girls were not in the least concerned about the matter. They were more interested in me than in the fact that their parents were slowly receding down a cracked sidewalk.

"Oh, just talking," the older girl said, with a dismissive flip of her hand.

"Tell me your names," I demanded.

They were delighted to be asked.

"Beverly Arber," the older one said crisply.

"B'linda Arber," the younger one said, not quite so crisply.

"*Bee*linda," Beverly corrected, shouting it into her sister's ear.

Belinda was undaunted. She looked at me closely, to see if I was willing to accept her at face value.

"Don't you know what a vowel is?" Beverly asked, trying to squeeze her little sister out of the window.

Belinda fought silently but grimly to hold her position, clinging with one tiny hand to the little knob that locks the door.

"She doesn't know what a vowel is," Beverly said, using that slim pretext to try and push her sister out of the van and into the crater.

I got a little worried. I could imagine decades of guilt for Jean and Jimmy if they came back and found their youngest daughter with a concussion.

"Hey," I said. "Would you girls like to get in my car?"

The struggle stopped at once. Two little faces looked at me solemnly; four blue eyes tried to gauge my intentions.

"What did you say your name was?" Beverly asked.

"Jack," I said.

"I want to," Belinda concluded, proceeding at once to try and climb out the window. Her decision caught her sister off guard. Before she could react Belinda somehow managed to turn around and pop her ass out the window. In a trice she was dangling by her hands and attempting to look over her shoulder to judge the drop.

Unfortunately her puffy red coat was in the way. She couldn't see over her shoulder. Besides the coat she had on blue corduroys and little red sneakers.

Beverly was outraged at such a breach of authority.

"Who told you you could?" she yelled, right into her sister's face.

Belinda didn't answer. Belinda simply hung. All I could see was her parka and her curls.

Then she dropped, landing right in the crater, which fortunately was only about two inches deep. In a trice she was up and scrambling into my arms, running from her sister, who had managed to open the door of the van and was scrambling out, ready to mete out punishment.

Unfortunately, she was the one who fell, misjudging the

steps and thumping down harder than her sister. Thanks to the parka she wasn't really hurt, but she got a harder lick than her sister, and when she looked up and saw Belinda smiling and unscathed, in my arms, the injustice of it overcame her and she burst into tears.

Sometimes it's not fun being the oldest.

I scooped her up in my other arm.

Belinda offered no sympathy—her coolness was too much for Beverly.

"Your fault!" she said, attempting to strike her sister.

Belinda ducked, grinning a big grin. "I jumpt,"she said happily, infuriating Beverly even more.

"How would you girls like a duck?" I asked, to change the subject.

"I would," the uncritical Belinda said. "Where *is* it?"

Beverly stopped crying but continued to gulp. I sat them both on the hood of my car for a moment.

"Is it alive?" Beverly asked.

"What *color* is it?" Belinda inquired.

"One duck," Beverly said. "Or two ducks?"

"Oh, two ducks," I said. "One for you and one for her."

"They're mostly blue," I said to Belinda. "Brown and blue."

That was not good enough.

"Jist the *feathers* part is blue?" Belinda asked, trying to get a workable picture of the duck.

"Don't you know anything?" Beverly said, punching her. "A duck is all feathers."

"Jist the *feathers* part?" Belinda asked again, ignoring her sister.

I caught them by the hands and swung them down. Compared to me, kids are astonishingly short, a fact I always forget until I come up against some. Two very short people in red sneakers and red parkas followed me around to the rear of my car, in the luggage compartment of which was a bag full of blue pottery ducks I had bought in McAllen, Texas, nearly a year ago.

Now and again a scout will buy something he has no

earthly business with, and such was the case with the ducks. I had been in the mood to buy something and the ducks, though just cheap pottery, were innocent and bright, so I bought them.

Probably I just bought them out of an impulse to pass money, that being the basic act around which my life is organized. I had stuck the ducks behind my spare tire and had forgotten about them, but the minute I found myself with two little girls on my hands they popped into my mind like a long-forgotten name.

Of course my luggage compartment contained everything but luggage. It was filled with such things as brass candlesticks, Hopi baskets, a big abacus that was possibly Turkish, and various other goods.

It also contained Valentino's hubcaps, four silver cobras with ruby eyes.

I swung the girls up and sat them on a Navaho blanket, next to the hubcaps.

"You've got snakes in here," Beverly said.

"Not *real* snakes," Belinda said, and then immediately repeated the remark. Except for her tongue, she might have been paralyzed.

"Not *real* snakes," she insisted, looking at me rather than the hubcaps, in case the snakes were more real than she thought.

"Not real snakes," I assured her.

Reassured, the girls looked at the hubcaps solemnly, so impressed they could scarcely breathe.

"The eyes parts are red," Belinda said, reaching out a finger to touch an eye part. With her other hand she retained a hold on my thumb, just in case.

When I gave them each a blue duck they took them without comment, not quite able to focus on such modest objects with the silver cobras only a foot away.

Once I got them safely ensconced in the front seat they regained their critical faculties and gave the ducks an intense scrutiny for about ten seconds, before turning their attention to the wonders of my car.

"Will these ducks float in the bathtub?" Beverly asked.

Belinda clutched her duck by the throat while rubbing her hand over the soft velour of my seats.

"Why is your car soft?" she asked.

"You girls ask a lot of questions," I said. "You must work in a question factory."

Beverly looked at Belinda and they both shrugged little nonchalant shrugs.

"We do," Beverly said.

A nonsensical question was not going to fool them.

Then the car telephone rang. Belinda grabbed it as if she were used to answering telephones in cars every day.

"I'll get it," she said, dropping her duck and grabbing it with both hands.

"Hello," she said, into the ear of the startled mobile operator, who promptly broke the connection.

"Hello, hello," Belinda said, annoyed at the silence on the line.

Then, with another shrug, she put the receiver back on its cradle.

"Nobody there," she said.

"You should have said whose residence it is," Beverly reminded her.

Belinda popped her hand over her mouth, as if suddenly remembering that that was standard practice.

Then the phone rang again. I reached to get it, as did Beverly, but Belinda was still the closest and she was in no way daunted by her first setback.

"I got it," she said, grabbing it again.

"Jist a minute, please," she said into the receiver. Then she looked at me, politely trying to cover the receiver with her small hand.

"Whose residence *is* this?" she asked, looking around the car.

"Mobile operator seven calling Mr. McGriff," a dry voice said.

Beverly, annoyed at being out-positioned, made a grab for the receiver, missed, and had to content herself with toppling Belinda over backwards.

As she toppled, Belinda coolly handed me the receiver. Anything to defeat a sibling.

"Mr. McGriff speaking," I said, watching Beverly pummel Belinda for her treachery. Fortunately the girls' coats were the equivalents of 16-ounce boxing gloves. As long as they had the coats on they could do one another little harm.

Naturally it was Coffee.

"Where have you been?" she said, in the proprietary tone that comes naturally to anyone I've been married to.

"I'm in Washington," I said. It wasn't what she wanted to know, but it was all I felt prepared to offer her. Once or twice I had mentioned other women to Coffee, only to be met with a silence suggestive of ice. I certainly wasn't about to mention Cindy, or Jean either.

Nonetheless, Coffee went into one of her silences. She was extremely passive, on the telephone, as in life, and was quite comfortable being silent. She would sit holding the phone for several minutes, waiting for me to entertain her with stories or trap myself with admissions.

This particular silence was not icy. I could hear her breathing into the phone, which did not occur when she was feeling icy. I could also picture her clearly, sitting there in an empty real estate office, a cup of coffee at her elbow, staring out the window at the sunny streets of Austin and waiting for me to tell her the latest about Boog and Boss, or else describe purchases she wouldn't approve of.

Before I could do that, Beverly got tired of pummeling Belinda and thought of a better tactic. She held Belinda down with one knee, unzipped the coat, plunged in both hands and began to tickle her sister mercilessly.

Immediately Belinda emitted a shriek of giggles, a shriek not lost upon my listener.

"What's that?" Coffee asked. "Where *are* you?"

There was real shock in her voice. She had never happened to call me before when there was anyone else in my car. I believe, in her sluggish vision, Coffee saw me as always alone, driving around America buying things, still essentially in love with her. In her imaginings the spell she cast had never really been broken.

"Oh, that's two little girls," I said. "I'm keeping them a few minutes while their parents run an errand. Their parents own an antique store in Wheaton."

"Where?" Coffee asked.

"Wheaton, Maryland," I said.

"Never heard of it," Coffee said, a silly remark—she had never heard of places no farther away than Waco.

At that moment I happened to glance around and see Jean and Jimmy walking toward us on the sidewalk to my left. This was startling, since they had departed to my right. It was as if they had walked around the world, though probably they had only walked around the shopping center. Certainly they were unlikely Magellans. Both had their hands in their pockets and were plodding along silently, not looking at one another.

"Well?" Coffee said.

"Can I call you later?" I said. I felt awkward. Jean and Jimmy were converging on my left, and Belinda was shrieking just to my right. I was in no position to tell my former wife any of the things she might want to hear.

"You better," Coffee said, an unusually stern remark for her. She never took much note of me when we were married, but since then I had never done anything to violate her vision of our relationship—such as having a personal life that she could imagine. The presence of two little girls in my car amounted to just such a violation.

"You don't need to sound like that," I said. "It's just two little girls."

"Yeah, but I bet they've got a mother," Coffee said, perceptively, just as their mother—and father—passed directly in front of my car. Coffee hung up. Jean and Jimmy walked on a few paces and stopped. Beverly stopped tickling Belinda, but kept her in place with her knee—she herself was watching her parents. Belinda had stopped shrieking and was catching her breath. I quietly hung up, too, aware that I was in deep trouble in Austin—the kind of trouble that occurs when you keep talking to a lazy woman you have divorced, thus encouraging her not to bother building a new life.

Jean and Jimmy seemed in much deeper trouble than I was. They almost started on a second circumlocution of the shopping center, but lost their momentum and just stood on the sidewalk, not looking at one another. Jean had a steely look in her eye, and she was directing it at Jimmy. It was a look I was very familiar with—the look of a woman who is not going to be conned even one more time by a beautiful boyishness.

Jimmy, of course, had the dejected look of a man whose beautiful boyishness has just failed him, leaving him uncertain as to what to try next. Probably a good part of his dejection stemmed from the suspicion that he had nothing else to try.

Then, fortunately, he spotted Beverly. It revived him in a second. His wife might be immune to boyish appeal, but his daughters weren't, and he knew it. He came over, opened the door of the car, and kind of dove into them, giving them many kisses and tickling them into ecstasy with his bushy beard.

"Hi," he said. "Thanks for keeping them." He raised his eyes briefly but looked at the steering wheel rather than at me.

"My pleasure," I said, concluding the formalities. It was obvious from the way Jimmy looked at the steering wheel that he assumed I was already fucking his wife.

Despite her pleasure at being tickled by her father's beard, Belinda was still hip to the main chance.

"Are we going to Baskin-Roberts now?" she asked.

"No," he said, looking embarrassed.

Both girls looked exasperated.

"Oh, Daddy," Beverly said.

"You *said* so!" Belinda reminded him, doubling up a tiny fist and squinting at him fiercely.

All this time, Jean was standing in front of the car, looking not at me, not at him, not at anything.

"I *know* I said so," Jimmy said. "But I can't do it today. We'll do it Friday."

Belinda stuck out her jaw. "Do you want a fat lip?" she asked, holding up a tiny fist.

The absurdity of the threat almost unnerved her father.

Beverly gave him no time to regain his composure. "When's Friday?" she asked. "How many days?"

"Four," he said. "Four days. We'll get double-dip cones to make up for it, okay?"

Belinda opened her fist and carefully counted out four of her own fingers, weighing them in the mind's eye against a double-dip cone. Beverly made the same judgment without resorting to fingers.

"Okay," they said in unison, flinging themselves back into his arms.

They should have hung tough. Their forgiveness was too much. Jimmy's eyes overflowed. I wanted to hide behind my Stetson. When he shut the door the little girls' faces were wet from his tears—not theirs. They themselves were serene.

He hopped in the tiny old Volvo and left, his cheerful daughters waving at him from my window, which I had obligingly lowered.

Jean stood where she was until the Volvo went through a traffic light and over a hill, making her safe from its rear-view mirror.

Then she got in and sat down, without a word to me. In a second she had a pile of daughters in her lap. She didn't say a word to them, either. She looked not so much calm as blank: emptied by the effort of rejection she had just made. Probably she didn't have a word left in her, just then. Rejecting a beautifully boyish, bushy-bearded father had clearly taken a lot out of her, a fact even her daughters respected.

For a moment we all just sat. I didn't even say hi.

I don't know how long we would have sat had it not been for the restive Belinda, who after a time scooted out of her mother's lap and began to point out some of the noteworthy features of my car.

"Look," she said. "He's even got a telephone."

Jean looked. "What do you know about that?" she said.

Then Belinda looked at me coyly.

"Do you like cheeseburgers?" she asked.

Jean slumped against the door, watching her daughter without comment, as if amazed that anyone could be so young and alive.

In watching Jean, I momentarily forgot that I had been asked a question. To jog my memory Belinda crawled over in my lap, seated herself comfortably on the steering wheel, and grabbed me by both lapels.

"Don't you ever listen?" she asked. *"Do you like cheeseburgers?"*

"Sure," I said. "I like cheeseburgers."

"Then let's go *get* some," Belinda said.

I looked at Jean, who was still slumped against the door, her eyes empty. She was beyond protest, or interest, or response of any kind. I knew just how she felt.

The cheeseburger decision rested with the girls and me, and their position was clear.

"Come on," Belinda said, as confidently as if she were eighteen and inviting me to buy her a milk shake.

Then she stood up, grabbed me by my doeskin lapels again, and brought two implacable blue eyes so close to mine that our noses almost touched. All I could see were eyes and curls.

"You *do* it!" she demanded.

Women know instinctively when they can boss me around. I know it instinctively, too. The fact that Belinda was a child was irrelevant to the matter, both in her view and in mine.

"Burgers it is," I said.

Belinda stepped calmly out of my lap and seated herself once again beside her mother and sister. She even gave me an approving pat on the leg.

I was so charmed that for a moment I just sat and looked at her.

For a moment too long, as it turned out.

"Jist *go!*" Belinda said.

Book III

Chapter I _____

    At the hamburger stand I dawdled much too long, listening to the girls prattle and watching them familiarize themselves with the wonders of my car, while Jean listlessly munched her way through a footlong hot dog.

"The good thing about having one like Belinda is that when you don't feel like talking you don't have to worry," Jean said, staring at Belinda as if she were something rare and curious, like a Fabergé egg.

"I'll talk," Belinda said, quickly.

"That's why I don't have to worry," Jean said. "You'll talk."

"She talks like a faucet," Beverly said. Then she pretended to be turning off a faucet, not looking at her sister while she did it.

Belinda gave her a cool look, then carefully selected a French fry, wobbled it around in the ketchup for a bit, and fed it to me.

"Not enough ketchup," she said blandly, ignoring her mother's and her sister's veiled criticisms.

"You don't have to feed him," Beverly observed. Belinda had positioned herself comfortably on the soft velour divider between my front seats, assuring that she and only she had free access to me.

Belinda wobbled another French fry in the ketchup, and ignored the comment. It was plain that Jean and Beverly relied heavily on irony in their dealings with her. It may have represented their only chance, but it didn't work. Irony means little to a natural winner.

Belinda looked at her sister, calmly turned an imaginary faucet back on, and went on with her prattle, giving me a pat or a French fry or a big smile from time to time, to keep me under control.

"Thanks," Jean said, when we got back. "I don't know why I ate that hot dog." She opened her door and got out, followed by Beverly.

"I still didn't get to see your antiques," I said.

Jean looked about to cry. "Oh well," she said. "It's just an excuse."

"What's an excuse?"

"My store," she said. "It allows me to pretend I know how to do something. Who would come *here* to buy an antique?"

"Me," I said.

She shrugged. "Yeah, but you're crazy," she said, peeping in at Belinda, who was waiting impatiently for the adult talk to be over.

"Coming with us?" Jean asked.

Belinda shook her head.

"He can take us home," she said. "Because it's not far."

"Maybe he has something better to do," Jean suggested.

Belinda thought it over, assuming a seductive look. Then she blew her mother a fine kiss.

"I think I'll just go with him," she said. "He can take me home."

"*Get out of that car!*" Jean yelled, suddenly. A good deal of rage, none of it really directed at Belinda, poured out with the yell.

Belinda hesitated for a moment, evidently contemplating a face-off. She read the impersonal nature of the rage as easily as I had. Then she thought better of it and turned and gave me a hug.

While we were hugging she put her hot little mouth in the vicinity of my ear.

"I want you to come back tomorrow," she whispered.

Then she popped a hand over my mouth, to keep me from making a reply.

"Can't I even ask why?" I asked, through her fingers.

Belinda glanced at her impersonally furious mother, then whispered the reason.

"So you can take us to Bask'n Roberts."

"You mean Baskin-Robbins, don't you?"

Belinda looked exasperated. She plainly didn't welcome quibbles at such a time.

"Jist *do* it," she said, and hopped out.

Chapter II ──────────

Getting from Wheaton to Georgetown during the afternoon rush hour is not the easiest short drive in the country. At 5:30, the hour at which I was supposed to be at Cindy's, I was trapped on the Capital Beltway, directly beneath the Mormon Temple.

The temple and my Cadillac were the only white things in sight. All the cars in my vicinity were dark green, and all the people in them were men in trench coats and small woolen hats, perhaps the very GS–12s who had been at the auction that morning.

Already I was getting the sense that Washington was a very cellular place. The motif of the cell recurred. All the men in trench coats and woolen hats probably spent their days in cell-like offices in vast gray buildings. Then when the government let them out they squirmed like larvae into small cell-like cars and rushed across the river or around the Beltway to vast gray apartment buildings, where they inhabited cell-like apartments.

During the day, in their cell-like offices, they probably spent their time hatching plots the size of microscopic organisms, directed at people in nearby cells.

While I was stuck beneath the Mormon Temple I bethought myself of Coffee, whom I had promised to call back. For some reason I felt guilty at the thought of her—an irrational guilt, since we had been divorced for years.

Anyway, just as the icepan of traffic began to break up—

with chunks of cars breaking off and swirling down the Belt-way for half a mile or so, until they hit the icepan again—I picked up the phone and called Coffee.

It was worse than I expected.

"Who are you fucking now?" Coffee asked, a wild, un-Coffee-like note in her voice.

Then she began to make sounds on the order of those a horse makes when it drinks. It was basically a sucking sound. Coffee hated any breach of bodily discipline, such as tears, vomiting, farts, etc. She never vomited and seldom cried, and the sounds now coming over the phone meant that she was fighting tears in the only way she knew, which was to suck them back up into herself before they could fall. It was a ghastly sound and didn't help my guilt at all.

"Coffee," I said. "Don't do that. Just go ahead and cry."

The strange sucking continued. It was something that should have been on the sound track of a horror movie.

The chunk of cars I was in broke loose and swirled all the way down into the vicinity of Bethesda while I was listening to Coffee fight back her tears.

Finally the sucking stopped. There was silence on the line.

"Do you feel better now?" I asked.

"No," she said. "I feel worse. There's never any Kleenex in this office."

"Why would there be? You never cry. You seldom even blow your nose."

Coffee was always thunderstruck when I pointed out some obvious fact about her. She regarded it as highly unnatural that I would notice something she hadn't noticed herself.

"I don't need to blow my nose," she said. "We have a really good climate here."

I couldn't argue with that. It was so typical of her mode of reasoning that I began to hope the conversation would become normal and cheerful. I was too optimistic.

"Nothing will ever happen to me," Coffee said suddenly, in a voice of utter hopelessness.

It is the statement I dread most from women, and now I

was hearing it twice within half an hour, for that was what Jean Arber had meant when she said her antique shop was just an excuse. What she really felt when she said it was that nothing would ever happen to her.

"Don't be ridiculous," I said. "A lot will happen to you. A lot has already."

But my statement was a lie. Coffee was not being ridiculous, just honest. Not much had happened to her, and unless she got lucky, not much would. Something had evidently just brought her face-to-face with her own insignificance, at a moment when nobody was around to distract her from it.

I had lied because I felt a little panicky. I didn't want Coffee to sit around Austin thinking about her own insignificance. Nor did I want Jean Arber to sit around Wheaton brooding over the fact that she didn't really know how to do anything except breed natural winners.

Jean herself was not a natural winner, but she *was* nice, and while Coffee was not significant, she too was nice, in a vacant sort of way.

For no clear reason I felt responsible for their common feeling that life was somehow lacking. This strange, irrational sense of responsibility is probably responsible for most of my problems with women.

At bottom I must think of myself as more like a chemical than a man. Once the chemical me is infused into the life of a woman the woman ought to feel competent and important, not skill-less and cipherlike, and if they don't I feel guilty. I realize such a guilt is arrogant and sexist, but I still have it. It comes over me whenever I hear a certain hopeless tone in a woman's voice, even though I know that hopeless tones are not permanent, and not really my fault, either.

The phone at my ear resonated with silence. Coffee had just said the truth and was now waiting for me to persuade her it was a lie.

"How can you say that nothing will ever happen to you?" I said, falling back on the Socratic method.

The virtue of the Socratic method, with women, is that it forces them to talk. Once they talk a little their natural volatility works in your favor. From talking about despair, meaninglessness, empty days, and loveless nights one can usually segue into talking about the movies they've seen lately or their agenda for the coming weekend.

Which is not to say I think the sorrows of women are shallow. The sorrows of women are deeper than mine—but their optimism and resiliency are also deep.

"How can you say nothing will ever happen to you?" I repeated.

"Because nothing's happened to me for over a year," she said. "I don't see how anything's gonna start."

"But things can always start," I reminded her.

"Not unless there's somebody to start them," she said, sighing like Eleanora Duse. The depth of the sigh surprised me. In all the time I'd known her Coffee had never given much thought to herself. She'd only cried once during the breakup of our marriage and that was because she couldn't get the hippo chair into the back of her car when she decided to go back to Austin.

Suddenly she was heaving tragic sighs. I had no idea what that meant. So far I had been very cautious in talking with her about her boyfriends, although when she had one she had no reticence about talking about them to me. In fact many of our hours on the phone were spent reviewing the inadequacies of Coffee's boyfriends.

"Has anything happened?" I asked, phrasing matters as vaguely as possible.

Coffee sighed again. "I haven't told you about Emilio, have I?" she asked.

She certainly hadn't. Most of Coffee's boyfriends had names like Richard or Robert, and almost all of them were lawyers. Somehow Emilio didn't sound like a lawyer. It was obvious things were changing, down in Austin.

"Who's Emilio?" I ventured.

"I guess he's my boyfriend," she said.

"You guess?"

"Okay," she said. "You don't have to jump down my throat."

"I've only been living with him a month," she added. "I thought you'd figure it out, but you didn't."

"Coffee," I said. "I haven't seen you in two months. How was I supposed to figure out you were living with someone named Emilio if you didn't bother to mention him?"

"You could have figured it out," she said, in her wannest tones.

I knew what was coming, and a second later it came.

"I guess you just don't care anymore," she said. "When we first broke up you figured out things like that even when I didn't want you to.

"You figured out practically every one of my boyfriends within a week," she added, with a bit more spirit. The reason for the spirit was because she had just summed up her case against me with incontrovertible logic: if I had stopped deducing the identities of her lovers it could only be because I had stopped loving her myself.

Actually, the reason the identities of her lovers had been easy to guess was because they had all been named Richard or Robert.

"Most of your boyfriends have been Texans," I said, in my own defense. "It's easier to sense Texans. My antennae don't work so well where Italians are concerned."

"Oh," Coffee said. The point seemed to exonerate me to some extent.

"He is Italian, isn't he?"

"Yeah," she said. "He comes from some place called Milan."

It occurred to me that Italians made very fine modern furniture, including chairs and lamps. They had probably decided Austin was where the money was and shipped over a lot of chairs and lamps. Emilio had probably won Coffee's absentminded favors with some Milanese abstraction he had convinced her was a chair.

"Does he sell furniture?" I ventured.

"I don't think so," Coffee said, surprised at the suggestion. "He hasn't sold any of mine. It's just that he beats me a lot."

Chapter III

I was so stunned I couldn't respond. What sort of man would beat Coffee?

Of course, being Italian, maybe he expected her to cook, something she hadn't any idea how to do, her culinary skills being pretty much encapsulated in her name. And even her coffee was far from world class.

"What does he do besides beat you?" I asked.

"He sells dope," Coffee said.

Some days bring many shocks. Not only was the Smithsonian for sale, Coffee was being beaten regularly by an Italian dope dealer. It seemed unfair. Coffee was just a girl from Baytown whose only mistake had been going away to school, where she had gotten kind of lost.

But she had stopped sounding wan and sounded merely conversational. I think she was looking forward to describing her beating in some detail, but that was nothing I wanted to hear. The traffic was beginning to break up and I had to decide whether to jettison all my fast-gathering Washington possibilities and go save her. I could be in Austin in about nineteen hours, time enough, probably, to keep Coffee from being beaten too many more times.

"I'm confused," I said. "Do you want the guy for a boyfriend, or what?"

"I guess so," she said. "Robert got married."

Robert had been the most recent lawyer.

Though not exactly a ringing endorsement for Emilio, it was enough to discourage me from a nineteen-hour drive.

In the shock of hearing about the beatings, I had forgotten several things, one of them being Coffee's profound passivity. If Emilio was possessed of even a normal amount of Italian volatility he would soon go off and find someone more responsive to beat.

"I wish you'd figured it out," Coffee said, remembering her original complaint. She sounded genuinely melancholy when she said it, so much so that it touched me.

"Aw, Coffee," I said. "Don't you remember? You used to hate it when I figured out things about you."

"Yeah, but people can change," she said. "Now I like it."

"Why?"

"Because it means something could still happen," she said simply.

It took the heart right out of me. Suddenly my most girlish girl had the voice of a grown-up, sad and only faintly hopeful.

The hope that something could still happen is the loneliest hope of all.

When I lived with her, Coffee had seldom been awake enough to notice that not much had happened yet.

"So when are you coming?" she asked, assuming that she had made her case.

"Maybe in about two weeks," I said weakly.

It was enough. Coffee brightened immediately and began to tell me about a dope ranch in the hill country where all the dope dealers went when they weren't beating their girl friends. In the course of the story it came out that Emilio only weighed 102 pounds.

"Yeah, and do you know what, he carries a purse," she added. From what I could gather, that exotic fact seemed to be his chief attraction.

When Coffee hung up I was almost to Georgetown. At the end of the conversation she was perfectly cheerful, having transferred her emptiness to me. I sang with it. It seemed to me I was beginning to pay for having failed to keep a clear distinction between objects and people. After all, I could start a relationship with a new object every day. Try that with people or—to be narrow—with women, and a lot of trouble would ensue.

It was rainy and gusty—wet fall leaves blew off the trees that hung over the road. Some of the leaves plastered themselves to my windshield—others sailed off toward the misty Potomac. In Georgetown the streetlights were already on.

For a moment I had the urge to pick up my car phone, call Cindy, and tell her some wild lie. I could tell her I had just mutilated myself through careless handling of some sharp antique, like a hangman's axe. It meant I had to rush straight to

Houston, to the world's best plastic surgeon, or else be disfigured for life.

I am not ungifted at the wild lie. A number of remarkable ones have popped out of me, when events or women make me really nervous. It may be because I seldom meet meek women. Or if I meet them I don't really notice them. I once thought Coffee was meek, but it turned out she was merely sleepy.

It might just have been that Coffee had so much Texas in her voice that it made me homesick. Innocent Texas voices are hard to resist. For the space of a mile or two I felt an urge to go back to her, watch her buy some more lamps and chairs. But then she had to hang up to take a business call, and the spell was broken. Instead of turning toward Austin, I sort of put myself on automatic pilot, and the Cadillac nosed on into Georgetown, to a parking lot one block from Cindy's stores.

Chapter IV ⸺⸺⸺⸺

The first thing I noticed when I walked up was that Harris seemed to be losing ground. Instead of being stuck astraddle of the threshold he was standing on the sidewalk near a parking meter, wearing a black raincoat and holding a rolled-up black umbrella. He was looking up at the sky, which was drizzling slightly into his face.

He wasn't really leaning on the parking meter, but he seemed to draw a certain comfort from the fact that one was near. He had a look of anguish on his face, only instead of directing it at the doorway he was directing it at the drizzling sky.

I felt I knew him, even though we hadn't been introduced.

"Hello, Harris," I said.

Being spoken to startled him a good deal. He gripped his umbrella a little tighter. His fingers were long enough to curl around it several times, like the toes of a sloth. He didn't answer me.

Meanwhile, Cindy's window had been transformed into a display case for my cowboyana. A bull's skull I had bought in Fort Stockton was the centerpiece, around which were piled horsehide lariats, Mexican spurs, a couple of Army Colts, and some horseshoeing tools. It was a nice display and almost everyone who walked in front of the shop stopped and looked at it. There were even two or three marshal's badges that may or may not have been worn by the Earp boys when they were working the Arizona territory.

Cindy was in her dress shop, opening packages of dresses. I felt like I had lived a life and a half in the hours since I had seen her last, but Cindy looked like she had only lived about five minutes. She was fresh, vigorous, and annoyed.

"Don't you ever listen?" she asked.

"I listen constantly," I replied, truthfully. "I'm sorry I'm late."

"I thought you kept your appointments," she said.

"I'm keeping my appointment," I said. "I'm not in Ohio or Mexico. I'm just a little late."

"When I say five thirty I mean five thirty," she said. "If you'd been on time we could be at a cocktail party at Oblivia's right now."

"I'm less than an hour late," I pointed out.

Cindy stopped talking. She turned her attention to a beautiful sleeveless black dress she had just taken out of a box. She opened two more boxes without looking at me or saying a word to me at all.

I began to wonder why I was still there. I think it may have been because I liked the alert way she read the Sunday papers, sitting naked and cross-legged on her bed. I also liked the way she smelled, night or morning, and I particularly liked the way she said words like "yeah" and "naw." She spoke in the tones of a real girl, however much she may have enjoyed social climbing.

"I bought a quadripartite icon today," I said, in an effort to change the subject.

"Big deal," Cindy said. Her irritation had not exactly subsided.

"It *is* a big deal," I said. "How many have you ever bought?"

Testy women seldom mind a little backtalk. In fact, they usually require it. Cindy looked at me as if I were a rock that had suddenly grown vocal cords and made a sassy remark. She apparently saw no point in answering a rock.

"How come you own an antique store if you're so fuckin' uninterested in antiques?" I asked, warming to my point.

"Listen, watch your language," she said hotly. A talking rock was one thing, a profane rock something she evidently didn't intend to tolerate.

"I have *employees*," she added, though none were in sight. I had noticed several thin-faced girls with fashionably frizzled hair in the various shops, but so far Cindy had not bothered to introduce me to any of them. They seemed to be silent minions. They all wore black sweaters and looked intelligent.

"It's a valid question," I insisted. "You own an antique store but you don't know a thing about antiques and what's more you don't really want to. How come?"

"Because I'm normal, that's why," Cindy said, in a voice full of very normal-sounding irritation.

"I'm normal, too," I said. "I just also know a lot about antiques."

Even as I was saying it I wished I wasn't saying it. Cindy put me away with a sharp volley, as if I were a tennis ball that had floated weakly up to the net where she was waiting.

"You were never normal a day in your life," she said, with such cool conviction that anyone listening would have been compelled to agree, though she had only known me for two days of my life.

"All you antiques people are kooks," she added. "I just bought this store in order to get the dress shop."

I began to feel depressed. Some hopeful part of me still wanted her to be an antiques person. In fact her attitude toward antiques was not much different from Coffee's.

"If I'm such a kook, what about us?" I asked.

Cindy walked past me to hang up some dresses. In passing she gave me a good swift jab with her elbow, as final punishment.

"I've fooled around with a lot of kooks," she said. "The good thing about you is that you're tall."

It didn't surprise me. I knew my height was an advantage —one of the most basic advantages, probably.

A second later, Cindy echoed my thought.

"It's basic," she said. "This town is full of shrimps."

Chapter V _____

At Cindy's house, while we were changing for the embassy party, some fooling around occurred. I started it. It's seldom a bad idea to fool around with women who've recently been mad at you. It may not lead to the heights of passion, but it will often suspend their memories and keep them from getting mad at you again over the same thing.

Besides, Cindy had very sexy shoulders—they were both strong and soft, rounded and dimpled, tanned and lightly freckled. In effect her shoulders were a kind of microcosm of the body that lay below them. I liked them a lot.

She was not loath to be fooled around with, either. I believe she felt I owed her something for having caused her to miss an important cocktail party. The dress she had chosen for the evening was a beautiful white one that covered one shoulder and left one shoulder bare—it was while she was considering it that the fooling around started.

It ended with Cindy having secured herself two orgasms, the second strong enough to send her into a form of repose. She didn't close her eyes, but she was in repose. Her eyes were bright, her body utterly still, and her face blank and smooth, like the face of a child who has just awakened from a nap.

My own exertions had been sufficient to induce a nap, though it turned out to be a very short nap. Cindy awoke me with her favorite tactic—an elbow. I felt very sleepy. Cindy had apparently just come out of the shower. She looked very awake. Like Boss Miller, she evidently had excellent cells. She looked ready for about three sets of tennis.

"You look pretty sluggish," she said. "I think you should watch your diet."

It was an absurd thing for her to say. I *was* sluggish but it was because she had just let me sleep about eight minutes. People who think everything is a function of diet give me a pain. In her preoccupation with waking me, she had forgotten to dry her legs and little streams of water were running down them onto her rug.

"Dry your legs," I said, "unless you want to drip."

She thought that was amusing and went over and got the white dress. Her closet contained more dresses than her dress store, which only contained maybe fifty dresses. They were costly dresses, but their numbers were not large.

An eight-minute nap disorients me. Instead of postcoital sadness I woke to postcoital surrealism. It seemed surreal to me that I was about to go to a party with a girl whose dress shop only contained fifty dresses. I don't know why that fact struck me, but it did.

I took a cold shower to try and reduce my disorientation and only succeeded in making myself feel sexy, which in itself was surreal. A cold shower is supposed to reduce one's ardor, and I had no reason even to have any ardor just at that time, but nevertheless I got an erection.

For some reason this made me reluctant to come out of the shower. I turned off the water, to see if that would have any effect on the erection, but it didn't. About that time Cindy came into the bathroom to look for a comb and noticed that the shower wasn't running and that I wasn't out. These facts struck her as novel.

"Hey," she said. "What's with you?"

I hardly knew what to say. I didn't really know. So I said nothing.

Cindy had no patience with mysteries. Also, it was her shower. She opened the door and saw me and my erection. At the time she was brushing her dark blond hair and she kept brushing it. A man in her shower with an erection was no big deal in itself. For all I knew it could have been an everyday sight.

"What was Harris doing standing by that parking meter?" I asked. I had meant to ask earlier but had forgotten to.

"He was trying to decide if it was raining enough for him to open his umbrella," Cindy said.

"Do you mind if I just stand here for a minute?" I asked, since she was still brushing her hair. I was beginning to be aware that I was probably only a temporary indulgence on Cindy's part. I wasn't exactly her chosen mate. I could feel my own temporariness, dripping like the shower. After a week or two of dripping I would be gone, probably.

At least her good humor extended to my erection.

"Why have you got a hard-on?" she asked pleasantly.

"I don't know," I said.

Actually, I felt a little blue. All at once I had the sense that I understood the workings of life. It worked through irony and paradox, like a metaphysical poem. The chief paradox seemed to be that what you most wanted was what you were least likely to get.

Cindy evidently sensed something plaintive in my attitude. The orgasms had eliminated her memory of my recent failings, as well as much of her natural combativeness. A faint sexual afterglow in her smooth cheeks was nicely set off by the white dress. She seemed willing to overlook the fact that I was standing in her shower with a hard-on just as she was almost ready to leave. She look girlish, friendly, and a little absent.

"If I told Oblivia about you she wouldn't believe it," she said.

"Why not?" I asked.

Cindy let her head hang to one side and brushed her hair that way for a while. The head hanging kind of kept the afterglow from fading.

"Oblivia doesn't understand people who don't do things at the right time," she said. "She was brought up among successful people."

"Come on." I said. "Nobody does everything at the right time."

"Oh yeah, around here they do," Cindy said. "Somebody like the Secretary of State isn't going to get a hard-on just before a party."

It was plain that my aberrant behavior intrigued Cindy a little. It might make me unfit for a Cabinet post, but I had a feeling that it kept me in the running with Harris, for at least one more day.

"I just don't know what she'll think of you," she said, laying down her brush. The uncertainty seemed to excite her. I was an ambiguous factor, socially and otherwise. On that provocative note, we left for the party.

Chapter VI _____

The first person I saw at the Embassy that I recognized was Boog. He was talking to the second person I recognized, Sir Cripps Crisp. The two of them were standing by a small tree that had somehow been coaxed up through the floor of the Embassy.

Apart from the fact that he was standing upright, Sir Cripps gave no sign of life.

Boog was wearing a raspberry tuxedo that would have nicely outfitted the maître d' of a dinner theater in Killeen, Texas, or somewhere.

"There's Boog," I said to Cindy, but she was by this time well out of her period of afterglow. Also she was pissed at me for having taken too long to park.

"Do I look like I'm blind?" she said.

At the time we were about eighty-sixth in the receiving line, a position Cindy clearly did not relish. Her natural impatience, deflected briefly by a little sex, had returned with a vengeance.

"At least Khaki's here," she said, having evidently spotted someone she knew.

Her impatience made me nervous. I myself evidently have too much patience—a useful quality if one spends half one's life waiting in auctions—and female impatience always makes me nervous, as if it were somehow my responsibility to hurry the universe.

"Khaki who?" I asked.

Cindy turned and looked at me. The friendly look she had given me when I had the hard-on in the shower might have occurred a year ago. My reluctance to park my Cadillac in the middle of Massachusetts Avenue had finished off the friendliness, at least for a time. She insisted that the middle of the street was under the protection of the Embassy, but I didn't believe her. I parked anyway.

"Haven't you ever heard of Khaki Descartes?" she asked.

"I may have," I said, trying to look thoughtful.

Cindy waited, skeptically. I kept looking thoughtful for about thirty seconds, and then gave up.

"I guess I haven't heard of her," I admitted sorrowfully.

"You could try reading a newspaper," she said.

In fact I often try reading newspapers. I'm just a flop at it. The only part that really interests me is the want ads. The news itself seems to be an interchangeable commodity: today's is seldom very different from last week's.

But want ads are ever fresh. What people are willing to try and sell or buy bespeaks the true variety of the human race. News only bespeaks the old constants: war and famine, earthquake and flood, politics and murder.

That very morning I had clipped a wonderful ad from the *Post*. "Authority on animal architecture wishes to sell approx. 10,000 nests" it said.

I thought that was wonderful. Some old person had actually spent a lifetime collecting nests. In all my years as a scout I had only seen one or two varnished hornet's nests for sale.

Naturally I called the collector at once and made an appointment to see his nests. He sounded like he was munching a nest when I called, though probably he was only eating Shredded Wheat.

Just having the appointment made me feel hopeful. A world that harbored a nest collector was a world that could be enjoyed.

The minute we got through the receiving line Cindy abandoned me.

The experience of the receiving line was not very enjoyable, either. A row of diplomats was planted at the head of it like small tuxedoed shrubs. Shaking hands with them turned out to be really creepy. Their hands were like fleshlike plants. Their plantlike fingers made no attempt to close around my hand, or any hand. We just rubbed palms—their hands swished slightly as the receiving line trotted by. Most of their palms were clammy, too.

The minute Cindy got through the line she made straight for a small ferretlike redhead in a khaki safari suit. Within seconds they were chattering like sisters. The redhead stared at me, but Cindy didn't beckon me to join them.

It was clear she was not the kind of girl who forgives a slow parker.

Feeling at a loss, I turned toward Boog, only to discover that he and Sir Cripps had left their position by the tree and disappeared. Like Brisling Bowker, they moved with stealth when the mood struck them.

I let a stream of people carry me through a door into a huge hall, where the first person I saw was Boss Miller. She was walking along talking to a tall, graying, tightly wound man with an aristocratic manner. I would have bet he was a squash player, squash being a game the tightly wound excel at.

Boss seemed greatly amused by him, but then she was greatly amused by most men, myself, Micah, and Boog being no exceptions. She was wearing a black silk dress and a magnificent string of pearls. Boog had expended a whole oil well on the pearls, in Paris years before.

Coming upon Boss unexpectedly, in the great hall of the Embassy, put life in a new perspective, suddenly. Boss seemed not merely beautiful, she seemed timeless. She could have been wearing that dress and those pearls in any capital, in any modern century.

Boss tossed her head in a way that meant I should come over, so I went over.

"Have you met Spud?" she asked, nodding toward the tightly wound aristocrat at her side.

Spud took me in at a glance. His glance did not have the radarlike qualities of Freddy Fu's, but it certainly had flash. When he looked at me I felt like I feel when a flashbulb goes off: exposed. Then he gave me by far the hardest handshake I had ever had from anyone in a tuxedo.

"Spud Breyfogle," Boss said, "meet Cadillac Jack."

"A pleasure," Spud said.

He nodded at me, gave Boss a knowing look, and turned away. For some reason he reminded me of Paul Henreid, in *Casablanca*, although he looked more like William Holden than Paul Henreid.

"He doesn't look like someone who would be named Spud," I said. The only other Spud I had known had been a small saddle-bronc rider from Junction, Texas. His name had been Spud Welch.

"Spud's a nickname," Boss said. "His real name is Newton. He's the most competitive man I ever met."

Then she slipped her arm through mine in a friendly way.

As we were promenading I noticed that Boss had an avid look in her eye. I followed the look, to see if there was a man in the crowd that she could be wanting, and discovered that we were actually promenading along beside a feast. One whole side of the great hall was given over to tables heaped with food. Three or four lambs lay atop great piles of rice, cooked to a crisp. Other tables were piled with seafood: shrimp, squid, smoked salmon, tiny fish. There was even a vast tureen of caviar. It seemed to be the caviar that prompted Boss's avid look.

Nearby was a vast tub of couscous, surrounded by platters of flat bread.

All the food was roped off behind thick velvet ropes. They were the kinds of ropes used in the foyers of movie theaters, to restrain eager crowds.

This crowd was eager, too. Most of the people in the receiving line had looked half dead, but the sight of a feast had brought them back to life. They were massed three deep behind the velvet ropes. Almost every eye in the house was shining, like Boss's, and a good many faces were shining, too. The sight of so much food must have released internal floods of gastric juices, causing sweat to pop out on many faces. The people were oblivious to one another. Lamb, caviar, and big pulpy shrimp were what they wanted.

I felt slightly revolted by the sight of so many avid, sweaty people—a totally unwarranted reaction, since I see avid sweaty people massed together at auctions every day. Also I felt an equally unwarranted jealousy of Spud Breyfogle.

"Is Spud famous?" I asked.

Boss chuckled. "Most famous editor in America," she said.

Then she lifted her head alertly. She seemed to be waiting for a signal. While she waited she adroitly edged into the crowd. All around us, alert men and women were edging into the crowd, skillfully displacing some of the people who were already there. Many of those who were already there seemed to be in a trance. They had made the mistake of edging in too soon and had sweated themselves out. They looked like exhausted runners, so wobbly as to be unaware that they were losing their positions to cool latecomers like Boss. Their unseeing eyes were still fixed on the food.

Meanwhile, Boss had taken my hand. She evidently had a use for me. As the crowd got thicker we were crushed together. Boss was sidling slowly toward the velvet ropes. Once in a while she gave my hand an encouraging squeeze. Crushed in the crowd, we were almost having an intimate moment.

As greed for objects welds crowds at an auction, greed for food welded this crowd. It was hard to imagine that such a well-dressed crowd could look so hungry. I've been to some wild barbecues down in Texas, where whole beeves were consumed, and yet I'd never seen a Texas crowd crammed up together, beaded with sweat. It didn't seem possible that a lot of people well off enough to own tuxedoes could be so hungry, and yet they seemed oblivious to everything but the food.

"Why are they so hungry?" I whispered to Boss, brushing back her dark hair so I could get to her ear.

Boss was uninterested in the question, but she seemed briefly interested in the fact that I had brushed back her hair. She looked at me curiously, as if she expected me to try and kiss her. It had not been my intention, but I saw no harm in trying. The crowd would never notice. It was oblivious to who was kissing whom. I bent to kiss her and it looked for a tenth of a second like it might work. But just at that moment, she smiled.

Chapter VII —————————

It feels silly to kiss a smile. At best you just sort of bump teeth. With Boss even that might be sexy, but as things stood, or as we stood, it seemed even sillier than it might have in another context.

I quickly lost belief in the notion that she had meant to kiss me. I felt embarrassed, but Boss seemed not the least bit embarrassed. She had a lot of confidence in her powers, it seemed.

"These people aren't hungry," she said. "These people are just bored."

She kept hold of my wrist and concentrated on edging ever closer to the velvet ropes.

She was a good edger, too. The trick seemed to be to move sideways, using one's lead elbow like a plow. As I watched, Boss plowed right between two short glassy-eyed Indonesians, her bosom passing just over their heads. A couple of tall, gloomy-looking Scandinavians had been blocking our view all along, but Boss somehow sidled right between them.

In three minutes we were standing next to the velvet ropes, directly in front of the tureen of caviar. Boss's eyes were shining and she was not even particularly sweaty, although there was a bead or two on her upper lip.

"You better get ready," she said.

Despite my constant immersion in the passions of auctions, I could not get over the avidity of this crowd. Even those who were glassy-eyed from the heat and the crush were trembling with eagerness.

Ten seconds later the ropes were removed. It was as if the roof had opened, dropping about five hundred people directly onto a feast.

I had no sensation of moving at all, but in an instant Boss and I were at the caviar bowl. I stood directly behind her, functioning like a rear bumper. People bumped into me, rather than her. A thicket of hands reached past me, trying to reach the bowl and slop a little caviar on some toast. There were little brown Indonesian hands, on arms long enough to reach around both Boss and myself. There were fat hands, mottled hands, be-ringed hands, skinny hands, and hands with sweaty palms. Having them waving all around me, like a sea of reeds, was creepy. I didn't even feel like I was among people. I felt like I was surrounded by a lot of wet plants.

While people were trying to reach around us, Boss and her peers were eating caviar. One of her peers was Sir Cripps Crisp, who must have been as good at edging as Boss was. He appeared out of nowhere and began methodically popping little caviar-heaped wedges of toast into his mouth.

Boss did the same, from time to time passing me a wedge. Once in a while she looked around at me and grinned, a fish egg or two momentarily stuck to her lips.

"Beastly," Sir Cripps said, while heaping himself another wedge. He was obviously a practiced man. In a second he could erect a neat pyramid of fish eggs on his wedge of toast. While his mouth worked on one pyramid his hand would be erecting the next.

His complaint was not lost on Boss.

"What's the matter with you, Jimmy?" she asked.

I was startled to hear Sir Cripps spoken to so familiarly, but he himself was not in the least offended. He actually raised his eyebrows when Boss spoke to him. They went up so slowly that it seemed they were probably powered by a little motor in his head, as if they were stage curtains. His eyes were an attractive and rather twinkly blue. It may have been the sight of Boss with fish eggs on her lips that caused them to twinkle.

"Beastly there's no vodka," he said. "Very irregular."

Boss opened a mother-of-pearl cocktail purse and took out a tiny silver flask. She opened it, took a swig, and handed the flask to Sir Cripps, who took a swig and handed it to me. They both looked at me impatiently, so I took a swig, too.

"You know Jimmy, don't you?" Boss asked, in much the way she had asked if I knew Spud Breyfogle.

I nodded, and Sir Cripps continued to erect pyramids of caviar.

"Jimmy writes the best cables in town," Boss said, giving him a little pat. "He used to bring 'em over and read 'em to me. Then we'd get drunk and he'd write a few in Latin. I think one of the ones in Latin nearly started a war, didn't it, Jimmy?"

Sir Cripps shrugged. "Only in Maseratu," he said. "Not difficult to start a war in Maseratu. Very excitable people."

Between the two of them they put away an amazing amount of caviar.

Being tall I was able to scan the crowd. Cindy was at the shrimp table, between Boog and Spud Breyfogle. Boog was gobbling shrimp, and Spud was dispensing a good deal of tightly wound charm for Cindy's benefit.

Meanwhile, Sir Cripps, whom I had considered to all intents and purposes a dead man, had come alive and was twinkling at Boss in a manner that suggested he might even still be capable of romance. He looked quite animated, perhaps because Boss was allowing him a snort of vodka after every wedge of caviar and toast.

Then I happened to notice the hapless Eviste Labouchere, a few steps away at the couscous bowl. Hapless is a word that might have been coined especially for him. In a room containing five hundred gluttons he still managed to stand out, thanks to the rate at which he was stuffing down the couscous. He ate like he was starving. Of course, he might have been starving. For all I knew he hadn't eaten since the Penrose dinner. Certainly he looked awful. He had clearly been living in his tux for several days, and at some point had come into contact with a dog, or at least with a place where a dog had spent time. His dinner jacket was covered with dog hairs. He had a wild, almost demented look in his eye as he scooped couscous out of the giant bowl.

Lilah Landry, his one-time date, was standing between the couscous and the caviar, watching Eviste go at it. She looked faintly sickened. Perhaps the sight of him gobbling couscous had brought home to her the fact that he wasn't really a star.

I think I must have looked at her at the precise moment when their romance ended. Eviste didn't notice it ending, but I did. Boss and Sir Cripps were having a tête-à-tête, and had forgotten me, so I had nothing to do but look. Also I was faintly worried about what sort of lubricity Spud might be whispering in Cindy's ear.

While I was pondering the general inconclusiveness of life, Lilah arrived at my side, tall, beautiful, and dizzy.

"How you?" she said, startling me.

"I'm fine," I said, trying to appear composed and at ease.

"How's Eviste?" I asked, in an attempt to make conversation.

Lilah just continued to smile her famous smile. The minute some women get through with a man their brains simply erase them, as tape recorders erase tape. Coffee had never bothered to erase me, but she had erased any number of Roberts and Richards.

I had the feeling that at the very moment the equivalent of an empty tape was whirling through Lilah's brain—a tape that had once contained memories of Eviste Labouchere.

To make up for my unnoticeable opening note, I offered her some caviar. This was possible because Boss and Sir

Cripps had quietly vanished, leaving me undisputed access to the bowl.

Instead of taking the wedge of toast and caviar I offered her and feeding it to herself, Lilah leaned over and nipped off half the wedge, in the process exposing much of the creamy bosom that had so recently harbored a pug.

Then she straightened up and chewed lazily for a moment.

"Well, I vow and declare," she said. "Look who's here."

Before I could look she caught my wrist, leaned over, and ate the rest of the wedge.

Chapter VIII ───────────

As a bosom-tilter, Lilah Landry was world class. By tilting adroitly she managed to make her bosom seem more interesting than anyone who could possibly have arrived in our vicinity, and even while I was enjoying the exhibition, I had the definite sense that someone was emitting heat waves of displeasure.

When I finally looked around I saw that the arrivee was the small redhead in the khaki safari suit.

"It wouldn't be a Washington party without you eating out of some man's hand, would it, Lilah?" she said.

The redhead had a face that put me in mind of a drill, and a voice that suggested sandpaper.

Lilah didn't seem in the least disturbed by the remark. She just gave me a blithe look and moved off toward the seafood table. Before I knew it I was alone with the redhead.

"Hello, Jack," she said, shaking hands. "Don't you think we ought to talk?"

I would have been more inclined to think so if I had some inkling of what she did. All I knew was that she put me in mind of drills. She had an intense, button-eyed manner, and she didn't let go of my hand.

145

"Do you want some caviar?" I asked.

The question stumped her momentarily. For a second or two her face lost its drill-like aspects and just looked like the face of a small hungry woman.

"George would kill me if I ate some," she said a little wistfully. "He doesn't approve of this regime. I don't think he'd tolerate it if I ate their caviar."

"It's difficult living with a moralist," she added. "George is not flexible. His moral vision is twenty-twenty. If I eat one bite of this caviar he'll throw a fit."

Instead of talking, we began to walk through the thinning crowd. While we were walking I saw a reporter's notebook sticking out of her handbag, which explained what she did, at least. She was a reporter, not a Cabinet member.

Most of the people in the thinning crowd looked sleepy. They had stuffed, now they wanted to sleep. In fact, some of the older diplomats had started sleeping already; they were being guided toward the exits by their well-trained wives.

Suddenly the spectral figure of Eviste Labouchere wobbled up. He spotted Khaki and rushed to embrace her as a colleague.

"Ah Khakee, Khakee!!" he exclaimed.

"Get lost, you little turd," Khaki said, in unsentimental tones.

Eviste looked a little hurt by Khaki's remark, which was more or less the rhetorical equivalent of a splash of acid.

"But Khakee," he said woefully. "I am going your way. I will give you a ride on Anouk."

"Like shit you will," Khaki said.

"George will probably strangle you when he hears about this," she added, in her sandiest tones. Once again she was burning with displeasure—her heat had a Saharan quality.

If Khaki was the pitiless desert, Eviste was the lost Legionnaire, the one who is never going to make it back to the fort. He stood looking woeful for a moment and then turned and stumbled away.

"Who's Anouk?" I asked, thinking Eviste might have a giant girl friend hidden away somewhere. After all, he had just offered Khaki a ride on her.

"That's what he calls his motor scooter," Khaki said, looking disgusted. "He named it after Anouk Aimée."

Chapter IX ───────────

"*He names all his* motor scooters after movie stars he's in love with," Khaki confided. "When I first met him he had one named Tuesday, after Tuesday Weld. Can you imagine a motor scooter named Tuesday?"

The thought depressed her so much that she walked along in a funk for a few minutes, occasionally emitting flashes of heat from her little black eyes. I walked along with her, past the emptying tables. She reminded me of one of those little mean rat terriers that are so common in the south. As long as you're looking at them they let you alone, but the minute you turn your back they bite you in the leg.

I was hoping we'd run into Boss and Sir Cripps, or perhaps Cindy and Boog, but instead we ran into Andy Landry and Freddy Fu. They were standing by what was left of a lamb, pulling crisp little pieces of skin off what was left of its hock and nibbling it. Freddy Fu had on a tuxedo and looked very merry. Being the best spy in Washington seemed to agree with him, and being with him seemed to agree with Andy Landry. She looked very healthful and had recently got her hair frizzed. Since she was very thin and had a cloud of frizzed hair she gave the impression of being slightly off the ground.

"Ah, Khaki," Freddy said, when he saw us. He left off eating lamb skin and came over and kissed the air about an inch from her cheek. He did it with merry self-assurance, as if that were precisely the way to greet a person such as Khaki Descartes.

"Charming of you to bring her over," he said to me, in Oxbridgian tones.

Khaki at once transferred her full attention to Freddy. I was immediately ditched. She and Freddy moved just out of earshot, leaving me with Andy Landry, who seemed a nice tall girl.

Andy fed me a piece of lamb skin, which surprised me. Food was the last thing I had come to expect from Washington women.

"Do you run?" she asked, after looking me over in a shy way that was rather appealing.

"Nope," I said. "I drive."

"Why?" she asked, looking a little shocked. "Driving isn't exercise."

"It may not be exercise but it gets you from place to place," I countered.

"Yeah, but it isn't *exercise*," she insisted. "What's your exercise?"

"Buying things," I said.

Andy looked a little hurt. I think she thought I was mocking her.

"No," I said. "It's true. Buying things is more strenuous than you think. A lot of exercise is involved. Also you have to carry the things you buy."

"It's not real exercise though," she said. "You should at least go to a gym once a week. I mean, you could do your body that favor."

Fortunately at that point she happened to notice that Khaki was scribbling frantically in her reporter's notebook.

"Khaki's a brain-picker," Andy said.

Suddenly Boog appeared at my elbow. Then he passed my elbow and gave Andy a big kiss. His didn't land on the air, either.

"Let's you an' me go to Bermuda for a day," he suggested. "We could ride motor scooters an' then fuck."

At this point Khaki and Freddy came back. Boog had been extremely cheerful, but at the sight of Khaki his cheer subsided.

"What about the Croat and the Senator's wife?" Khaki said, getting right to the point. "I know you know, Boog. I know you know."

Boog widened his eyes and tried to look like an innocent millionaire from Winkler County.

"Whut Croat?" he said. "Hail, I don't even know whut a Croat is."

"The Croat who's buying the helicopters," Khaki said, through clenched teeth.

Boog cast his eyes heavenward, as if he expected to see a helicopter beneath the Embassy roof.

"I don't even care about the helicopters," Khaki said. "I know you set up the deal but I don't care. George is the one who doesn't think the Croats ought to get helicopters. I just want to know about the Senator's wife."

I felt a subtle touch at my elbow. It was Freddy Fu.

"Whut Senator's wife?" Boog said.

"The one that's fuckin' the Croat," Khaki hissed. "Was she in on the deal? I want to know!"

At this point Freddy sidled back about ten feet, and his look suggested that I accompany him. Since I don't know how to sidle I just turned around and walked.

"I wouldn't ordinarily set her on him," Freddy said, "but of course the Booger-man can take care of himself."

"You mean there's no Croat?" I asked.

Freddy just smiled. "There are always Croats," he said. "And there are always Serbs. How would you like to buy a warehouse full of baskets?"

Chapter X _____

"*Did you say a* warehouse full of *baskets?*" I asked.

"That's right," Freddy said. "Approximately 190,000 baskets, representing virtually all cultures and all periods."

I love baskets, almost indiscriminately. I like the cheap bright basketry of Mexico, and the somber expensive basketry of the Apaches. I've also seen some wonderful Peruvian baskets, but in all my scouting I may have now owned 150 baskets, surely no more. Now I was being offered 190,000.

"The Booger-man mentioned that you know baskets," he said. "He thought you might be able to take them off our hands."

Freddy never stopped smiling, but his smile had nuances, cadences almost. Sometimes he smiled the smile of the inscrutable Oriental, at other times the smile an old Princetonian might adopt when confiding in a slightly doltish friend.

"Is there a price?" I asked.

"The price is four million," Freddy said. "I think when you've seen the baskets you'll find it a bargain."

I could easily believe that, since one really good American Indian basket, from almost any tribe, will bring anywhere between $1,500 and $10,000 dollars these days.

"Are you interested?" Freddy asked.

"Yes," I said, reduced to a monosyllable by the audacity of it all.

Of course even my monosyllable was a bluff. I didn't have $4 million, or even a significant fraction thereof.

Besides that, I didn't have any place to put 190,000 baskets. The volume buy had never been my style. It was Big John's style. My style was to buy the solitaries, such as the single best Sung vase in the '77–'78 auction season, for example. Or the only known Brancusi hood ornament. Or, possibly, the boots of Billy the Kid.

Nonetheless Freddy has just offered me an opportunity to fulfill one of the great scouting fantasies: getting inside the Smithsonian warehouses. It was a chance not to be missed.

"How do I get a look at them?" I asked.

"You want to see a man named Hobart Cawdrey," he said. "He's in the Department of Transportation, extension 1000. Easy to remember. I suggest you call him tomorrow. Things are beginning to move."

It seemed odd to me that a man responsible for the fate of 190,000 baskets would be in the Department of Transportation, but then what did I know?

"I'll call him tomorrow," I promised.

Freddy shook my hand again, still smiling. "I hope it works out," he said.

It had all seemed kind of odd. We had stood there surrounded by some of the most famous journalists in America and talked openly about the sale of part of a great national institution. Any passing journalist could have heard us—even a deranged stringer like Eviste. And there was another thing to consider: what my purchase would do to the basket market.

That question at least had an obvious answer. The basket market would be finished for a generation. It would suffer the fate the Boy Scout knife market had suffered when Big John bought the warehouse in Poughkeepsie. All the basket scouts I knew, and I knew some good ones, would have to find new careers.

It was a sad thought. As people tend to resemble their pets, so scouts come to resemble the objects they scout for. Basket scouts are among the nicest people I know. They tend to be simple, spare, graceful, unaggressive. They have a kind of dry quiet humor that I like.

"You better watch out," Boss said. She had come up behind me and seemed to be regarding me with a motherly eye. It annoyed me a little, that she was looking so motherly.

"I'm watching out," I said.

Boss smiled. Worse still, she ruffled my hair.

"You're cute when you're huffy," she said. "What time does Cindy let you out in the morning?"

"I do as I please," I said, wishing I could think of something wittier or more original to say.

"I don't know who you think you're fooling, but it ain't me you're fooling," she said. "I'm going out to see Cyrus in the morning. He's selling his second-best horse farm. You could come if you can talk Cindy into letting you out."

Boss was a master of the taunt. It is not exactly a rare skill, among women, but she had developed it to a very high level of subtlety. At times I tended to forget that she employed both of my former wives, and thus knew more than most about my behavior with women.

"Did you mean Cyrus Folmsbee?" I asked, remembering

that he was supposed to be the power behind the sale of the Smithsonian.

"Yeah, Cyrus," Boss said. "You better come and meet him before you let Boog and Freddy get you in trouble. Cyrus is no one to fuck around with. Come by about nine, if you can get loose."

"I can get loose," I said.

Boss looked amused. "We'll see about that," she said.

Chapter XI ─────────────

Bravado always backfires, with me. Every time I make a bold claim, particularly if I make it with a woman, fate blows it back in my face like a piece of wet newspaper.

The fact that Cindy had been up and ready to hit the street at seven the morning before had misled me into thinking early rising and the efficient dispatch of business was a pattern that could be relied on.

The minute we got home from the Embassy she konked out and slept like a baby, while I sat on the bed feeling restive and indecisive. Life was looking more and more complicated. Cindy was even more beautiful asleep than awake—slumber added an almost ethereal shapeliness to her face and body. Of course she was shapely asleep or awake, but the minute she was awake enough for her impatience level to rise to its normal mark on the gauge she stopped seeming ethereal and began to seem like a big beautiful Santa Barbara girl who was used to getting her own way.

Cindy slept evenly, peacefully, untroubled by the thought of tomorrow or the memory of yesterday, while I sat and fidgeted for hours, worrying about all manner of murky eventualities.

When I finally dozed for a bit I had my backward driving dream. It was early morning before I had it, because when I awoke from it fall sunlight was filtering through Cindy's long windows. About that time, Cindy, who had been sleeping with her back to me, turned over and curled against me. She slept with her mouth partly open, which for some reason made her seem far more helpless than she really was.

She might not have been helpless, but she was warm. She flopped an arm across my chest and the arm was hot as a stove. Having a long warm girl stretched out against you as the October sunlight is beginning to come through the windows in the morning is a good way to overcome the fidgets. After cooking for a while in Cindy's body heat I became genuinely drowsy and went to sleep, only to have, once again, little flash cuts of myself driving backwards.

Then I began to have a vague but sexy dream involving Boss Miller. As it got sexier the flash cuts of backward driving gradually stopped. Boss took the dream and it got sexier and sexier, although I could not tell that we were actually doing anything. Unfortunately, as the sexiness increased I began to wake up. I tried to stay asleep but I couldn't. I woke up and looked at Cindy, only to discover that she had slipped down in the bed and was quietly and rather speculatively performing an oral sex act, in which I had been playing an unwitting but cooperative part.

I was very surprised, since in our previous lovemaking she had been energetic without being either aggressive or inventive. She went straight to the point and made it. After a bit she might recoup and make it again, but it was essentially the same point. Her lovemaking was like I imagined her tennis game would be: a matter of serve and volley. She was not into drop shots, topspin, or elaborate baseline strategies. She went for the ace, and then went for another ace.

But a change had come over her. Perhaps the fact that I had been deeply asleep had made her feel that a little harmless experimenting could be done. She was experimenting rather tentatively, as if she hoped to learn a new game without the embarrassment of having someone watch her practice.

Being compliant by nature, I went along with what I judged to be the requirements of the situation and pretended to be asleep, although for a time I watched what was going on through lidded eyes. It only had the effect of making me feel like a peeping Tom. The longer Cindy's experiment went on, the sillier I felt, though thanks to her natural impatience it probably only went on a few minutes. The fact that it was early morning and that I couldn't decide whether to be asleep or awake made it seem longer.

I guess Cindy concluded that oral sex might have its interest but was not likely to get her any aces. She soon decided she preferred the old game of serve and volley and hopped on top of me. I opened my eyes just long enough to glimpse a narrow band of bright sunlight between her body and mine. Cindy must have been pretty excited because she looked like a big strawberry. She came in no time and collapsed on my cheek in a kind of victor's trance. Her breath, warm from her exertions, ruffled the little hairs on my arm while I cuddled her a bit.

As for me, I felt as distant as if I were in the middle of Wyoming. My mind was as sere and dry as the flats along the Wind River, and they are very sere and dry.

Then she began to want to be kissed, which surprised me a little. After all, she hadn't spoken to me at all the evening before. But she definitely wanted to be kissed. Her breath was always fresh as a green grape—breath that was blowing straight off some absolutely tiptop cells. Even in the early morning she had a clean, grapelike flavor that was very appealing.

After a while my Wind River mood passed and I began to feel not so empty. Also I began to feel curious about what might be going on with Cindy. It was true that we had made love on previous occasions, but there hadn't really been much amorousness involved. Cindy had just wolfed down a little sex much as she had wolfed down Brie and salami. The wolfing had had no real character. It had been all vigor and no tone.

Now all of a sudden, on a morning when I was supposed to go somewhere with Boss, she was developing an interest in tone.

"Let's fuck all day," she said. "I never have."

"What do you mean?" I asked.

"I never have just spent a day in bed, doing things," she said. She said it almost meekly, as if it were a shameful confession.

"You never will, either, if you start this early," I said. "Not unless you can arrange for a string of fellows. No one fellow is going to last all day."

"It doesn't have to be just fucking," Cindy said, still meekly. "We could do other kinds of things."

"What other kinds of things?"

She shrugged her beautiful freckled shoulders. "Orgy-like things," she said. "You probably know more about them than I do. I never get to do those kinds of things."

"That's hard to believe," I said, though in fact I could believe it perfectly well. A lot of brash girls who will fuck you in an instant turn out not to have done much sexually—they often live a life of very simple fucks.

"But you're the toast of Washington," I said. "How come you haven't had better opportunities?"

"I told you," she said, wiggling a little. "These are successful people. They can't lay around in bed all day."

She looked slightly depressed, as if it had just occurred to her that she had missed a lot because all the successful men she knew were off running the country, leaving no one to do what she called orgy-like things with her.

"What about the reporters?" I asked. "They don't have to run the country."

Cindy shook her head. "They always fall in love and then they never leave their wives," she said. Then she reached down between my legs to see if there were any signs of recovery in that region. I could hardly believe what was happening. The efficient social-climbing woman of the weekend was fading out and being replaced by an almost lovestruck, partially innocent Santa Barbara girl who wanted nothing more than a day of slightly out-of-the-ordinary sexual adventure.

"Come on," she whispered. In my confusion I had not exactly launched into doing things.

Clearly I had to do something, so I repaid her what might be called a favor—I guess it counted as an orgy-like thing, because Cindy had an orgasm so strong that an observer might have thought she was being electrocuted. After that she fell into a deep sleep and I got up and shaved and took a shower. From the force of the orgasm I judged she might sleep long enough for me to go off and spend a few hours in the country with Boss.

That plan had a life-span shorter than a gnat's. While I was standing there, half adrowse in the shower, the door opened and Cindy stumbled in, half asleep also. I woke up but she didn't. She hugged me and resumed her nap. The shower poured down over both of us. Cindy didn't have on a shower cap. I don't think she cared that her hair was getting wet. She had just got out of bed and sought a body to be near. Some homing device had brought her straight to me. She seemed to be sleeping soundly, her wet face against my wet chest.

After that we stood there for a while, one of us asleep and the other wide-awake and a little confused.

Chapter XII _____

My confusion lasted over an hour, most of which time I spent trying to provide Cindy with enough sexual pleasure to knock her out again. In this I failed. Once she had her little nap in the shower she became extremely wakeful and nothing I did in the way of orgy-like activities put her back to sleep. Her hair was so wet that every time I put my face in it I got water in my eyes. When things were going slow she rubbed at it vigorously with a towel. Once when she was wiggling around I slipped out of her, only to be immediately rein-serted.

"Stay in there," she said.

It was only thirty minutes before I was due to meet Boss. Although I seemed to be glued into a day-long embrace, I still had faint hopes that I could somehow escape and keep my date. I had stopped feeling romantic about the date—I seemed to have all the romance I could handle closer to hand—but I was determined not to let Boss think I couldn't get away from Cindy when I wanted to.

However, I was far from certain as to how I was going to get away from Cindy. At the moment she had one hand on the base of my cock, to see that I didn't slip out again.

Since she was looking quite friendly I decided to try a frank approach.

"I have to tell you something," I said.

I guess she was looking friendly because she was sort of tuned in to her own pleasures, listening to them as if over a radio. When I interrupted the radio she raised her head briefly and gave me a kiss.

"What?" she asked.

"This is not a day we can spend all of in bed," I said. "We could do that tomorrow," I added quickly.

I meant it, too. I had nothing against a day in bed with the new Cindy. But that didn't mean I wanted to lose face with Boss.

"What's wrong with today?" Cindy wanted to know. She didn't look mad. She didn't turn loose of my cock, either.

"I have to go somewhere," I lied. "I have a very big deal lined up."

"Un-uh," she said.

To strengthen her point she wrapped her legs around me and hooked her ankles. She was a strong girl, too.

"I don't know what's come over you," I said.

"I don't either but you can't go," she said.

"But this is important," I said. "It's a deal that could make me as rich as Boog."

Cindy shook her head.

"Naw," she said. "You'll never be rich. You aren't even successful. You better just stay here and fuck me. It's the best you're gonna get.

"Don't try to be like everybody else," she said, raising her head for another kiss.

"Why not?"

"It will just spoil everything," she said. "I don't want it spoiled. I want it like this. I'm tired of everybody else."

That's when I knew the day was lost. Boss was right, I couldn't get away. Cindy and I looked at one another for a while. I didn't feel in love, but I felt extremely fond.

In ten minutes Boss was going to expect me to start for Middleburg with her. Meanwhile Cindy and I were floating along on a slow boat, sexually. We weren't doing much but we were definitely united.

For some reason I decided to be honest, a rare decision with me. I guess it was prompted by the deep ephemeral feeling of closeness I had with Cindy. I didn't feel like lying to a face that was only two inches from mine.

"I have to make a call and break that appointment," I said.

"I bet it was with a woman," she said.

"You better not lie," she added, looking at me closely.

I hadn't meant to, but she did well to warn me. Sometimes I cut into a lie at the very last moment, even when I have every intention of telling the truth. An instinct for the protective falsehood seems to take over.

"It was with Boss," I said.

Cindy regarded me solemnly for a second. I think she was genuinely surprised that I had told her the truth. I was surprised myself, since I knew she was jealous of Boss.

In terms of womanly power, Boss was far ahead of her, and Cindy knew it. Boss had a husband, children, many lovers—a depth of gesture Cindy just didn't have. Against Boss she was overmatched.

Thus it was kind of a big deal that I had told her the truth. For once I had gambled on the potency of honesty. Cindy's only immediate response was to flex her hips.

"I feel embarrassed," I said. "I have to call. It's not fair not to break the appointment."

Cindy didn't say a word. She was leaving it to me. So call, her look said.

"Put your fingers in your ears for a minute," I said, in a cajoling tone. "Then I won't have to get up. I can use the bedside phone."

"You're not getting up," she said, flexing her hips again.

"I've never talked on the phone at a time like this," I said.

For an answer I got a kiss. Then she wiggled her head down between two pillows and raised her arms to squeeze the pillows against her ears. She didn't really squeeze them very tight, though. Her armpits were lightly stubbled. Evidently she had decided to rely on her eyes alone to detect any treachery.

I called Boss, who answered on the first ring.

"I can't come today," I said, wasting no words.

Boss was silent for a moment. In the background I could hear Micah giggling and the outraged voice of Desi Arnaz. An early morning rerun was in progress.

"What a surprise," Boss said. "How about tomorrow?"

"What?" I asked, surprised myself.

"Cyrus canceled," Boss said. "Bessie couldn't come today and he won't do anything without Bessie. Do you think she'll let you out tomorrow?"

"I don't know," I said, risking another venture into truth. Further bravado seemed pointless.

I expected gloating, but Boss didn't bother.

"Give it a try," she said. "Same time same station."

Cindy hadn't taken her eyes off me. She smiled as she watched. Then she began to stroke one of my legs with one of her heels.

Boss seemed to have no more to say. Neither did I. Desi Arnaz was screaming at Lucy when I hung up the phone.

Chapter XIII _____

Cindy's all-day sex-fest only lasted half a day. Of course it started at dawn, so it was a long half day. During the half day I attempted to help her do all the things she had never got to do with men more successful than myself. They were not really very revolutionary things. In fact, they were sexual staples, familiar to millions, if not billions. But for some reason they had not yet become staples to Cindy, and she enjoyed them a lot.

We had to go out to lunch, since we were both ravenous and there was not enough food in Cindy's larder to feed even one of us. So we went out and wolfed down some bacon cheeseburgers and happened to notice that there was a Humphrey Bogart double feature at a movie theater two doors from the restaurant. *To Have and Have Not* and *Casablanca* were the movies.

"We could go see them," I suggested.

Cindy was delighted. It fit in perfectly with the unconventionality of the day. Seeing movies in the afternoon was an even greater defiance of the laws of success than lying around fucking. The latter was at least tinged with romance—the former was just lazy.

"We can eat popcorn and hold hands," I added.

"Naw, I hate popcorn, it's not good for you," she said. "But we can hold hands. I've never seen either of those movies."

"You must be the only person in the world who hasn't seen *Casablanca*," I said.

She looked at me as if I had just made a serious assertion.

"I don't think I am," she said.

If she was, she still is, because the minute we sat down she fell asleep and slept contentedly through most of both movies. I slept through most of *To Have and Have Not* myself—it had been a strenuous morning—but I woke up in *Casablanca* just as they were singing the "Marseillaise." Not Cindy. She was snoozing soundly, her head on my shoulder, her mouth open. On the screen Ingrid Bergman was looking her freshest, her eyes liquid with the dew of youth and life. Cindy looked the picture of vulnerability. I kissed her and when she opened her eyes they were just as dewy as Ingrid Bergman's. We abandoned the movie, bought a huge sack of groceries, and went back to her house.

Cindy went in the kitchen and began to put the groceries away, yawning big healthy yawns as she did it. She had bought five or six kinds of soup. Leek soup, turtle soup, gazpacho, split pea, lentil, and Manhattan clam chowder. She was happily stuffing them into her shelves, which already seemed to contain a lot of soup.

"It's my favorite thing," she said, a bit defiantly, when she caught me looking at the soup. Somehow it was a winning touch. Behind the poised social climber was a girl who liked to stockpile a lot of soups. Probably having a lot of soup made her feel secure. In an odd way it sort of made up for her lack of interest in antiques.

In effect she was a soup collector, a realization which cheered me, for some reason. I went over and kissed her just as she was starting a yawn. It was a happy move. A woman who is just getting into being awakened is usually eager to have the awakening continue.

"I'll make you some soup," she remarked, after the kiss.

Chapter XIV _____

At 11:30 that night I remembered Belinda Arber, who had been expecting me to come by that afternoon and take her, her mother, and her sister to Baskin-Roberts, as she called it. Of course Belinda was only three and might have forgotten that I was supposed to come, but I had a feeling she hadn't. Natural winners are not forgetful where their own interests are concerned.

Beside me, Cindy was sleeping deeply, in her pink nightgown, recovering from a long day of sexual awakening. Actually she had gone to sleep with one of my hands squeezed between her legs and it was still there, slowly growing numb. It was already numb nearly up to the elbow. Once I had pulled it out, to give my blood a chance to circulate through it, but Cindy had grunted and succeeded in stuffing it back against her fundament without even waking up.

I felt an inward disquiet, although it was a quiet night, so quiet that I could hear Cindy's steady breathing. True to her word, Cindy had given me some soup, and I had given her some love. I don't know that it was an unequal trade. The soup was probably as good on the soup level as the love was on the love level, all things considered.

Cindy took my feeling and swirled it around in the blender of her body, absorbing it instantly, as if it were a healthy mixture of sugar, orange juice, and raw eggs. Sex was the raw eggs. Since she herself didn't have to bother feeling very much she got the full and immediate benefit of emotion that might otherwise have been doled out over several months of domestic life or social partnership, like a balanced meal.

Cindy didn't want a balanced meal. Like Belinda, she just wanted a quick trip to Baskin-Robbins.

For the second night in a row, I fidgeted, while my hand went to sleep against Cindy's cunt. At some point she rolled over and spread her thighs and my hand tingled for about twenty minutes, as it came back to life. While it tingled I tried to imagine the future.

What my imagination prefers to do with futures is furnish them. I see large airy rooms, filled with all my most treasured and spectacular things, and then I see myself and the woman of my immediate dreams living in them.

I lay in bed and furnished a few rooms, but my imagination couldn't keep Cindy in one of them for more than a tenth of a second. My imagination is more realistic than I am. Cindy wasn't going to be in any of those rooms. My objects held no interest for her and my towns and roads would bore her.

Though for the moment she was asleep beside me, in her pink nightgown, Cindy really was just waking up. Once she was really awake she wasn't going to want me around. She would go out into the capital, as Boss had, and pick the men she wanted, from the berry bushes of diplomacy, politics, journalism, the arts, the law firms, or whatever capital bushes she might be passing. The juice of many men would stain her lips for a time, before she reduced them to mulberry-colored pulp.

In the morning she was up at 6:30, and she punched me five times before leaving for her high-level exercise class at 7:30. All five were unpremeditated punches that occurred whenever she remembered that I was going to Middleburg with Boss. She punched me once in bed, once in the shower —which she insisted we take together in memory of our romantic yesterday—twice while we were dressing and once in the kitchen. The last punch caused milk to slosh out of the bowl. She didn't wipe it up, or explain any of the punches. I might only be the berry-of-the-week but I wasn't supposed to be anybody else's berry during that time.

"You better be back here by six," she said, from the door. "We're going to Oblivia's tonight. We have to try and act like normal people."

"My gosh," I said. "We *are* normal people. Even the most normal people in the world are sometimes late."

"That's not true," she said.

"Of course it's true. Punctuality is not synonymous with normality."

If it hadn't been 7:25 I think we would have had a terrible fight. Cindy was itching for one. I wasn't, but I realized one was practically inevitable, in view of the fact that I had a sort of date with Boss.

The minute she left I dug out a Maryland phone book and called Jean.

Belinda answered on the second ring.

"I'll get it," she said, having got it. Then she breathed into the receiver for a bit.

"Who *is* it?" she asked, having caught her breath.

"*That's* not what you're supposed to say," her sister said, from somewhere nearby.

There was silence on the line as Belinda tried to remember what she was supposed to say.

"Is this the Arbers' residence?" I asked.

Belinda wasn't listening.

"I know what to say, Beverly!" she said.

"Then say it!" Beverly yelled.

More silence.

"Can't remember right now," Belinda admitted, though in clear and unrepentant tones.

"Are you Belinda Arber?" I asked. "I'm the man with the big white car."

"Are you gonna take us to Baskin-Roberts today?" she asked, coming straight to the point.

"You better," she added.

"Why had I better?"

"You jist better come over here," she said.

"I just better talk to your momma first," I said. "She might not want me to."

"She cried," Belinda remarked, apropos of nothing.

"Uh-oh," I said. "When?"

"Two times," Belinda said. "Are you coming over here?"

"Let me have that phone," Jean said, from somewhere behind her.

"I'm *talking!*" Belinda insisted.

There was silence while a struggle took place. I could imagine Belinda clinging grimly to the receiver.

Jean, however, was stronger.

"Hel—" she said, just as we were disconnected.

I immediately called back.

Jean answered. In the background I could hear loud howls. Belinda had lost a round.

"I can't believe she did that," Jean said, sounding a good deal strung out. One of the times she cried had not been long ago.

"What'd she do?" I asked.

"Disconnected us," Jean said. "The little bitch. If she can't win she makes sure everybody else loses."

"Did you spank her?" I asked.

"Of course I spanked her," Jean said. "You think I'm gonna let her get away with that?"

"I couldn't come by yesterday," I said. "I just called to apologize."

Jean was silent for a moment.

"I didn't expect you to," she said. "There's no reason you should rearrange your life just because I have a bossy daughter."

The howls came closer. The bossy daughter was returning to the attack.

"Don't you hit me," Jean said soberly.

"But . . . I . . . was jist *talkin*'," Belinda insisted, her voice bubbly with sobs.

"So? There's no justice," Jean said, in the voice of a mother who was not very impressed with the tragic little figure standing before her.

"Is . . . he . . . comin' over?" Belinda asked.

"I don't know, are you?" Jean asked.

"I was thinking I might come over this afternoon," I said. "I'd still like to see your antiques."

It was actually true. I was eager to see what kinds of chests Jean had managed to dredge up.

Also I wanted to see Belinda, Beverly, and Jean—they seemed a likable and promising trio.

"You realize that if you come it means Baskin-Robbins," Jean said.

"I can live with that," I said.

At mention of Baskin-Robbins Belinda fell silent. There was a rustling sound, such as a little girl might make when she's climbing up in her mother's lap.

"Jist *tell* him," Belinda said.

"You don't tell people, you ask them," Jean said.

"I'll tell him then," Belinda said, repossessing the phone.

"You're rude, Belinda, you grab," Beverly said. "I don't grab, do I, Mom?"

"Nope," Jean said. "You're my well-mannered daughter."

Her other daughter was not interested in such distinctions.

"You come an' take us to Baskin-Roberts, okay?" she said.

"Okay," I said. "I'll come."

"I tolded him," Belinda said.

"I heard you," Jean said. "I didn't hear you say thank you, though."

"No, 'cause I didn't say it yet," Belinda said blithely.

Then she held the phone close to her mouth and breathed into the receiver, as if to make it clear that her will had not relaxed one whit.

"Is you the one with the soft car?" she asked.

"I'm the one," I said.

Belinda giggled. "What's your name again?" she asked.

"Jack."

"It's Jack," she said, to her mother.

Then she breathed into the receiver some more.

"You're coming *today?*" she asked.

"That's right," I said.

"Okay, but no forgets," she warned.

"No forgets," I said.

Chapter XV _____

    The first thing I saw when we drove into Cyrus Folmsbee's second-best horse farm, near Middleburg, was a wooden-sided Rolls-Royce hunting brake. It was sitting on a beautifully kept gravel driveway, and a small man in striped pants and a neat little black cap was waxing its wooden sides, rubbing them gently and expertly with a soft cloth.

"I can't believe it," I said to Boss. "That's a Rolls-Royce hunting brake."

It sat in front of a beautiful red brick house, beneath trees whose leaves had just turned, in the midst of rolling green country filled with white fences and sleek horses.

Just seeing it there gave me a feeling akin to nausea. It's a feeling I only get when I have to go onto the properties of the very rich and see wonderful things that I can't possibly buy.

Boss noticed that I immediately fell in love with the car.

"Don't try to buy it," she said, smiling a little, in a motherly way, which was the way she had been smiling all the way to Middleburg.

We were in her Lincoln rather than my Cadillac, because Boss was afraid the sight of a Cadillac would send Cyrus Folmsbee into a rage. Evidently he harbored a long-standing grudge against the Cadillac division of General Motors because they had once sent him a car whose color had been slightly wrong.

"Cyrus is picky," Boss said. She was in a cool but cheerful mood. She let her eyes rove a bit over Cyrus Folmsbee's second-best horse farm before getting out.

"He's probably just selling it because the fences need painting," she said, pointing at the miles and miles of white fence that stretched over hill and dale, to vanish in the foothills of the Blue Ridge. In the crisp fall morning the Blue Ridge mountains were living up to their name. They were as blue as the flame of a welder's torch.

"The fence looks okay to me," I said.

"Un-uh," Boss said. "It's dingy. Not really up to standards."

We got out and strolled over to where the little man in the striped pants was polishing the heart-stopping car. He made a little bow when he saw Boss.

"How are you, Herbert?" she asked, putting her hand on his shoulder in a friendly fashion.

Such kindness made Herbert look like he might cry.

"Very well, thank you, Mrs. Miller," he said. "It's kind of you to ask."

"What does he intend to do with you, if he sells this place?" Boss asked.

Herbert shook his head, a little forlornly. "I expect I will go with the cars," he said. "That probably means Connecticut. I shouldn't think he'd require seven cars in Maine, though of course that *is* a possibility. He does like the way I do these cars."

I could see why. The hunting brake had probably been made in the late twenties, from the look of it, but one would have had to crawl underneath it to find any evidence that it had ever been used.

"Why hasn't he painted the fence?" Boss asked. "It's not like Cyrus to let things run down."

Herbert was not happy to have been asked such a question. His horrified look reminded me of my old friend Goat Goslin, who also hated to be asked questions, though in all other respects no one could have been less like Goat than Herbert. The latter had all his fingers, and had probably never seen a rodeo.

Herbert looked carefully around before answering. After all, his boss had once run the CIA. His caution was understandable.

"It's the neighbors," he said finally. "I'm afraid Mr. Folmsbee has fallen out with them. He says they deserve to have to look at a dirty fence."

He stopped polishing and stared with something like shame at the long line of fence, which looked perfectly white to me. It wasn't as white as my Cadillac, but it was still pretty white. Nonetheless, its condition was obviously a matter that weighed on Herbert.

"There's been a great deal of talk," he said mournfully. "No one is happy about the situation. Mr. Folmsbee has received complaints. But, as you know, he is not a man who bends to public opinion."

"Yeah, he's a stubborn son of a bitch," Boss said, giving Herbert a comforting pat. "If he ever fires you you come to work for me, okay?"

Herbert's face was a study in confusion. It was plain he regarded the prospect of working for Boss rather than Cyrus Folmsbee as sort of a dream of heaven, not a life that was likely to happen here on earth.

It was hard for me to imagine, too. A little man who wore a black apron and striped pants when he polished cars wouldn't stand much of a chance in the Miller household. He reminded me of diminutive servants I sometimes caught glimpses of in Beverly Hills, all of whom seemed to spend their time watering down acres of Mercedes. At least Herbert had a Rolls-Royce hunting brake to polish.

"So is the Squire up?" Boss asked.

"Oh yes indeed," Herbert said. "I think you will find them with the ferrets."

On our way to the ferrets, wherever they were, we passed a large garage with six more cars in it, five of them covered with neat canvas car covers. The car that was uncovered was an ancient Pierce Arrow, the size of a bus.

"A family could live in that Pierce Arrow," I said.

"That Herbert's really sweet," Boss said. "I got a soft spot for men like him."

"Why don't you just hire him?" I asked. "He doesn't look very happy."

Boss chuckled. "You don't go stealing servants from the Folmsbees," she said. "Cyrus would have one of his Koreans assassinate me."

Just as she said it, two Koreans popped out of a small arbor we happened to be passing. Like Herbert they wore striped pants and neat little caps. They stopped, deferentially, until we passed, and then made off toward the house. I had to admit that they looked pretty efficient.

"Cyrus says they make the best assassins in the world," Boss said. "They also make pretty good bartenders."

Once we passed the little arbor the estate opened up before us. It stretched without interruption across a gentle valley to the Blue Ridge. There were a couple of red-roofed barns and several small trellised houses, all ivy-covered, that looked as if they ought to contain little English ladies who read Dorothy Sayers. There was a lake to the northwest, and the pastures beyond it were crisscrossed with white fence that had evidently not been kept up to standards. Several bay thoroughbreds grazed in one pasture, while another held a scattering of black Angus cattle. The horses were swishing their tails and gamboling a bit in the crisp morning, but the black cattle were just standing there. I never saw one move. The landscape before us was so perfectly composed, with green grass setting off blue mountains, white fences setting off orange leaves, and bay horses contrasting with black cattle, that it occurred to me that perhaps the Angus weren't allowed to move. Perhaps they had been trained to spend all day in one place, for the sake of perfect visual composition. If they had bunched up in one corner of the pasture, as cattle frequently do, the whole balance of the landscape would have been spoiled.

"Why does he have ferrets?" I asked.

"Cyrus likes little quick things, like Koreans and ferrets," Boss said.

The ferret run turned out to be a fair distance from the house. We passed a gazebo in a modest grove, a small pond with willows around it, and a skeet range. Down the hill we could see a tall man in tweedy garb standing by a fence watching a bunch of small animals dart around. A lumpy woman was with him, Bessie Lump no doubt.

When we got closer I saw that the ferrets had a very nice run to disport themselves in, with holes for them to pop in and out of and a number of small humplike structures reminiscent of Dutch ovens, which may have been ferret houses. The ferrets that weren't busy darting moved along with a peculiar sidling motion, sniffing at the fence.

"Ah, Boss," Cyrus Folmsbee said, when he turned and saw us. He had very red cheeks and wore a blue silk neckerchief around his throat. He also had a monocle dangling from his tweed jacket, but he mostly just let it dangle.

Bessie Lump was wearing the same nondescript dress she had worn at the auction.

"Well, is this our buyer?" Cyrus asked, when he shook my hand. He had skinny hands—the bones in them pressed mine like a vise. His pale blue eyes peered at me out of his red face.

"Have you got four million, won't take a cent less," he asked, acting at once on the assumption that I was a buyer.

"Slow down, Cyrus," Boss said. "This is my nephew, Jack. He's up from Texas for a few days. I thought I'd show him Middleburg while he was here."

"As well you might," Cyrus said, looking at me thoughtfully. "As well you might. Good place to buy. People are damned bores, but then most people are damn bores. You won't find a gazebo as good as mine, I'll tell you that. Man who built the Brighton Pavilion built that gazebo. Besides, there's this run. Best ferret man in England built me this run. They *know* ferrets, in England. Only place they *do* know ferrets—as a matter of fact. I've had good luck with my gray ferrets—can't say that I care much for my browns. You won't find a decent ferret handler in these parts, I'm afraid, but that's your lookout, assuming you've got the four million, of course."

Bessie Lump had turned and was looking at me with eyes that would have been right at home on a dead fish.

Cyrus pressed on relentlessly, ignoring both Bessie and Boss.

"I'm glad you've come straight to the point," he said. "I like a man who doesn't beat around the bush. Speaking of which admittedly my boxwood is not all it might be, but if you coax it along I think it will do. I shan't take these ferrets. I have other ferrets. Be careful with the grays or you'll get bit, I can assure you."

I looked at Boss, hoping she'd stop him, but Boss was making no effort to stop him. She was surveying the acreage. Cyrus had a staff of some kind, leaning against the fence. It was as tall as he was, and made from some kind of gnarled wood. I had never seen one like it and I looked at it admiringly. Cyrus immediately picked it up.

"Can't have this," he said. "Yugoslavian shepherd's staff, in case you're wondering. Tito gave it to me. Yugoslavians whack their sheep when they want them to do something. Far simpler. Admirable thing, isn't it?"

"I say it was cheap," Bessie said. "He should have given you an estate."

Cyrus looked startled. Then he whirled on Bessie.

"Absolute nonsense," he said. "Why would I want an estate in Yugoslavia? Can't speak the language, don't like the food. The people are damned bores. Stolid peasants, worse than Virginians. I'd rather have this staff. I can whack those damn black cattle with it, when I feel like it. Much satisfaction to be had from whacking a black cow. They don't move, you know."

Bessie was not convinced.

"I still say it was cheap," she said.

"Sorry, forgot to introduce you," Cyrus said. "Actually, I can't introduce you because I don't know your name."

"Jack McGriff," I said. "Actually I met Mrs. Lump yesterday."

"How astonishing," Cyrus said, looking hard at Bessie. "I heard nothing about *that*. What's going on here? More plots, eh Bessie?"

Bessie stared at me with her dead-fish eyes.

"We don't know him," she said.

I was about to remind her that Boog had introduced us, when Boss gave me a hard pinch. I interpreted it to mean I had better keep quiet.

"You deny it, do you?" Cyrus said heatedly, looking at Bessie.

"Stay out of it but buy the horse farm," Boss whispered, while Cyrus was glaring at Bessie.

"Did you meet this man or didn't you?" Cyrus asked loudly, thumping the ground a time or two with his Yugoslavian staff.

I was supposed to buy the horse farm? I looked at Boss and she smiled and nodded.

"I want to know what's going on," Cyrus yelled. "You know better than to keep things from me!"

Though Cyrus looked ready to whack her with the shepherd's staff, Bessie didn't change expression. None of us seemed to interest her in the least. She was carrying the same little-old-lady handbag she had had at the auction. She just stood there, gazing at Cyrus idly, as if he were of no more interest than a boxwood bush.

Cyrus' face was getting redder. His skinny hands gripped the stick tightly. He was clearly not a man who liked to have his stick-thumping ignored, but that is precisely what occurred. Bessie just walked off from us and ambled slowly up the hill, without saying another word. There was something about her silence that was very unsettling.

"Absolute nonsense," Cyrus said. "Utter and complete bosh. That woman's a liar and always has been!"

He shouted the last sentence, evidently hoping Bessie

would hear it and turn around. She didn't turn around. She just continued her slow, inexorable progress up the long green lawn.

"She likes to get my goat," Cyrus said, more quietly. "Always has. Worse than my wife. Much worse, in fact. My wife only likes to drink."

"I hear you've been traveling," Boss said. A couple of ferrets stood up on their hind legs and sniffed at us curiously.

"Oh well, it's Peck and his museums," Cyrus said. "He builds them in the most inconvenient countries. Was building one in Uganda but of course that's gone a bit haywire. I'm generally required to consult, you know. After all, blood is thicker than water."

For a moment we stood and watched the ferrets.

"Bessie's a damned snob, that's what she is," Cyrus said. "Denies knowing half the people we know, including people we've known for forty years. Bessie doesn't know them. Not good enough for her. That's because she's a Shipton. Absolute snobs, all of them."

"Boog gets along with her, though," Boss said.

"He flatters her," Cyrus said. "Anyhow she makes exceptions for certain males, if they're rich enough. Or if they flatter her. I'm the opposite. Can't stand flattery, don't have to be a snob."

"Why not?" Boss asked, with a smile.

"Perfect bosh, snobbery," Cyrus said. "Of course, I'm lucky. Nobody's as good as me, so I escaped it. I might as well know everybody. Saves energy. Are we set then, young man?"

I glanced at Boss, who was inscrutable.

"I guess we're set," I said.

"Bully," Cyrus said. "Couldn't be more delighted. Never liked this place. The lake is the wrong shape: L-shaped, you know. Perfect bosh. Lakes should be round, not bent in the middle. Incidentally, you don't get the sailboat. I've plenty of round lakes, you know. Got one not ten miles from here. Keeping that one. It's got a helicopter dock, too, though I don't keep a helicopter anymore. The Agency's been very good about lending them to me, when I need one."

During this whole speech he was squeezing my hand in his skinny fingers. Then he turned, bent in a courtly fashion, and gave Boss a kiss before seizing his Yugoslavian staff and starting for the house.

"I'm glad you're not one of those types that have to be driven around and shown things before settling a deal," he said. "Decisive people, Texans. I've always said it. Buy what you like and live with it, that's been my motto. Middle class, I say, all this peeking and inspecting. Bessie's the same. Detests the middle class as only a Shipton can."

"You might ask Boog what she's up to," he said to Boss, after a pause. "He'll know. I've great respect for Boog. You ask him, will you? I hate it when Bessie goes about plotting. I think she's hired her own Koreans, which is a damned impertinent thing to do, if you ask me. *I* introduced her to Koreans—taught her all she knows about them. Cheeky of her to hire some for herself. I'll tell you one thing, they can cause no end of trouble if they aren't managed right. Not for amateurs, I can tell you that."

By the time he had told us that we were rounding the corner of the big red brick house. Bessie was shuffling around the hunting brake, still holding her handbag. Herbert was standing more or less at attention, and looking extremely nervous.

"Look at that woman!" Cyrus said. "What do you suppose she's up to now?"

Chapter XVI _____

"*I don't know, but* Herbert looks worried," Boss said. "I love that Herbert. If you ever fire him I'm gonna snap him up, Cyrus. I just thought I'd warn you."

Cyrus looked puzzled. "Sporting of you, of course," he said, looking at Herbert as if he were noticing him for the first time.

"I hardly suppose I'll fire him," he said, as if the very notion were surprising and droll. "Herbert has always worked for me. I'm surprised anyone's noticed him. *I* haven't in years, now that I think about it. But you're right, *there* he is. Bessie will have him in a state, I suppose. Keeps all the servants in a state, actually. Knows what to expect of servants and won't settle for less."

We all stood and watched as she shuffled around the beautiful car. When she finished she shuffled into the house, not saying a word to anyone. Herbert remained at attention. He looked as if he were waiting for a firing squad to march out of the house and dispatch him.

"All right," Cyrus said, slapping his thigh briskly. "Very good morning's work indeed. Never liked that L-shaped lake. You'll attend to the details, won't you, Boss? Draw up the papers and send them along to my people. Then this lucky young man can write his check and that will be that."

"Fine," Boss said. "I'll be in touch with your people. See you later."

"Months later, unless we're very lucky indeed," Cyrus said. "It's Peck, you know. No head for trade, though I suppose his museums are nice enough. Could have stayed home and been a gentleman, but nothing could persuade him."

Then he turned and strode into the house I had just bought.

As they strolled past the hunting brake, Boss winked at Herbert.

"I wish I could give him a kiss, but of course Bessie is watching," she said.

"I don't have four million dollars," I pointed out.

"I do," Boss said. "I had no idea Cyrus was thinking so cheap. Bessie must have him going around in circles."

"Are you planning to loan me the money?" I asked.

"Yep," she said. "You're my decoy. We'll paint the fences and sell the place for six million. Maybe six and a half."

That put matters in a different light. "How much do I get?" I asked.

Boss laughed. "You'll get something," she said. "I haven't decided how much, or even what."

Boss was a very fast driver. A big sale had a good effect on her, just as it did on Kate. The little Virginia roads that border $4-million-dollar horse farms are narrow and windy, but Boss roared over them at a high speed, the windows down and the cool fall air rushing through the car.

Boss had a wonderful complexion. She could look tanned and rosy at the same time. That was how she looked with the cool air rushing through the car.

"Did you really want to kiss Herbert?" I asked, jealously.

"Boy, did I!" she said. "You know why? Innocence. I just can't keep away from innocent men."

"That explains Micah," I said. I had long wondered what explained him.

"Yeah," she said, giving me a look. "Only Micah never wears striped pants and a little black apron. Neat little innocent men in striped pants are the cat's meow, so far as I'm concerned."

"I guess that lets me out," I said, hoping she would contradict me.

She shot over a little hump in the road and swerved around a man on a tractor as if she'd known he'd be just over that hump. Then she grinned at me.

"Don't worry about it," she said. "I might like you better once you've been despoiled. Despoiled innocence is kind of cute, too."

"I don't understand your criteria very well," I said.

Boss just shrugged. "I'd like a hamburger," she said.

She got it in Chantilly, Virginia—basically just a wide space on Route 50, not far from the flea market where I had met Beth Gibbon, the flea marketer's daughter.

Beth had been sitting on the tailgate of her father's old pickup when I spotted her, her five young children piled around her like little possums. Beth's father was a quilt man, although he also sold pocket knives, old bottles, and a smattering of knickknacks, when he could find them. Beth was only twenty-four when I met her and had a wildness in her eyes that was the result of feeling frightened and out of place in what she called "big ol' towns." She had a husband somewhere, the one who had given her five kids in five years, but he hung out in Cincinnati when he wasn't giving her a kid.

The thought of Beth mingled with the smell of cooking hamburgers in the little place Boss had chosen. The hamburgers were excellent, but I was distracted by my memories. I hadn't seen Beth in almost a year, which probably meant that she had another child.

On the jukebox Tanya Tucker was insisting that, if it came to it, she would prefer Texas to heaven. The song prompted a moment of nostalgia for Coffee, which mingled with the hamburger and mustard in my mouth and my nostalgia for Beth.

Boss was cheerfully munching her hamburger and making eyes at a booth full of truckers, who on the whole were greasier than the hamburgers. The truckers were mildly abashed at being the object of her attention.

"Penny for your thoughts," she said.

"I have about a million," I said. "I can't sort them out."

Boss swallowed too big a bite and hit herself in the breastbone a time or two, to help it go down.

"I'll tell you what's wrong with you," she said. "You're too romantic on the one hand. On the other hand, you don't know the first thing about romance."

It seemed to me an arguable point. After all I had two ex-wives and several girl friends and/or potential wives. I must know *something* about romance.

Boss was wobbling a French fry in some ketchup. For a moment she reminded me of Belinda Arber. She gave me a cool look. Belinda was much like Boss, only forty-nine years younger.

In fact, the women I sometimes inaccurately think of as *my* women were always reminding me of one another. There were plenty of differences between them, but somehow the correspondences outnumbered the differences.

Boss didn't say anything for a while. She ate her hamburger and French fries and occasionally let her gaze drift over to the truckers, who continued to be mildly abashed. They were evidently not used to even such light attentions as Boss was paying them.

The waitress kept refilling Boss's coffee cup, with coffee so hot that a wreath of smoke rose from it. When Boss lifted it to drink she gently blew aside the smoke.

"I don't think you really know how to get girls," Boss said, breaking her silence. "It doesn't matter, though, because any girl would know how to get you."

She looked hard at the truckers suddenly, causing them to shift nervously in their booth.

"What's cute about you is that you're kind of chaste," she said.

"I'm not chaste," I said, automatically. She knew enough about me to know that I didn't exactly avoid carnal relations.

"There's just two romantic relationships," Boss said, fingering a strand of her black hair. "All the rest are what my granny used to call common doings."

"Which are?"

"Sexy friendships and adultery," Boss said, opening her purse and scattering change on the table. "I got the tip, you can get the ticket."

Then she got up and headed for the door, walking right past the truckers all of whom fell instantly silent. They almost cringed, in fact, though Boss didn't give them another look. She got a toothpick and went outside. I paid the ticket. As the door closed behind me the truckers, grown suddenly confident, began to laugh uproariously.

Book IV

Book IV

Chapter I _____

When I walked into Jean Arber's antique shop, in the cracked shopping center in Wheaton, Jean was on the phone, talking in such low tones that I assumed she was talking to her husband. Belinda was sitting on a beautiful Pennsylvania dower chest, swinging her heels, which as usual were in tiny red sneakers. Her sister Beverly sat over in a corner by a larger but less remarkable chest, attempting to fit a paper dress she had just cut out onto a paper doll.

At the sight of me Belinda leaped from the chest and dashed to her mother's lap. She was not seeking shelter—she merely wanted her mother to get off the phone.

"He's here, Mom!" she said loudly. "Let's go."

Jean continued to talk in low tones, ignoring her daughter to the extent that such was possible. She cupped a hand over Belinda's mouth, cutting off further orders. Belinda countered by bouncing up and down in her mother's lap, impatiently and not gently. Annoyed, Jean opened her legs and managed to roll Belinda to the floor, where she bumped her head. The head bump was not gentle, either.

Belinda got up and snatched a metal-cased tape measure off the desk and drew back her arm as if to throw it at Jean, at which point Jean covered the receiver with one hand.

"If you throw that you're going to get spanked," she said, with a flash in her eye. "And no Baskin-Robbins, either. Put it down."

Thus confronted, Belinda compromised. She didn't throw the tape measure, but she ignored the order to put it down. Instead she marched around the desk and advanced on me.

"Stand still," she said. "I'll jist measure you."

"Do you think this dress goes with her hair?" Beverly asked, holding up a paper doll dress.

"I think so," I said.

Belinda kicked me. "Stand still, I said," she said.

"I *was* standing still," I protested.

"You talked," she said serenely. "Let's see your boots."

Beverly scooted over to help her and Belinda carefully measured my boots from heel to boot top.

"Tall boots," Belinda said. "Did you bring the soft car?"

"I brought it," I said. Meanwhile my eyes were roving scoutlike over the antiques. Except for the dower chest none of them looked really expensive, but they were well chosen. There was a wooden snow shovel that I liked, and a charming silver ewer that I would have liked to look at. Unfortunately it was right next to the phone and I couldn't look at it because I didn't think Jean would welcome me that close to the conversation.

However, I could look at Jean, and I liked what I saw. There was a nice color in her cheeks, perhaps caused by the heated argument she was having. Beverly and Belinda went to the door to make sure the soft car was really there, then, after whispering a bit, began to work on their mother. Belinda put the tape measure back on the desk and began a slow, easy, seductive ascent back into Jean's lap. Beverly followed, and Jean soon had two girls in her lap, their wild ringlets obscuring her modest bosom, their clean little ears not a foot from the phone. Inevitably, she was forced to take notice.

She took it with a huge sigh, covered the receiver again, and looked down at the undemanding curly heads just beneath her chin. At that point they turned and smothered her with kisses. She peered at me from between them, the receiver momentarily hooked on her shoulder.

"I hate to ask," she said, "but could you just take them?"

She opened a drawer and scattered two or three dollar bills on the desk.

"Take some money," she said. "I'll feel less guilty for doing this to you. I really have to finish this call. He won't stop unless I explain. If you'll just take them they can have anything they want. Stuff them till they burst. All I've heard is Baskin-Robbins for thirty-six hours."

"I hope you both bust!" she said, to her daughters. "I hope you eat so much ice cream you vomit. It'll serve you right."

Then she looked at me with silent appeal.

Belinda popped out of her lap and laughed merrily.

"Ice cream don't make you vomit," she said, marching around the desk and catching one of my fingers.

"Don't you want to come, Mom?" Beverly said. When Jean shook her head she slid down and ran to join us.

For tiny people the girls had ferocious appetites. Giant banana splits were not much beyond their capacity. In ten minutes they had reduced two of them to a trough of rich strawberry-streaked chocolate syrup.

While they were mucking around with their spoons in the gooey troughs of syrup I pumped them. It might have been an immoral tactic, but I didn't care. He who hopes to find out about women can't be too picky about tactics. Besides, the girls were easy to pump. They were quite without reticence, and saw no reason why the world—or at least myself—shouldn't know all about their family life.

"What does your daddy do?" I asked.

"Teaches people to dance," Belinda said. "He already teached us."

"Old dances," Beverly said. "That people did in olden times."

"He has pigs, too," Belinda said, holding up one fist and slowly opening her fingers until four of the five were sticking up. "Four pigs. I feeded them."

This information merely confirmed the opinion I had already formed of Jimmy from my one glimpse. A man who taught archaic dances and kept pigs was bound to possess extensive charm.

"I bet he's a nice daddy," I said.

"He is," Belinda said, puddling her syrup.

"Only he forgets," Beverly said.

"Yeah," Belinda said. "Once he forgetted *me!*"

"And me," Beverly said. "We had to spend the night with Mary."

"Who's Mary?"

The girls shrugged.

"Daddy's friend," Beverly said.

"She's got the longest hair," Belinda said, waving her spoon at me for emphasis. When she waved it a small rivulet of pinkish chocolate syrup ran down into her sleeve. I grabbed the spoon just as the first drops went under the sleeve.

Belinda coolly looked down her sleeve. "Not much spilled," she said, ripping five or six more napkins out of the napkin holder. She got most of the goo off her coat and then licked her wrist until it was more or less clean.

When the three of us marched back into the shop Jean was slumped in her chair, staring forlornly at the crumpled one-dollar bills she had meant for me to take. The girls dashed around and jumped in her lap.

"Give me some kisses," Jean said, "so I'll know what you ate."

The girls happily complied. Jean pretended to be stumped, requiring a good deal of kissing as she tried to puzzle out the flavors. While they were kissing I looked closely at the dower chest, which was a really wonderful piece. It had everything it needed to have except a price tag.

"I think I've got it," Jean said. "Beverly had chocolate pineapple and Belinda had pineapple strawberry."

Both girls laughed cheerfully and lolled like tiny harem girls across their mother's lap.

"Banana spluts, four flavors," Belinda said yawning.

"Three," Beverly corrected.

Belinda studied her fingers to see if it was four flavors or three, but lost interest in the question before she made up her mind.

When I looked around at Jean she was watching me quizzically. It was not lost on her that I was deeply attracted to the dower chest. The look in her eye made me feel awkward. It was obvious that the chest was her favorite thing. If I bought her favorite thing, at this stage of her life, I would probably take a small part of the heart out of her, something I was loath to do.

On the other hand, she *did* have an antique store, open to the public, and the point of a store is to sell. Probably Jean had just begun to edge over the wavery line that separates the long-time collector from the novitiate dealer. If I didn't buy the chest somebody else would.

"Nice chest," I said. "What'll you take for it?"

Jean yawned and slumped down in her chair, as relaxed as the girls. They were all sprawling more or less voluptuously. She still had the nice color in her cheeks.

"What am I offered?" she asked, grinning.

"You're the seller," I said. "You have to make the price."

Jean yawned again. She seemed to be fading before my eyes, but she was not uncheerful. She had fine green eyes and at that moment they were alight with merriment, although I didn't know why. She wound a finger through Belinda's ringlets.

"I'm too tired to price a chest," she said. "Besides, it's my favorite thing. If you buy it I'll cry."

I walked over to the desk and picked up the silver ewer. It didn't have a price either. There were a number of small white price tags scattered on the desk, but so far none of them had prices on them.

"How long have you been open?" I asked.

"About a month," Jean said, sleepily. "It's an old established business we have here."

"We run *it*," Belinda said.

"You don't," Beverly pointed out. "Momma runs it. Besides, you broke a cup."

"Shut up about that cup," Jean said. "She didn't mean to break it. Anybody can break a cup."

"Would you take a thousand for the chest?" I asked, sort of testing the waters.

"I guess so," Jean said, without much conviction. "However, I think it's mean of you to force me to be professional when I've just spent two hours on the phone. I'm not myself. Anything I do I'm liable to regret tomorrow."

185

She had such nice color that she appeared to be blushing when she wasn't. What she was doing was flirting, which was not what I had expected, exactly. Previously she had seemed too involved with the end of her marriage to be capable of flirtation.

"Is *he* coming home with us?" Belinda asked, divining as if by magic her mother's newest mood.

"I don't know," Jean said. "He's welcome, if he likes. I'll even make him dinner when I wake up."

"Goody," Beverly said.

"With peas?" Belinda asked, poking her mother.

"With peas," Jean said. "Don't poke me."

"Of course he's undoubtedly a popular gentleman," she added, sinking deeper into the chair. "He's probably too busy to come to our house tonight."

"No, he *isn't*," Belinda said, glaring at me. "Are you?"

"I am tonight," I said, remembering Oblivia Brown. "But I'd love to come to your house."

"He doesn't really want to," Jean said, from behind Belinda. "He just wants to see all the things I haven't brought to the store. He wants our goodies, not us."

Both girls looked at me solemnly, to see if this could be true.

"No fair," I said. "I'd love to come to your house."

With a sigh Jean roused herself and sat up. She looked at me studiously. I've been looked at a lot of ways, but never quite so studiously. She had very clear eyes.

"Well, tomorrow night's open," she said. "Along with the next twenty or thirty years. Take your pick."

"I'll take tomorrow night," I said, instantly casting about in my mind for a lie I could tell Cindy. After all, we were still vaguely planning to set off for New Mexico once we had discharged our obligations to Oblivia Brown.

Jean was still watching me. I got a strange feeling. I can tell when I'm being sized up.

"You don't have to buy a thousand-dollar chest just to impress me," she said.

"I wasn't," I said, which was true. I could move the chest for two thousand easily.

"Are you sure?" she asked.

"Of course," I said. "I was just worried that you might be attached to it."

She grinned. "I've got another one," she said. "This one is second best."

"Oh good," I said. "Then I can buy it."

Actually, I felt trumped. If the one I was buying was worth a thousand, how good was the one she was keeping? My reputation hadn't been built by buying second-best things.

I sat down and wrote the check anyway. The second-best chest was worth every penny of it, though it was already fading in my favor. I no longer felt it was exceptional—just first rate. I would get rid of it quick, and the purchase might further other purposes.

Also, it would accustom Jean to *selling* things, which was important. The thrill of the sale might get her in gear, and once she got moving as a dealer she might keep moving. She would learn the first great lesson, which is that there are always more things to buy.

Of course, on another level I *was* doing it to impress her. At least it might impress her. Women seem to detest parsimonious men, and yet they often marry them. They seem to adore men who spend money like water, but I don't know that they take them very seriously. Perhaps they secretly believe that tightwads have the right slant on life, or at least the right slant on money.

Jean picked up the check and looked at it for a while.

"What do you know?" she said, to the girls. "He bought my chest. It's not mine anymore. I think I'll cry."

The girls, who were still in their harem-girl loll, straightened up and looked at their mother, to see if it was true. It wasn't. Jean looked slightly stunned, but not tearful.

"You're not cryin'," Belinda pointed out, with a touch of sternness.

"Nope," Jean said. "Guess what this means?"

"What?" Beverly asked.

"New clothes for all," Jean said.

"Bloomingdale's?" Belinda inquired hopefully.

"I'm gonna have you sheared," Jean said, ruffling her daughter's ringlets. "You got too much hair."

Belinda reached in the desk drawer and pulled out a mirror. It was an old, silver-backed mirror. As I left, their three heads were squeezed together, as they all contemplated new hairstyles with the aid of one mirror.

"You can change your mind about coming if you feel like it," Jean said. "You don't have to let us bully you."

"You didn't bully me," I said.

"I did!" Belinda said.

Chapter II _____

Oblivia Brown only lived three blocks from Cindy, so we walked to the party, holding hands. It was a sharp, clear night. Clouds of frozen breath streamed behind us as we walked, like vapor trails.

Oblivia's house was only slightly smaller than the Executive Office Building, and hailed from about the same period. The butler who let us in was a dour little shrimp, the antithesis of Benson. He was so fish-eyed and uninterested in life that he didn't even change expression when I handed him the Stetson with the diamondback hatband. He reminded me of the croupiers in minor casinos in places like Elko, Nevada.

As we started to go down a hallway hung with not very good mirrors in not very interesting frames I saw a dog standing in our path. It was black and extremely shaggy and seemed to have a hump of some sort. It looked like a miniature buffalo.

"That's Felix," Cindy said. "Hi, Felix."

Felix retreated in a hurry. He went bounding up some stairs. As we passed he was standing on a landing, looking very much like a small buffalo.

A large number of people were assembled in a long living room. Our hostess immediately spotted us and swam through a sea of pinstripes to our side. I had expected her to be beautiful, or at least stylish, but she was neither. She had a thin face, her hair was limp, her complexion blurred, and her look vague. She wore a dowdy-looking gray dress and a string of imitation pearls that looked like they'd been bought at Woolworth's.

"So tall," she said, looking at me. "Adore those yellow boots. I just hope they're not made from the skin of some pathetic endangered creature. *My* charity, you know. *Very* partial to creatures here. *So* yellow. I've never seen such a yellow creature."

Oblivia stood at a kind of angle to us, so that she could speak to us and yet keep an eye on the crowd, which I noticed included both old Cotswinkle and John C. V. Ponsonby.

"The boots are just armadillo," I said. "They're not endangered."

"Oh," Oblivia said. "Armadillo. I thought that was where Prub lived."

Cindy smiled. "That's Amarillo," she said.

Oblivia smiled. "*So* far," she said. "Can't keep places straight unless I've been to them."

Prub I knew. He was a crazed liberal trial lawyer who lived in Amarillo. His real passion in life was collecting minor league baseball teams. At the time he owned eight, scattered from Puerto Rico to Vancouver. I had once sold him a baseball autographed by Heimie Menusch, one of his true heroes.

"Is Prub here?" I asked hopefully.

"Well, I hope not," Oblivia said. "Of course, the man's brilliant, but *so* difficult. Won't eat asparagus. Insulted my chef so badly he almost quit. Told him the sauce had curdled. Of course it *had*—even Jean-Luc has an off night once in a while. Nobody but Prub would have dared mention it. Jean-Luc had one of his rages—*so* fierce. Didn't bother Prub."

"Why won't he eat asparagus?" Cindy asked.

"Claims he ate it on his wedding night and a bad thing happened," Oblivia said.

Actually Prub had been married six times. Every time he won a big case his wife of the moment divorced him and took half of his fee. One of them had been a friend of Coffee's, so I was no stranger to stories about Prub Bosque.

Cindy had had enough of such chitchat. She started into the crowd, only to be immediately embraced by a short man in a tweed suit. The short man stood on tiptoes and kissed whatever she would allow him, which was just a cheek.

"*So* lecherous," Oblivia said. Something like a spark of hatred appeared in her otherwise unfocused eyes.

"Who's that?" I asked.

"George," she said. "Can you imagine those tweeds?"

I remembered that someone named George Psalmanazar was the boyfriend of Khaki Descartes, but that didn't explain the spark of hatred. George also had snow-white hair. His teeth were clenched as if he had a pipe in them, but he didn't.

"*Such* a crowd," Oblivia said, taking my hand in order to lead me into it. Her hand was damp, as if it had been left in a dim room in a tropical clime too long. I was puzzled as to why old Cotswinkle might be fucking her, when he had a wife who was fifty times more beautiful. His wife was standing nearby, in fact, looking even better than she had at the Penroses'.

The clammy hand of my hostess pulled me deeper into the pinstripes. The crowd sucked at us like an undertow and before I knew it we were over in a corner, far from safety, where Khaki Descartes was in earnest conversation with John C. V. Ponsonby.

"*Knew* I'd find you together," Oblivia said. "George is drunk."

"Don't be silly," Khaki said.

John C. V. Ponsonby said nothing. He appeared to be in a hypnotic trance. Perhaps over the years he had learned to sleep on his feet, like a horse. His silence had an equine quality.

"*George* is drunk," Oblivia repeated. The flash of hate came in her eyes again.

"Moreover," she said, "he is talking about Iran. I consider that ominous."

"Well, go tell him to shut up about it," Khaki said. "You know him as well as I do.

"*Not* the case," Oblivia said. "*That* was long ago.

"I put him at my table only because he gave his word not to talk about Iran," Oblivia continued. "He gets so pettish if he's not at my table."

George seemed to be clinging to Cindy like a small tweedy burr.

Meanwhile Andy Landry and Eviste Labouchere had just stepped into the room. Eviste was wearing a white suit. From a distance it made him look a little like Claude Rains.

"My god," Khaki said. "Where'd he get that suit? Look at that suit."

"More to the point," Oblivia said, "where did he get Andy? I thought Lilah was the one who liked him."

"You're slipping a little, Via," Khaki said. "Lilah just took him home by mistake. She thought he was Jean-Luc."

"My chef?" Oblivia said. "Why that's an outrage. Much as I like the woman I won't have her sleeping with my help."

Khaki allowed herself a trace of a smile. "Not your chef," she said. "Jean-Luc Godard."

Since neither of them were paying any attention to me I edged away. I wanted to try and have a word with John C. V. Ponsonby, who was still holding his position in the corner, staring hypnotically at an ugly green drape.

However, I was a little slow: a tall, aquiline young man in impeccable pinstripes reached Ponsonby just before I did.

"Hello, Jake," he said. "I've been in Riyadh. That place is really shaping up."

This piece of information made absolutely no impression on Ponsonby. Thinking, perhaps, that he was hard of hearing, the young man repeated it. Ponsonby continued to stare at the drape. Having taken two called strikes, the young man gave up and edged off into the crowd.

The reason I wanted to speak to Ponsonby was because I happened to know that he was the world's foremost collector of truncheons and it so happened that I had an excessively rare truncheon, one of the very few Ponsonby did not possess.

"Mr. Ponsonby," I said, "are you still buying truncheons?"

The word "truncheon" penetrated his hypnosis more effectively than the word "Riyadh." The film over his eyes quickly burned away. He turned his head and looked at me with marked distaste.

"Why are you here?" he asked. "This is an eminently civilized occasion."

"I just came here to sell you a truncheon," I said. It was more or less true.

"That in itself is reprehensible," he said. "This is a social occasion. If you are a tradesman you should apply to me at my home."

"I like to deal catch as catch can," I said.

"Then deal with someone else," he said.

"Well," I said, "I have one of the Luddite truncheons."

That gave him pause. In fact, he seemed to find it a real pisser. If he had had my Luddite truncheon in his hand at the time I think he would have bashed me with it.

In fact, Luddite truncheons were originally used to bash the Luddite rioters—their rarity is a result of the fact that many of them were used for firewood, in the grim aftermath of the Luddite riots.

I had not really taken the time to delve deeply into the matter, but I did know that Luddite truncheons belonged to that small class of objects, the true rara avis, for which all scouts continually search: *cire-perdue* Lalique, rosethrow whimsies, Sung vases, and great historical artifacts such as the boots of Billy the Kid.

"I believe you are lying," John Ponsonby said. "No Luddite truncheon has changed hands in this country since 1946. There are, in fact, only two in this country, one in the Metropolitan Museum, where it doesn't belong, and the other in Boston, in a private collection."

"You're well informed up to a point," I said. "The one in Boston changed hands last year. I bought it. It's in my car."

Ponsonby, who looked somewhat like a frog, also looked like he'd just swallowed one. A person he didn't like had just informed him that he had missed out on one of the rarest truncheons in the world—a truncheon he had probably been plotting to get since 1946.

"Am I to understand that you have bought the Eberstadt truncheon?" he said. "That in itself is an outrage. Who are you?"

"Just a scout," I said.

The fact that, in defiance of all appropriateness, the Eberstadt truncheon had come to me rather than him, had left him too dazed for speech.

"But I knew Woodrow Eberstadt," he said, almost plaintively. "We went to the same school. I knew his wife, Lou Lou. I sent Lou Lou flowers once. I think it was when Woodrow died. They knew of my interest in the truncheon. Lou Lou knew, I'm sure. It is very distressing. She might have given it to me. I'm sure I sent her flowers once."

In fact, Mrs. Eberstadt had told the antique dealer she sold the truncheon to that she would have it carved into toothpicks rather than sell it to Ponsonby, since he had pestered her and her husband about it for thirty years.

"Regrettably, Lou Lou had a will of her own," Ponsonby said, with a sigh. "There was talk when she married Woodrow. No one was in favor of the match, as I recall. I always felt Woodrow lacked judgment, an opinion that has now been borne out."

Before my eyes, Ponsonby's spirits began to droop. The thought of his old schoolmate's lack of judgment weighed on him visibly.

"I'm afraid this means the end of Western civilization as we know it," he said, turning away.

For no good reason, unexpectedly, I began to get my Harbor City feeling. What was I doing in a room full of blue suits and Empire furniture with Harbor City slightly less than a continent away?

While I was mentally calculating the most satisfying route across America, Felix, the buffalo dog, reappeared. He stood about ten feet away, looking at me through his hair.

At that point the little butler who should have been a blackjack dealer in Elko came and called us in to dinner.

Chapter III ───────────

As I was walking into the dining room a small and somewhat sinister maid presented me with a seating chart. Evidently I was supposed to take a little sticker of some sort, which would legitimize my seat, but before I could do this Lilah Landry walked down the hall and walked up, took my arm, and walked right on into the dining room with me. She wore a dramatic black dress and was in very high color.

"You're by me," she said. "And if you aren't we'll just switch the place cards and pretend the help made a mistake."

That sounded like serious mischief, to me. Cindy had been at pains to explain that the reason Oblivia prevailed, season after season, as the hostess with the mostess, was because of the brilliance of her seatings. According to Cindy, her seatings were masterpieces, in which age and beauty, brains and egos, pomp and pomposity were blended as delicately as flavors in a sauce.

As it turned out, I was seated between Lilah and Oblivia anyway—Lilah didn't even have to change the place cards.

As I was arranging my napkin I had a chance to look around me, and it struck me that Lilah, Cindy, and Cunny Cotswinkle all shared one remarkable attribute, which was the ability to arrive at a dinner party looking like they had just arisen from the happiest of fucks. Somehow they got their blood up for the occasion.

With Lilah glowing on one side of me it was hard for me to be properly attentive to my hostess, who did not glow and gave no evidence that she even had any blood.

"*So* worried about you," she said to Lilah, who had evidently arrived just in time to sweep into the dining room. "Not like you to be so tardy."

"Shoot, I wasn't late," Lilah said. "I didn't even miss the soup."

At that very moment servants were slipping soup bowls in front of us. The bowls contained a thin green film, evidently a minute serving of soup of some kind.

George Psalmanazar, who was seated just across from me, was quick to note the minuteness of the amount. He got one good spoonful, but had to scrape the bowl to get even a half spoonful by way of a second bite.

"What is this supposed to mean?" he asked, glaring at Oblivia. "*Cuisine minceur? Cuisine infinitesimal* if you ask me."

George had turned quite red in the face, as if he had just received a personal insult, He grabbed his knife and fork and stared at the door to the kitchen, as if he expected to see a huge beefsteak arrive at any minute.

Oblivia Brown was not impressed by his color. She sipped a drop or two of her soup before replying. Various of our tablemates were trying to figure out how to get a spoonful of soup without indecorously tipping their bowls.

"*So* testy," Oblivia said, looking at George.

"Well, goddamn, Oblivia," George said. "People have to eat."

"But *you* are the champion of the Third World, George," Oblivia said. "You do write constantly about world hunger. So much starvation to worry about, one is not sure where it may break out next."

"It's going to break out in fuckin' Georgetown if this is all we get to eat," George said.

"*So* sorry," Oblivia said. "But it was your principle that guided me, of course. Not every day I get a man of the people at my table. The rest of us tend to get complacent. I feel sure we would be quite capable of stuffing ourselves with wasteful delicacies if we didn't have you to uplift us. We might sit here eating like pigs while five million Cambodians starve. That was the figure, wasn't it? You quoted it just this morning."

"Listen, Oblivia, cut it out," George said. "Nobody is impressed with your sarcasm."

"Well, I was," Lilah said.

"Excuse me, Lilah, but you're not exactly the hardest sell in town," George said. "A complete sentence impresses you."

George did not seem to be a favorite of the ladies. Both Lilah and Cunny Cotswinkle were watching him alertly, their heads cocked slightly to one side. I got the sense that they were lying in wait for their victim.

"Are you calling me dumb?" Lilah said, after a moment.

"Well, if I get nasty, blame it on Oblivia," George said. "She knows better than to starve me."

"A man of the people?" Cunny said, catching Oblivia's phrase as if it had been a high lob that had hung in the air all this time. "Which people?"

"Any people except you rich snobs," George said.

"*So* foul, when he's like this," Oblivia said.

The maids slipped in like cats and removed the soup bowls. A set of slightly taller maids, who may well have been bred for that very purpose, came in and began to fill the wine glasses. As soon as one sloshed a little wine in George's glass he picked it up, swirled the wine around with a deft little flick of his wrist, smelled it, and shook his head in resignation.

"You and your California wines," he said, giving Oblivia a look of disgust. "It's a comment on Washington."

"*So* particular," Oblivia said. "But then you live in the Adams-Morgan. *So* lucky. I believe they have real life over in the Adams-Morgan."

"It's not *the* Adams-Morgan," George said. "I hate people who call it *the* Adams-Morgan. It's just Adams-Morgan."

"Oh," Lilah said. "It's like Albany, in London. If you say *the* Albany people know you don't belong there."

"George knows *so* much about wine," Oblivia said to Cunny.

"Oh, *vino*," Cunny said absently, as if nothing could be more boring than a man who knew a lot about wine.

"That's right," Lilah said. "How many bottles you got now, George?"

"None of your business," George said.

"Not nice to hoard, George," Oblivia said.

"I've heard you have six thousand bottles," Lilah said.

"That's strange," George said. "I've heard you've had six thousand boyfriends. I wonder how these rumors start."

"Newspapers," Cunny said. "All the terrible things are invented by newspapers. Look at vat they say about me. Dese affairs I have with the President. Whose business is dat?"

The table digested that in silence for a moment. At least it was something to digest. So far the tall maids with the wine had not been followed by any short maids with food.

"But George is a famous columnist," Lilah said. "He writes for hundreds of newspapers himself."

"Now, now," George said. "Only 146, and most of them hate every word I write. They don't want the truth, in this country."

"Who are you to talk?" Lilah said. "You won't even 'fess up to owning six thousand bottles of wine."

"*So* trenchant," Oblivia said. "He could sell his wine and buy rice for the Cambodians."

George sighed. "Remarks like that appall me," he said. "What they reveal is that you have understood nothing about the geopolitical realities."

At that point the maids poured in, carrying our entrees. These consisted of the breasts of some very small bird, floating in a lemony sauce.

Disregarding etiquette entirely, George stabbed his bird with a fork, picked it up whole, and ate it in about two bites, while the ladies watched in their alert but patient way.

"Down in Georgia we cut our food," Lilah said, cutting herself off a delicate slice.

George scarcely looked up. "Down in Georgia everything is so overcooked it must be like cutting cinders," he said.

"It didn't stop you from eating like a pig when you were there," Lilah said.

"My body is like a little motor," George said. "It must have fuel, even if the fuel is overcooked. Besides, eating overcooked food is better than talking to your relatives. Your relatives are a bunch of redneck facists."

"*So* critical," Oblivia said. "*Hard* to travel with."

"Going to Georgia is not traveling," George said. "Anyway your relatives are no better. A bunch of wimpy snobs. They seem to think the Garden of Eden was just west of Philadelphia."

My Harbor City feeling was getting stronger. Also, I would have liked a hamburger. If the women at the table wanted to tear George apart, that was fine with me. I was trying to remember if I had read any of his columns. If they appeared in 146 newspapers it would have been hard to miss them, but somehow I seemed to have missed them.

"I don't suppose anyone here has read my Monday column, have they?" George asked, letting his eyes do a slow pan around the table.

"*So* hard to tell them apart," Oblivia said.

"Anyway, why do we have to?" Lilah asked. "We all know what you think. We all oughta be in jail, that's what you think, just because we're fun-lovin' Americans."

"Fun-loving Americans?" George said. "Do you mean that seriously? Do you think of yourself as a fun-loving American?"

"Why, yeah," Lilah said. "I believe in fun. So did my momma and daddy. I enjoy fun. Ain't that's what life's for?"

"No wonder America's in trouble," George said, twirling his fork.

"Well, don't sound so happy about it," Lilah said. "You *are* an American, George, even if you were born in Detroit."

"If you were in Russia they would shoot you," Cunny said. "How would you like dat?"

"He wouldn't like it because he's a sissy," Lilah said. "Down in Georgia he was afraid to say anything because he thought my brothers would beat him up. They might have, too. All he did was talk communism."

"Your brothers are rabble," George said. "And if you don't stop talking about Georgia I'm going to throw up, although I didn't eat anything worth vomiting. You'll all have to watch a case of the dry heaves."

Oblivia's eyes sparkled with hate for a moment. "*So* contentious," she said. "*Don't* know why I ask you."

"That's easy," George said. "You ask me because I have a first-rate mind. Not too many of those bopping around Washington. You hate my guts but you can't afford to leave me off your guest list. At least when I'm here Jake has someone to talk to in the rare moments when he's awake."

"Yes, but your precious mind doesn't entirely make up for your deficiencies in other quarters," Lilah said, with unusual crispness. She gave George the kind of look that in itself constitutes a sexual insult.

"While your brain was swelling up the rest of you was shrinking," she added, neatly driving home her point just as the maids whisked away our plates and brought in the salad.

Chapter IV _____

At that precise point in the dinner party, while the maids were carrying out bowls full of lemony sauce and carrying in a few leaves of endive on crystal salad plates, I stopped listening to the women snipe at George Psalmanazar and slipped into a road revery.

In this particular road revery I seemed to be crossing the high plateau of northern Arizona, going west out of Flagstaff. It was a clear day, with a few high white clouds, brilliant sunlight, and nothing to see along the road except an occasional Indian boy sitting on a rock.

Usually in my road reveries I turn up not too far from one of my favorite bargain barns, so that added to the pleasure of imagining myself on the road I get the little tickle of anticipation that precedes a chance to buy something.

I have such reveries all the time, and they are not just wispy daydreams. Most of them are so intense that they create little gaps in my life. Since most of them hit me when I'm involved in social situations—such as Oblivia Brown's dinner party— my memories of social situations contain many gaps. In effect, I blank out, and later have no memory of what may have taken place at the party I was at when the revery began.

Fortunately I seem to have a sort of automatic pilot that moves me along fairly smoothly at such times—it even prompts me to make appropriate sounds to hosts and hostesses, so that I seldom disgrace myself, even in the midst of a very long revery.

Something of this nature seems to have happened to me at Oblivia's party. While I was dreaming myself in Arizona I somehow became popular with a number of ladies. When the revery petered out, instead of finding myself somewhere around Kingman, Arizona, I was standing on a sidewalk in an unfamiliar part of Washington. Cindy, Lilah, and Khaki were with me, and we were all watching George Psalmanazar yell at a very drunk black man.

I don't snap out of my reveries instantly—I sort of fade in, like a television set warming up. As my focus improved I saw that the black man was standing there quietly taking a leak against a telephone pole.

"Button up, man, button up!" George yelled, but his yelling had no effect. The man went on pissing. In fact, once I got the scene in focus, his pissing came to seem like a remarkable performance. He seemed to go on at full flush for about five minutes. At one point George went so far as to shake his arm, which only caused the stream of urine to miss the pole for a second or two. It splashed against a Volkswagen that happened to be parked very close to the curb.

The three women were watching all this happen in bemused silence. It was clear that the sight of a man taking a leak didn't bother them, nor did George's efforts to get him to button up impress them.

George eventually gave up. "He won't button up," he said. The man had slowed a little, but he was far from through.

"Isn't that interesting," Lilah said. "I never saw anything like that happen before."

"This is a ghetto, Lilah," George said.

"It is not," Khaki said. "This is a perfectly nice neighborhood."

"Well, it's more of a ghetto than Georgetown," George insisted, opening his door.

Cindy was silent and seemed a little detached.

"Do you think that man was a rapist?" Lilah asked, once we got inside.

"Who knows?" George said cheerfully, yanking off his coat and flopping down full length on a long Danish chaise longue.

The whole spotless apartment was full of extremely modern Danish furniture. The chairs all had lots of chrome on them. Coffee would have loved the place.

"How about some Irish coffee?" George said, kicking off his shoes. "And see if there's any of those doughnuts left. Some cheese wouldn't be amiss either, and a couple of pears. I hate dinner parties where I don't get fed."

To my surprise all three women trooped off to the kitchen, leaving George to the delights of his chaise, which he rolled on like a baby in a baby bed. He had a fat little body, under his tweeds.

He popped up briefly, ran into another room, came back with a brocade pillow, lay back down on the chaise, and put the pillow under his head.

"I wish those women would hurry up," he said. "Not one of them would make an adequate housewife, you know. Too selfish. It's hard to find an unselfish woman in this town. Lord knows I've looked."

Just as he said it the three women trailed back in, bringing an array of goodies. These included cookies, doughnuts, apples, and pears. Also several cheeses. Lilah had one tray and Cindy another. Khaki brought up the rear, bringing the Irish coffee.

George was not terribly appreciative. He grabbed a doughnut, ate one bite, and dropped it back on the tray, glaring at Khaki as he did.

"Those doughnuts are stale," he said. "What happened to the crullers?"

"I guess you ate them," Khaki said. "I didn't see any."

"Shit," George said. "I want a cruller. Go look again. They must be there."

"They aren't there," Khaki said. "You ate them."

George threw a doughnut at her but missed. Then he picked up four or five doughnuts and threw them all at her. His face had suddenly gotten red.

"Don't talk back to me, woman," he said. "Get your ass in the kitchen and find those crullers."

All three women stared at him with hostility. Khaki's eyes

were like little ingots of hate. Though all of them had trotted off obediently at first and done a quick turn as harem girls, the role had suddenly worn thin. The sight of George flinging doughnuts at Khaki from his reclining position had evidently reminded them that they were liberated women.

"Don't order me around," Khaki said. "I'm not your slave, you know."

George ran his fingers through his hair. "Oh boy," he said. "This is what I get. I might have known this would be what I got. This is *really* what I get."

"Hey, change the record," Cindy said, snapping out of her detachment suddenly. "What do you mean it's what you get?"

"In plain English it's what I get!" George yelled. "I work my ass off year after year trying to be the conscience of this country and this is what I get."

"Come again, honey?" Lilah asked, in surprise. "What is it you been doin'?"

"Working my ass off!" George yelled. "Living down here in the ghetto, trying to practice a little social justice, hoping in a small way to be a voice for the oppressed, hammering away at the need for economic sanity and better relations with the Third World, and now I end up with a woman who can't even find a cruller in her own kitchen."

"It isn't the ghetto and it isn't my kitchen," Khaki said. "It's your kitchen. Go find your own crullers."

"I won't!" George said, stretching out on the chaise like a defiant child. "This is a partnership we have. You have to do your part, and your part is getting me crullers when I want crullers."

"Fuck your crullers," Khaki said, with a certain vehemence.

Then the women exchanged looks. It was as if the instinct for mischief had awakened at the same instant in the three of them. Without another word they marched out of the room, in the direction of the kitchen.

George exhibited no surprise.

"That's impressive," I said. "It looks like you're going to get your way."

"I always get my way," George said. "All you have to

remember about women is that they have weak egos. People with weak egos love to take orders from people with strong egos. I have a strong ego. It's that simple. All this liberation bullshit makes me giggle. I could boss Gloria around, if I wanted to. I could even boss Bella around, if I wanted to."

At that he stopped, evidently startled by what he had just said.

"Though I doubt that Bella would bring me a cruller," he added, wrinkling his freckled brow.

Just as he said it the three women came rushing back into the room empty-handed. Before George could open his mouth to berate them for their empty-handedness all three flung themselves on top of him.

This was a surprising thing to observe, and it surprised George at least as much as it surprised me. In a second he lay pinned to his Danish chaise by three bodies, two of which were fairly hefty bodies. Cindy, who lay across his chest, glanced over at me.

"You keep out of this," she said. "We're getting our revenge."

George said nothing, perhaps because one of Cindy's strong Santa Barbara forearms was pressed against his Adam's apple.

"Hurry up," Lilah said. "Unzip his pants."

This job fell to Khaki, who was lying across George's midsection. When she started to unzip them George started to wiggle, and wiggled violently for perhaps thirty seconds, before he wore himself out. He was not in very good shape and grew extremely red in the face, a fact none of the women took the slightest notice of.

Watching, I had a strong sense of *déjà vu*. I seemed to be seeing a scene the like of which I had not witnessed since my pre-teen days in the Texas Valley, when gangs of giggling girls were always ganging up on some hapless boy and unzipping his pants.

In fact all three women were giggling, much like girls. The object of their attack seemed to be to fish George's penis out of his underwear and stick it through a doughnut. Khaki, as his lover of the moment, was required to do the fishing.

203

To a detached bystander like myself, the results were anticlimactic, just like most of the unzippings I had witnessed in high school. About all that happened was that George got a lot of powdered sugar in his pubic hair.

The women regarded the attack as highly successful, though. They laughed like banshees and continued to hold George down, perhaps hoping that he would get a hard-on and impale the doughnut in a more colorful manner. It didn't happen.

The minute the women let him up George marched out of the room without a word to any of us, and was never seen again, at least by me. Khaki made the prudent decision to spend the night with Lilah. The doughnut they had tried to stick George's penis through lay on the floor.

"He never admits defeat," Khaki said, speaking of George's silent exit. "It's one of his facets."

"He'll claim he was high and didn't notice," she added. "We better not let him catch one of us alone for a while, though."

"I'm not scared of George," Cindy said, calmly. "I could always handle him and I still can."

"Ah well, he broke my heart," Lilah said, unexpectedly, as if she had just remembered it. Neither Khaki nor Cindy responded to the remark, but they responded to the taxi driver, who had just taken a turn they didn't like. The man looked like he had just left Pakistan a few days before. His turban was dirty, and I doubt he was used to being bossed around by women, because he looked pretty surly when they all started yelling at him.

Then he started muttering. I think his pride was hurt. He was not in his own country, and three women were giving him a hard time.

"He'll break yours, too," Lilah said to Khaki, referring to George's penchant for breaking hearts.

"That's all right," she added. "Then we can be best friends again. I can't be best friends with anybody who's sleeping with George."

Cindy was looking out the window of the cab. The conversation seemed to hold little interest for her.

It held none for the Pakistani taxi driver, either.

"Be quiet!" he said, turning suddenly to glare at Khaki and Lilah. While he was turned the taxi narrowly missed a head-on collision with a city bus. When the driver saw the bus he honked and shook his fist at it, although he was on the side of the street that rightfully belonged to the bus.

"I kill it!" he said menacingly, looking at the women again.

Unfortunately his ferocity did not impress them. He was a little fat man, not unlike George.

"Listen, just watch where you're going," Khaki said. "And you know what? You ought to wash that turban sometime."

"One took me to the Iwo Jima monument," Lilah whispered. "Just last week. I wanted to go to the F Street Club and he took me to the Iwo Jima monument. I don't think they should let them immigrate if they can't learn their way around any better than that.

"Why would I want to go to the Iwo Jima monument anyway?" she asked, after a moment.

"Maybe he wanted to hang you from it," Khaki suggested, as the driver let them out.

Chapter V ────────

"*Did George ever break* your heart?" I asked Cindy, the minute we were inside her door. Unfortunately, I was developing a curiosity about her past.

Cindy looked at me as if I were only slightly less dumb than the Pakistani taxi driver.

"Naw," she said.

She was looking intensely beautiful. She had looked great at the party, but now she looked subtly better. Something had happened to elevate her a notch or two, beauty-wise.

I knew enough about beautiful women to know that when

that happens their prospects have changed. A new and better future suggests itself, causing their already excellent cells to radiate at an even higher level.

That must have happened to Cindy. Deep down inside her, some prospect was throbbing. Even as I watched it was being weighed on the scales of her instincts. That was why she looked so detached. I remembered that she had been seated by Spud Breyfogle at Oblivia's.

She went upstairs without another word. Her new mood left me out to such an extent that I felt a little hesitant about even following her up to the bedroom. I was no stranger to such occasions. Often I had temporarily ceased to have an existence in the consciousness of a particular woman. One minute they're talking to you, the next minute you could just as well be in Tibet, where they're concerned. Sometimes you fade back in in a few minutes, other times it might take months.

Once I had followed Coffee into the bedroom, when she was in such a mood, and when she looked around and saw me sitting on the bed taking my boots off she was as shocked as if I had tried to rape her.

The only way to determine Cindy's attitude, in such a situation, was to go on upstairs, so I did. She had already washed her face, and she came out of the bathroom with her nightgown in her hand. She was neither hostile nor welcoming. She behaved as if she were alone, yet she never registered the slightest objection to my presence.

"Do you want me to leave?" I asked, just to be sure.

Cindy looked at me curiously. She had put on her nightgown.

"Why would I want you to leave?" she asked.

"I have no idea," I said.

"You're really goofy," she said, turning down the covers.

I sat down on the bed and took off my boots.

"Brush your teeth," Cindy said.

When I came to bed, Cindy took my hand. She liked to hold hands at night. It allowed her to be sure that somebody was there. We lay side by side, holding hands. There was just enough light from the streetlight that I could see her profile. Her eyes were wide open. While she was holding my hand she was thinking about whatever it was that had happened at the party—the thing that had detached her, and elevated her, beauty-wise.

"I think Spud wants to go out with me," she said.

I felt touched. She had actually spoken her mind to me. It seemed a considerable act of trust, all things considered.

"I think so, too," I said. It had been obvious to me at the Embassy party that Spud was interested in Cindy. I had noticed him feeding her a shrimp. Men seldom feed shrimp to women they aren't interested in taking out.

Cindy sat up in bed and looked at me.

"How would you know about it?" she asked.

"I saw him coming on to you at the Embassy party," I said. "He fed you a shrimp."

"Yeah," she said, startled that I had noticed something she had registered only subliminally.

"You must have a good memory," she said, rubbing my stomach. "I didn't even remember that.

"So what, though?" she said. "It was just a shrimp."

"Feeding people is sexy," I pointed out. "It's a form of coming on. If I had a shrimp I'd feed it to you right now."

Cindy looked at me silently. That shrimp eating could be a form of sex play had evidently not occurred to her. I decided to see what could be accomplished without the shrimp, which proved to be an excellent decision.

"It's getting better," she said, in a surprised voice, when we were resting and holding hands again. The surprise in her voice was extremely appealing.

"Do you want to go out with Spud?" I asked, pleasantly.

"Don't browbeat me," she said meekly, sounding like a little girl who was about to be sent to bed without her supper.

"I'm not browbeating you," I said.

She pursed her lips, as if irritated by the complexities life springs on one.

"I like Jennie," she said.

"Who's Jennie?"

"Spud's daughter," she said. "Jennie's my friend. I don't know about Betsy."

"Is Betsy another daughter?"

"Betsy's his wife," she said. "He's from an old family, you know."

"Actually, his family is better than Harris'," she said, again with a touch of surprise in her voice. The thought that a man from a family better than Harris' might want to take her out had never occurred to her.

Now that it had, the complexities of life were gathering fast. One of them obviously was that Spud had magnetism, while Harris only had a good family. Spud could walk through doors and feed ladies shrimp at Embassy parties.

"Harris is sweet, though," she said, as if answering a question I had asked. "He takes me to every single Marx brothers movie that comes to town."

"If you like the Marx brothers that's got to be a factor," I said.

"I got too much to think about," Cindy said. "I hate having too much to think about. I can't even sleep when that happens."

"You don't really have to think about it," I said. "Spud hasn't done much yet. Maybe he's just flirting."

"He better not be," she said, indignantly. "He could get me in a lot of trouble, you know." Her brow wrinkled at the thought of the havoc an affair with Spud Breyfogle could wreak.

"I hope you stick around," she said.

"Why do you hope so?" I asked, though I was touched that she hoped so, whatever the reason.

"I like you," she said simply. "If you stick around maybe nothing will happen."

Chapter VI _____

In the morning I felt peculiar, unlike Cindy, who bounced out of bed, all worries forgotten, and went off to swim three miles. I hate to swim, and the fact that I was sleeping with a woman who swam three miles every other day made me feel even more peculiar.

I dressed and drove up to the Millers', hoping Boog would be gone so I could sit around in peace with Boss for a while. Naturally, Boog was still there, sitting at the breakfast table in a vivid yellow suit, a quart full of red liquid in front of him. Boss, as usual, was engrossed in *The Wall Street Journal* and hardly looked up when I came in.

"You're just in time for a red draw," Boog said, hefting the big glass at me.

A red draw was a mixture of beer and tomato juice—a popular drink in West Texas.

"I'm disserpointed in you, Jack," he said. "You never bring me no worthwhile antiques no more. All you do is hang around hopin' to fuck my wife."

Boss got up and took some biscuits out of the oven. She hadn't said a word to me. I mixed myself a red draw, just to be companionable.

"Sell me that icon," Boog said. "Or ain't you give it to the woman you wanted to fuck yet?"

"She wouldn't take it," I said.

"Anyway, sell me somethang," Boog said. "I ain't bought nothin' in days. That makes me restless as all get out."

"What do you want, Jack?" Boss asked.

"He wants to fuck you, like the rest of mankind," Boog said.

"I'm gonna sock you, Boog," Boss said. "I wasn't asking you."

"If he's so nice he ought to sell me somethang," Boog countered. "What's the use of a scout if he don't bring you nothing?"

He had a point. I had not exactly been piling up treasures, during the last few days. The icon and Jean's dower chest were my only purchases. I had begun to drift, slightly. Partly it was Cindy's fault, since she didn't recognize my profession and didn't care whether I was drifting or not. I hadn't hit a flea market in a week, which was most unusual for me.

While I ate some biscuits, Boss watched me closely. I didn't meet her eye, but I knew she was watching me. The fact that I interested her that much was faintly reassuring.

Then I remembered that I had an appointment to meet Mr. Cawdrey, the man who was presumably selling the Smithsonian baskets. Buying 190,000 baskets would certainly pull me out of my slump.

"I'm looking at the baskets today," I said, to Boog.

He looked blank.

"The Smithsonian baskets," I said.

"Oh, them," Boog said. "I thank them already sold. That's what I hear."

"I just talked to the man yesterday," I said. "How can they have sold?"

Of course I knew my question was stupid. The first law of life is that anything can be sold at any time.

I suddenly felt very unconfident. A scout's confidence is like an athlete's confidence, essentially irrational. The old, beautiful conviction, which was that I could persuade anyone to sell me anything, was slipping away.

"You sat on your ass where them baskets was concerned," Boog said. "There was probably a lot of them baskets that I could have used. What's the matter with you?"

"Cindy is the matter with him," Boss said.

"I wisht she was the matter with me," Boog said. "But I never was lucky."

He belched a deep belch and stood up. "Gotter go," he said. "Gotter see a man."

"That's odd," Boss said.

"Whut is?"

"You seeing a man," she said. "I thought you usually saw a couple of little fat hookers this time of day."

"I wouldn't know where to find one if I was to want to," Boog said, straightening the knot on his bright blue tie.

Just as Boog went out the door Micah Leviticus walked into the room, looking bleary. He hadn't shaved. Somehow stubble looked worse on such a small face. His whiskers were larger than his features. As usual, he had a small television set in his hand. He got a spoon from a drawer and came over to the table, where he began to eat jam right out of the jar.

Boss sat with a cheerful look on her face, watching him eat jam. It was a good thing I had already taken all I wanted, because Micah polished off the jar. It was excellent strawberry jam.

"Micah's writing an epic poem," Boss said.

"What's it called?" I asked, to be polite.

"It's called *Soap Opera*," Micah said. "Only it may not be an epic. It may be a verse drama."

"Boog's gonna get it put on TV," Boss said. "He knows a lot of TV people."

"*If* we can get the right actors," Micah said. "I think I'll wash my hair."

This he proceeded to do, at the kitchen sink, using Ivory liquid and the dishwashing nozzle. Boss went over and gave him a scalp massage while streams of white suds ran down his face.

I decided to leave. Watching Boss give Micah a scalp massage was not exactly what I had had in mind for the morning, thought what that was might not have been easy to say.

When I started out Boss gave Micah a dish towel to dry his hair with and walked out with me. "You're always in a hurry," she said, linking her arm in mine.

"I don't understand what you see in Micah," I said.

"Well, he's never in a hurry, like you," she said. "Give him a TV set and a jaw of strawberry jam and he's happy. I like happy fellows. Can't stand men that get down in the mouth.

"Most men don't have the energy to be happy," she said. "That's what I like about ol' Boog. He's got the energy."

Then she tickled my ear a little, looking happy. It was a

windy fall day. Leaves were rustling over the concrete of the Millers' driveway.

"Do you think I was wrong to leave Coffee?" I asked Boss. I don't think I really needed an answer. I just wanted to stand around with Boss and mooch off her spirit for a little while.

"I got no opinion," Boss said, with a grin. She was well aware that I was mooching off her spirit. She gave me a little sock on the shoulder and then went back up the driveway through the swirling leaves.

Chapter VII _____

I still had a lot of time to kill before my meeting with Mr. Hobart Cawdrey—a pointless meeting anyway, if the basketry had already been sold—so I drove down and wandered into Brisling Bowker's auction, where it was setting-up day.

The pace of setting-up day was in marked contrast to the frenzy of auction day. A gangly black youth was pushing a big broom up the floor, so slowly it was hard to detect his movement. A couple of minions were pulleying a big dusty Oriental rug up on one wall. The rug had several holes in it, a matter of no moment whatever to the minions. Near the back of the room, other minions were unloading lawn mowers and bags of fertilizer. Probably some lawn-supply store had gone broke, and Brisling was getting ready to auction what assets it had left.

Tuck was standing near the front of the room, receiving a shipment of tweedy-looking chairs. The chairs were all fat, and all the color of George Psalmanazar's tweed suit. A big moving van parked in the street was smack full of them. A couple of movers were shooting the chairs down a little ramp straight to Tuck, who was functioning like a post in a pinball machine. He scarcely seemed to touch the chairs with his hands. When one shot down he would give it a little bump with his hip, sending it straight over to the wall, where it would pop in line next to the one that had preceded it.

I didn't bother him. The chairs were coming along at the rate of one every twenty seconds, so he needed his concentration. A number of boxes of bric-a-brac had been dumped helter-skelter along the wall, and I began to pick through them, though I knew at once that they just contained junk glassware. Still, going through bric-a-brac was a kind of warming-up exercise. It was relaxing. At least I was back in a place where things were bought and sold. I poked through the residue of a lot of lower-middle-class dining rooms, lulled by the slide of tweed chairs across the floor, or the thump of falling bags of fertilizer.

Then I went back to the farthest reaches of the room, where the true junk was sold—broken washing machines, treadless snow tires, similar flotsam and jetsam. The best thing I saw was an ancient snowmobile, so old that it looked like it might have been the patent model. I studied it for a bit, since I knew a rich lady in Chicago who collected patent models. Her name was Sally Reed, and her life consisted of a search for patent models interspersed with drinking.

Unfortunately, the snowmobile wasn't a patent model. It was just old and worn out. When I finished inspecting it I looked up to see Brisling Bowker, standing in his own service elevator. Brisling had a habit of simply materializing, mysteriously. He reminded me of a Cape buffalo.

Then I spotted an old tricycle, wedged in with a litter of household goods. It is unusual to find a tricycle earlier than the forties, and this one was definitely earlier than that. I knew plenty of tricycle collectors, including a man in Oregon who had over five hundred.

"Too rusty," Brisling said, while I was looking at the tricycle. As usual, he was right.

"Want to buy a Henry?" he asked, staring at me impassively.

"Do you mean a Henry rifle, or a person named Henry?" I asked.

Brisling was not a man who appreciated witticisms. He nodded and I got on the service elevator with him. We went slowly upward, through the several floors of his empire, most of them crammed with consignments waiting to be auctioned. The floor we got off on was almost pitch dark, though I could see huge shapes looming in the darkness.

When Brisling turned the lights on I saw that the dark shapes were furniture, of a very ponderous sort. We were on the heavy furniture floor. Most of the pieces were Victorian or Edwardian and not much smaller than the average log cabin. There was an oak pantry against one wall so commodious that a small family could have probably lived in it.

A long object was lying on one of the side tables, wrapped in an old army blanket. Brisling handed it to me. Sure enough, it was a Henry rifle, in a saddle scabbard so beautifully worn that it looked like mahogany. I had never sold or owned a Henry—in good condition one could be worth upwards of $15,000.

They were heavy guns. I eased this one out of the scabbard and hefted it. It's strange how good objects immediately communicate a certain authority when you hold them. Of course the Henry was a weapon—authority was its business. It was meant to knock down buffalo, or anything else you pointed it at. When I put the gun to my shoulder and sighted it at the pantry I saw a herd of buffalo in my mind's eye, standing in a valley of Montana or Wyoming. It was happening more and more—objects functioning like time machines, effortlessly removing me from my time and inserting me briefly in theirs. The longer I looked at the Sung vase the more I had imagined China. Little eighteenth-century porcelain snuffboxes invariably made me think of Voltaire, although I knew practically nothing about him. And Elizabethan wine bottles, of which I've owned only three or four, made me think of Sir Walter Raleigh, sitting in the tower waiting to get his head chopped off.

Brisling Bowker was not disposed to grant me my vision of buffaloes for very long. Scouts were nothing new to Brisling. He had seen the great ones of the profession come and go. I knew he harbored a sneaking affection for Zack Jenks, but I wasn't so sure that it extended to me.

"Buy it," he said, meaning the Henry. "If I put it on sale somebody'll break it."

He was probably right. The public that flocks to auctions can't resist guns. They love to work levers, snap triggers, and pull back hammers. Pretty soon they've messed up the gun.

"What do you know about the warehouse full of baskets?" I asked, out of curiosity. "I was thinking about buying it, if it isn't already sold."

Brisling sighed. I looked up and found him looking at me almost fondly.

"You don't want to buy no warehouse full of baskets," he said. "You just want to see it. You don't want to buy no warehouse full of nothin'. You do an' you'll end up like me."

He nodded at the vast room, which must have contained about ninety tons of obsolete and mostly graceless furniture.

I was startled. A personal comment from Brisling was an unheard-of thing.

"I was like you, once," he said. "On the road all the time, making a score in every town. Now lookit. Five floors of this junk I'm responsible for. Selling fertilizer. Lawn mowers."

He stared at the huge Victorian pantry as if he would like to take an axe and chop it to kindling.

"Look at that," he said. "It'd take a damn crane to move it, and who's going to buy it?"

His point was not lost on me. If you open a store you have to stay and run the store. And then, instead of buying things you really love, you start buying what people bring you, in order to fill the store and have something to sell. If the store is successful, pretty soon you get a warehouse, and then more warehouses, and the next thing you know you're Brisling Bowker, commander of an empire in which there might not have been ten objects he really liked.

I had not even known he had been a scout.

He took the Henry from me, hefted it just as I had, sighted down the long barrel. Perhaps he too was taking the time machine, back to the time of buffalo.

"I wasn't born nailed down," he said, slipping the gun back in the scabbard. He handled it with a light touch.

"I went everywhere," he said. "California, New England. Canada. Europe. You know what did me in?"

He did not look done in, but I knew better than to argue with a man in a nostalgic mood.

I just waited.

"Bargains," he said. "You guys doing it today, you ain't seen nothin'. Bargains everywhere. In the thirties this gun would have cost me two bucks. Maybe five at the outside. That icon you bought, I would have got that for a quarter, back in the thirties."

It was the song of the Old Scout. I had heard it from many of them: tales of days when a fine Sung vase would have cost 50 cents instead of $20. No doubt they were right. There must have been unbelievable bargains lying around America in the days before swap-meets had been thought of. There still are unbelievable bargains lying around America, though nowadays every third person is some kind of scout.

"I found a Rubens in Idaho, once," Brisling said. "Gives you an idea. Idaho. In the only antique store in the whole state. Gave the old lady $200 for it and she thought she was robbing me. Then I went and robbed myself. Sold the fucking thing for seventy-five thousand dollars. Be worth three million today."

"So what?" I said. "You got your profit."

Brisling nodded. "Always," he said. "I had one of those big Pierce-Arrow roadsters. It would hold a lot of stuff, but not enough. I bought a truck, and made it follow me around. Then when the truck got full I rented a warehouse."

He stopped. The rest of the story was obvious. Dealers become slaves to their objects, just as farmers are slaves to their land. Being enslaved to beautiful objects is one thing, but being enslaved to ordinary or even ugly objects is something else.

Brisling had paid me the great compliment of perceiving me as I was: a scout, such as he had been, such as he might have remained. Offering me the Henry was not only a warning, it was almost a paternal act.

"How much for the gun?" I asked.

"Twelve thousand," he said.

That was fine. He had carefully left me a 20 percent profit, if I was good enough to get it. I wrote him a check for $12,000 and he stuffed it in his shirt pocket without looking at it.

"I sold this gun three times," he said, as we were riding down. "It came in during the war and I didn't do nothing about it till '46. Brought $400. The guy that bought it brought it back in '56 and it brought $1,250. The guy that bought it in '56 died last year."

He paused. "Why I gave you a bargain," he said. "Bad luck to sell the same piece more than three times. You get my age, things start following you around. Pets, I call 'em. Take that thing to Texas and sell it. I got enough pets. Pretty soon I'll be like Bag Hopkirk."

Bag Hopkirk was an aged dealer in Cleveland who had made a fortune by outliving his customers, and their heirs, and their heirs' heirs. His shop was filled with objects he had owned several times. His sales were more like rentals. No one who knew him supposed he would ever die. He had sold things to customers forty years younger than himself and then outlived them.

The bankrupt lawn store had had a lot of leftover fertilizer. Even in bags it didn't smell too great. A huge pyramid of it had risen in the auction room, while Brisling and I were upstairs. The pyramid separated forty or fifty shiny new lawn mowers from about a hundred tweed chairs. Brisling regarded the arrangement gloomily. If some pesky customer punctured one of the sacks of fertilizer the auction room was going to be fragrant for a while. When I left, Tuck and one or two of the minions were erecting a sort of barrier of lawn mowers between the public and the fertilizer.

"Thanks for the gun," I said, but the gun was history, just a droplet in the river of objects whose flow had been Brisling's life. He was contemplating a huge stack of dusty Oriental rugs, and he didn't look up.

Chapter VIII _____

As I was cruising along in what I hoped was the general direction of the Department of Transportation, where I was to meet the mysterious Hobart Cawdrey, I suddenly found myself in front of a Wax Museum. The reason I noticed it was because I was behind a bus and the bus suddenly stopped and disgorged about a hundred high school kids with cameras. Other buses were disgorging elderly couples, also with cameras. I politely stopped and let a stream of young and old cross the street in front of me.

The old women had on print dresses and the old men had the collars of their shirts turned back over the collars of their sports coats. Some of the old men were holding hands with their wives. Most of them looked keen to see the Wax Museum, outside of which was a sign advertising WATERGATE FIGURES.

The kids seemed a good deal less eager. They looked like they had been up all night, smoking dope and trying to fuck one another. Several bedraggled teachers were grimly herding them along, watching to see that none of the kids made a break for freedom. Having bussed them to the capital from remote parts of the country they meant to make sure that they saw every damn thing they were supposed to see, including wax replicas of Watergate figures.

"I hope they've got Martha Mitchell," one old lady said. "I wanta see Martha."

A couple of blocks past the Wax Museum I bumped right into the Department of Transportation. It occupied a full city block, from corner to corner. It was 10:25 and I was supposed to meet Mr. Cawdrey at 10:30. I found a phone and dialed the Department. When the operator rang extension 1000 Mr. Cawdrey answered at once.

"Ho-bart Cawd-rey," he answered, in a very slow voice.

"Hi, Mr. Cawdrey," I said. "I'm Jack McGriff."

He didn't say a word.

"I was going to meet you in regard to the basketry," I reminded him.

"Well, you're too late, much too late," Mr. Cawdrey said. "The baskets are being moved today. Arrangements have been finalized. I'm surprised you called."

"We had an appointment," I said. "That's why I called."

"Wait a minute," he said sternly. "I better check my book."

"Oh lord," he said, a moment later, aghast at what he'd found in his book.

"What's the matter?" I asked.

"You're right," he said. "I'm wrong. I'm due to meet you in the cafeteria in two minutes. You'll look like a cowboy."

"That's right," I said.

"Oh dear," he said. "I've been guilty of miscalculation. I can't possibly get to the cafeteria in two minutes. I can seldom even get down in the elevator in two minutes. It often takes four. I'm very sorry about this. It's not like me at all. I forgot to look in my book. I suppose you'll want to reschedule the whole business."

"Oh no," I said. "I'm in no hurry. I've got plenty of time."

He was silent for a long time. The thought of a cowboy with lots of time seemed to strike him as curious.

"All right, could you just stand near the ice," he said. "I'll be there in four to six minutes."

Pretty soon I was following a stream of people which was pouring down into the basement of the building, toward the cafeteria. The stream was not exactly meandering aimlessly, either. I felt like I had wandered into an ant colony, or perhaps a beetle colony. The people around me had an insectlike quality, though it would have been hard to name the insect they suggested. Wood lice, probably. They moved along at a rapid clip and seemed to be responding to the directives of a collective brain. All of them seemed to be dressed not merely poorly, but terribly, in the cheapest available synthetic fabrics of the worst colors. None of them looked like they owned so much as a good pair of socks.

There was a lack of light in their eyes that would have won

someone an Academy Award for great special effects if they had all been in a zombie movie.

By the time we actually got down to the cafeteria I had begun to feel odd. After all, I wasn't part of the colony. I felt like a wasp that had accidentally gone down an anthill.

Fortunately the ice-maker where I was supposed to meet Hobart Cawdrey was easy to spot. It was in the center of the room, near a counter that seemed to contain millions of styrofoam cups. The workers—I guess they should be called bureaucrats—poured off the food line carrying hamburgers on styrofoam plates. Then they grabbed a styrofoam cup, scooped up a few ice cubes, and moved past a row of spigots that dispensed liquids on the order of iced tea and Pepsi-Cola.

I don't eat in cafeterias much—just being in the middle of such a vast one was a little daunting. The people shuffling along in the food line didn't have the anticipatory look people usually have when they're waiting to be fed. Most people assume that if they're going to be fed the food will probably taste good, but nowhere in the cafeteria did I see a face lit with the prospect of eating something that might taste good. Instead of looking like people who were about to eat they looked like people who had lined up to get polio shots, or something.

Someone touched my elbow and I looked down into a round unwrinkled face under a woolen hat.

"Hobart Cawdrey," the face said.

From the first glance it was clear that Mr. Cawdrey was a man of his profession. It wasn't merely that he wore a woolen hat and a trench coat, but that he failed to wear an expression. His eyes lacked many of the qualities that one normally associates with eyes. Though he was looking right at me, I could not tell that he regarded me with the slightest interest or curiosity.

"We better get in line," he said. "This place is going to fill up soon."

Without further ado we joined the nearest food line. At close range the people in line looked even more depressed than they had from a distance. Mr. Cawdrey did not seem to feel the need to say anything. His round face and blank eyes did not change expression, though since they had not really attained an expression they couldn't very well have changed it.

"How's the food?" I asked, to be conversational.

This simple question startled Mr. Cawdrey. He looked around at me with something like a look of puzzlement—then he glanced at the food counter as if he were being forced to take cognizance of it for the first time.

"Why the food's right there," he said. "You'll see for yourself. We're a new department, you know. I understand they have more things over at State. I ate at the Treasury once and they had quite a few things, too. But we seem to have all the normal things. I usually eat a hamburger."

With that he picked up a styrofoam plate and ordered a hamburger and French fries. I did the same. When I asked if I could have everything on my hamburger the woman who was doling out burgers looked at me so truculently that I didn't repeat my request. As a result I got two buns, a patty of meat, and one leaf of lettuce. Mr. Cawdrey got a Pepsi, I got iced tea, and then we stood in line for about ten minutes at the cash registers.

Mr. Cawdrey had been right. People were pouring into the cafeteria like beetles, armored with carapaces of total indifference. The streams of beetle-people were beginning to back up into the stairwells.

I was beginning to get depressed, partly because I hate styrofoam. To me, styrofoam plates aren't even objects—they belong in a revolting subclass of some kind, well beneath the level of an honest paper plate. The one I was holding seemed to have pores. Also, it was taking an awful long time to get to the cash registers, though I was the only one who seemed to mind. Everyone else seemed to think it perfectly natural that the food they were buying would be cold long before they could even pay for it, much less eat it.

Finally we got past the cash registers and took our food into another vast room, this one filled with tiny tables. The tables and chairs were of some sort of plastic that was itself not far removed from styrofoam.

The ice had long since melted in my tea, which was watery, and when I took a bite of my hamburger it was as if I had taken a bite of my plate: it tasted like styrofoam. When I picked up a French fry it folded limply down my finger, like a dead worm. I couldn't bring myself to eat it so I eased it off my finger, back into the pile, and contented myself with a little sip of watery tea. I felt dismal. No wonder the people in the food line didn't look anticipatory. They knew perfectly well the food they were waiting for would consist of impotent French fries and hamburgers that tasted much like a styrofoam plate.

Mr. Cawdrey was clearly not bothered by these dismal reflections. He munched his way right through a tasteless hamburger, eating every crumb.

"It's a pity you weren't a little quicker," he said. "If I were a buyer I would have wanted the baskets, because they're so easy to move. Baskets are light. We have many other things, but they aren't very light."

"What sorts of things?" I asked.

"Well, the weapons, for example," he said. "You could buy the weapons, but they aren't light, you know. We have two thousand cannons, and they have to go with the weapons."

"How much are the weapons?" I asked.

"Six point two million," Mr. Cawdrey said. "But you have to take the cannons."

"What else do you have that's light?" I asked.

"Well, the pottery," he said. "Much of it is light, but unfortunately the sarcophagi go with the pottery and sarcophagi aren't light."

Then he noticed that I hadn't eaten my food.

"My goodness," he said. "You didn't eat."

"It got cold while we were standing in line," I said. "I don't like cold hamburgers."

"I guess mine got cold, too," he said, as if trying to remember the hamburger he was even then digesting.

Then he fell silent. I fell silent, too. I was getting very depressed. All at once I couldn't think of any reason to go on doing what I was doing, if what I was doing could bring me to such a place. The mere sight of the round blank face of Hobart Cawdrey was discouraging. For a moment I saw my life in its most ridiculous light: here I was, in a city I had only come to on a whim, talking to a man who wanted to sell 2,000 cannons, among other things. For the course of perhaps twenty seconds I felt I must be virtually insane, not to have found a more sensible occupation in my thirty-three years.

Mr. Cawdrey was looking at my hat. A faint flicker of expression crossed his face.

"I was sent to a dude ranch once," he said, as if surprised at having been invaded by a memory. "I was fourteen. It was in Wyoming. I had never been in Wyoming before."

He paused. "Come to think of it, I've never been since."

"Did you enjoy yourself?" I asked.

"No," he said, a little sadly. "The cowboys laughed at me because I wore pajamas. Then they stole my pajamas. They also put a skunk in my bed. It didn't stink, but it was a skunk."

Then he stopped talking as abruptly as he had begun. The memory of his embarrassments at the dude ranch apparently faded somewhat. Then he looked at his watch and it faded completely.

"My goodness," he said. "I've dawdled. Are you quite sure you don't want the weapons?"

"I'm quite sure," I said, feeling slightly nauseous, either from my one bite of styrofoam hamburger or from the thought of 2,000 cannons.

"It's odd that you came," Mr. Cawdrey said. "Though of course you did have an appointment."

A second later he was gone.

Chapter IX _____

Escaping from the Department of Transportation cafeteria into the bright fall sunshine was such a relief that it made me feel dizzy. It was a joy to discover that the world was still there. I felt a tremendous urge to be with people who were as different as possible from the thousands of numbed souls still waiting in line in the depths of that vast building.

Accordingly, I headed straight for the Little Bomber's Lounge, where I was immediately rewarded by the sight of Lolly and Janie Lee, sitting in their favorite booth giggling like mad. This time they were drinking piña coladas. Their girlish laughter seemed to be something of an irritant to a couple of sullen-looking customers who probably just wanted to sit in a bar and nurse a beer and be quietly depressed.

They waved me over the minute they saw me.

"I knew he'd come back," Lolly said, when I squeezed in beside them.

"Yeah, he can't resist us," Janie Lee said.

"Well, so what, I can't resist them yellah boots," Lolly said. "Have a piña colada. We're celebrating."

"Don't tell me you finished secretarial school already," I said.

"Naw, we quit," Janie Lee said. "I couldn't stand that shorthand."

"I bet Boog's disappointed. He had high hopes for you girls."

"Yeah, he was," Lolly said. She was wearing a red peekaboo blouse over a pink peekaboo bra.

"We made it up to him, though," Janie Lee said. "We kept him in the Jacuzzi all afternoon and didn't charge him a dime."

"He was all wrinkledy when he got out," Lolly remembered.

"Am I too late for the Double Bubble Brunch?" I asked.

"Aw yeah, you missed it," Lolly said. "That's okay,

though. We can just give you the Soap Opera special. It ain't supposed to start till one, but Penny ain't here today."

"Who's Penny?"

"The manager. Shoot, she don't care. We got some special going 'bout every hour of the day."

"We even got a Midnight Special," Janie Lee said. " 'vailable till 3 A.M. on Friday and Saturday nights."

Ten minutes later I was in a large, warm whirlpool bath drinking pink California champange with two fat naked girls. A big color TV sat across the room, providing the soap opera part of the Soap Opera special. *As the World Turns* was on, Janie Lee's favorite soap, as it happened. She watched it intently, her elbows on the side of the big tub and her pinkish body floating more or less on the surface. From time to time she sat her plastic champagne glass on her stomach.

Lolly evinced little interest in *As the World Turns*. Beside the deep whirlpool was a heap of green snorkeling gear.

"What's the snorkeling stuff for?" I asked. Lolly was trying to get some water out of her ear.

"Aw, that's for Congressmen," she said. "Representatives mostly. Sometimes two or three of them get in here and want to watch what's going on from under water."

"Shoot, that ain't the worse of it," Janie Lee said, looking our way, during a commercial break.

"What's the worse of it?"

"When they put that stuff on an' expect us to suck 'em off while they're sitting on the bottom," she said. "I never did like to swim underwater."

"First time I tried it I swallert so much water I like to drowned," Lolly said. "I don't know who thought up this snorkeling business, anyway. It don't mix with fucking very good."

A minute later she got out of the tub and pattered wetly over to the icebox where they kept the champagne.

"Oh Janie Lee, you drunk all the pink," she said.

Janie Lee didn't hear her. The soap had started again and whatever was happening struck her as deeply wrongheaded.

"Now that ain't gonna work," she said. "That's just gonna make trouble all around."

Lolly came back with some white champagne and hopped back in the bath.

"Janie Lee, you don't never help if there's a soap opera on," she said, a little testily. "I end up doin' just about every bit of the work."

With that she began to blow in my ear. Janie Lee looked briefly guilty and worked her way around the pool to us, with the result that I was soon floating between two sizable girls both of whom were slick as seals. The scene was too companionable, if not ridiculous, to provoke anything resembling passion, and anyway Janie Lee couldn't really get her mind off the soap opera.

"You wanta get on the floatie?" Lolly asked.

The floatie was a huge rubber air mattress. It lay over by the snorkling gear.

Without waiting for an answer Lolly drug the big mattress into the pool.

"You won't hold us both up?" Janie Lee said.

"Janie Lee, you don't never wanta try nothing," Lolly said. With the floatie in the pool there was not much room for the three of us. It covered at least three quarters of the surface of the tub.

"Now I can't see," Janie Lee complained. "This is the Soap Opera special. What's so special about it if we can't even see the soap opera?"

Lolly ignored this complaint. She managed to get on the air mattress by the simple expedient of straddling it and then flopping backwards.

"Come on up here, Janie Lee," she said. "It'll hold us up."

Though not as enthusiastic as Lolly, Janie Lee finally complied. With my help she managed to get on the floatie, too. The two of them lay there looking as innocent as babes but a lot larger, while *As the World Turns*, unnoticed now, filled the big color screen, occasionally sending an orange or green shadow over their bodies.

Both girls had fat thighs with dimples in them, smallish

breasts, and fat white shoulders. Somehow as they lay there with their legs squeezed together and their wet blond hair stuck to their necks they reminded me of Beverly and Belinda Arber. They had the aspect of two slightly mischievous little girls.

"You could pour some champagne on us, I guess," Janie Lee said. "That's real popular, seems like."

"I don't think so," I said. "I'd rather drink the champagne."

"See, he's normal, like us," Lolly said.

"You girls are too friendly," I said, apropos of my own lack of raging passion.

"Yeah, we are," Lolly agreed. "It's our only trouble. My husband's always tellin' me that."

"Your husband?"

"Yeah, Bobby," she said. "He's best friends with Janie Lee's husband."

"I wisht you hadn't reminded me," Janie Lee said. "We don't never get to see them. They stay on the road a lot."

"What do they do on the road?"

"We wisht we knew," Lolly said. "I guess they mostly chase girls, unless they're smuggling dope. They stay in Florida just about all the time. Shoot, me and Janie Lee's got to have a life, too. That why we work at the Double Bubble. I'd rather suck off Congressmen than sit around the house."

"What do your husbands think about all this?" I asked.

Both girls looked solemn for a moment—neither of their faces were meant for solemnity and it had the effect of making them look younger than they were.

"I don't know," Lolly admitted. "We ain't asked them."

"Shoot, why ask them?" Janie Lee said. "They don't ask us if they can go to Florida. They just get in the car and take off."

"Yeah, and they don't call, neither, unless the car breaks down and they need money."

"We don't never know when to expect them," Lolly added somewhat forlornly.

"Do you reckon they've got mistresses?" she asked. "A lot of men around here have mistresses."

"Yeah, I wish I could be one," Janie Lee said. "I'm getting tired of staying in a tub half the time. I get water up my nose nearly every day."

"We had a double wedding," Lolly said, somewhat more cheerfully. "But no double honeymoon. Shoot, that wouldn't have worked. Me and Bobby went to Ocean City and Eddie and Janie Lee went to Norfolk."

"Reason it wouldn't have worked is because they're always trying to get us to swap," Janie Lee said. "Or worst than that. Four in a bed is what they really want. Pretty soon they'd get us so mixed up we couldn't remember who we was married to. It'd be just like a soap opera."

"If they've got mistresses I bet they do it four in a bed," Lolly reflected.

"Shoot, I'm not going through that," Janie Lee said. "I'd rather not do it at all."

This was going too far for Lolly, who looked at her friend with a shocked expression. The notion of celibacy was clearly one she had never entertained.

"Not do it at all?" she said. "With your own husband? You better be glad Eddie didn't hear you say that. Shoot, Bobby would run me over with a car if I was to tell him I didn't plan to do it at all."

Janie Lee looked unrepentant. "We could still dance," she said. "That's about all me an' Eddie like to do together, anyway, and we can't even do that if he stays in Florida all the time. Me an' you paid our own way into the disco every night last week."

"Yeah," Lolly said, as if a sad truth had just been revealed to her.

"I don't like to think about it," Lolly added. "I'd rather do almost anything than think."

My heart went out to her. In general, it was a heart that went out at odd moments. It had gone out to Coffee while she was trying to stuff the hippo chair into her blue Chevelle. It went out to Cindy because she liked to sleep holding hands, and now it was going out to two fat wet girls on a rubber mattress in a fairly low-grade pussy parlor.

"Aw," I said. "Then don't think."

"Can't help it," Lolly said, with a little gulp. "Janie Lee got me started and when I get started I can't stop."

She was silent for a moment. Janie Lee was silent too, evidently chastened by having caused her friend to think.

They floated quietly for a while. True to her own prophecy, Lolly had not been able to stop thinking. While Lolly thought, Janie Lee paddled in the water with one foot. I realized she was trying to turn the floatie so she could watch her soap. I helped her turn it. When I did Lolly nudged me intimately with one of her plump little feet.

"Lookit," she said. "You ain't even got a hard-on. You shouldn't never have got us talking."

"We don't usually talk," Janie Lee said.

"We knew you'd come back," Lolly said. "I even had dibs."

"Dibs on what?"

Lolly looked surprised. "On fuckin', what else?" she said. "Janie Lee don't care 'cause she don't like it as much as I do, anyway."

"I do *sometimes*," Janie Lee said, defensively. "But sometimes I don't."

"Anyway, I had dibs," Lolly said.

"Sometimes I don't care if I never do it again," Janie Lee said, reflecting on her periods of sexual disinclination.

"Then why'd you wanta quit secretarial school I'd like to know?" Lolly asked. "If you don't wanta fuck a lot you oughta get another job."

Janie Lee was silent. Lolly's logic was more or less irrefutable.

"I do *sometimes*," she said, a little plaintively.

Lolly sighed. "We ain't usually gloomy," she said.

"I don't know why he'd believe that," Janie Lee said. "All we've done is lay on the floatie and talk depressing."

"Well, it's his fault, too," Lolly said. "He coulda done something."

Four eyes, all blue, looked at me with faint reproach. I had stood by and let a whole Soap Opera special fizzle away into sobering thoughts.

"Well, it's too late now," Lolly said. "Penny's coming with a whole station wagon full of Representatives. That Penny knows a bunch of people."

"Okay, but she is twenty-six," Janie Lee said. "If this keeps up you an' me will know about half the world by the time we're twenty-six."

Then their spirits bobbed up, as buoyant as the mattress.

"Least I didn't get water up my nose," Janie Lee said.

When I left, the two of them were giggling again and slipping into billowy blue negligees, in anticipation of the station wagon full of Representatives.

Sure enough, as I was sitting out front studying a road map, trying to figure out the quickest way to Riverdale, Maryland, where I was to meet the nest collector, whose name was Bryan Ponder, a green station wagon pulled up right beside me, a tall woman at the wheel. She glanced at me briefly through sunglasses as black as tar, and then got out and marched into the Double Bubble, followed by five or six nervous men in ugly suits. Lolly and Janie Lee had obviously called their next shot.

Chapter X _____

Riverdale, Maryland, is one of those American places that seem to stand outside the stream of time. It is just a little grown-up-around town way out Rhode Island Avenue, and what has grown up around it is postwar America. Nothing in Riverdale is either really old, or really new, and the home of Bryan Ponder, the nest collector, was no exception.

It was just an ordinary white frame house that stood in a cul-de-sac near the railroad, across the street from one of the oldest laundromats I'd ever seen. Two large women were standing in the ancient laundromat, watching diapers swoosh around. They looked like they had had about eighteen children each and might have a few more, if only to have an excuse to come and visit one another at the laundromat.

When I knocked on Bryan Ponder's door only silence answered. Then, through the silence, I could hear the distant sound of a TV—a baseball game was on. In fact, the World Series was on. I heard the crack of a bat, the roar of a crowd.

I knocked again, harder.

"Mr. Ponder," I said. "Are you there?"

A sound that I took to be a grunt of assent came from somewhere deep in the house. The door was not locked, so I pushed it open a little way, far enough to enable me to look into a room that was cluttered even by the standards of a person like myself—which is to say someone long accustomed to the kind of clutter human packrats gather around them.

The living room was entirely full of nests, except for a narrow track down the middle and a space over in one corner. The space in the corner contained a black-and-white TV, of a vintage comparable to that of the washing machines in the nearby laundromat. It also contained a large stuffed chair with a small stand beside it, the sort off which people eat TV dinners. A very tall old man sat in the chair, watching the TV set.

Beyond the chair another narrow trail wove between more stacks of nests, into another room.

The living room was filled with nests to a depth of about three feet, with more nests piled and stacked on mantel and windowsills. Most of them were birds' nests, of every size and description, though one corner was filled with cones of dried mud that resembled the cones crawdads make, except that crawdad cones were smaller.

The old man in the chair didn't look around. He wore a white undershirt and old khakis. Mud-dauber nests were stacked against the back of the chair.

"Mr. Ponder?" I said, tentatively.

"Come in and shut up, goddamnit," he said.

I stood quietly in the little lane between the piles of nests. Hardened as I was to bizarre collections of objects, I still felt a little odd. There must have been five thousand nests in the room, ranging from ordinary bird nests to great sacklike objects hanging from hooks on the wall. The sacks seemed to be made of Spanish moss.

The TV set across the room had a picture almost as white as the old man's hair. I could vaguely detect the figures of ballplayers on the screen, but since the ballplayers were in white too they seemed extremely ghostlike. The old man didn't seem to mind.

"Only thing that hasn't changed, since my childhood," he said. "Baseball. Only thing I recognize, out of what was once a healthy civilization."

On the screen a ghostly pitcher threw a ghostly pitch, and a ghostly batter missed it. The crowd cheered and the old man rose out of his chair.

"Got him on a breaking ball," he said. "Seventh inning stretch."

He looked at me for the first time and held out his hand. He was almost five inches taller than me, which put him close to six feet ten inches.

"Ever see so many goddamn nests?" he asked. "These here are relatively uninteresting. Just nests I picked up along the way. Better nests in the dining room. Go take a look."

He was right. In the dining room were cocoons the size of footballs, and nests so spiky it was hard to see how a bird could sit on one without being impaled. The small path led through the dining room to the kitchen, where more nests were stacked on the cabinet. A big gray hornet's nest was on top of the icebox.

Out the back door I could see a big barnlike garage, much larger than the house. I knew that meant yet more nests. Collectors don't let space just lie around empty. So long as there's a cubic inch they can cram stuff in, they won't stop buying, and they won't stop buying even when there isn't.

Bryan Ponder had followed me into the kitchen. He seemed fairly relaxed himself, at least during the seventh inning stretch.

"What's in the garage?" I asked.

"Fossilized nests," he said. "That's what got me started. I bought my first nest in Baghdad. How about that?

"I was in the spying trade," he said. "Bought a bustard nest, fossilized. Most people don't even know bustards nest, but they do. That nest is probably fifty thousand years old. I saw it and thought to myself, 'My god, a bird sat in that nest fifty thousand years ago.' That's what got me started."

Then he went back to his chair. The eighth inning was starting.

"What do you do, son?" he asked.

"I'm kind of a trader," I said.

"You want to buy my nests?" he asked.

"Are you sure you want to sell them?" I asked.

He nodded. "Damn right I want to sell 'em," he said. "I'm tired of nests. Make me an offer."

"I don't know what I'd do with them," I said.

"Why, you'd *have* them," he said. "What do you think I do, lay eggs in them? Go out in the garage and look at the ant cones. I've got five digger ant cones out there. You won't find another one in America. The only other cones in private hands are in Orvieto, which is in Italy."

"What are they doing in Orvieto?" I asked.

"Just being had, like my cones," he said, a little impatiently. "Guy there collects them. Count Guiccoli. Between us we've got about all the nests worth having, although there's a mechanic over in Sussex who has a few nice nests."

"Have you seen the Count's nests?" I asked.

"Of course I've seen them," he said. "Used to live in Italy. Spied on the Vatican for Harry Truman. Harry didn't trust the Pope."

Then the conversation lagged. The baseball game was close and Bryan Ponder was reluctant to turn his attention from it.

I wandered out to the garage and poked around awhile. It was truly an amazing place. It was clearly where Bryan Ponder kept his larger nests. Several of the nests in it were immense. There was a condor nest from the Andes—I know that's what it was because it had a little piece of paper stuck in it that said "Condor nest from the Andes." One whole side

233

of the barn was filled with fossilized nests. Some were large and some were small but all were definitely old.

At the back of the garage there was part of a large tree. Its leaves and vines had long since turned brown but up in it was a kind of abstract nest, made of branches. The tree was thicker than a telephone pole and the branches that formed the nest looked like they could have held up a gorilla. I couldn't imagine what kind of bird could have needed such a nest. It would have needed to be a great deal larger than any bird I had ever seen.

As I wandered through the garage I began to feel flatter and flatter. I felt something resembling postcoital sadness, without having even had sex. Something had suddenly gone wrong in my relationship to objects, and my relationship to objects was more or less the basis for my life. Women came and went from me, or I came and went from women, but there were always objects, in their endless, infinite variety. In many years of scouting, I had never really tired of them.

Now, suddenly, I was tired of them. Somehow I had suddenly lost my appetite for the bizarre. Here I was, in a truly amazing place, looking at perhaps the preeminent nest collection in the whole world, and I didn't really care. My response was dried out and a little abstract, like the dead tree in Bryan Ponder's garage. I had just O.D.ed on objects. I didn't want to get up and dig through the thousands of nests in the hopes of coming out with a half-dozen so extraordinary that I could sell them immediately to any great dealer or great museum. A day there had been when I would have moved every nest in the place to find those half-dozen, but that day had passed. The whole pursuit suddenly seemed empty. What did I want with nests? What did I want with anything?

I sat down on one of the huge, hard, fossilized nests and rested a bit, hoping the mood would pass.

While I was sitting, I heard the slap of a screen door and in a minute Bryan Ponder appeared in the door of the garage. The World Series must be over, at least for the day.

"I've got the nests, don't I?" he said, gazing happily around the garage.

"You've got 'em," I said.

"What kind of nest is that?" I asked, pointing at the strange tree.

"Oh, that's a gorilla nest," he said. "It don't look right—oughta be green—but that's what it is. Gorillas like to sleep up high, where they can get a little breeze."

I felt terribly sad, for no reason that I could explain. I felt like I had unexpectedly reached the end of my road, the one I had been traveling haphazardly but enthusiastically all these years. It ended at a gorilla nest in Riverdale, Maryland. So far as I knew, no scout in America had ever found a gorilla nest, and what's more it was for sale. I could buy it, capping my whole strange enterprise and making myself unique in the annals of American scouting.

But then what?

"Well, I hear they're selling the Smithsonian," Bryan Ponder said. "You gonna get in on that?"

"I don't think so," I said, listlessly.

That I had no urge to was in itself sort of terrible. I hadn't even pressed Hobert Cawdrey to let me look at the Smithsonian warehouses that might still be for sale. Even if I didn't want to buy 2,000 cannons I could still have gone and looked at the weapons. I had fantasized about those warehouses for years, and then had not really even tried to worm my way into one of them. Actually I felt like the sight of a warehouse full of anything would have filled me with despair.

"What's the matter, son?" Bryan Ponder asked. "You look a little down."

"I guess I am," I said, offering no excuse.

"Well, this town'll get you down, if you ain't used to it," he said, in a rather kindly tone. "It's fine for spies and newspapermen but it ain't everybody's cup of tea. Maybe you oughta move to Minnesota."

"Why Minnesota?" I asked, curious.

"I'm from Minnesota," he said. "A good climate but not many nests. The tropics is where you go to find your best nests. Who's gonna buy my nests if you don't?"

"Well, I guess you can't sell them to the Smithsonian," I

said. "They'd have to make reproductions of all of them so they could sell the originals."

He grinned a big gaunt grin. The notion of someone making reproductions of his thousands of nests didn't startle him at all. I wondered vaguely if there were nest forgers, just as there were hubcap forgers, but I didn't ask.

"Maybe you're in the wrong trade," he said. "Maybe the spying trade would suit you better. Traders make the best spies, anyhow. In my younger days I was a trading fool. When I was in the Balkans I even traded for a wife."

"What'd you trade?" I asked.

"Well, I traded a secret," he said. "It was a fake secret, actually, but it got the job done."

"How did it turn out?"

He looked at me solemnly, in a way that made me wish I could take the question back.

"It turned out fine till last year," he said. "Then she died. She put up with me and these nests for thirty-four years. Then she died. I never knew a human with a lovelier voice. Ain't that strange? I spent thirty-four years just listening, I liked her voice that much."

"What was her name?" I asked.

"Sophie," he said. "Don't you know anybody that'd buy these nests? Now that Sophie's dead I've lost patience with 'em."

"Well, there's Big John," I said.

Five minutes later I had him on the phone. He wasn't in his antique barn in Zanesville, but they said I might catch him at a certain chili parlor in Cincinnati, and I did. Naturally he was eager to buy the nests. His plan was to spray them with some kind of liquid varnish and disperse them through a network of roadside produce stands in the midwest. Travelers who stopped to buy a few tomatoes could buy a varnished nest as a souvenir. Of course that would only work for the small nests. The large nests would require different merchandising skills, but I was sure Big John had them. He could sell anything, and was willing to buy anything, too. The thought of having several thousand nests excited him a lot. He said he would leave for Washington as soon as he finished his chili.

He believed in the instant strike, which is probably why he is such a successful trader.

I envied him his excitement, his zest for the buy. I had had the same zest until quite recently, but it seemed to have utterly vanished. I walked back through the house with Bryan Ponder, feeling absolutely zestless.

"I wonder what the floor will look like, when he moves all these nests?" Bryan Ponder said.

I think it had just occurred to him that he really was going to lose all his nests. The sound of Big John's voice had convinced him he was dealing with a serious man, who would soon come and take his nests away.

It was probably a surprise. Many collectors fantasize about selling their collections, without really expecting it to happen. Sometimes they go so far as to set wheels in motion, only to balk at some point in the transaction. They think of it as a fantasy, or a dream they will soon wake up from, but often they don't come fully awake until some dealer is carting their collection out the door. Then they get really upset. Sometimes they stop the deal, much to the dealer's disgust. Sometimes—if the dealer is adamant—they even buy their own collections back. Or else, unable to bear the sight of their own space, they begin a new collection the next day.

It didn't seem likely that Bryan Ponder was going to start picking up nests again, though. His surprise was mild. He walked me out to my car, more bemused than anything.

"Think about Minnesota," he said, noticing that I had not exactly perked up. "It's a wonderful place. New, mostly. I favor new places."

He glanced down the street, in the general direction of Washington, scratching his ribs through his undershirt as he looked.

"Now you take Washington," he said. "It's old. People in old places get picky. They run out of energy so they make do with taste, which is not as good a thing. What you've got in Washington is a nineteenth-century town wishing it was an eighteenth-century town. It's just a damn graveyard of styles. That's why I live in Riverdale."

It seemed an odd speech, coming from a man who lived

across the street from the world's oldest laundromat. But then it would have been odd to hear a normal speech from a man who claimed to have 11,000 nests.

"If Sophie had lived I would have kept them," he said. "Sophie finally got to liking nests, but then the cancer killed her off. I think I'll just sell them to that fellah. Find out what the floor looks like."

He gave me a friendly wave as I drove away.

Chapter XI _____

It was only about four in the afternoon when I left Bryan Ponder's—nearly three hours before I was due at Jean Arber's for dinner. Ordinarily I would have nosed around the Hyattsville–Riverdale area, seeing what I could find in the local antique shops. But I wasn't in an ordinary mood.

What I did instead was drive out to Greenbelt, Maryland, where I sat in the parking lot of a Safeway for two hours, watching people come and go with their bags of groceries. I felt blank, neither depressed nor elated, neither interested nor bored. Watching the humble citizens of Greenbelt carry out their equally humble bags of groceries was not an exciting way to pass the time, but it was sufficient. One woman's sack burst as she was passing in front of my car and she looked so distressed that I got out to help her. The sack contained mostly Spam, plus a few cans of frozen orange juice and a stalk of celery. I guarded the Spam while the woman went back to get another sack.

I knew that at some point I had to call Cindy and tell her a lie, but no lie came immediately to mind and I kept putting it off. That proved to be a mistake, because while I was sitting watching the afternoon traffic back up on the street in front of me the car phone rang and it was Cindy.

"I thought you were going to call in," she said. "Where are you?"

"I'm out in Frederick," I said, instinctively placing myself about fifty miles from my actual location.

"Come on back," she said. "Lilah's throwing a little party. She wants us."

"Uh-oh," I said. "I don't know if I can make it."

There was a moment of silence. It was not a pleased silence, either.

"I told her we'd come," Cindy said, as if that fact rendered the matter closed.

"I thought you were dependable," she added. "What are you doing in Maryland, anyway?"

"I'm waiting to see a man about a gun," I said.

"Are you kidding me?" she said. "You're going to screw up this party because of a gun?"

"I didn't know there was going to be a party," I pointed out.

"You would have if you'd called in."

"I called in several times but the line was always busy," I said. It wasn't true, but it was plausible.

Cindy was silent again. She was not particularly contentious—argument for argument's sake didn't really interest her. Her view of life was grounded in certain simple verities, the main one being that she should get whatever she wanted. It was not so much a facet of selfishness as of extreme good health. To be denied might mean being unhappy, and she was too healthy to allow herself to be unhappy.

Unfortunately she had caught me in a rare mood. I wasn't particularly looking forward to having dinner with Jean Arber and her daughters, but neither did I want to go to a party at Lilah Landry's. I felt like I might just sit in the Safeway parking lot for several days, watching people carry out bags of groceries. I had settled in nicely to that life, and I wasn't ready to leave it.

Consequently, I met silence with silence. Cindy didn't say anything and neither did I.

I didn't expect that to last long, and it didn't.

"Aren't you going to say anything?" she asked.

"I already said it," I said. "I really have to see this man about the gun. It's a $20,000 gun. I can't get him on the phone, either. He's on his way here from Pennsylvania."

It was not bad, for a spur-of-the-moment lie. After all, I did have a fine gun in the car. The right collector might pay me $20,000 for it. It meant I had something to show when I finally went back to face the music.

"I can't believe you're doing this," Cindy said. "I *told* Lilah we'd come to the party."

"Yeah, but you didn't know I had a previous engagement," I said. "And I didn't know about the party. Things don't always mesh."

"They do in my life," she said.

"Look," I said. "Just go on to the party. I'll get there when I can."

"No way," Cindy said. "I can't show up without you."

"Why not?"

"People are getting interested in you," she said. "You're being talked about. Lilah just asked *me* to get you. She's not gonna want me showing up by myself."

"That's pretty insulting," I said. "I don't think we should go at all, in that case. Why go to a party where you're not wanted?"

"But I *am* wanted, if I bring you," she said.

"Well," I said, "I think you're subtracting yourself. If you're not wanted unless you're with me, then *you're* not wanted."

"I hate you," she said suddenly. "You just got here last week and you don't understand anything. Just shut up and come on back. You don't have to buy a gun.

"I don't appreciate this," she went on, with a quiver in her voice. "I've done a lot for you. If it wasn't for me people wouldn't even be interested in you."

"I don't think they're very interested," I said. "I think I'm just a new face."

There was another silence. During my life with Coffee I had become something of a connoisseur of silences. During the latter, Coffee was simply more or less absent. In fact, her genius was for the absent silence. Hers could go on for days.

Cindy's present silence seemed to have elided from angry to hurt. It might have been strategy. Women can usually figure out when tears will get them more than blows.

"I didn't think you'd do this to me," she said, with a kind of dying fall in her voice. "I thought you were nice," she added.

"I guess I'm not," I said. It was all I could think of to say.

"I'm not going without you," she said. "I'm going home. You just better come."

Then she hung up.

I immediately called back, but the line was busy.

This was an unfortunate turn of events. Cindy had adopted, instinctively, the smart tactic of making me feel guilty. I had no doubt that she would do exactly what she said. She would go home and wait, expecting that guilt would bring me back in plenty of time for the party.

However, after sitting for a while, I found that I wasn't feeling guilty. The parking lot of a Safeway in Greenbelt, Maryland, is in some ways a remote place. It was not literally a desert, but sitting in it I felt some of the remoteness that I might have felt had I been in a desert. Greenbelt seemed to be a kind of enclave for people who were not quite right. None of the people who were moping around in the parking lot were monsters in any way—in fact, they seemed rather pleasant—but on the other hand they weren't quite like people in other places, either. A great many of them were stooped, whether with the weight of cares or because of arthritic conditions I don't know. Many were smiling, and yet they didn't look like the sort of people who had much to smile about. They didn't seem to be smiling at anyone, or for any reason, unless they were secretly delighted to be carrying home shopping bags filled with Spam or Spaghetti-Os or other treats. I don't think that was the case, though. I think they were just smiling out into the universe, in a rather child-like fashion.

In fact, the longer I watched them shuffle out of the Safeway and push their grocery carts slowly off to their nonde-script little cars, the more it seemed that the parking lot in Greenbelt had developed its own indigenous life forms. You wouldn't have seen a single person who looked like them in the parking lot of a Safeway in southwest Houston—to give only one example.

The effect of watching them for an hour or so was to make me feel extremely remote from Georgetown, Cindy, and all social obligations of a normal type. The people moving around my car all seemed to be slightly bent, slightly handi-capped, slightly gaga, or just depressing to look at. As dusk fell I began to feel that I had wandered into a garden of grotesques. They were not aggressive grotesques—they all looked rather soft, rather helpless. I saw four men get off a bus and start across the parking lot and all four of them walked oddly. Instead of pointing forward their legs pointed at angles to one another.

Also, unfortunately, I notice clothes. All the hideous syn-thetics worn by the people in the Department of Transporta-tion had depressed me that morning, and now the clothes of the people in the parking lot in Greenbelt were depressing me just as much. They looked like remnants that had been handed down through generations of bottom-grade civil ser-vants. Overall, they reminded me of what people wear who work in the charity stores I used to work: Goodwill, Salvation Army, St. Vincent de Paul, Disabled Vets.

The longer I sat the more convinced I became that there must be some connection between the customers of this par-ticular Safeway and the thrift stores of the D.C. area. Perhaps Greenbelt was a service town for all the thrifts, thoughtfully established by someone for just that purpose.

It was a snobbish thought, as I was well aware. But no one can be a successful scout without being a visual snob. The ability to spot beauty even in bad light is the first essential—perhaps the only essential. When I had first come to the park-ing lot the people had sort of matched my mood. I felt I must be slightly off center, for living the life I did—being sur-rounded by people who were slightly off center had been a kind of comfort. But the comfort was only temporary. I might be off center, but the people in the parking lot now were way off on the edge somewhere, in a time zone of their own. I might be adrift, but I didn't want to drift any farther in their direction.

Besides, I had come out of my depression sufficiently to feel that I might be capable of dealing with a live current again. I picked up the phone and dialed Jean, and a live current answered.

"Hi," I said. "I'm the one with the soft car."

"I *know*," Belinda said, impatiently. "You jist come on. We're havin' peas."

Chapter XII ⎯⎯⎯⎯⎯⎯

Jean Arber and her daughters lived in a small two-story frame house in a somewhat run-down neighborhood in Wheaton. Actually, the neighborhood was not unlike my neighborhood in Houston, which attracts a lot of more or less educated hippies, most of whom start out with grand ambitions in regard to their houses. The ambitions involve restoring the houses to their original purity and simplicity, which means that paint has to be scraped off and walls knocked out. But the hippies generally turn out to have more purity and simplicity than the houses—or else they just lose interest, or stop being hippies. The houses may pass from owner to owner, half-restored and sort of damaged looking.

It was that way with the houses of Jean's neighbors, and in fact her own house had a pile of lumber beside it that had clearly been there for some time.

Jean came out to greet me, a daughter on either hand. The girls had on new red dresses and looked dressed up, whereas Jean just had on a simple gray sweater and a blue skirt. They all looked fresh, friendly, and cheerful. Just looking at them made me feel better.

"We got new dresses," Beverly reported.

"They're nice," I said.

"I *know*," Belinda said.

Jean was simply watching me. Perhaps traces of my recent mood still lingered, detectable to her instincts.

"If you're scared of girls you've come to the wrong place," she said.

Both girls were watching their mother, who was not looking at me, particularly. She was just standing on the front steps of her house, smiling. Following the girls' lead, I watched her for a moment, too, marveling as I often have at the capacities of women. One of their most amazing capacities is that of looking different from one day to the next, or even one hour to the next. My memories of Jean Arber were that she mostly looked wan. She had certainly looked wan the day she had the argument with her husband—wan and a little beaten.

But she looked anything but beaten standing on her steps in the gray sweater. She had undergone some internal transformation, and the external sign of it was that she looked beautiful. The girls were as alert to this fact as I was. Beverly was watching her appraisingly, as if her mother's sudden loveliness was a little more than she had bargained for.

"Penny for your thoughts, Mom," she said, tugging at one of Jean's fingers.

"Cheapskate," Jean said. "My thoughts are worth more than a penny, and anyway you don't have a penny."

"*I* don't," Belinda said cheerfully.

"Jack might like refreshments," Beverly pointed out.

"He might at that," Jean said. "I'm glad one of us has some social graces."

They led me into the house, which was filled with trunks, just as I had expected. A number of nice, flat-topped trunks, covered with cushions, took the place of chairs. I was hoping to see the dower chest Jean claimed was better than the one I had bought, but it wasn't in sight. There was a low couch covered with a dark nineteenth-century lap robe, and lots of small things to look at. A few miniatures hung on the walls, plus a couple of small primitives that looked Haitian.

The refreshments consisted of some excellent *nachos*, which Beverly served and Belinda helped me eat. The *nachos* had jalapeños, except for five or six for the girls which did not.

"I ate one and I cried," Belinda said, pointing at a pepper.

The *nachos*, which were unexpected, tasted so good that I ate about fifteen. The girls sat beside me on the brown couch, their feet sticking straight out. None of the major women in my life had been able to cook a bite, and I was faintly unnerved to have encountered a woman whose domestic skills included not only two lively daughters but also Mexican food.

"Where's the other dower chest?" I asked, since I was really curious about it.

"In my bedroom, which is where it's going to stay," Jean said.

"What do you do, jist buy things?" Belinda asked, patting my leg.

"That's what I do," I said.

"You could buy us things," she pointed out.

"And you could offer him one of your *nachos*," Jean said. "He's eaten all of his."

"Who's your wife?" Belinda asked.

"I don't have one," I said.

"Jist a soft car, I guess," Belinda said.

"Have you ever had a wife?" Beverly asked.

"Two," I said.

Jean was watching her daughters interrogate me, amused.

"Can you read stories?" Belinda inquired.

"I guess so," I said. "I can read."

Belinda was off the couch in a flash. We all watched her disappear up the stairs.

"Come on, Beverly," Jean said. "Let's go make dinner. I don't want to hear any of these stories."

Belinda soon returned with six or seven books and I read her a story about a buzzard named Hugo. Far from listening passively, Belinda kept up a running commentary, elaborating on both the pictures and the text. We were in the middle of a story about a frog when Jean interrupted.

"We're reading," Belinda pointed out.

"That man's read you enough stories," Jean said. "Let's eat."

The dinner consisted of *carne asada*, guacamole, and cheese enchiladas.

The dinner was delicious. Jean and I ate heartily, while the girls ate English peas and picked at a cheese enchilada Jean had divided between them.

"Sometimes I think I should take these girls and raise them in Mexico," Jean said.

"You must have lived there," I said.

"I lived there," she said, but didn't say when or with whom.

Evidence of Mexico was everywhere, in the kitchen. The blue tablecloth we were eating on looked Mexican and there was a huge colorful Mexican basket in one corner.

"He could take us to Disney World in the soft car," Belinda suggested, to our surprise.

"She's always looking for action," Jean said.

"You said we could go to Disney World *someday*," Beverly said, throwing her weight behind her sister suddenly.

"This man is a virtual stranger," Jean said. "We can't just demand that he take us to Florida."

Both girls ignored the remark. They had stopped regarding me as a stranger, obviously, and were looking at me as if they expected I might be able to make this glorious possibility come to pass.

Jean was looking at me thoughtfully.

"Two marriages but no kids, huh?" she said.

"No kids," I admitted.

"I have a feeling this is a man who keeps on the move," Jean said, to her daughters.

"So?" Belinda said.

The kitchen was a wonderful room, actually. Besides the Mexican basket it had a huge cheeseboard that looked Greek, a butcher's block made from the knot of a gum tree, a hanging bronze scale that was probably Italian, and a row of wonderfully rough wooden apothecary's bowls, not to mention a

French towel rack and a gaudy ceramic teapot. The girls' crayon drawings adorned the front of the refrigerator. Jean and I drank tea out of big glazed mugs that had come from Finland.

"We just about live in this room," Jean said, blowing on her tea. "We don't really need the rest of the house."

"We need *my* room," Belinda reminded her. "It's got the toys in it."

"Who says we need you?" Jean said.

Belinda giggled at the absurdity of the thought that life could go on without her. Beverly was drawing small ducks on a napkin, holding it up frequently for her mother's inspection.

"I think you're going to be my talented daughter," Jean said.

It was very pleasant to sit in the nice kitchen with Jean and her two daughters. When Jean let her eyes dwell on her girls, I let my eyes dwell on her. Seeing her in her own domain was different from seeing her in the outside world. In the outside world she didn't seem very happy—perhaps because she was small, she didn't seem quite equal to the outside world.

But in her own kitchen she seemed more than equal, both to the world and to me. Listening to the flow of chatter between her and the girls I began to experience absurd but intense guilts. If I had only had the nerve to give Coffee a couple of daughters she might not be drifting around Austin, being beat up by a tiny dope dealer. A daughter might have relieved Kate of her obsession with real estate, or might have made Tanya Todd a little less angry. And if Cindy had a couple of kids she'd at least have to keep something in the refrigerator besides salami and Brie.

For a few minutes, sipping tea, I tried to imagine how the various women I knew would be if they had children, a difficult act of the imagination. The children kept disappearing from the picture, leaving Coffee or Kate or Cindy relatively unaffected.

"Why don't you offer Jack a penny for his thoughts?" Jean suggested, to Beverly.

Beverly shook her head. "I don't know him well enough," she said.

Jean and I sat in the kitchen, drinking more tea, while the girls went up and got ready for bed. In no time they were back, in red bathrobes, looking delightful but not very sleepy. Beverly climbed up in her mother's lap, Belinda in mine.

"What's this?" Jean asked. "How come you're in his lap?"

Belinda shrugged. "Jist am," she said.

"Let's read some more stories," she suggested, looking up at me.

"Let's put you to bed," Jean said. "I'm never going to find out anything about this man with you two around."

"*I'll* find out," Belinda volunteered, looking straight up at me.

"What about you?" she asked.

"Nothing to say," I said.

"He don't got nothing to say," Belinda reported.

"He knows better than to talk to a blabbermouth like you," Jean said. "Are you coming over here or not?"

"Did *you* want to read the stories, Mom?" Belinda inquired.

"Come over here and maybe I'll tell you," Jean said.

Belinda gambled, one of her rare mistakes. All Jean did, once Belinda was in her lap, was steal kisses from the vicinity of her neck. Belinda burst into gales of laughter, subsided into giggles, and then stopped and yawned heartily.

"Are you getting sleepy?" Jean asked.

"No," Belinda said.

In fact, despite herself, Belinda was fading. Once her energy began to go, it drained out of her like water out of a bathtub. When she saw Jean had no intention of reading a story she squirmed out of her lap and struggled back to me, only to lie lifelessly in my lap.

"Jist one story," she said.

"Let's go," Jean said, nodding at me.

I carried Belinda upstairs, following Jean and Beverly. Belinda was as helpless as a windup toy that had just run down. "Jist one story," she repeated faintly. Her eyes were still open, but the force was gone.

She and her sister had tiny adjoining rooms in the small

upstairs. Beverly's was blue, Belinda's yellow. Both were full of dolls and stuffed animals, the stuffed animals mostly being of ancient vintage. Belinda slept with a raggedy beaver that looked to belong to the forties.

Jean bent over and went about getting her out of her robe, a process Belinda didn't assist in any way. When Jean picked her up her head lolled back as if her neck were broken.

"God, you're made of rubber, Belinda," Jean said. "Not very good rubber, either."

"You didn't brush my hair," Belinda protested, faintly.

"Well, you sat in the wrong lap," Jean said. "Live and learn, kid."

"I wanted you to brush my hair," Belinda insisted.

"Nope, your hair's too sleepy," Jean said. "I'll brush it in the morning."

Jean gave her a kiss.

"He didn't give me one," Belinda said, sitting up suddenly. Lack of fair play had briefly restored her.

I gave her a kiss, receiving a hug in return.

"Are you going to take us to Disney World?" she asked, in the midst of the hug.

"Not tonight," I said.

"Okay, but *sometime*," Belinda said.

"I wouldn't make her any promises, if I were you," Jean said. "She has a memory like an elephant."

"Jist do it *some*time," Belinda said, just as her mother turned off the light.

Chapter XIII _____

It was only about 8:30 when we put the girls to bed. By Georgetown standards the evening was just beginning. If I had been dutiful I could still have salvaged Cindy's evening. All I would have had to do was thank Jean, dash back to Cindy's, endure a bit of a fit, and proceed on to the party. We would hardly even be thought late, and Cindy's reputation would be secure.

But an hour and a half later I had made no moves at all toward securing her reputation. I was still sitting in Jean's pleasant kitchen, drinking brandy and soda. Jean had another large mug of tea, but no brandy and soda. I guess she didn't need it because she wasn't nervous. I was very nervous and drank more than I usually drink.

I don't know why I was nervous, because Jean was quite relaxed and merely told me the story of her life—a life so normal its story didn't take long to tell. Her father worked for the Department of Agriculture, which is how she had happened to get to live in Mexico. Other than that, she had always lived in Maryland, not far from where we were at that moment. She had gone to the University of Maryland, married Jimmy when he was a graduate student, had two daughters and various not very interesting jobs, and that was it. For years she had spent all her spare time at flea markets and swap-meets, buying things and sticking whatever wouldn't fit into her house in her parents' garage, which was a few miles away, in Poolsville.

"I've always been a junk junkie," she said. "I don't know if I really want the stuff, or if it's just a good way to pass the time. A little of both, I guess."

"You don't buy junk," I said. "You buy very nice things."

"Oh well," she said, dismissing the compliment. "I've never had any money. I don't think I've ever spent over fifty dollars for anything."

"But you were ready to spend several hundred on the icon," I reminded her.

"It was an act of defiance," she said. "I get a little crazy about objects, sometimes. Also it makes me mad that I never have any money. Jimmy has plenty of money but he's obsessive about not spending it. If I had spent six hundred dollars on an icon while I was married to him he would have cut my throat."

That was surprising. Jimmy hadn't looked rich.

"Oh, he's rich, all right," Jean said. "You'd never guess it

250

from how we lived, though. Jimmy's all screwed up. He has all the attitudes of a rich person but he won't spend money. He wants to be waited on hand and foot and he can usually find some woman that will do it. I even did it for a while, but no more. I'm not waiting on anybody hand and foot again."

She looked at me rather severely, as if she expected that I might reveal myself to be a person who wanted to be waited on.

"The only redeeming thing about Jimmy is that he loves the girls," Jean said. "He's easy to replace as a husband but not so easy to replace as a father. Although even there you can't count on him for the practical stuff, like taking them to the dentist and buying them shoes. But he does love them a lot."

"And he uses them to try and get you back, right?" I said, since I thought I had observed that very tactic being used the day I had seen him.

"Oh, yeah, but he's not getting me back," Jean said. "Jimmy's incapable of learning a new trick, and I'm not susceptible to the old tricks anymore."

She stared off into space when she said it, and then turned her eyes suddenly and caught me looking at her. All evening I had been becoming progressively more impressed with her, and more attracted as well, but at the same time I felt unusually cautious. I had sense enough to know she was not the kind of woman I knew much about. For one thing, she was two years older than me and up to that point I had never had a single girl friend who was older. Besides, Jean had been a mother for five years, and I had never been a father. I had never had a single girl friend who had a child, either. In a way, they and I were the children, our relationships probably not much more serious than a trip to Disney World.

Watching Jean gave me the sense that there were probably reaches of womanhood I hadn't experienced. Jean's world seemed quite modest, but it also seemed to have a density and an intricacy that I wasn't familiar with. It wasn't just the girls, either. It showed itself even in the way the objects in the kitchen had been placed. It wasn't overplanned, but at the same time it was subtle.

"Why are you looking that way?" Jean asked.

"I don't know what way I'm looking," I said.

"Worried, that's how you're looking," she said. "What have you got to be worried about? You seem to be free as the breeze."

"I guess I am," I said.

Jean looked faintly disgusted.

"I guess I have no right to pry," she said. "It was nice of you to come to dinner. In theory I like for the girls to know there are other men in the world besides their father, in case I end up with one. But in practice I never bring anyone home."

"Do you think you'll end up with one?" I asked.

"Oh, sure," Jean said. "I probably will. I could use some help with these girls. It's hard to maintain the kind of enthusiasm it takes to stimulate two kids, if you're just one person. That's why I asked you to dinner. The girls think you're interesting."

She grinned.

"Maybe you are," she said. "But how am I gonna know if you're just gonna sit there drinking brandy and looking worried?"

"Are you divorced already?" I asked.

It sounded like a silly question, and Jean looked slightly disgusted again.

"No, but I've filed," she said. "The hearing's in about a month. Jimmy gave me a lot of trouble. He can't get it through his head that I really want to leave him. His immediate conclusion was that I was insane, since in his view only someone insane could want to leave him. He's got a nice girl friend—or nice enough—but that doesn't seem to affect his thinking. Then when he decided I meant business he got vindictive and did a lot of childish things."

"Like what?"

"Like canceling all the credit cards and taking all the money out of the joint account," she said. "He even changed the lock on the Volvo door, so I couldn't get in and drive it."

"Gosh," I said. "He seemed kinda nice."

"He is nice, except when he's threatened with the loss of a possession," Jean said. "Then he reverts to being a rich child."

She fiddled with her mug, looking at me speculatively.

"He knows all about you," she said.

"What do you mean? We haven't even really met."

"Yeah, but he took your license number, the other day at the store," Jean said. "His family's famous around here, you know. His father has a very important job."

"Doing what?"

"At the CIA," Jean said. "Besides that his family owns a detective agency that does a lot of work for the government. So Jimmy called the family detective agency and told them to find out everything about you."

That was surprising. It was hard to believe that a man with a nice face, overalls, and an old Volvo would simply do things like that.

"What did he find out?" I asked. Actually I was curious to know how my life might look to a total stranger, such as a detective.

"Oh well," Jean said, shrugging. "I don't know why I'm telling you this."

"Tell me anyway."

"Well," she said, "he found out who your girl friend is, and that you just bought a horse farm in Middleburg from one of his father's old rivals."

"I didn't really buy it," I said. "A good detective would have found out right away that I don't have that kind of money."

She nodded. "He told me that, too," she said. "He thinks you're just a front for somebody. Jimmy's very scornful of people who don't really have money. Also, he hated your car."

"Well," I said. "He doesn't have to ride in it."

There was quite a long silence, after that.

"So did you stand her up?" Jean asked. "Is that why you're worried?"

I finished my brandy and took my glass to the sink, to wash it out. It's a finicky habit of mine, which seems to be getting worse. I have a compulsion to wash out my glasses. When I set it on the cabinet I looked down at Jean, who was looking at me with a slightly expectant smile. I didn't know whether she wanted a comment or a kiss. Since I didn't have a comment I leaned over and kissed her, though the kiss was so hesitant that it barely reached her. She quickly put a light hand on my neck. Her hand was warm, from having been holding the tea mug all this time. I was bent over awkwardly, which she seemed to realize, because she too stood up. Even so I was a lot taller than she was.

"The first thing I ever really wanted was stilts," she said, drawing back for a moment.

"You really are worried, aren't you?" she said, leading me out of the kitchen. I assumed we were going up to the bedroom but instead she led me to the couch with the brown lap robe, where, in a very short time, we had managed to make love. I wasn't in a hurry, but Jean was. I think she was in such a hurry that she cheated herself out of an orgasm, but I couldn't be sure.

"No woman likes to be upstaged by her own daughter," she said, by way of comment, afterward. "I shouldn't have drunk so much tea. I could feel it jiggling."

The ends of her short hair were damp with sweat. She stuffed a blue pillow under her head and kept her eyes on the stairway.

"No woman likes to be caught in the act, either," she said. "Particularly if she's got a daughter like Belinda."

Actually we had only managed to get undressed in the most basic areas.

"She's got an instinct for hanky-panky," Jean added. "Only there hasn't been any for so long she may have lost it."

After a bit she went up to the bathroom and came down wearing a blue bathrobe. She was extremely appealing and I grew hopeful of more lovemaking, but Jean seemed rather reserved. She was listening. Some instinct had been awakened. After a bit she tucked her robe about her, very demurely. A moment later Belinda appeared at the foot of the stairs, clutching her beaver.

"You shutted my door," she said to her mother.

"We were thinking of playing some records," Jean said. "We didn't want to wake you up."

Belinda came over and crawled up in her mother's lap. Jean attempted to smooth out a few of her curls, an impossible task.

"Is he spending the night?" Belinda asked.

"Nope," Jean said. "Wanta kick him out?"

Belinda yawned. "Don't care," she said. She buried her face in her mother's bathrobe and was soon asleep.

"Where's the trunk I sold you?" I asked.

Jean reached across Belinda and took my hand. "Why, it's in my bedroom, where all the really super things are," she said.

"I don't guess I'm going to get to see it tonight, am I?"

"I wouldn't think you'd have the time," Jean said, dryly. "You probably ought to be getting back to the lady you stood up."

"I don't think it matters whether I get back or not," I said. "I imagine the damage is done."

"Oh, ho, ho," Jean said. "You underestimate us ladies. We're forgiving creatures. We don't banish a man for five minutes' indiscretion.

"Jimmy said she was engaged," she remarked. "That seemed a little odd."

"Yeah," I said. "Seems that way to me too."

"Well, maybe it isn't," Jean said. "Maybe you just like women who aren't available."

That was such a surprising suggestion that I didn't answer.

"Seeing me with Jimmy might have given you the notion that I wasn't particularly available, either," she said. "Your girl friend's not quite married, and I'm not quite divorced. Maybe that's what attracts you to us."

"It is not," I said. "It could just be something normal, like your eyes, that attracted me to you. You have wonderful eyes."

Jean immediately looked chastened, and moved closer to me. She shifted Belinda so that her feet were in my lap. We kissed for a bit.

"That's a bad thing I do," Jean said. "I posit the abnormal

255

in everything that happens to me, now. I guess there's no reason why you couldn't have a normal attraction, whatever that is. It just doesn't seem to be your pattern."

"I don't really have a pattern," I said. "I just let things happen."

Jean gave me a dig with her elbow. "Well, if you want to see my bedroom you're gonna have to be a little more active," she said. "I've reached the stage where I require gentlemen to earn their privileges."

"Well," I said, "I could take you out to dinner. We could go to a movie."

"Keep talking," Jean said. "You're making progress. I haven't been taken out in so long that the very words sound quaint. Jimmy and I never went out."

"Why not?"

"Because he's too tight to spend money in restaurants," she said. "Buying the girls burgers is about as extravagant as he ever gets. He would never buy anything that wasn't necessary to his pleasure. Magazines, for instance. I think the reason I broke up with him is because he yelled and screamed every time I bought a magazine. I happen to love to read magazines. But Jimmy couldn't see wasting money on something you'd just throw away in a couple of days."

At that point I remembered that I was technically scheduled to leave for New Mexico in the morning. Of course my defection might have turned Cindy against that plan, but if it hadn't, things looked complicated.

I guess the thought of this complication made me frown, because Jean put a hand on my forehead and rubbed gently.

"You just got a crease in your brow," she said.

"Yeah, because I just remembered I was supposed to go to New Mexico in the morning," I said. "It might interfere with my taking you out for about a week."

Jean's look was rather noncommittal.

"We could make a date, though," I said. "I won't be more than ten days. Why don't we make a date for ten days from tonight?"

"What's in New Mexico?" she asked.

I told her all about the boots of Billy the Kid, which fascinated her. Then we kissed some more, over the recumbent, peacefully sleeping Belinda. I thought she might take me upstairs for the night, which would eliminate the problem of New Mexico, but Jean balked.

"Why not?" I said.

"Oh, I don't know," Jean said. "I think I'll just keep you waiting until you take me out. It seems kind of Victorian. It's been about five years since I was taken out. It's funny how the most normal things come to seem the most exotic, if you stop doing them."

"I guess I'm a poor judge of people," I said. "Jimmy looked normal, the one time I saw him."

"Well, he's a charmer," Jean said. "He charms everyone. He even charmed me, once upon a time. Naturally most people think I'm to blame for everything. Even my folks think it, since he's totally charming whenever he gets around them."

"Does that bother you?"

"Sure," she said. "You can't win against charm. The fact that he's intensely selfish, phobically tight, and has had girl friends practically from day one doesn't mean anything. People look at that winning little face of his and two minutes later they're making excuses for him."

Jean leaned over the back of the couch and peeked very cautiously through the blinds.

"I'm sure there's a detective out there somewhere," she said. "Jimmy can't bear to have his curiosity thwarted. He'll spend thousands, if necessary, to find out what's going on."

She draped Belinda over her shoulder and went around peeping out windows, but of course she couldn't see a thing.

"Maybe the detective will follow you all the way to New Mexico," she said, grinning. "Think how much that will cost. Jimmy's going to be furious."

Then she wished me a pleasant trip and kissed me goodnight.

As I was driving through Wheaton I happened to pass a newsstand that was open, so I stopped and bought her sixty dollars worth of magazines. I bought one of practically every magazine they had: fashion magazines, political magazines, movie magazines. I even bought her a surfboarding magazine. Then I tied them in a bundle and went back and left them on her porch, inside her screen door. The house was dark but there was a faint glow from what must have been her bedroom window—the kind of glow made by a TV set. The glow made me wistful. I would have liked to be in bed with Jean, watching TV. I went back and sat in my car for a while, feeling indecisive. Maybe Jean would like it if I knocked. Maybe she was feeling wistful, too. My sudden reappearance might come as a happy surprise.

On the other hand, it might make her mad as hell. Jean hadn't looked wistful at all when she said goodnight. She had looked cheerful and friendly. Now she was probably just lying in bed watching a late movie, not missing me or anyone. I kept sort of hoping the glow would go out, so I would know she was definitely asleep, but it didn't and I finally just drove off, feeling very half and half.

I drove all the way to Washington fantasizing about what might have happened if I had gone back and knocked on Jean's door. In fantasy the gamble was wildly successful and led to a night of passion and coziness in the mysterious bedroom containing the wonderful dower chest. I knew it was only a fantasy, but I kept fantasizing it right up to the moment I let myself in Cindy's door.

Chapter XIV _____

Cindy was sitting in the middle of the bed in her night-gown, surrounded by piles of damp Kleenex. I was prepared for anger, but not for such a picture of devastation. She looked like she had been crying for about six hours. At some point she had run out of Kleenex and had simply let the tears run down the front of her nightgown, which was soaked. Her tear ducts were evidently just as healthy as the rest of her, but she had finally emptied them and was just sitting blankly when I walked in. When she heard me she looked around and cringed, as if she were a dog who had just been beaten and was about to be beaten again.

"What's the matter?" I asked, aware that the question was inadequate. I couldn't think of any other way to start.

"I've never been treated like this before," she said, in an exhausted little voice very unlike the voice she normally used.

I sat down on the bed and put my arm around her, which she accepted passively. She had several damp Kleenex wadded in one hand and I made her let me have them so I could throw them in the wastebasket. My first project was to clear the bed of damp Kleenex.

"Gosh," I said. "I'm really sorry. It was just one party. I had no idea you'd be this upset."

"Were you with another woman?" she asked, looking up at me. The skin around her eyes was puffy, but it didn't stop her from asking the right question. Instinctively, in about a tenth of a second, I lined up all the lies I might tell her, but then I didn't use any of them. It's difficult to lie to a person who has just been humbled to the degree Cindy had. Lying to her strength was easier than lying to her hopelessness.

"Yeah," I said.

She didn't seem surprised or any more hurt. Her brain had figured it out anyway and confirmation may have been a small relief.

"I've never been rejected before," she said. "Not in my whole life."

"I'm not rejecting you," I said. "I was just asked to dinner by a lady who owns an antique shop, so I went."

"You planned it in advance and you didn't tell me," she said.

"Well," I said, "I didn't know Lilah was going to throw a party."

I was well aware that my response did not exactly dovetail with her accusation.

"I bet you fucked her, too," she said numbly.

I just nodded.

"She's probably just some little hippie that sells junk," Cindy said.

Her statement had practically no energy in it. I saw no point in trying to explain that Jean was a nice woman. The notion that I had been sleeping with a hippie seemed to provide a modicum of comfort. An excess of truth needn't be rushed, it seemed to me. Truth can be counted on to arrive under its own power, where women are concerned.

"Now I don't know what to do," Cindy said. A minute later she got up, went to the bathroom, washed her face, and gave her teeth their usual careful brushing.

I considered that a good sign. Though devastated, she was not so far gone as to neglect her teeth. For Cindy to have gone to bed without brushing her teeth would be an indication of profound despair. She did not neglect to use dental floss. When she realized her nightgown was soaked at the neck she took it off and put it neatly into her clothes hamper.

Then she rummaged around in a drawer and found a huge T-shirt, which she put on.

"I got it from Maurice," she said. Maurice had been the NBA guard.

I watched her warily, expecting that as her generally healthy instincts slowly reasserted themselves anger would suddenly make its appearance. I expected it to strike with hurricane force, whenever it struck, and I wanted to give myself at least an even chance.

But Cindy came meekly back to bed. "You ought to go brush your teeth," she said, as if we were getting into bed on a normal night.

When I got in bed she immediately took my hand.

"I wish you hadn't done this to me," she said. "Is she a hippie or what?"

"No," I said. "She's a nice woman with two little girls."

"You couldn't have picked a worse time," she said. "I saw Spud this afternoon."

Although I had sensed that Spud was in our future, I hadn't expected him to check in quite so soon.

"What do you mean 'saw' him?" I asked. "Are you telling me you slept with him?"

"Don't be so mean," Cindy said. "I thought you were kind, only now everything you do is mean."

I hadn't meant to sound mean. It was more surprise than anger that had prompted the question. I had been feeling very guilty—illogically—and now the illogical basis of my guilt was starkly exposed. Cindy had had Spud, and I had had Jean. We had betrayed one another almost simultaneously, although since our own relationship was sort of accidental and our feelings undeclared betrayal might seem too strong a word.

On the other hand I felt betrayed, not to mention confused. Why had she cried for six hours because she suspected I was with another woman if she had just started an affair with another man?

The longer I thought about it, the more confused I felt. I couldn't even think of what questions to ask. Neither could Cindy, evidently. We were both locked in silence. It was strange to feel both guilty and abused at the same time. In a sense I ought to have welcomed Spud's interest in Cindy, since my interest in Jean had risen so rapidly. On the other hand, my interest in Cindy hadn't really sunk.

In a little while the wistfulness I had felt when I was waiting indecisively outside Jean's house came back and transferred itself to Cindy. I had a sort of innocent wish that we could just cancel the day and be as we had been the day before. The feeling got so strong that I turned to Cindy and tried to kiss her. She turned gratefully toward me, perhaps with the same need, but the kiss proceeded to die. Instead of a rising of the blood all we came up with was friendly puzzlement. We were just sort of bumping mouths in our confusion.

By mutual agreement we gave up on the kiss.

"I thought you'd want to talk," Cindy said.

"I do," I said. "But you said I was mean when I didn't have a mean intention."

"Couldn't you be more patient?" she asked. "I just said it because you scared me."

"So what about Spud?" I said.

"Don't berate me," Cindy said.

I had spoken as mildly as I knew how. I didn't know what to make of things at all. What had happened to the big, confident social climber? She had been there that morning, but all that was left was a healthy body.

"I'm just asking," I said, in my gentlest voice. "I don't have the right to berate you."

"That's right," Cindy said, as if the thought surprised her. "I shouldn't let you get away with it."

"But I'm not *doing* it," I insisted. "There's no question of getting away with it."

Cindy fell silent again, evidently discouraged by the conversation, which I also found peculiarly discouraging. Our attempts to talk were just as inept as our attempt to kiss.

"Just talk about Spud," I said. "I'm not judging you. You're free. Just talk about him a little."

Cindy sighed. "He's a lot sexier than you but he scares me," she said.

That hadn't been exactly what I had been expecting to hear.

"Where does Harris fit into all this?" I asked.

"He doesn't fit in at all," Cindy said. "That's the nice thing about having Harris as a fiancé. Harris is really sweet. I wish you didn't have such a problem about him."

It was nothing to the problem I was about to have with Spud, but I didn't tell her that.

"Does that woman have big tits?" Cindy asked.

I did not see Jean's breasts, but I knew they weren't large.

"No," I said. "She's a small woman."

"That's one good thing," Cindy said.

"Why does Spud scare you?" I asked.

Cindy thought for a while. "Spud's very successful," she said. "He's about as successful as anyone gets around here. I don't think he has much time for me.

"It was his secretary that called me," she added. "I guess he doesn't call people himself."

"I'm surprised he even fucks them himself," I said, bitterly. I had been worried about Spud all along, although all along only amounted to one day.

"He does, though," Cindy said. "That's the problem. Now I feel like doing anything he tells me to."

"I don't see why it's a problem," I said. "You don't owe me anything. You can do anything you want to do."

Then she began to cry again, sobbing hard and gasping for breath. I put my arms around her and she cried on my chest. It was a hard cry, but finally it ended.

"Oh, I hate being confused," she said. "I've never been this confused. If you'd just come home when you were supposed to and not gone and fucked that woman things would be a lot better."

"Maybe I secretly knew what you were doing with Spud," I suggested. "Maybe I was secretly just sort of staying even."

The statement was total bullshit, but it gave Cindy something new to think about. She sat up in bed and wiped the tears off her face with the bottom of the long T-shirt.

"Okay," she said. "I can accept that if you'll just promise not to see her again. I can't stand being rejected."

"Are you going to stop seeing Spud?" I asked.

Cindy looked shocked. "Why would I stop seeing him?" she asked. "I've never had sex that good before. I could still feel it two hours later, while I was at the shop."

"Oh," I said. "Then what am I supposed to do?"

"Be my best friend," she said. "I told you he made me feel scared. Anyway, he won't leave his wife."

"This is getting pretty odd," I said.

"I know," she said, "but it's just the way things are now. Actually I like a lot of things about you. If you were my best friend I'd probably be all right."

"Am I ever supposed to get to fuck anybody?" I asked.

She was silent for a while. "I just don't want to think about that right now," she said. "I feel rejected enough."

"Are you sleepy?" I asked.

"No," she said. "I'm wide-awake."

So was I—zingy with wakefulness, in fact.

"Do you want to just head for New Mexico?" I asked. "We were going in the morning, anyway."

Cindy looked surprised. "Oh yeah," she said. "We were going to get those boots. You really want to go right now?"

"I don't see any reason not to," I said.

"I guess there isn't any reason not to," Cindy said. She switched on the bedlight. The thought that there was no reason not to leave seemed to strike her as sad.

"I don't know, Jack," she said, looking at me. "You didn't even promise not to see that hippie again."

It was true. I had evaded the issue.

"It's too complicated to talk about right now," I said. "Let's just go."

Cindy was a supremely quick packer. In fifteen minutes we were in the car and across the Potomac. It was a clear night. The Washington monument shone very white as we crossed the river. Cindy was lost in thought. In twenty minutes Washington was behind us. We passed the dark Manassas battlefield. Cindy's worries were soon absorbed by her healthy body—she slumped against the door of the Cadillac, peacefully asleep, as I drove on toward the west.

Chapter XV _____

Two hours later, as I was crossing the Blue Ridge in a heavy white ground fog, Cindy got tired of sleeping against the door. She curled up in the seat, her cheek against my thigh, and reached for my hand. But holding hands was difficult, since I kept changing hands to drive, so eventually she stuffed one hand under my crotch, in a way that evidently made her feel safe.

I just drove. Soon I hit I–81 and had to contend with small convoys of trucks. Time sped as I sped. In Christiansburg I stopped and got gas and when I came back to the car Cindy was sitting up, looking as blank and puzzled as a sleepy child. I doubt she had the slightest idea what she was doing out in the middle of America, in the middle of the night. I asked her three times if she needed to go to the bathroom, but she didn't say a word. The minute we left the station she curled up again and stuffed her hand back under my crotch.

Despite a lot of experience, I am always underestimating the vast resources of doubt and insecurity that can lurk beneath the surface of even the most vibrant women. I had just done it with Cindy, and when I tried to think of what I might do to bring her confidence back my mind went blank. I just drove, conducting a quiet *mano* with the streams of trucks. I zipped along at a steady ninety, passing them in bunches. Once I got to Tennessee, where the cops are more tolerant, I upped it to ninety-five, shooting past the trucks so fast that the truckers hardly even had time to get annoyed.

As the sun was coming up I pulled into a gas station in Nashville. More than eight hours had passed, and yet I had no sense of having been gone from Washington more than a few minutes.

During the last eighty miles or so, Cindy had shown signs of restlessness.

"Jesus, I need to pee," she said, sitting up suddenly and looking with no comprehension at the Nashville skyline.

I had noticed already, in my few nights with her, that she had the rare ability to wake up looking perfect, or as close to perfect as human flesh can get. When she stepped out of the Cadillac and strolled across the dirty concrete to the john, the two sleepy, cynical gas station attendants, used to an all-night stream of argumentative travelers from Michigan, New York, and California, stopped moving and looked at her with open wonder, as if a true American Venus had stepped out of my pearl-shell Cadillac.

When she emerged, having done no more than splash a little water on her face, they practically stood at attention. She was wearing a T-shirt, jeans, and sandals, and she looked wonderful. The two guys would have probably given us the gas if Cindy had asked for it, but in fact she got back in the car without even noticing them.

"Jesus, this place is ugly," she said, looking around her. It was true. A strong wind was blowing and Nashville looked particularly gritty. Little waves of dust sailed down the empty streets.

Cindy stared at the town in surprise, faintly indignant that she had been exposed to such ugliness so early in the morning. It's not easy for people brought up in Santa Barbara to accustom themselves to the rest of America.

"Yuk," she said, as we sped out of town. For a time that was all she said.

I knew an excellent little country café, about an hour down the road, and since we were both starving we stopped and ate huge breakfasts. Everyone in the café, male and female alike, stared at Cindy the whole time we were eating. The café was full of truckers, mechanics, and local farmers trying to put off having to go out and farm—none of them had probably ever seen a woman as beautiful as Cindy.

The troubles of the day before had somehow settled in in such a way as to raise her beauty a dimension. Riding through the night in a state of emotional collapse would have made most women look sort of blasted, but Cindy had awakened from it so surpassingly beautiful that it was quite understandable that people stared. The traumas had added an element of gravity that she had previously lacked. It overlay her normal energy and health, which of course were still abundant. Three or four truckers at the counter were as stricken by her beauty as the filling station attendants. They kept turning cautiously on their stools, toothpicks in their mouths, to stare at her.

Also, she wore no bra. Though her breasts were smallish, she had prominent nipples, and bra-less women with prominent nipples were not an everyday sight in central Tennessee. The men stared openly, except for two or three who were with women. The best those could do was cast an occasional glance.

"How many states before New Mexico?" Cindy asked, when we were on the road again. Her knowledge of the geography of mid-America was minimal.

At the café we had bought both the Nashville and Memphis papers, and Cindy was indignant that neither of them contained a thing that she considered news. The front-page story in both papers was about a bizarre incident in which a Tennessee farmer had gone berserk and tried to drive his tractor into the local courthouse, in order to run over a county agent he didn't like. The county agent had escaped, but the tractor had got stuck in the door of the courthouse so firmly that no one could figure how to get it out without pulling down the courthouse.

It seemed like a funny story to me, but Cindy was annoyed that such trivia would be given front-page space. There was nothing more relevant to the world situation in either paper. The one syndicated gossip column contained gossip that Cindy had known for weeks, which just increased her indignation.

"I wish you'd stop in the next town, so I can get the *Times* and the *Post*," she said.

"They don't get the *Times* in the next town," I said. The next town was Cuba Landing, Tennessee. "You'll be lucky if we can find one in Memphis."

Actually we did find one in Memphis, but only because I had the forethought to whip by the airport. Cindy had scarcely said a word since breakfast. She was looking out the window rather hostilely, and it seemed to me resentment might be building. After all, I was the one who had brought her to a place where *The New York Times* wasn't sold.

Finding one at the Memphis airport was a big relief. I could barely get Cindy to stop reading it long enough to glance at the Mississippi River. The Father of Waters made little impression on her. She read the *Times* through most of Arkansas, obviously reading slower than usual in order to make the news last. An occasional glance at the dreary Arkansas flats probably convinced her she'd be lucky ever to see another copy of *The New York Times*.

West of Little Rock I began to tire. I had driven a thousand miles, not an exceptional drive for me, but long enough. Also, there was the factor of Cindy. The fact that she was along, and feeling resentful, affected my mental pacing. Although she had not spoken fifty words, her presence took a certain amount of dealing with.

"You want to drive?" I asked.

"You could have asked me sooner," she replied.

Before she had driven twenty miles I dozed off, only to be awakened by the sound of a siren. It felt like I had only slept a few minutes, but when I looked out the window I saw that we were in Oklahoma. The grass had changed.

A big, shy young cop was standing by Cindy's window with a ticket book in his hand, but he didn't seem to be saying anything. Apparently the sight of Cindy had struck him dumb with awe.

The fact that Cindy had inspired the awe did not mean that she was prepared to be tolerant of it.

"So what's the deal?" she asked. "Was I going too fast, or what?"

"Uh, yes ma'am," the cop said. "You were runnin' along there at about ninety-seven m.p.h."

Cindy said nothing.

"Yes ma'am, you were kinda speedin' along there," the cop said, sighing heavily. A consciousness of his professional duty obviously weighed heavily upon him at that moment.

"Well, I had the radio on," Cindy said, by way of explanation.

"Aw yeah," the cop said, as if he had been offered a sufficient excuse.

"Anyway, I didn't hit anybody," Cindy pointed out.

The patrolman agreed that that, too, was the truth. Then, unable to think of a next move, he just stood and looked. Cindy didn't pander to the look—she neither smiled nor made excuses. But she was so beautiful that the young cop had probably already forgotten that she had been going ninety-seven. He may even have forgotten that he was a patrolman. He hadn't so much as asked to see her driver's license. He just stood and looked.

"Listen, we have to get to New Mexico today," Cindy said. "Could we just go?"

"Oh, you sure can," the cop said. " 'Preciate it if you could just take it a little slower."

"Okay, thanks," Cindy said, immediately pushing the button that raised the window. She was off so quick that gravel splattered against the officer's pants leg. It did not affect his decision to exercise leniency. He just stood there watching us go, as transfixed as the gas station attendants in Nashville.

Once we were safely off Cindy gave me a lovely how-about-that smile, quite aware that her beauty and nothing else had spared us a trip to the Muskogee courthouse.

"I like this," she said. "I've never driven a hundred miles an hour before."

When I woke again we were well past Oklahoma City, bearing down on the Texas Panhandle. Cindy didn't offer to surrender the wheel—she didn't even acknowledge my waking. She was on a little driving high of her own, keeping her foot down and letting the Cadillac eat up the road. We were far beyond the trees now, on the high plains. There was nothing between us and New Mexico but road and sky. The sun had just gone down and the plains were shadowed and somber, with vapor lights just beginning to wink on in the yards of ranch houses. Far to the south a patch of yellow light indicated a small town.

"Getting tired?" I asked.

"No," Cindy said. "I like this. I want to drive all night."

"It won't take all night," I said. "We're almost there."

"I ought to go visit my folks sometime," Cindy said. "They won't leave California."

"Why not?"

"Because they like California," she said, as if it were a stupid question.

"I'd like to meet them," I said.

But Cindy was interested in driving, not talking. However, she proved to have one thing in common with Belinda, namely a tendency to the quick fade. I noticed the fade just as it began and got her to stop at a motel on the west edge of Amarillo. She had become sleepy so suddenly that she went to sleep at the wheel while I was registering at the motel. The minute we got in the room she fell on the bed in a deep sleep, without even having brushed her teeth. I ordered myself a steak from room service and watched a little TV over her sleeping form.

Just as the steak came a call of nature woke her. She went to the bathroom, brushed her teeth thoroughly, and came back to the bedroom just as I was about to eat my steak.

"Can I have a bite?" she asked, and proceeded to eat the whole steak, fat, gristle, and all, plus the rolls and most of the salad I had ordered.

"Didn't you even order any milk?" was her only comment. I ordered some, as well as another steak. I told them to rush the milk, so Cindy could drink it before she went back to sleep. In a sense she wasn't really awake, she was just stoking her body after a long day's drive. Long before the second steak came she was in bed in her T-shirt, sleeping soundly.

When I awoke the next morning she was watching me solemnly, so solemnly that it made me a little nervous.

"Hi," I said, since she was watching me.

"Did you try anything last night?" she asked.

"No," I said. "You went right to sleep."

"I still thought you'd try," she said.

"I don't know why I came on this stupid trip," she added, looking miserable. "I think you're in love with that hippie."

"The trip is to get boots for your exhibition," I said. "It's not stupid at all. This is where the boots are."

"What's the point, if you're not even gonna try anymore?" Cindy asked. It was clear she was in the grip of a major attack of insecurity. I got her to turn her head so I could kiss her. I didn't expect matters to go very far, but Cindy was interested. I hadn't really expected to get to make love to her again, and the fact that I got to filled me with relief. I became very enthusiastic, but Cindy didn't, particularly. She had encouraged the lovemaking, but she herself was in neutral. I figured that had to change soon—Cindy was too selfish to cheat herself out of a nice early morning orgasm—but I was wrong. I had one and she didn't, which immediately depressed me.

"I don't understand you," I said. "I guess this *is* a stupid trip."

"I don't see why you always want to argue," she said. "I'm starving. If you ate a good breakfast you might feel better."

We got up and showered together. Cindy had a little rubber

thing with prongs that she used to massage her scalp. After she had massaged hers she massaged mine, assuring me that my hair would be grateful. She used a lot of shampoo—streams of foam coursed down our bodies. She was apparently in an excellent humor, whereas I was in a real depression. My emotional life was becoming ever more surreal, and it had always been surreal enough. So far as Cindy was concerned, we were perfect pals. I was even a pal with sexual privileges, perhaps even sexual responsibilities. She didn't want me not to try, nor did she really want me to succeed.

Meanwhile, she was hungry. The only shadow on the morning was that the newspaper dispensers outside the coffee shop did not dispense *The New York Times*. The best she could do was *The Wall Street Journal*. While she made her way through the *Journal* she consumed two eggs, a breakfast steak, and several glasses of milk. I was eating pancakes with syrup and butter.

"No wonder you're so grumpy, if you eat stuff like that," she said. "Your body needs protein."

"I don't believe in protein," I said. "I think it's a myth, like vitamins. I don't believe in nutrition, in fact. I think it's all a myth."

Cindy greeted that little outburst with silent contempt, finishing her steak. She put on her sunglasses and insisted on driving. The sunglasses made her seem doubly inscrutable, but I could tell from her mouth that she was rather happy. We sped south, over the Staked Plains, and in not very long were in Clovis, New Mexico, with Fort Sumner the next stop down the road. As we were passing out of Clovis Cindy used the car phone to check her service.

"Are you sure?" she asked, with a slight frown. Then she hung up. I felt better immediately. Spud hadn't called.

Cindy reached over and took my hand.

"Are you sure that woman isn't a hippie?" she asked.

"She's not a hippie."

"Why'd she leave her husband?" she asked.

"How come you're so interested?"

"Don't berate me," she said. "Just answer my question."

"Her husband was a spoiled rich boy," I said.

She thought that one over for a while.

"That's good," she said. "He'll probably get her back."

"I doubt it," I said.

"He probably will," Cindy said. "It's harder to leave a rich person."

"Is that your philosophy of life?" I asked.

She didn't answer, but she kept holding my hand. It was a beautiful day, with high fleecy clouds racing over New Mexico. It all seemed to be strange preparation for a visit to Uncle Ike Spettle.

"It's a good thing we left town," Cindy said.

She didn't elaborate, and I didn't answer.

Book V

Chapter I ―――――――

It was just past midday when we pulled into Fort Sumner, passing a big antique shop that functioned as a kind of home-made Billy the Kid museum. We stopped at a little café on the main street and ate lunch. Cindy consumed her third steak in less than twelve hours.

"That's your third steak in twelve hours," I pointed out.

"So what?" she said. "Did you expect me to ask them for veal niçoise?" She was slightly belligerent, in her insecurity.

The waitress at the café was named Myrtle. I knew her slightly, from past visits. She was a big rawboned woman who took life lightly. This last was an uncommon trait in eastern New Mexico, at least in my experience.

"Seen Uncle Ike today?" I asked, when Myrtle brought up two orders of peach cobbler and a little pitcher of cream to pour on them.

"Yeah, he come in and gummed on a doughnut awhile," she said. "I don't see what keeps the pore old sucker from starvin' to death. He hasn't had a tooth in his head since 1956 and he won't wear his dentures 'less he's on the TV."

"What sort of mood's he in?" I asked.

"Bad," Myrtle said. "Hoot's been beating him at dominoes, day after day. Uncle Ike ain't won in two weeks. Losing always makes him feisty. He peed in the street three times last week—I don't know what we're gonna do with the old sucker."

As we were about to cross the street to the little domino parlor where Uncle Ike spent his days we heard my car phone ring.

"Answer it," Cindy said. "It might be my service."

I didn't think it was her service, and I was right. It was Coffee.

"Where are you?" she said. "You never call me anymore."

"I'm in New Mexico," I said. "I'm very busy but I'll call you a little later."

Cindy was standing two inches away, listening to every word.

"I'm very disappointed in you, Jack," Coffee said. "You used to call."

"Well, I'm very busy," I said.

"Oh, you always are, now," Coffee said, with a heartbreaking little crack in her voice. "You used to treat me with kind respect, but now you treat me awful."

I wanted to deny that I treated her awful, I wanted to tell her I'd come and see her, I wanted to ask her why she sounded so unhappy, but I didn't want to do any of those things with Cindy two inches away, waiting with palpable annoyance for me to get off the phone.

"I'm just trying to make a big buy," I said. "I'll call you when I can."

Coffee sighed. She put her whole strange little heart into the sigh.

"I thought I could count on you," she said. "I thought you'd be the one who was always nice."

I was beginning to think it was time to get rid of the car phone. It was bringing me nothing but awkwardness.

"Coffee, will you just wait," I said. "I'll call you when I can. It's not the end of the world."

"How would you know?" she said. "It might be."

Then she hung up.

"Why do you let her call you if you're divorced?" Cindy asked immediately. As we crossed the street she put her sunglasses back on, a signal that she was very annoyed. Two cowboys in a pickup stared at her as they went by, and then made a U-turn in order to come back by and stare at her again.

"The fact that you've divorced somebody doesn't mean you stop knowing them," I pointed out.

"It would if I did it," Cindy said with finality.

After the windy brightness of the street the little domino

parlor was cool, dim, and dark. Only three people were in it: Uncle Ike, a man named Hoot who looked older than Uncle Ike but was thirty-five years younger, and a man they called Junior, who might have been in his late sixties. They were concentrating hard on their play and we did nothing to disturb them until Hoot started to shuffle the dominoes.

"You're a goddamn cheater," Uncle Ike said, addressing Hoot. "That's how come you're winning."

"I'm smart is how come I'm winnin'," Hoot said.

"Well, I've known a lot of smart men that was domino cheats," Uncle Ike said. Of the three he looked much the most alert, and was also the most spiffily dressed. He had taken long ago to wearing a clean white shirt every day, and to polishing his boots once a week, just in case a TV crew from Clovis or Albuquerque happened to wander in hoping to get a few shots of him on his home ground. His shirt was starched to such a crispness that it crackled when he moved his dominoes. In contrast, both Hoot and Junior were dressed in dirty khakis. They both wore oily dozer caps, whereas Uncle Ike had on a neat, small-brimmed Stetson.

Uncle Ike had originally been of a fair complexion, but 110 years in the wind and sun of New Mexico had gradually freckled him to an unusual degree. He consisted of layer upon layer of freckles, overlapped and interwoven into a mosaic so thick that he seemed actually to be brown, rather than fair. What was left of his hair was snow white. When we came in his teeth were out, resting beside his elbow on the domino table.

"It's Jack," Hoot said, recognizing me. "I guess he finally got marrit."

Uncle Ike swiveled around at once to inspect my wife, and took a good long look at Cindy. His blue eyes had not lost any of their keenness. He looked mostly at her nipples, which were puckered from our walk across the cold street. He snapped his gums a few times, reflectively.

"Air you his wife?" he asked Cindy.

"Un-uh," Cindy said, not very impressed with the domino parlor or the three men in it.

"I guess you're from Hollywood then," Uncle Ike said.

"Wanta make a motion picture about me? It wouldn't be the first chanct I've had to be in a motion picture."

"Howdy, Uncle Ike," I said. "You're looking feisty."

"He peed in the street three times last week," Hoot remarked. "They're gonna put him away if he keeps that up."

"Who's gonna do the puttin'?" Uncle Ike asked belligerently. "I doubt they'll send in the National Guard just because I took a piss."

"If that fat deputy ever gets the cuffs on you they won't need no National Guard," Junior remarked.

The threat of arrest did not seriously interest Uncle Ike. He had not yet taken his little blue eyes off Cindy's nipples.

"How much is she gonna pay me to be in the motion picture?" he asked, addressing me. "If it's just a talk show I ain't interested. Get enough talk show business right around here."

"She's not from Hollywood," I said.

Uncle Ike worked his gums several times.

"Air you a libber?" Uncle Ike said. Cindy had definitely caught his interest.

Cindy didn't reply. She was waiting for me to begin negotiations for the boots, that and nothing more.

"You'll be right at home around here, if you're a libber," Uncle Ike said.

"Yeah, Myrtle's a libber," Hoot said.

"She's always been sassy," Uncle Ike said. "That woman's sassed me about enough."

"She may sass you some more, before she's through," Junior said.

"Somebody ought to take and break a bed slat over that woman's noggin," Uncle Ike remarked.

"I wish you'd hurry up," Cindy said, to me.

"This lady's got an art gallery," I said. "It's in Washington, D.C. She's gonna put on a big exhibition of cowboy boots in about a month. We thought maybe you'd loan us the Kid's boots for a week or two, if we made it worth your while."

"Okay," Uncle Ike said, without a moment's hesitation, surprising us all.

"I guess he's finally gone round the bend, Junior," Hoot said.

Though surprised, I was not immediately euphoric. From the way Uncle Ike was staring at Cindy I knew he had something up his sleeve.

"Well, great," I said. "It's just like we'll be renting them for about a month. How much do you want?"

"I always did want to go to Washington, D.C.," Uncle Ike said. "Hell, ol' Geronimo got to go. All them old mangy Indian chiefs got to go."

"A hunnert and ten and all he wants to do is travel," Hoot said.

"Whose else boots was you gonna get for your show?" Uncle Ike inquired.

"Well, maybe Pancho Villa's," I said.

"I never cared for Mexican boots," Uncle Ike said.

He snapped his gums a few times.

"You can rent them boots for five hunnert a month," he said. "But where they go I go. You gotta rent me with 'em. I'll cost you another five hunnert plus expenses. And the hotel room better have color TV."

"He's hopin' for one of them dirty movie channels," Hoot said. "They got 'em in Albuquerque now."

It was an unexpected turn of events. Uncle Ike wanted to go to Washington.

"Why should a goddamn mangy Indian get to go someplace I ain't been?" he asked. Evidently he had been brooding about the matter for seventy-five or eighty years.

"I guess we could manage that," I said. Cindy was inscrutable, behind her dark glasses.

"If you see the President tell him to cut out this socialism," Hoot said.

"Well, I might not get asked to the White House," Uncle Ike said. "I ain't no Indian chief."

"Aren't we even gonna see the boots?" Cindy asked.

There was silence for a moment.

"She's got a mind of her own, ain't she?" Uncle Ike said. "You best take a bed slat to her before she takes one to you."

I knew the boots were in a bank vault in Clovis.

"We do have to go right back through Clovis," I said. "Maybe we could just stop and look at the boots."

"I'll take the five hunnert for the boots in advance," Uncle Ike said. "And I ain't gonna do but one talk show a day. Too many talk shows fog up my system."

His system looked clear as crystal to me. He had scarcely taken his eyes off Cindy the whole time. I tried to get him to discuss a few details but he was mainly interested in staring at Cindy's nipples.

"I guess you're one of them bra-burnin' libbers," he remarked. Then he put his teeth in, called his banker, and arranged for us to look at the boots. We agreed to send him a plane ticket Albuquerque–to–Washington once the exhibition date was set.

"Don't forget about the color TV," he said, as we turned to walk back to the car.

Chapter II _____

On the way back to Clovis the car phone rang. I was reluctant to pick it up, fearing it would just be Coffee again, but Cindy insisted so I did. In fact it was her service, informing her that Spud Breyfogle had called and wanted her to meet him in Miami the next day.

Cindy instantly became so nervous she all but broke out in a rash. She began to scratch her hair, although her hair had been thoroughly washed just a few hours earlier. Spud had made a reservation for her at the Fontainebleau. By the time we drove into Clovis, Cindy had lost all interest in seeing the boots we had come so far to see. She had begun to scratch under her arms. She was really nervous.

"Why Miami?" I asked, a little nervous, too.

"I don't see that it's any of your business," she said. "I hope there's an airport around here somewhere."

Actually there was one in Lubbock, which was not too far,

but it turned out to be impossible for us to make any flights that would get her to Miami that day.

This frustration was almost more than she could bear. She kept the phone tied up for fifty miles, trying to find an air route that would get her to Florida sometime that night.

"I don't see what's the hurry," I said. "He isn't coming till tomorrow. You can easily get there in the morning."

Cindy glared at me. "He wants me to be there when he arrives," she said. "My service said so. It's your fault I'm here, anyway. Normally I'd be in Washington and I could get there tonight."

As we were rushing across the plains a norther struck, so strong that by the time we reached Lubbock we could barely see for the blowing sand. In Lubbock this is no big deal—the town is usually knee-deep in sand anyway—but it played havoc with Cindy's very tentative schedule, since the flight that was to have taken her to Dallas was canceled. Sand beat against the windows of the Cadillac, and swirled in waves down the flat streets. Cindy couldn't believe it. She had never seen a real sandstorm and she seemed to feel I had conjured it up just to prevent her reaching Spud.

"Why would you do this?" she asked.

"I didn't do anything," I said. "I can't make a sandstorm happen."

"Yeah, but you're glad," she said. "You're already trying to make Spud mad at me. You're terrible when you're jealous, do you know that?"

"I guess we better try and find a motel," I said.

Cindy was scratching her armpit. She was still pretty nervous. She looked at me suspiciously. Then she looked out the window at the rivulets of sand, flowing endlessly off the hundreds of miles of plowed cropland that surround Lubbock. The sand blotted out the lower sky. The streetlights had been turned on and shone a weak yellow against the brown sky.

"Just make sure our room has two beds," Cindy said.

I got a room with two vast beds. Emotional tension had exhausted both of us. I lay on one bed, Cindy on another.

281

When we roused ourselves and fought our way through the sand to the motel restaurant I was too tired to eat, but Cindy rapidly consumed her fourth steak. I offered her my steak too but she only took my baked potato.

"At least you can't accuse me of denying you protein," I said. "That's four steaks."

"I wish you'd stop counting," she said. "I hate people who count."

After dinner we went back to our room and lay nervously on our two beds, fully clothed. There was a Don Knotts movie on TV. It was idiotic but it was better than total silence. Cindy's plane left at eight in the morning, which seemed a long time away.

"What are you going to do after I go?" she asked.

"I don't know," I said. "The only collector I know here collects bumper stickers and I don't need to see him."

The bumper sticker collector was named Hank Rink. He worked in a shoe store downtown and spent his vacations poking around in auto junkyards all over the south and southwest, looking for early bumper stickers. Sometimes when he found one he floated it off, but often it was easier just to buy the bumper with the sticker still on it. Hank's garage was so full of bumpers he couldn't get his car in it anymore, but he had some wonderful bumper stickers, including four or five from the thirties, the incunabular period for bumper stickers.

However, in her present mood, I didn't think that Cindy would appreciate hearing much about Hank Rink, and I was right.

"I don't want to hear about any of those nuts," she said. "Are you going to see your wife?"

"I don't have a wife."

"You might as well," she said. "She calls you all the time."

I didn't answer. When we stopped talking we could hear the sand beating like fine birdshot against the windows.

"This is an awful place," Cindy said, in a weak voice. "I think it's the worst place I've ever been."

Then I heard a strange sound and looked over and saw that

she was crying. She lay flat on her back, fists clenched, tears rolling out of her eyes. At the same time she was trying to stop crying by sniffing the tears back, which wasn't working. I went over and put my arms around her, which she accepted gratefully. She pressed her face into my shoulder, crying so hard that it was as if I had a faucet running on my arm. Finally her crying slowed and she was able to catch her breath.

"Oh, I wish I'd never done it," she said.

"Never done what?"

"Fucked Spud," she said. "I didn't know he would frighten me so much. I should have just stayed with you, even if you aren't very sexy."

"Well, you still can," I said.

She shook her head.

"Why can't you?"

"Because he's got me," she said.

She lay quietly for a while, hugging my arm.

"I don't trust you very much but at least I'm not scared of you," she said. "I did trust you until you met that hippie. You should have told me your wife still calls you."

There was no more talk of separate beds. Cindy clung to me all night. She didn't allow an inch of space between us. We had arranged for a wake-up call two hours before her flight, although the airport was just a few minutes away. She didn't want to take any chances. But we didn't really need the wake-up call. Both of us woke up an hour before it was due, meaning we had three long hours to get through, somehow. Cindy started scratching the minute she woke up.

"I hate this," she said. "I never felt like this in my life. Usually I enjoy guys."

My own most fervent hope was that the hand of the clock would move faster. It seemed to have been about two weeks since we got the news that she was going to Miami.

"You didn't try anything last night, while I was asleep, did you?" she asked, after a bit.

"No," I said.

"I wish you were more understanding," she said. "I

thought you were, at first, but now you've just totally stopped trying anything."

"What good would it have done me to try?" I asked. "You were worried stiff about Spud. You still are."

"Yeah, but I notice things," she said. "I'd notice if you tried. You don't seem to understand that little things make a difference."

"It's not such a little thing," I said. "I would try, except I'm depressed that you're going to see Spud."

"The other day you acted like you couldn't get enough of me," she said. "That day we fucked so much, remember?"

"Sure," I said. "That was before you decided I wasn't sexy."

"I didn't *decide* it," she insisted. "After I fucked Spud I just *realized* it."

"Why would you want me to try anything if I'm not sexy?" I said. I had been saving that question for a while.

"It would reassure me," Cindy said. "It reassured me yesterday."

"That's funny," I said. "What happened yesterday made me feel insecure. I still feel insecure."

"I don't know what to think of you, Jack," Cindy said. "You weren't so selfish, at first. You thought of me once in a while."

I was getting a strong sense of *déjà vu*. There was no reason why such illogical words should ever be exchanged by man and woman, and yet the conversation was very familiar to me. It was quite consistent with conversations I had had with Coffee, Kate, Tanya, and others.

"You could at least kiss me," Cindy said.

I kissed her. She accepted it eagerly, too. Evidently she wanted to be reassured by a repeat of yesterday's performance. While I kissed her I wondered why I had ever mistaken such a bottomless pit of insecurity for a confident woman. Probably it was just that she had ripped a check out of her checkbook confidently. I've often been misled by clues no larger than that.

I would have been content just to kiss for a while, but

Cindy wasn't. She wanted the whole works—or rather part of her thought she wanted the whole works. Her body didn't really want any works, to speak of. When I tried to penetrate her I couldn't. She felt like she was sealed. I pushed for a while but I wasn't getting in. It made me feel ridiculous, so I stopped.

"We better just quit," I said. "This isn't working."

Cindy looked depressed.

"Don't look that way," I said.

"It's depressing to have to give up," she said.

"It's not such a big deal," I said. "You just don't want to make love right now."

"I do and I don't," she said.

"You mostly don't," I said.

"It's because I'm so scared," she said, clutching my penis. "I'm not my normal self."

"Can I make a suggestion?" I said. "Call Spud and tell him to forget it. Then we'll go buy some classy boots."

She was silent.

"Why see a man you're deathly afraid of?" I asked.

She shook her head helplessly. Denying him a single wish seemed to be beyond her.

"Just help me," she said. "Try some things."

While I was trying what she wanted tried I got so depressed I lost my erection. By the time it was technically possible for Cindy to have sexual intercourse, I was technically unable to perform the act. I began to get a headache, just from confusion and anxiety.

"Uh-oh," Cindy said. "Now you're impotent."

"Not really," I said. "I just have a headache."

"You look impotent to me," she noted.

I gave up, both on sex and talk, and just lay beside her.

"Maybe it's just as well, with your wife on the loose," Cindy said, in a cheerful voice. My impotence had restored her spirits more effectively than my potency could have.

"I think I'll have one more steak," Cindy said. "I don't like to start the day on an empty stomach."

By the time she had polished off the steak much of her glow

had returned, and some of her interest in life. She looked around the coffee shop, which was full of insurance salesmen and wheat farmers, plus a few cowboys.

"People probably eat a lot of protein here," she said. "That's good."

It looked as if she was going to fly cheerfully off, but as we were standing in the terminal, waiting for her flight to board, traces of anxiety began to reappear.

"I hope I don't make any mistakes," she said. She was so beautiful in her doubt that I could hardly bear to look at her.

"You could come," she said, suddenly. "You could get a car and drive around buying things. Then you'd be there if something went wrong."

"I better not," I said. "I better stay here and look for boots for your exhibit."

"You could be more flexible," she said. "If nothing went wrong you could fly back here and get the boots."

Most women make their own rules, where love and language are concerned, but Cindy's rules were so oblique that I could only now and then discern them. Spud seemed to have been the first destructive possibility she had ever encountered, and she was far too healthy to welcome destruction. The mere possibility of it played havoc with her nerves.

"I keep getting nervous," she said. "I think I won't and then I do. I can't control it.

"I hate it," she added. "I wish you'd come."

"I know why, too," I said. "You just want to have one person around that you're sure you can control."

"Yeah," she said, brightening. She was pleased that I had made such simple sense of her fears.

"That's exactly right," she added. "What's wrong with that?"

There was nothing wrong with it, really. A strong self-preservationist instinct was functioning healthily.

"So why won't you come?" she said.

"I'd like to see you have to take a few risks," I said.

She looked at me more closely than was her custom. "You better promise you'll come if I get in real trouble," she said.

"Of course I will."

"Do you want to buy your ticket now, just in case?" she asked.

"No, I may not stay in Lubbock," I said. "Just call me on the car phone, if you need me."

"Boy, I never expected you to behave like this," she said, just before she turned and walked onto the plane.

Chapter III _____

When I got to the motel I slept all day. I don't think I even turned over—I just slept, awakening to a gloomy plains dusk and the sound of sand beating against the windowpanes. A second norther had struck, weaker than the first but still strong enough to move the sand around a little.

I felt so puzzled that there didn't seem to be any real reason to even get up. I tried to think of a next step, but it wasn't easy. My trading instincts were at a low ebb. I was supposed to go buy boots, but I didn't really feel up to it.

Boot collectors are tenacious by nature. Trading with them takes some energy, though most of them aren't really collectors in the true sense. They're just rich people who tend to buy a lot of boots while they're buying a lot of other things, too.

On impulse I picked up the phone and called Jean Arber. I think I just wanted to know if she still liked me.

Belinda answered on the first ring.

"You must live on the top of the phone," I said.

Belinda was silent a moment.

"I like to get *it*," she said. "Is this you?"

"You who?"

"I forgot," she said. "What's your name?"

"Jack," I reminded her.

"Who is it, Belinda?" I heard Jean ask.

"It's Jack," Belinda said, as if I were someone who had been hanging around the house for weeks.

"He wants to talk to *me*," she added.

"He *has* talked to you," Jean said.

Belinda decided to yield gracefully, in this instance.

"What a surprise," Jean said. "Where are you?"

"I'm in Lubbock," I said. "I miss you."

I had not meant to be so direct, but the words popped out.

"It serves you right," she said. "Poor planning, this trip of yours."

"I may come back sooner than I had planned," I said.

"Does this have anything to do with me?" she asked.

"Sure," I said. "Is that okay?"

"It's a free country," she said. "I'm still amenable to being taken out. What happened to the friend you were traveling with?"

"That didn't work out too well."

"So now you're in the mood for a normal woman," she said. "That's understandable."

"Do normal women spend all their time buying trunks?" I asked.

"Listen," she said. "A few eccentricities like that doesn't mean you're not normal."

"How are the girls?" I asked, to change the subject.

"They're fine," she said.

I couldn't think of anything else to say. I didn't know Jean well enough to be talking to her on the phone. On the other hand I loved her voice. Even when she was jousting with me she sounded kind.

"You sound quite depressed," she said.

"I am quite depressed," I said.

"That doesn't surprise me," she said. "I could tell you were a potential depressive the minute I met you."

"Would you like to bring the girls out west?" I asked.

"I certainly wouldn't," she said. "What a bizarre suggestion."

"Well, we could take them to Disney World, then," I said.

"Ssh!" Jean said. "Whisper when you say that. A person with big ears is sitting in my lap."

"What'd he say?" Belinda asked. Fortunately her attention had wandered.

"He says you ask too many questions," Jean said.

We were silent for a bit.

"I think you ought to learn not to be so spur-of-the-moment," Jean said. "It can cause enormous trouble. I'd like to be taken to a few movies, if you don't mind, before we start planning any road trips. Then I'd know if our tastes really jibe.

"Besides, there's no big rush," she added.

"It feels like there is," I said. It was true. I was conditioned to rush. At estate sales the best pieces go in seconds. At flea markets there's nothing good left ten minutes after the dealers set up. It seemed to me the same was probably true of women. One as good as Jean could hardly be expected to last a day on the open market.

"If I don't rush someone else might find you," I pointed out.

"Someone already has," she said, cheerfully.

"Who?" I asked, my fears confirmed.

"A man," she said. "Fortunately for you he's very shy. He hasn't asked me out yet."

"He'll probably ask you tomorrow," I said.

"Nope," she said. "I'm not divorced yet, and he's very proper."

"I'll probably head back there tomorrow," I said. "Just as soon as I buy a few boots."

"This call is costing too much," Jean said. "I'm from a family that doesn't believe in spending money just to talk. Jimmy didn't believe in it, either."

"I believe in it," I said.

"I wish I did," Jean said. "I hate being tight-assed about anything, but the fact is I still get anxious when long distance calls go over three minutes."

"I'll cure you of that," I said. "Tell the girls goodnight for me."

"You better not try to exploit my mother's heart," she said. "These girls will pursue you to your grave, if you wrong me."

"*I* will," Belinda said. "What is it you said?"

"Never mind," Jean said.

Chapter IV ─────────

Talking to Jean made me feel considerably better. I felt I had contact with a live person. Of course, another live person, Cindy, had left only a few hours before, but I was far from confident that I still had contact with Cindy. I could easily imagine never hearing from her again, if things went well between her and Spud.

Talking to Jean hadn't really answered any major questions but it had at least restored my energies. I didn't want to waste another night in Lubbock, listening to a second-rate sandstorm. In ten minutes I was up, dressed, checked out, and on my way. I wasn't exactly sure where I was going next, but I knew it had to be east, so I drove in that direction.

Often the strings of homey roadside businesses—pizza parlors, muffler shops, hairdressers, cheap cafés, and 7-Elevens —appeal to me as I drive around. Their overall tackiness is part of the charm of America. But seen through a screen of sand these same little businesses can seem intolerably bleak. Lubbock seemed particularly rich in muffler shops. I passed about forty of them as I was leaving town. Just passing them depressed me. They seemed to bespeak the many disappointments of life. Then I became slightly less depressed. At least I wasn't working in a muffler shop in Lubbock. My fate was more intricate, and less oily.

I soon dropped off the caprock and proceeded through the night, slipping through a number of small silent towns. All of them were one-street towns, and the buildings of their one street were pale under the streetlights. The wind finally blew the clouds away and left a cold sky, sprinkled with stars. My thoughts kept slipping back to Jean. I didn't really think anything very specific about her, I just sort of had her in mind. Thinking about her blanked out two hundred miles. Before I really took note of myself I was buying gas in Wichita Falls, at one in the morning.

It occurred to me as I was paying for the gas that I wasn't far from the home of Little Joe Twine. His home was just down the road, near a town called Henrietta. In some parts of the world Little Joe would be called Joseph Twine II, but in Henrietta he's called Little Joe, to distinguish him from his father, Big Joe. The situation is further confused by the fact that Little Joe is married to a small blonde named Josie.

The Twines owned the largest ranch in that part of the world, a lovely ranch whose thousands of acres are dotted here and there with oil pumps. I had met Little Joe and Josie about a year earlier, at the home of a gun dealer in Amarillo. They had driven up to sell the gun dealer all the Twine family guns—and since the Twines had been a pioneer family that meant quite a few.

"These ain't the only guns in the world, Little Joe," Josie said several times, as I sat drinking beer and watching the transaction. The whole floor of the house was covered with rifles, pistols, and shotguns.

"No, but they're the handiest," Little Joe muttered. He was fat, long-haired, and depressed.

"Listen," Josie said with authority, "if I need to shoot you I'll shoot you. I can buy plenty of guns on a credit card."

"This don't mean I expect to live forever," Little Joe replied.

Then he snorted some cocaine.

Later I ran into Josie in the kitchen, where she was pouring vodka into a large pitcher of tomato juice. She was good-looking, but unhappy in the eyes, and had cut her blond hair too short.

"Let's go upstairs and fuck," she said in a friendly tone. "Shoot, it'll take them all night to finish this deal."

"That might be dangerous," I said. "Little Joe might load one of the guns and come up and shoot us."

"He ain't about to," Josie said. "The reason he's selling these guns is to stop me from shooting him."

"Why would he think you'd do that?"

"Because Momma Twine shot Big Joe two weeks ago," she said. "Don't you read the papers?"

"I guess I missed it," I said.

"I don't see how, it was on the TV too," Josie said. "Big Joe was down in the lots working some cattle and she walked down with a 30-30 and shot him right off his horse. She took good aim, too. Ten cowboys standing around and nobody even noticed her until she pulled the trigger."

"Was he hurt bad?"

"He was killed deader than a sonofabitch," Josie said. "It worries Little Joe. He's afraid it'll give me ideas. Shoot, I ain't even mad at him. Little Joe's real paranoid."

Then she told me about her life, which consisted of driving down to Dallas—as she put it—almost every day. It was only 85 miles to Dallas, a short toot in that country. In Dallas she bought things for a while and then went to a city billy bar, had a few beers, and looked for boyfriends. Little Joe spent his days playing cassettes of dirty movies on his wall-size TV. Sometimes the cowboys came in and watched, and a lot of dope was enjoyed. Now that Big Joe was dead nobody saw any reason to do much work, least of all Little Joe.

Instead of fucking we went out and sat in my car awhile, drinking vodka and tomato juice and watching the wind blow. While we were drinking Little Joe and the gun dealer came out, got in the gun dealer's pickup, and drove off, destination unknown.

"I don't know why I come on this trip," Josie said. "Shoot, I don't even know why I married Little Joe, except he's rich. Wanta go to Dallas? We could stop off at the ranch and have breakfast. I can cook."

The house was the Twine ranch headquarters, about 300 miles away.

"Or we could have the pilot fly up and get us," Josie said.

"Little Joe probably went to Lubbock to buy some dope. No telling when he'll be back. We keep this pilot to fly us around but we hardly ever call him. I think he's about bored to death."

She was wearing a wonderful pair of red ostrich-skin boots with elaborate flame stitching, and when I complimented her on them she smiled. "I got about three hundred pair," she said. "Me and Little Joe just buy boots all the time."

Since Little Joe and the gun dealer had not returned in an hour, I drove Josie home. The Twine ranch house was done in typical degenerate third-generation style, with ugly shag rugs and dozens of telephones and TV sets. Little Joe never wanted to be out of sight of a TV set or out of reach of a phone, so he had put several phones and TVs in every room. The phones were all different colors and sizes, from fake antiques to Mickey Mouse phones. There was not one good thing in the house, except the boots. Upstairs there was a walk-in closet the size of a presidential suite, all filled with boots. The Twine family had evidently never thrown away a pair of boots, or worn one out, either. There were boots in the closet going back to Big Joe's father's early days, most of them in fairly decent condition.

It was the boots I remembered, as I was getting gas in Wichita Falls. If Josie hadn't shot Little Joe yet maybe I could buy their boot collection and fulfill my obligation to Cindy at one swoop.

I had the Twine number in my book, and I called it, hoping for Josie. Instead, I got Little Joe.

"You got any hash?" he asked, once he figured out who I was. Though clearly disappointed when I said no, he invited me over anyway.

When I knocked at the door, twenty minutes later, he met me. He was wearing cut-offs, a purple T-shirt, and a look not far from idiocy. In the year since I had seen him he had gained another fifty pounds, and managed to avoid barbers. His hair was really long.

"Got any dirty movies?" he asked. "If you got any I'll buy 'em as long as there ain't queers or niggers in them. I mainly like to watch heterosexual activity between members of the white race."

When I stepped into the large, ugly living room I saw that that was exactly what he had been watching. Several pale bodies were bobbing and weaving on the wall-size TV screen, but Little Joe was so high he had let the set get out of focus. The bodies were just a blur, though a pale blur.

There was a huge blue suede couch along one wall, beside which sat a large tube of gas of some kind. It looked like the tubes that welders have on their trucks, but it was hard to know why Little Joe would need acetylene in his living room.

"Aw, that's just laughing gas," he said. "Want some?"

He offered me a little mask, such as dentists use when they give gas, but I declined so he plopped down on the couch and put the mask on his own face, opening the nozzle on the tube of gas so that he would get a strong stream of nitrous oxide right up his nose.

"Where's Josie?" I asked.

"Upstairs watching the cable," he said. "She don't like dirty movies."

As I started to leave the room I almost stepped on a cow-boy, stretched out on the floor by one of the doors. He had on boots, spurs, and chaps, but he lay so limply that for a moment I thought he must be dead. His eyes were open, but they weren't fixed on anything.

"What's wrong with him?" I asked.

Little Joe had forgotten about the cowboy.

"Is he still there?" he said. "I thought Josie called the ambulance to come and get him. He took some horse medicine by accident.

"He'll be all right," he added. "Only thing is we may have to cut his boots off. That horse medicine makes your feet swell."

The vast hall upstairs was lined with extremely bad oil paintings of Texas rural scenes. Far down the hall I could hear the sound of a television set. It proved to come from the master bedroom, which was about the size of a tennis court. Much of it was filled with one of the largest beds I had ever seen. Josie sat in the middle of it, in a nightgown, watching *Benjy* on another wall-size TV.

"Why howdy," she said, when she saw me. "You're the one that buys things. I wisht you'd buy me." She touched a control and the sound went off on the big TV. Benjy's antics continued in silence.

"Actually I was hoping to buy some boots," I said.

She was still drinking vodka and tomato juice, and had begun to let her hair grow out. Since it had to grow through various levels of dye it was not yet easy to predict what color it would be.

"Did you call the ambulance about that cowboy?" I asked. "He didn't look too healthy."

"Well, it's what he gets, for tryin' to get high on horse medicine," Josie said. "It's real boring around here. I've started taking dope too. What I'd like to do is take a trip. Are you going anywhere?"

"I am," I said. "I'm just not sure where."

"Anywhere will do me," Josie said. "I'm even afraid to drive now, Little Joe's hid so much dope in all the cars. If I was to get stopped for speeding I'd go to jail for years. It ain't worth it. Are you going north or south?"

"North," I said.

Josie got out of bed, went to a large closet, selected a yellow cowboy shirt, peeled off her gown, and put on the shirt. She got into some Levi's and yellow running shoes, found a purse, dropped a comb in it, and was ready to go.

"You don't care if I go, do you?" she said. "You can just kick me out whenever you get tired of me. I'll just call the pilot and make him fly up and get me."

I felt paralyzed. All I had meant to do was buy boots. Josie had not been part of my plans. Even so, it seemed a pity to disappoint her. I knew I ought to be forceful and just say no, but I didn't. I just stood there feeling vaguely wrong, creating by my indecision the assumption that it was fine for her to go with me.

"Do you think I can buy some boots?" I asked, feebly.

"Sure," Josie said. "We got a few to spare."

We went to the boot closet and turned the light on. I made a careful count, determining that the closet contained 262 pair of boots. I began a tasteful selection. My first choice had the Alamo embossed on them in white pigskin. Another had the San Jacinto monument in mother-of-pearl. Several pairs were covered in rhinestones, and many pairs were at least seventy-five years old.

"Little Joe got the rhinestone ones when he was trying to be a singer," Josie said.

The closet was a boot scout's paradise. The Twines had been eclectic, evidently buying almost any boots they ran across. There were boots with the impossibly high heels that had been in vogue in the twenties. There were Mexican boots, Montana boots, and a pair of boots that had been awarded some Twine at a steer-roping contest in Tucumcari in 1918. In no time at all I had picked out forty pair, all old. Then I selected five pair of garish boots from Little Joe's assemblage, and several pair of Josie's. Her taste ran to exotic skins: armadillo, warthog, shark. Also, she had a passion for yellow. At least two-thirds of her boots were yellow, regardless of the skin.

"Yellow's the only color I feel sexy in," she said, looking at the yellow shirt she was wearing.

"We better just throw them out the window," Josie said. "Then maybe we can just drive around in the car and pick them up."

The suggestion did not surprise me—I knew it would probably not be easy simply to buy the boots from Little Joe. He might appear to be a total dopehead, but the one thing that had to be remembered about him was that he was very rich. The rich don't sell easily. If they have something someone wants they automatically assume it's got to be worth much more than the person is willing to give. Also, they don't need money—even extravagant sums don't tempt them. If you offer them a million they figure that what you're after is worth five million; and if you persuade them it's worth only a million they may decide to keep it anyway, on the grounds that it's pointless to sell something that's only worth a million.

Besides, I had heard Little Joe bargaining with the gun dealer in Amarillo, and the dealer later told me that the deal had taken four days to complete. He had paid too much for almost every single gun, and had stopped even wanting the guns by the time Little Joe was satisfied. All the dealer wanted by that time was for Little Joe to go away.

I didn't want to stay in Henrietta four days, haggling over boots.

"He likes to gamble," Josie said. "If you're willin' to bet you got a chance."

We went down to discover Little Joe rolling around on the blue couch in a strange contorted manner. He appeared to be doing exercises of some sort.

"It's yoga," Josie whispered. "Somebody told him if he learned yoga he'd eventually get limber enough so he could suck himself off. Did you know that less than one percent of human males can suck themselves off?"

"I didn't know that," I said.

While Little Joe exercised, laughing gas poured into the room from his unused mask. Also, the pornographic movie was still going on, behind our backs, and the cowboy who had taken the horse medicine still lay on the floor, glassy-eyed.

Josie switched off the pornographic movie and flipped channels until she found Benjy. She wanted to be sure the little fellow was still all right.

Little Joe stopped exercising, sat up, and popped the mask back over his nose. He was sweating profusely.

"I'm taking a trip," Josie said. "I might be back next week."

Little Joe received this news without apparent interest.

"Jack wants to buy a few boots," Josie added.

"Which boots?" Little Joe asked, a faint gleam of perception lighting his pupils.

"Boots, boots," Josie said, snapping her fingers at him as if she were a hypnotist, trying to bring someone out of a trance.

Little Joe got up without a word and went upstairs. We followed. I had lined all the boots up in the hallway. He squatted down and looked at them carefully. I knew from

297

experience he was going to try to estimate the precise dollar value of each pair.

"Don't be so slow, Little Joe," Josie said, impatient to be on the road.

Little Joe didn't reply. He was studying the boots.

"How about if we gamble?" I said. "One toss of the coin. If I win I get the boots."

"What about if I win?" Little Joe said. "What do I get?"

"Let's go out to the car," I said. "Maybe I've got something that would interest you."

We went out into the cold moonlit night. I could hear the chug-chug of oil pumps, each of them chugging through the night to make Little Joe richer. I showed him the Henry rifle, thinking perhaps the family passion for guns had returned, but it hadn't.

"We solt the guns," he said.

Then his eyes lit on the Valentino hubcaps. He picked one up and looked at it.

"Where'd a thang like this come from?" he asked.

For a second I was tempted to lie. I didn't really want to gamble the hubcaps against the boots. The hubcaps were truly rare. Only four sets existed. Not only were they worth more than the boots, they were also my legacy from Beulah Mahony. She had treasured them a long time and had finally chosen me to have them. It had been an act of love, of a sort.

The boots I was merely getting for Cindy Sanders, whom I might never see again.

Besides, the gamble involved an imbalance of class. The boots were good, but the hubcaps were simply in a different, and a higher, class.

Little Joe was clearly in love with the cobra hubcaps. I knew right away that he'd take the gamble, if I agreed to it.

I told him about Valentino, about the hubcap forger, about the fact that only four sets existed. Every word I said made him more eager.

"I'll flip, but not for an even trade," I said. "The hubcaps are worth too much more than the boots. If you win I want $5,000 to boot."

Josie had grown cold and was sitting in the car going through my collection of eight-track tapes.

"Okay," Little Joe said. "I like them snakes."

We went back inside. Little Joe rolled the glassy-eyed cowboy over and dug in his pockets until he found a quarter. Then he went back to the couch and popped a few pills, while he considered.

"You flip," he said, pitching over the quarter.

I felt a little strange. I wasn't really taking the bet because I wanted the boots all that much—the problem was that I wanted the hubcaps *too* much. In five years I had never put them up for sale, which was a breach of discipline. One of my firmest principles is that those who sell should not keep. The minute a scout starts keeping his best finds he becomes a collector. All scouts have love affairs with objects, but true scouts have brief intense passions, not marriages. I didn't want to own something I loved so much I wouldn't sell it. That would violate the logic of what I was doing. The game is about selling, as much as buying: if you have the courage to sell a really great object today you may be rewarded with the opportunity to buy an even greater object tomorrow.

The truth was, I had had the hubcaps long enough. It was time to risk them, and this was as good a way as any.

I flipped the coin.

"Tails," Little Joe said.

The coin landed. It was heads. The hubcaps were still mine, and I had won some fifty pairs of boots.

Little Joe was not in the least discouraged. After a moment he went over and looked at the glassy-eyed cowboy.

"That son of a bitch took himself a real dose," he said. "If he'd come to he could help you load the boots."

I loaded them myself, making several trips. Josie had started the motor in order to keep warm. Streams of white exhaust poured out into the cold night. I had to make several trips. Little Joe went back to watching the movie, the gas mask still back over his nose. Josie played a Willie Nelson tape on my stereo. Finally I got all the boots into the luggage compartment, tucking them carefully around the various other objects that were there. As I was fitting in the last of the boots the glassy-eyed cowboy walked out of the house. His spurs jingled slightly as he walked across the gravel driveway. He no longer looked glassy-eyed. When he saw the rear end full of boots he stopped a moment, looking at them.

"Now what would anybody want with that many boots?" he said, in a slow drawl. "A man ain't got but two feet."

Then he went to the nearest pickup, got in, and drove off.

"I guess Mitch got all right," Josie said, when I got in. "If the ambulance shows up now all they'll get is Little Joe."

She was snapping her fingers quietly, in time with the music. As we drove out of the driveway, dust from Mitch's pickup rose ahead of us, white as the moonlight.

Chapter V _____

At the end of the Twine driveway I turned left, toward Washington, D.C.

"I hope you'd just as soon go to Washington," I said to Josie.

"Why not?" she said. "That's my motto, why not. Little Joe got me some license plates with that on 'em, for my birthday once. That was one of the nicest presents he ever gave me."

Josie began to watch me as we drove toward Dallas. I had a feeling she was more intelligent than I had first supposed her to be. Also, she seemed kind.

"How come you're not happy?" she asked. "You sure got a nice car."

"Do you think anybody's really happy?" I asked. I had a feeling that the one person I knew who was really happy was Belinda Arber. Her sister Beverly had traces of doubt in her eyes, traces of anxiety, but Belinda had none. In all likelihood, Belinda simply wouldn't tolerate unhappiness; for all I knew it might never touch her, or touch her at most momentarily.

"Shoot, my baby sister's happy as a frog," Josie said. "She's real pretty and she knows how to take up for herself. She ain't but eighteen and she's already had more boyfriends than I've had my whole life. She don't take nothing off any of them, either, unless it's something she wants. If one of them don't do right she just kicks him out of bed and gets another."

"Was Little Joe ever nice?" I asked.

Josie considered for a moment, looking out at the pale plains.

"Well, he wasn't mean," she said. "Little Joe ain't never been mean. That's something. All he really wanted to do was get away from Big Joe. We was gonna run off, but shoot, we never stood a chance. They wasn't about to let Little Joe loose or nothing."

Josie sighed. "Actually, he was kinda sweet for a while," she said. "He still is kinda sweet, only now he just takes dope all the time. You wouldn't believe how much that man spends on dope. If he was a normal person he'd be broke in no time."

She sighed again, a small quiet sigh. The next time I looked at her she was asleep.

I hit I–30 and drove across East Texas, leaving the plains and entering the pines. By four in the morning I was into Arkansas, and a little tired. The first real stopping place inside Arkansas is a little town called Hope, where I often stopped. Why Hope was called Hope has always interested me. The pioneers who settled it must have been in a good mood the day they arrived there, so they named it Hope. But most of their descendants, the residents of present-day Hope, looked as if they wished their ancestors had kept on trucking. They did not seem rich in the quality for which the town was named.

In the faint light of the dashboard Josie Twine looked very young—a girl, really. One whose hair had recently been dyed several times.

I drove over to the Holiday Inn and asked for a room with two beds.

When I came out, Josie was sitting up, looking blankly at the motel.

"I went to sleep," she said, in the tones of a child. "Where are we?"

"Arkansas," I said.

"My momma was born in Fayetteville," Josie said. "Are we anywhere near there?"

"It's not too far," I said.

"I'm gonna send her a postcard," Josie said. "She loves to get postcards. You think it's too late to buy one now?"

"No, but it won't go off until tomorrow," I said.

"Okay, but don't let me forget," Josie said. "I gotta take advantage of my opportunities."

In the room, Josie went right to the TV set and turned it on. Naturally all she got was snow. There is nothing happening on TV at four in the morning in Arkansas. Josie flipped through all the channels with mild disbelief.

"Shoot, we *are* out in the sticks," she said. "They ain't even on the cable. We've been on the cable for over a year. Now little Joe's got one of them $7,000 discs and we can get 120 channels. He can watch live fucking straight from Denmark. I don't know what we'd do without the cable."

At the mention of fucking she looked at me with sort of a puzzled expression, as if she were not sure what ought to happen next. The mere fact that we were driving around America together did not necessarily mean we were going to get involved. However, the fact that we were also in a bedroom together carried implications. I sat down on one bed, drained of will. Josie stood in front of the TV set, as if she hoped a program would suddenly come on and break the silence. What I mostly felt was an urge to brush my teeth, only I had forgotten to bring in my traveling kit.

"Excuse me," I said, getting up. "I forgot my toothbrush and stuff."

Just as I opened my car door to get my kit from the back seat the phone rang.

"Where *are* you?" Cindy said. "I called you a lot of times yesterday. Then I called you tonight. You said I could call you any time but it isn't true."

She sounded very distraught.

"I've been driving for most of the last eight hours," I said. "You could have got me."

"Yeah, but I was afraid to call then," she said. "Spud was supposed to come and I didn't want him to walk in and find me talking to you. I only can call at times when I know he's not supposed to come. And then I never get you even though you said I could get you anytime."

"I'm sorry, I'm sorry," I said. "Now and then I'm out of the car. What's the matter?"

"This is the most terrible thing that's ever happened to me," Cindy said. "I wish it had never happened."

"What happened?"

"Nothing," she said. "He hasn't come to see me yet. His secretary called and said he was coming about four this afternoon, but he didn't."

I was secretly glad, but I thought it best to conceal this.

"How soon can you get here?" she asked.

"I don't know," I said, a little surprised. "I've got to sleep for a while. I guess I could get there in a day and a half."

"You don't have to drive everywhere," she said. "Just go somewhere and take an airplane. I'll be crazy in a day and a half."

"Why don't you just go on back to Washington?" I said. "Why sit around Miami if the man isn't even going to come and see you? He made you go there, you know. I think it's terrible behavior."

"I didn't call to listen to you criticize him," she said, anger replacing hurt in her voice.

"Well, you have to admit he's behaved terribly," I said.

"I don't know why you think you have any room to talk," Cindy said. "You said I could get you anytime but it wasn't true.

"You were impotent, too," she reminded me. "You have no right to criticize anybody."

"I was impotent *once*," I pointed out.

There was silence on the line. Our conversation was getting nowhere.

"I cried for hours," Cindy said. "Now I'm puffy. He probably won't sleep with me now even if he does come."

"I doubt he'll come this time of night," I said. "What do you suppose he's doing?"

"He's with Betsy," Cindy said.

"Who's Betsy?"

"His wife. I told you that. Can't you remember anything?" Cindy said.

"Why did he bring his wife if he wanted to see you?" I asked. "I think you should leave on the first plane in the morning."

"I didn't ask for your advice," Cindy said. "Just come and help me."

"Help you do what?" I asked.

"Help me wait."

"How's that supposed to work? If I'm sitting there helping you wait and Spud shows up he might be a little annoyed, don't you think?"

"You won't be in the *room* with me," Cindy said.

"Then where will I be?"

"You could be somewhere in the hotel," she said. "In another room."

"How would that help you wait?" I asked.

"I never thought you'd ask so many questions," Cindy said. "God, you ask a lot of questions."

"Well, it seems strange," I said. "What help can I be if I'm in another room?"

"Because you'll be there if I give up," she said. "I don't want to give up, but I might."

She said it in a voice that was not quite in control of itself. It was clear she was not that far from giving up, even as we spoke.

I was silent for a moment.

"Jack, are you there?" she asked.

She had rarely used my name in speaking to me.

"I'm here," I said.

"Can't you just do it and not ask questions?" she said. "That's our problem, you know."

"What is?"

"We talk too much," Cindy said. "We should just do things and not talk so much."

"Can I just ask you one more question?" I said.

"What?"

"What if I start to Miami and Spud shows up while I'm in transit? He may just be planning to let you suffer and then surprise you. How am I gonna know?"

"I wish you didn't make everything so complicated," Cindy said.

I was silent again.

"I feel like I'm about to give up," she said. "You know how you sometimes feel you're about to vomit? I feel that way, only I'm about to give up."

"Listen," I said. "I've been driving too long. I've got to sleep. You should sleep too. Then call me. If you give up you could fly to someplace and I'll meet you."

"Okay," Cindy said, meekly. "I hope you're gonna be reliable this time. I hope I can get you if I call."

"I have to eat," I said. "I'm sometimes out of the car for a few minutes. But you can keep trying. You'll get me."

"Okay, Jack," Cindy said. "Do you love me?"

"Yeah," I said.

"Okay, Jack," she said again, and hung up.

Chapter VI _____

When I came back to the room Josie was lying right in the middle of one of the two large double beds, staring at the ceiling. She had the covers pulled up to her chin, and she looked perplexed.

I felt sympathetic. Only a few hours earlier I had been

staring at the ceiling of a motel in Lubbock, feeling perplexed. Even Cindy Sanders, who seemed to have nearly everything going for her, was probably lying in bed in Miami, staring at the ceiling and feeling perplexed.

"I'm sorry," I said. "I got a phone call on my car phone."

"I don't know why I come," Josie said.

She looked like she had spent too much time asking herself questions that had no answers.

"Maybe you just wanted a change," I suggested.

"Yeah, but this ain't a change," she said. "I feel lonesome at home and I feel lonesome here."

She looked at me quizzically, to see what I could offer. I didn't have a thing to say. The truth was, I felt lonesome too.

"Little Joe just about never comes upstairs anymore," Josie said. "I never thought I'd spend my whole life watching TV, but that's how it's worked out. It's a good thing we can get 120 channels, otherwise I wouldn't have nothing to do at all."

Then we both fell silent. Our adventure, if that was what we were having, was turning out to be miserable all around.

I excused myself, as if I was leaving a dinner table, and brushed my teeth. I felt very awkward, and had no one but myself to blame for feeling that way. I almost never use good judgment, or any judgment, when it came to personal relationships. What was I doing in Hope, Arkansas, with the wife of a millionaire rancher from Henrietta?

I brushed my teeth for quite a while, but came up with no good answer to that question.

When I came out, Josie was still staring at the ceiling.

"Do you know a lot of rich people?" she asked.

I sat on the other bed and began to take off my boots.

"Quite a few," I said.

"I never knew any till I married Little Joe," she said. "My dad's just a carpenter. What are the ones you know like?"

I tried to think, but it was hard to come up with a general analysis of rich people.

"The thing about Little Joe is that he expects a lot," Josie said. "I guess that's the difference. I guess I just never expected very much."

I took off my socks.

"I still don't expect very much," Josie said, sadly. "Seems to me like the less I expect the less I get. I was just sittin' up there watching *Benjy* and you walked in. I thought I'd just run off with you before I had time to start expectin' anything. Once you start expectin' something then it's sadder if you don't get it, don't you think?"

At that point I decided to try and sleep with Josie, as a means of stopping her from saying such heartbreaking things. She seemed to have tapped a pure spring of sadness inside herself, the result no doubt of several years spent sitting around the Twine ranch watching Little Joe grow dopier and dopier.

I particularly didn't want to hear her say any more about expectations, since I too spent a lot of time expecting things that didn't happen. My fantasies were just little séances of expectation.

"Can I come to bed with you?" I asked, before Josie could say another word.

Josie seemed surprised. She had evidently abandoned that expectation so completely that it startled her.

"Did you just get horny, or what?" she asked.

"I ain't been doin' much fuckin' lately," she added, as if that had a bearing on the question.

"It doesn't matter," I said.

"I don't know what happened," Josie said. "I used to do a lot. Then gradually I stopped. I don't buy much anymore, either. All the stuff looks the same to me now."

I turned off the light, undressed, and got in bed with her.

"Was the reason you wasn't horny before because my hair's so funny looking?" she asked, sliding over to me. Her tiny body was hot, from having had covers on it for the last half hour.

"Had nothing to do with it," I said. "Your hair looks fine."

Chapter VII _____

The next day Josie and I drove across Arkansas and Tennessee. Josie had never seen the Mississippi and got very excited when we approached it.

"Shoot, I don't see how they got a bridge across it," she said, when she actually saw the river. She looked the happiest I had seen her, and she tried to get me to stop on the bridge so she could take a picture of it.

"I can't stop on the bridge and anyway I don't have a camera," I said.

Josie looked disappointed. Practically her first trip and already she was being denied things. Simple American needs, too, such as getting to take a picture of the Mississippi to send to her mother, who liked postcards.

By the time we got into Memphis I felt so bad that we stopped and bought a Polaroid and we went back to the river and took pictures. We also bought a lot of postcards at a newsstand by the river. She wrote five or six and sent them right off to her mother. Most of them just said, "Hi, Mom, wish you were here!" Josie has not had much practice composing postcards.

I spent most of the day expecting the phone to ring. Undoubtedly the phone *would* ring and Cindy would demand that I rush to Miami. Josie would enjoy seeing Florida and her pilot could easily fly there to get her. I had begun to like her more and more, actually. She was affectionate, generous, and kind. We got to Nashville and the phone still hadn't rung so we just kept going east.

By this time I was very puzzled by Cindy's silence. Something had to have changed. Spud must have come, after all. I felt quite disappointed. Cindy wasn't affectionate, generous, or kind, but she was absolutely beautiful, and I had been looking forward to having her back.

Then, just as we were approaching Oak Ridge, Tennessee, the phone *did* ring, only when I picked it up it wasn't Cindy's voice I heard.

"Is you still in the car?" Belinda asked.

"Why yes, I am," I said. "Where's your mother?"

"She wants to talk to you. Bye," Belinda said.

"We just wanted to find out if this phone-in-the-car stuff really works," Jean said.

Josie had stopped tapping my leg and was trying to pretend she wasn't there.

"Where are ya?" Jean asked.

"Tennessee," I said. "I'm on my way back."

"Buy any nice trunks?" she asked.

"No," I said. "However, the trunk of my car is full of interesting boots."

"There's no such thing as an interesting boot," Jean said. "Are you alone?"

"Yep," I lied.

"If you weren't you'd be in trouble by now," she said. "You're not very wary or you wouldn't have given me this number."

"I'm not very wary," I said.

"Well, there's not much news," Jean said. "I sold sixteen dollars worth of cups today. A big day for me. When may we expect to see you?"

"Probably in a day or two," I said. "Although there's a distant prospect that I might have to go to Miami. I've heard of an estate that sounds interesting."

"Are you sure it's an estate, and not a woman?" Jean asked.

"Oh well," I said, made cautious by the tone of her voice.

Jean was silent.

"It might be a little of both," I admitted.

"And then again it might be a woman and not an estate," Jean said. "Am I right?"

She had cleverly trapped me in a situation in which I had to admit to a lie, or else keep lying. Neither option was very palatable, particularly not with Josie sitting there pretending not to hear a word I said.

"You're right," I said, deciding she would probably rather have a rival than a liar.

"Then how come you mentioned the estate?" she asked.

"I guess I was just being tactful," I said weakly.

"No, you were being dishonest," Jean said, anger in her voice. "I hate dishonest men. Jimmy lied to me practically every day. I wish you hadn't done it. We aren't involved enough for you to need to lie to me."

"I apologize," I said. "It was stupid."

"More importantly, it was wrong," Jean said. "Stupidity I can forgive."

She was silent again. I didn't know what to say. I had already apologized once—apologizing twice wouldn't help.

"I wish I hadn't called," Jean said. "It was just a spur of the moment fancy Belinda and I had. Beverly thought it was weird to call someone in a car, and she was right. Beverly's got a lot of sense."

"Whereas you and Belinda can't resist your impulses," I said lightly.

"Unfortunately not," Jean said.

"I met you at a complicated time of my life," I said.

"Shut up," she said. "I hate men who make excuses like that. *All* times of my life are complicated, as it happens."

"I don't think I'm really going to Miami," I said. "I don't know why I even mentioned it."

"You mentioned it to leave yourself an out," Jean said. "I wish I could find a man somewhere who didn't constantly feel the need to leave himself an out."

"Don't you ever do that?"

"I'm a parent," Jean said. "When you're a parent, there's no out. But then how would you understand that?"

"Well, I make an awful lot of mistakes," I said.

Jean laughed a rather harsh laugh.

"You sure do," she said, and hung up.

I felt very depressed. First Cindy had vanished from the radarscope and now I had witlessly and needlessly alienated Jean. All I had to show for a perfectly pointless three-thousand-mile drive was Josie Twine and a trunk full of boots, neither of which I had any notion what to do with. Besides that, I had entered into an agreement with Uncle Ike Spettle, who was going to show up in Washington in a month's time, expecting to become a national celebrity, as a reward for his

century-long stewardship of a pair of boots. People had become celebrities for far less, but that didn't solve my problem.

Josie was looking at me curiously, in a kindly way.

"Shoot," she said. "You must know some picky women."

"Yep," I agreed.

"How many girl friends you got?" she asked.

"I don't know," I said honestly. "Maybe none. Or maybe
as many as five or six. It depends on how you define girl
friend."

"That ain't very complicated," she said. "It's just somebody
who'll sleep with you if you happen to be around.

"Much as you travel I can see why you'd need quite a few,"
she added, in a kind voice.

In my depression it seemed an amazingly humane and
worldly judgment, coming from a young woman from Henrietta.

"You don't think it's wrong to have several?" I asked.

Josie shrugged. "It beats tryin' to learn to suck yourself
off," she said. "I've been trying to get Little Joe to go to a
psychiatrist, but he won't."

"Have you ever gone to one?"

"Aw, yeah," she said. "I went to one down in Dallas for
nearly a year. He said I oughta leave Little Joe, only he didn't
tell me how I was supposed to get energy enough to do it."

"Maybe you *have* left him," I suggested. "Maybe that's
what this trip's about."

Josie scooted over enough that she could hug one of my
arms.

"I hope so," she said. "I was getting so lonesome staying
upstairs all the time I was about to go crazy. Shoot, I'd rather
drive around and see the country."

Chapter VIII _____

We stopped for the night in Knoxville and woke up to a world so fogged in with Appalachian fog that neither of us wanted to get out of bed and deal with it. The white mist was so dense that it looked like it had been painted on the windows of the motel.

"Shoot, I don't see how people get around," Josie said, rubbing on the window as if by doing so she could rub a little hole in the fog. It didn't work so she came back to bed and snuggled against me.

"It'll go away when the sun comes up," I said.

"Yeah, but what happens on a cloudy day?" she wanted to know.

At certain levels of tension and uncertainty the least little things make a difference. Sunlight, for example. If I wake up in a borderline mood and see the sun shining it might lift my mood several notches. I might get up feeling optimistic and go out and buy something wonderful.

Total fog has just the opposite effect. I felt like never getting out of bed. In such a fog it would be difficult to find my car, much less a junk shop or an antique store. I had been to several flea markets that opened in the early morning, when the mist was still rising. The flea marketers moved through it like ghosts, setting up tables and putting out old bottles and other objects, oblivious to the fact that the customers couldn't see the tables, much less the objects. Certain well-equipped scouts carried big miner's lights for just such occasions. I had a miner's light myself, and had used it to good effect at several dawn flea markets. Once I had bought a marvelous Pennsylvania butter spreader by the light of my miner's light, in the days when I scouted obsessively.

Lying in bed in the fogged-in motel in Knoxville, with Josie's arms locked tightly around me as she stared at the very un-Texas fog surrounding us, I began to feel nostalgic for the days when I had scouted obsessively. I had had a lot of discipline, once. In fact I had had a good bit of it right up until the moment I had met Cindy Sanders. Of course there had been lapses, when my passions for Coffee, Kate, and Tanya had been at their heights. But Coffee, Kate, and Tanya were fixed entities, each of them easily located and quite predictable once found. In my mind they had become so closely indentified with their respective Texas cities that they could have been called Austin, Houston, and Dallas. Their qualities and the qualities of their three cities were very similar, their rhythms the rhythms of those places. To the extent that I understood the places, I understood the women, and vice versa.

Nothing like that applied to my relationship in the District of Columbia and its environs, where I understood nothing, neither the women nor the place. So far my every move had been wrong, womanwise. I felt like I was on a down escalator where women were concerned, though fortunately the small warm one with her arms wrapped around me didn't think poorly of me yet.

"What kinds of people live here?" Josie inquired.

"Just the usual kinds," I said. "It's not always this foggy."

"It seems like a long way, back to Henrietta," she said. "Do you think I could get a job, up in Washington?"

"I guess you could," I said. "But I thought you were just going to send for your pilot. It's not a long flight."

"It is if you don't really want to go back," she said.

"Don't worry, I ain't gonna be a burden," she added. "I know you got all them picky girl friends to think about."

"I wasn't thinking of you as a burden," I said.

"You wasn't thinking of me at all," Josie said quietly. "That's okay. I wasn't thinking of you, either. It's just an accident, ain't it?"

"What?"

"That you come by and that I run off with you," she said. "Just an accident. It ain't like we met one another in high school and fell in love."

"No," I said. "You're right. Did you meet Little Joe in high school?"

"Yeah," she said. "Everybody was trying to get him because he was so rich. Lucky me, I got him."

Relieved by the accidental nature of everything that was happening, we made love, had a big breakfast, and dashed out of Tennessee into Virginia. The fog burned off when we got to Bristol and we drove north through Virginia on a beautiful fall day. The leaves had turned in my absence—the slopes of the Blue Ridge were exhibiting their most brilliant fall foliage, a sight that Josie managed to take in stride.

"I was never much interested in leaves," she said. "Momma likes 'em, though."

Near Wytheville we stopped to see an elderly Virginia aristocrat I knew, named Mead Mead IV. Mead lived in what appeared to be perfect leisure in a beautiful old eighteenth-century manor house, attended by tactful servants, all black. The lifestyle of the Mead manor was so eighteenth century that there was no way of knowing whether Mead or any of the servants knew that the Civil War had occurred.

Both Mead and the servants were more than a little shocked by the sight of Josie, in her yellow shirt and tricolored hair, but fortunately their manners were adequate to the situation.

I had only stopped in order to sell Mead a nineteenth-century lightbulb. He was a passionate collector of nineteenth-century lightbulbs, his one concession to modern times. He had over four hundred and kept each one in an individual wooden case which one of his handymen made.

I had found a beautiful nineteenth-century lightbulb in South Dakota. It had been the living room lightbulb of a family who had only used the living room once or twice in the twentieth century. Consequently, the bulb still worked. I knew Mead would be delighted, since only about 10 of his 400 lightbulbs still worked. He had a nineteenth-century light fixture in his study, and when he screwed in the South Dakota lightbulb it shone with a pure if feeble light.

"Perfectly beautiful," Mead said. He loved the pure feeble light of nineteenth-century lightbulbs. A look of pleasure lingered on his features as he wrote the check and handed it to me. His thin silver hair was neatly combed and the effect of perfect elegance was marred only by a few traces of egg on his necktie.

As we were driving out of the manor's long driveway, Josie reached over and got the check out of my pocket.

"I just want to read it," she said. "You mean he paid you five hundred dollars for a lightbulb?"

I nodded.

"I never seen such a creepy house," she said, and the rest of the way to Washington she brooded about the elegant creepiness of manor houses in Virginia.

When we got to Washington I headed straight for Boog's, the one place in Washington I was fairly sure Josie wouldn't think was creepy.

I was right. Boog had just flown in from Kansas City, bringing some barbecued ribs. Micah had his little TV set on the table and was giggling helplessly at a *Sanford and Son* rerun.

"Hi, like your hairdo," were the first words out of Boog's mouth, when he spotted Josie. In two minutes she was eating ribs like one of the family and helping Micah watch *Sanford and Son*. Micah liked her almost as instantly as Boog had, since she was the first person to come along in months who knew reruns as well as he did.

Boss seemed to be in a somber mood. She was not unfriendly to Josie, or to anyone, but she didn't say much.

I had meant to ask if Josie could stay at the Millers' for a night or two, until we got our bearings, but before I could even mention it Boog invited her to stay as long as she wanted to.

"Oh great," Micah said. "I hope you like Bob Newhart."

Half an hour later they all went off to Georgetown to see a double-feature Bogart rerun. Josie went with them, looking younger and happier than I had ever seen her.

Boss didn't go. She sat at the table, idly fingering her long black hair.

"I didn't mean for her just to move in," I said, thinking Boss might be annoyed that I had brought a young woman into their lives.

"I don't care if she moves in," Boss said. "She seems like a nice kid. Why didn't you go see Coffee when you were in Texas?"

"I meant to," I said. "I know I should have."

"Coffee depends on you," Boss said. "She's also about the only woman who gives a flip about you. You ought to be a little more loyal."

Boss's hair was extremely beautiful. She stood up and began to clear the table. I helped her.

"I'm glad you showed up," she said. "I've got some papers for you to sign. I sold the horse farm today. Spud bought it."

"Spud?" I said, shocked. "I thought he was in Miami."

"When's the last time you heard from Cindy?" Boss asked.

"A couple of days ago," I said.

"Spud just left his wife and moved in with her," she said. "Naturally her engagement to Harris is off. They need the horse farm for a weekend place, since Betsy will get Spud's weekend place, if they divorce."

"My gosh," I said. "Cindy and Spud are planning to marry?"

"Yep," Boss said. "Spud's like Boog. He's been good at his job too long. He's just at the right age to leave his wife for someone half as good."

I was so stunned I couldn't think of a thing to say.

Boss went about cleaning up, perfectly self-assured.

"I guess I ought to go," I said.

"You're welcome to stay," Boss said. "Plenty of beds. But then a bed's not what you want, is it?"

I shrugged. I had no idea what I wanted. The fact that my life lacked purpose had never been more obvious.

"I think I'll just hit a motel," I said. "I'm getting where I can't sleep, in house."

She seemed at least slightly sympathetic, but not sympathetic enough that I dared approach her. I stopped as I was going out the door, looking back to see if Boss had anything else to say.

Chapter IX _____

I drove to Georgetown and cruised past Cindy's house. Sure enough, a light was on in her bedroom window. I felt like dumping the fifty pairs of boots on her doorstep, but if I did that someone would just steal them. I wasn't despairing enough to want to lose fifty pairs of boots.

Despair or not, I had difficulty accepting what had happened. Once Cindy's confidence had collapsed, our relationship had begun to seem almost real. Women were often accusing me of only choosing weak, insecure, dependent women. It was the weak, insecure, and dependent women I chose who flung the accusation at me most often. A good percentage of the women I chose spent most of our time together explaining why it was wrong for me to have chosen them. Cindy had even done that, although she did it in a rather oblique way, by explaining to me constantly why I wasn't successful enough for her.

Now that she had the most famous editor in America maybe she could relax, on that score.

I drove to Alexandria and sat in the parking lot of a motel for twenty minutes but I didn't go in and get a room. While I was sitting there I called Coffee, but her dope dealer answered so I hung up.

The next time I killed the motor I was in front of Jean's house. The downstairs was dark but a light was on in her bedroom. I have a theory that women love surprise arrivals, and now I had an excellent opportunity to test it. Despite this theory, I didn't jump right out of the car and run over and ring the doorbell. I sat in the car almost as long as I had sat in the motel parking lot.

On the other hand I knew I had to act. It was getting late. The light in Jean's bedroom could go off any second, in which case it would seem ten times more difficult to go up and knock on her door. A woman who had just gone to bed might destroy my theory. She might not welcome a surprise arrival from someone she was mad at anyway.

Finally I got out and walked up her steps. For perhaps a minute I just stood there, looking at the door. Then it occurred to me someone might see me and mistake me for a burglar, so I knocked.

The knock rang loudly in the quiet neighborhood. At least it seemed loud to me, but nothing happened. Jean didn't come downstairs.

I knocked again, more loudly still. That got results. Lights began to go on in the house. An upstairs light came on, illuminating the stairs. Then I saw Jean scamper downstairs, in a bathrobe, but she didn't head for the front door. She headed for the kitchen. A light came on in the dining room. Then she peeped into the living room and switched that light on too.

Only then did she approach the door, crossing the living room cautiously.

"Who is it?" she asked, without opening the door.

"Me," I said.

"Jack?" she said. "Is that you?"

"Yep," I said.

She opened the door a crack and looked out at me, her eyes very large. When she saw it was me she heaved an enormous sigh.

"Jesus, you scared the piss out of me," she said.

"I'm sorry," I said. "I should have called."

It only occurred to me then that I could have called from across the street. In my anxiety I had forgotten my own telephone.

"Why did you turn on so many lights?" I asked.

"So I could see who I was being murdered by," Jean said. "Why do you think? Nobody's knocked at my door this time of night in several years. I get scared, you know."

She opened the door a little bit more, but just to get a better look at me rather than to let me in. It was not a friendly appraisal, exactly. As her fear subsided, anger took its place. It came to her suddenly that she was very mad at me.

"What are you doing here anyway?" she asked. "Who told

you you could come and knock on my door in the middle of the night?"

"It's not that late," I said, although it was.

Jean opened the door and came out on the porch, brushing against me as she did but not looking at me again. She stood on her top step and looked at my car, which was sitting innocently in the street.

"Why are you looking at my car?" I asked. She really looked angry.

"It's parked in my street," she said. "I'll look at it if I want to."

"There's no point in hating a car," I said.

"How stupid do you think I am?" she said.

"I don't think you're stupid."

"You have no right to show up here," she said. "It's my house, I like to *invite* the people that show up here."

"I know," I said.

"You don't, you don't!" she said emphatically. "You don't know how it scares me when people I'm not expecting show up at my door. I hate it. I get totally scared."

"You shouldn't be living alone if you're so scared," I said.

Jean looked at me contemptuously.

"I'm sorry I said that," I said.

"Go on," she said, after a moment. "Tell me you make a lot of mistakes."

Then she sat down on her top step. She was barefoot and it was a cold night. I sat down, too, but not too close to her. I was worried about her feet.

"Aren't your feet cold?" I asked. "Don't you have some house shoes?"

"My feet are none of your business," she said.

"Don't be so mad," I said. "I won't lie to you anymore."

"Yes you will," she said. "Can't you even be honest about the fact that you lie?"

Actually, it wasn't easy to be honest. Despite almost constant lying, I think of myself as pretty honest. There seems to be some paradox, pitting truth against literal statement, that I have never understood. My view was that I only lied in the hope of achieving a better truth, but that was never the view of the people I lied to when they discovered the lie.

It seemed to me a complex subject, but it didn't seem so to Jean, or to most of the women I knew. To them a lie was a lie, invariably bad. I have never been able to persuade a single woman that certain lies were the route to a happier truth.

"It was a minor lie," I said, deciding not to try and argue ethical theory with a woman whose feet were freezing on the cold steps.

"All the more reason it was disgusting," Jean said. "A major lie, such as concealing that you have a wife or something, I could understand. You might conceal that you had a wife in order to get to fuck me, which is at least an understandable motive. Why tell me some stupid little lie about Miami?"

I didn't answer. I didn't want to try and re-create the grounds of that lie.

"You better say something," she said. "I'm not going to sit out here freezing if you won't even talk to me."

"Why do we have to sit out here?" I asked. "Couldn't we go in the house?"

"No," Jean said. "You're not getting in my house. I don't want it. I don't trust you anymore."

"How about my car?" I asked.

"Why should I trust your car?" she asked.

"I mean how about getting in it. It's warm."

"You'd think it was below zero," she said. "If I leave the house one of the girls might wake up. And anyway I don't want to sit in a car with you."

She didn't seem quite so mad.

"Let's hear about the woman in Miami," she said. "I assume this was your glamorous friend."

"Yes," I admitted.

"Why was it so important that you go see her in Miami?"

"She was in trouble. At least she thought she was. It turned out she wasn't."

"The plot thickens," Jean said. "He likes women who appear to be in trouble but actually aren't. If they appear to be in trouble then you can appear to come to the rescue."

I didn't say anything.

"That's one of the worst syndromes," Jean said. "It's revolting it's so sexist."

"Maybe I can outgrow it," I said.

"No, I have a feeling you need to feel you're coming to the rescue," she said. "Otherwise why did you follow me out of the auction that day when I was crying. It's probably an unbreakable pattern with you—coming to the rescue."

I didn't argue. For all I knew she was right.

"I don't need rescuing," she said. "You're dishonest and you can't stay put."

We sat for a bit.

"Finish the story," Jean said. "How come the glamorous friend in Miami got out of trouble so quick?"

"A very important man fell in love with her," I said. "I'll probably never see her again."

"Unless the very important man falls *out* of love with her," Jean said. "In that case she'll *really* need you. You can *really* come to the rescue."

She looked at me for a minute, a little disgusted. I think she was mostly disgusted with herself for letting the conversation continue for so long.

"I don't think she'll need me again," I said. "They've bought a six-million-dollar horse farm already."

Jean stood up. "Six million, huh?" she said.

I nodded.

"Well, so what?" she said. "I had a guy that rich once. Jimmy could buy a horse farm if he wanted to. Catching a rich guy is not an impossible feat."

"You don't have to compete with her," I said. "That's over."

"Just until she needs rescuing," Jean said. "That gives her an edge, in my book. I certainly don't intend to get in a position where I need rescuing by the likes of you. And if I do I won't tell you."

"I'm going to come back and show you the boots I got," I said. "Sometime when you've got shoes on."

Jean looked over her shoulder, but didn't say anything. She

didn't seem to be softening much. She went in, and the lights in the downstairs went off, one by one. Then the light over the stairs went off. But the light in her bedroom was still on when I drove away.

Chapter X _____

I didn't even consider sleeping. I was far too frustrated. Generally women soften, no matter how badly you've treated them, if they see you more or less mean well and that it was mere human frailty that made you treat them badly.

But Jean had been adamant. Not totally hostile, just adamant. There was a chance, but it was going to take work.

I knew if I checked into a motel I wouldn't sleep. I was on a kind of driving high, and my thoughts were spinning. When your thoughts are spinning it's horrible to lie in bed.

So I hit the Beltway and headed for Baltimore. It's a deeply decayed city, but the very fact that it was decayed made it perfect for the mood I was in. Many people in Baltimore are so far gone into urban neurosis that they make no distinction between night and day. They drag themselves around at all hours of the night, doing odd things and looking depressed.

The reason I decided on Baltimore was because I knew an antique collector there named Benny the Ghost, a name he acquired because of the habit he has of materializing out of nowhere at country auctions only a few seconds before the best lot is being sold. You never see Benny until just after he has bought something you wanted, and then, almost at once, he melts away. Very few people have ever spoken to him, including auctioneers whose sales he has frequented for years. Benny the Ghost keeps his own council.

I was one of the privileged few who actually knew Benny, whose real last name was Higgins. The way I got to know him was by outbidding him for an Isnik dish. It was a won-derful dish; God knows what it was doing in Pennsylvania, where the auction was held.

Benny has money and usually gets whatever it is he wants at auctions—his reputation takes the competitive spirit right out of most bidders. It's not that he has obvious auction macho—he looks like a men's room attendant in a second-rate hotel—but he does persist. However, I really wanted the Isnik dish, so I ignored him and kept bidding.

I think Benny was startled—he's not used to being strongly challenged—and I got the dish for $950. It was an extraordi-nary dish, and while I was paying for it Benny came over and stood looking at me sorrowfully. Like many Baltimoreans, he looked like he had a headache, a toothache, and sinus trouble. He did not look happy, and seemed stunned by the fact that he had lost the dish.

"That dish was the only thing I came for," he said to me, looking like a dog who has just been unjustly kicked. "I drove sixty miles."

"Benny, you should have kept bidding," I said.

"But the next bid would have been a thousand dollars," he said. "Isnik dishes don't cost a thousand dollars."

"This one did, nearly," I said.

"It's very reckless," he said. "Paying that much for an Isnik dish."

"It's beautiful though, isn't it?" I said.

Benny just looked gloomy. He had a long heavy face that could hold a lot of gloom, too. He didn't want to admit that the dish was beautiful, since if he did his regret over losing it would just deepen. His regret was already pretty deep.

"I wonder if I have anything you'd like to trade for it," he said. The words obviously cost him an effort. I was intrigued. No one I knew had ever heard Benny the Ghost offer to trade for anything. No dealer that I knew had even the faintest idea of what the nature or scope of his collections were. He bought almost exclusively at auction, almost never from dealers. But his territory was wide. He mostly hit country auctions in the Baltimore–Washington–Philadelphia area, but he had been known to strike as far north as New Hampshire, and as far south as Florence, South Carolina.

No one knew when or where he might appear, but everyone knew what his habits were, the principal one being that he only bid on a single item at each auction—almost always the best item, although many an auctioneer hadn't realized he was selling his best item until Benny had bought it.

"Sure, we might trade," I said. "What sort of things do you have?"

"Well, I just have odds and ends," Benny said. "I've never traded anything. But I hate to lose that dish."

"It's for sale," I assured him. "I didn't buy it to keep. I'll trade if you have something I like better."

"It's hard to say," Benny said. "I just have odds and ends."

While I was writing out a check for the dish, Benny dematerialized. He just vanished. Nobody had seen him leave, but he definitely wasn't there, and I didn't see him again for over a year. I was at an estate auction near Richmond and I sensed a gloomy presence at my elbow. There stood Benny, wearing the old khaki shirt and faded green slacks that he wore everywhere.

"Have you still got that Isnik dish?" he asked.

"I sure do," I said.

In fact I had held on to it solely in the hope of someday running into Benny the Ghost again.

"I liked that dish," he said gloomily.

"We can still trade," I said softly. I know how shy certain eccentrics are around their collections. They approach the thought of showing them as cautiously as deer approach a waterhole.

"I guess you could come and look," Benny said, hopelessly. "I live in Baltimore."

He gave me a phone number and two days later I called it. I was in Baltimore at the time.

"I guess you could come and look," he said, even more hopelessly. It turned out I was only two blocks from where he lived, which was in a narrow, five-story building in a decaying block of North Howard Street.

When I knocked on Benny's door I had no idea that I was about to walk into one of the greatest hoards in America: hoard was the only word for it. All five floors of the building were shelved floor to ceiling with green library shelving, and every shelf on every floor was crammed absolutely full of antiques.

When the shelving along the walls of the five floors had been filled, Benny had simply extended rows of shelves at angles out into the rooms, creating in miniature an effect like that of the tangled streets of certain old cities like Boston. Shelves wound through the large rooms with no rhyme or reason, all of them stuffed full of antiques. Piles had begun to build up in front of the shelves, antiques in almost unimaginable profusion and variety: everything from crocks to buttons to frakturs to silver, gold, brass, bronze, pewter, copper, jade, ironware, paintings, porcelain, tools, stuffed animals, barometers, rifles, carvings, pots, baskets, toys, lamps, etc.

I have seen some hoards, but never anything to equal what Benny the Ghost had crammed into the house in Baltimore. There may have been twenty or thirty thousand antiques in it, all of them good. Some were tiny and some were huge— he had an iron pot you could have cooked a hippopotamus in —but very few were mediocre.

The only light in the building came from plumber's lamps, which hung everywhere, thirty or forty to each floor.

Benny lived in the house, apparently. In time I toured each of the five floors but saw no evidence of a bed, a TV set, a couch, or any of the other things that normally go in a home. Doubtless these things had gone long ago, judged inessential and jettisoned to make room for more antiques. There was what once had been a kitchen—I could tell that by the sink in it—but it had no stove and there was not so much as a hot plate, that I could see. Benny took his meals out, if indeed he had not dispensed with the need for meals. The sink was piled with Zuñi pottery and a tiny bathroom on the second floor was almost full of Eskimo bows, arrows, and harpoons. If a seal had suddenly appeared in the john it would have been easy to get.

Living as I do in a world of goods, I thought that I had long since grown jaded to objects in the mass, but Benny the Ghost's secret hoard taught me better. I had never seen such an exciting gathering of antiques. Generally hoarders on Benny's scale get one good item out of every one hundred things they buy, and the good idea items are soon obscured by piles of junk. Benny's case was just the reverse: out of every hundred he bought there was one that was merely good. The rest were exceptional. Many were great, and five or six on each floor were supreme. He had the greatest star Kazan I had ever seen, and a George I teapot than any silver dealer in America would have given a quarter of a million dollars for. It was surrounded by perhaps three hundred other silver teapots, each worthy of prolonged attention. An even tinier bathroom on the fourth floor was filled with *Kiseru-zutso*, the wonderful delicately decorated Japanese pipe cases.

The hoard was so staggering that on my first visit I never got above the first floor—and there were five floors. There were so many fine things that my eyes couldn't take them in, or distinguish between them properly.

When I walked in with the Isnik dish Benny was twitching and looking extremely gloomy. I knew why. He might have twenty thousand objects, but Benny was a collector, not a dealer or a trader. The thought of having to part with any one of them made him extremely unhappy.

"Well, I just have odds and ends," he said. "I don't know what I could trade."

I immediately put his mind at ease by selling him the Isnik dish at my cost, plus 10 percent, a very fair price. Isnik crafts had nearly doubled in value in the year that I had owned the dish, and Benny knew it.

When he learned that he could have the dish and not have to give up anything he looked almost happy for a few minutes. His collection need not be violated. He wandered off down the long rows of shelves, dodging the hanging plumber's lights, and in a minute was back with the cash, precisely $1,045 of it.

"I'll put it on the fifth floor," he said. "I've got my Isnik things up there."

Then, to my relief, Benny the Ghost gradually became friendly. In all the years that he had been collecting, I may have been the first one to see the collection. He had been its sole appreciator all along, and when he discovered that I knew things about some of his pieces a tentative opening process began. We spent the whole night on one section of shelves on the lower floor, while Benny lectured me on the objects in it, most of them pewter. Once he started talking I was trapped: the knowledge he had been storing up for his whole life began to pour out.

From then on, whenever I was in the vicinity of Baltimore, I made a point of stopping by, so Benny could lecture me about his antiques for a few hours. Usually I sold him something good, at a reasonable price. He always paid in cash, and pretty soon he began to expect my visits. I came to realize that Benny was a kind of frustrated professor. He should have opened an Academy of Antiques somewhere and shared his knowledge with eager students. With the knowledge he carried in his head he could have trained an army of scouts and sent them to pick America even cleaner than it has been picked already.

There was no need to call ahead when visiting Benny at night: he was always there, and always up.

I knew Benny looked terrible, but when I rang and he worked his way down to the door, through the maze of his shelving, it was always a shock to see how terrible. The circles under his eyes might have been painted with charcoal. He had only a few teeth left, most of them in his upper jaw. He rarely shaved but his salt-and-pepper stubble wasn't long enough to be thought of as a beard.

"Hi, Benny," I said, when he peeped suspiciously out of his peephole. "I was in Washington and happened to have something I thought you might want."

It was an American Indian carving of a bear—I had bought it in Chicago. I knew Benny loved Indian woodcraft, and had bought it with him in mind. It was a peculiar piece, almost abstract, and very beautiful.

"Oh yes, Pequot," Benny said, glancing at it. "I have several in this style but I don't think I have a bear. We better go see, though. I might have a bear. The others are on the top floor."

All five flights of stairs were piled with things that wouldn't fit in the shelves. One landing held a brass diving helmet and some weighted brass shoes.

We found the Pequot carvings way at the back, on a high shelf.

"I was right," Benny said. "I don't have a bear."

I agreed to let him have it for $800 and while he was going to get the cash I poked around a little. While I was wandering along a long section of shelving containing lighting devices, lamps mostly, I noticed a door I hadn't seen before.

When Benny came back with the cash I nodded toward the door.

"What's in there?" I asked.

"Oh, I keep my unicums in there," he said. "I have forty-seven now."

A unicum, of course, is a unique thing: not a freak, but the only surviving example of its class.

Assiduous collectors—usually the dominant collectors in their fields—will occasionally secure a unicum. A collector of American prints, if he's lucky enough, might get a unique example of a print by some obscure artist. Most unicums, in fact, are paper items: stamps or broadsides that exist but in a single copy.

"I didn't know you have a unicum collection, Benny," I said.

Benny looked modest. "It's just some unicums I picked up," he said. "Someday I'll show them to you."

While we were looking at the Pequot carvings the doorbell rang. I think I was more surprised than Benny. It had never rung before during my visits, and I had taken to making the lax assumption that I was the only person admitted to Benny's house.

"That must be August," Benny said.

We worked our way laboriously downstairs. The thing that worried me most about Benny's collection was that he might get trapped in it. It is not unheard of for elderly collectors to fall victim to their own collections. A magazine collector I knew slightly had met his death that way. He had a largish house in St. Louis, but it was filled with magazines, heaped in towering stacks in every room, with only a narrow path between the stacks, like the paths between Bryan Ponder's bird nests. One day the old man had dislodged a stack, that stack had struck another stack, and he had been buried beneath an avalanche of magazines. Since, like many collectors, he was a recluse, he was not found for nearly a month.

Indeed, I knew many stories of collections turning on their collectors. A man in Fort Smith, Arkansas, who collected tractors, was killed when his latest acquisition reared up and fell on him.

Something like that could happen to Benny. There was only one exit to his house: the front door. All the windows had long since been covered with shelving. The front door itself was getting harder to open, as Benny carelessly piled more and more things in the front hall until he could get time to sort them. Eventually, if he wasn't careful, he was going to wall himself in. If there was a fire, or if he simply pulled some shelving over on himself, he would be in big trouble. Nobody would be likely to miss him, since nobody ever saw him anyway.

The doorbell rang steadily, as we worked our way downstairs.

"August must think I'm deaf," Benny observed mildly.

When he opened the door August still had his finger on the doorbell. He was a short man, as broad as he was tall, dressed in old overalls and a grimy red baseball cap. He was about Benny's age, but so thick that he could have made three of Benny. One unusual aspect of his appearance was that his white chest hair extended upward to his jaw line. It was thick, white, and curly. August looked like a primate, but not exactly like a man. More disconcerting than the chest hair was the fact that his eyes were not in synch. One looked straight at us—the other pointed off toward the left.

"Hello, August," Benny said.

"Got a nice gong," August said.

"Oh well," Benny said. "I've got quite a few gongs. About forty. What kind of gong is it?"

"Dinner gong," August said. "Got a turtle shell with a picture on it."

"What?" Benny asked, perking up a little.

"Big turtle shell," August said. "Picture ain't too good though."

Through the door I could see an old black pickup parked at the curb. It had wooden sideboards, but whatever it may once have boasted in the way of springs had long since had the spring crushed out of them. The pickup sagged far to one side with the weight of goods piled in it.

On the sidewalk near the pickup were two thin men dressed as August was. They were watching a dusty-looking mongrel relieve itself against the rear tire of the pickup.

"I better take a look at that shell," Benny said.

August took no interest in me at all. He led us out to the pickup, lowered the much-dented tailgate, and began to dig objects out of the clutter of goods the rear end contained. To my surprise, the objects were good. The dinner gong was silver, with a nice little felt mallet. The two thin men and the dusty mongrel came over and stood silently as we inspected it.

"Hello, Sept," Benny said. "Hello, Octo."

The two men nodded shyly, but didn't speak.

"How's your dog?" Benny asked. The dog was scratching at a tick. The two thin men looked down at it, embarrassed by Benny's politeness.

Nice as the gong was, it was a trifle compared to the turtle shell with the picture in it. The shell was the size of a washbasin, the shell of a sea turtle, obviously. The picture, on the inside of the shell, was a primitive showing two little black children with flowers in their hair. It was painted on the scraped surface of the sea turtle's shell. I had never seen such a painting, never heard of such a technique. It was a wonderful thing, but I carefully muted my interest. After all, it was Benny's buy, and the qualities of the painting were not lost on him either.

"My goodness," he said. "My goodness. Where'd you find this, August?"

"Down Carolina," August said.

"Well my goodness," Benny said. "Did they have any more?"

"Only one," August said.

"What would a man have to give for a thing like that?" Benny wondered.

August looked unhappy. Having to think up prices for oddities like a turtle shell with a picture on it was wearisome work. He fixed his one good eye on the two thin men, but they were carefully noncommittal. They kept their eyes on the dog.

"Only one they had," August said. "Would you pay seventy-five?"

Benny didn't have to think that one over long.

"I'll go get the money," he said. "I don't really need the gong. I have quite a few nice gongs as it is."

He went in the house to get the money and silence fell. The three men were not very talkative. The dog, more animated than the rest of us, jumped up in the back of the pickup and crawled over the miscellaneous heap of goods to where it had a bed.

I was wondering if I ought to buy the gong, simply as a means of breaking the ice. It was obvious that I had stumbled on a little family of American traders, men who got around. The pickup had an Ohio license plate.

"My name's Jack," I said. "How much do you want for the gong?"

August looked unhappy. Some people are as shy about selling as others are about sex. Although he probably spent his whole life buying and selling, the making of prices did not come easy, particularly if the customer was a stranger.

"Silver gong," he said finally.

Then I noticed the end of a trunk, wedged beneath a pile of quilts. I could barely see it, but it looked like an interesting trunk. It looked very old, and it didn't look American.

"Hey," I said. "Can I see that trunk? I need a trunk."

331

The two tall men blinked. My erratic behavior made them nervous.

August was not so volatile. He was thinking about the gong and did not allow himself to be distracted. His left eye gazed off into Baltimore, while his right studied me.

"Like to get a hunnert an' twenty-five," he said.

I immediately handed it over.

"Thank you," I said. "That's a good price. What about the trunk?"

"It's under them quilts," August said, after a moment. Having $125 materialize in his hand startled him, and he waddled off around the pickup and put it in a safe place.

"I sure would like to see that trunk," I said, when he came back.

Benny arrived with $75 and took the turtle shell with the beautiful primitive on it.

"He wants that trunk," August said. "You want it?"

A true trader, he was sticking to protocol. He had come to see Benny, therefore Benny had first refusal on everything that was for sale.

"My goodness," Benny said. "I don't think so. I have over two hundred trunks."

It was true. Benny's house had trunks everywhere, most of them serving as storage bins for medals, seals, coins, watches, paperweights, *netsuke*, or other small objects.

August looked at the trunk thoughtfully.

"Take it out I won't be able to get it back in," he said, to test my seriousness. Removing the trunk would disrupt the balance of his load, which in his mind possessed an order not visible to the casual eye.

"I'll probably buy it," I said.

Looking resigned, he extracted the trunk, while his companions stood by like two nervous birds, watching his every move but not daring to offer any assistance. August was clearly the boss.

The trunk, when it finally emerged, was wonderful. I couldn't immediately place the wood, but it was not American. From the leather and brass work I thought it was probably seventeenth century, though it might have been sixteenth. There was a crest stamped into the leather and the inside was lined with an ancient purplish velvet, dried to the thinness of Kleenex, but velvet still. Probably the trunk was Spanish, possibly Portuguese.

"Do you know this crest, Benny?" I asked. If it was a royal, as opposed to a ducal, crest, the chest might be worth thousands.

Benny was no help. Like many collectors, he is completely indifferent to objects he is not interested in buying.

"It's not familiar to me," he said rather formally. He had got what he wanted—an astonishing primitive—and a Spanish trunk could not interest him less.

August's good eye watched me unblinkingly as I studied the trunk.

"Gosh, I like it," I said. "Where'd you get it?"

"Over't Pensacola," August said.

"What would you take for it?"

"Two hunnert," August said. His expression didn't change at all, but the figure caused his companions to blink several times. I had a feeling August thought he was shooting for the moon this time.

"Fine," I said, paying him as quickly as I had paid for the gong.

My rapid acceptance caused a slight look of worry to cross his broad face. He had meant to overprice the trunk, but the fact that I hadn't even bothered to bargain could only mean that he had underpriced it after all.

Nonetheless, the deed was done. No doubt it would be discussed endlessly, as the three men rode up the road. They might debate the sale for weeks, and even persuade themselves eventually that they could have got an unheard-of sum, like *three* hundred, for the trunk.

In the meantime they closed the tailgate and got ready to leave for the next stop up the road, having just made four hundred dollars—not bad for Baltimore in the middle of the night. The tires of the old truck were so treadless they were shiny.

Watching it creak away up the bumpy street, the side-boards swaying with the weight of goods piled in it, I felt better for a moment. The three strange traders had made me feel that I was in touch with my vocation again. It was warming to think that all over America at this hour people were loading pickups and vans and setting off for flea markets and swap-meets. It was a peculiar solution to life, perhaps, but a surprisingly effective one. The treasure hunt must never stop, even if most of the folks who pursued it were only able to offer humble treasures.

"Who were the thin guys?" I asked Benny.

"Sept and Octo," he said. "Octo's the youngest. That's as far as the old man got."

I looked puzzled.

"Named his kids after the months," Benny said. "He was hoping to get twelve but the old lady died after Octo."

"Were there any girls?" I asked.

"Why yes," Benny said. "April, May, and June. They run a nice flea market outside of Cleveland. You ought to stop and see them if you're up that way."

"I'll do that, Benny," I said.

Chapter XI _____

It was 4 A.M. when I pulled back into Washington—too late to sleep, too early to go to Jean's house. It wouldn't do to show up that early, even armed with an extraordinary trunk.

Thinking of Jean, I went into the cafeteria where I had persuaded her to eat breakfast with me the morning we met. It was an all-night cafeteria, but 4 A.M. was not its busiest hour. A few tired delivery men were drinking coffee, and two young hookers were hanging around the pay phone as if it were their office. There were a few pale young men in poly-ester suits who looked like they might have come off the graveyard shift in some far-flung wing of the bureaucracy. They were so pale as to be almost translucent. Perhaps they were only allowed out in the dark of night, and never experienced sunlight at all.

As I was about to sit down and eat a big plate of scrambled eggs I happened to look out the window and see Eviste Labouchere. He was chugging slowly up the sidewalk on an ancient motor scooter, wearing evening clothes and a blue crash helmet.

Eviste carefully parked his scooter and came in, still wearing the blue crash helmet. The hookers didn't give him a glance—perhaps he often straggled through their office at four in the morning. He stood pensively in front of about fifty yards of food, a small solitary figure contemplating almost infinite gastronomic choices, but all he got was coffee and a croissant. Beneath his crash helmet he looked a little melancholy. I waved at him and he came over.

"Must have been a late party," I said.

Eviste shook his head. He tried to grin, but was too tired even to lift his small mustache.

"I speek to Poland," he said.

I didn't know if he meant the country, or if he had a new girl friend named Poland.

It turned out to be the former. Thanks to the fact that he spoke Polish, Eviste had a job at the USIA. Every morning from 2 A.M. to 4 A.M. he broadcast in Polish, for the benefit of the oppressed masses.

"Sometimes I read poems," he said. "Tonight I was reading Adam Mickiewicz."

To my horror, he began to cry. He had not taken off his crash helmet, either. Tears ran out of his eyes and dripped into the smudge of his mustache, then ran on beneath the chin strap of his helmet and stained the front of his dress shirt.

"I don't like to speek to Poland," he said, wiping his eyes with a paper napkin. "I am a re-porter! I need the sources. All the sources are taken up."

He was too disheartened even to be able to break his croissant in half.

Across the room the phone rang and one of the two hookers answered it. Their wait had paid off. A minute later they were going out the door.

It occurred to me that perhaps I could help Eviste out. I could be a source. After all, I knew what seemed to me like an important secret, although it wasn't too secret and no one else in Washington seemed to think it was important at all, or even unusual.

"Do you know about the Smithsonian?" I asked. "Do you know it's being sold?"

Eviste looked blank. In his tired state the concept didn't really penetrate.

"Here's your scoop," I said. And I explained to him about the sales to Third World countries, Peck Folmsbee's museums, and all the replicas being manufactured in secret factories in Hodges, South Carolina.

"It's the truth," I said. "I don't know why it hasn't been in the papers."

I really didn't know why. The only person I knew who considered the Smithsonian sale an important secret was Brisling Bowker, and that was probably because he hoped to auction some of it. The one journalist I had mentioned it to, George Psalmanazar, had dismissed it contemptuously. "It's a page-six story in the *New York Post*," he had said, with some disgust.

Eviste was a fresher spirit. The minute I mentioned the Third World his eyes began to light up. In no time he had sluffed off his fatigue. This was it, the "sceup" he had come to America to find. He began to scribble on napkins. Since he used a felt-tip pen with a broad tip his scribbles soaked into the napkins and became illegible almost immediately, but Eviste kept scribbling. Soon he had such a pile of ink-soaked napkins that it became embarrassing. Fortunately, the one busboy in the cafeteria was asleep, slumped against the milk machine.

Then, while I drank a second cup of coffee, he dashed off

336

to a pay phone to phone in his story. This did not prove simple. While he was trying to get his paper in Rouen another hooker came in and looked indignant when she discoverd a small Frenchman using the telephone.

The call took a long time. Eviste's editors probably weren't convinced. In all likelihood they had forgotten the very existence of Eviste. Eviste became excited. He was yelling in French into the phone.

I kept drinking coffee and thinking about Jean. Though small she had seemed rather demanding. Probably the least she would demand was stability, a quality I wasn't sure I had to offer.

While I pondered, Eviste chattered in French to his editors. They were probably sitting over in Rouen trying to decide if they wanted to make themselves the laughingstocks of world journalism by printing a story emanating from a stringer so obscure they had long since forgotten him. As Eviste tried to persuade them, the city grew light. A street-sweeping machine, just finishing its nightly run, parked outside. The driver came in to have his breakfast. It was a misty morning, the streetlights amber circles in the mist.

Eviste finally came back, looking resigned. His editors had had no interest whatsoever in the Smithsonian or its fate.

"They want to know about Nanceey," he said. "They want to know about Haig. They think Haig will shoot a bomb."

He slumped in his seat, defeated. His sceup had fallen on deaf ears.

"Let's take a ride," I said, thinking a trip to the Millers might cheer him up. The Millers were early risers.

Sure enough, they had risen, or at least Boss, Boog, and Josie had. Boog was sitting glumly at the table holding a telephone to his ear, while Boss cooked a sausage omelet. Josie was cheerfully making biscuits. She and Boss looked as friendly as sisters.

"I wondered where you went off to," Josie said, when I came in. "Boy, you brought me to the right place, all right. We seen a movie and then we went dancin'. Me and Micah danced half the night."

337

"Hi, Eviste," Boss said. "Welcome to breakfast."

Boog hung up the phone and sighed.

"What's wrong with you?" Boss asked. She looked somewhat testy.

"What ain't?" Boog said. "We got any tequila?"

"He's a little like Little Joe," Josie said to Boss. "Gets depressed all the time, right?"

Eviste was watching Josie, who was still wearing her yellow shirt. She had exchanged her Levis for some running shorts she had found somewhere.

"You wanta buy a Henry rifle?" I asked Boog, thinking a little action might lift his gloom.

"For how much?" he said listlessly.

When I introduced Eviste to Josie, Eviste bowed, which surprised Josie no end.

"I guess I better make some more biscuits, now that we got company," she said. In two minutes she was teaching Eviste the fine art of biscuit making. The fact that he was wearing a tuxedo didn't faze her at all.

"Eviste tried to break the story about the Smithsonian being for sale, but no one's interested," I remarked.

Boog shrugged. "I'm puttin' Winkler County up for sale pretty soon," he said. "If I was to buy that gun who could I shoot with it?"

"You might as well shoot yourself if you don't cheer up," Boss said. "The one thing I won't tolerate is a gloomy man."

"Micah's gloomy," Boog pointed out. "He lays around crying half the time."

"Yeah, but it only takes Bob Newhart to cheer *him* up," Boss said. "I thought you were going to Saudi Arabia today."

She sounded put out with her husband—a normal thing for a wife to be, but Boss had never seemed like a normal wife. It had never occurred to me that the Millers' marriage might fray, like other marriages. Their long defiance of convention had been so successful that you tended to forget that no success is necessarily permanent.

The life of their household went on, as expansive as ever,

accommodating Josie easily, and now Eviste, but the life of Boog and Boss seemed to have changed subtly.

"It's an unsubstantial pageant," Boog said. "A sleep and a forgetting. There ain't no peace nor help from care. Ignert armies clash by night, so's it's hard to sleep."

"Shut up," Boss said. "Go back to bed if that's the best you can do."

"I never went to bed," Boog said. He looked at me angrily.

"What's the matter?" I asked.

"You wouldn't sell me that icon," he said. He was quite greedy, actually—not fond of being denied anything his eye had lit on.

"I've still got it," I said.

"I don't care," he said. He drank two beers in quick succession.

"It's hard to get drunk in the morning," he said. "Particularly on beer."

Boss was looking at him coldly, so coldly that he subsided, sat gloomily for a minute, and then went out in the yard.

"It's probably just a phase," Josie said, washing the biscuit dough off her hands. "Do you want orange juice, Eviste?"

Eviste just smiled. It was plain that he was enchanted with Josie. I decided it was a good time to leave.

I found Boog in the front seat of my car. The icon was in the back seat but he wasn't looking at it. He was just sitting.

"What's the matter with you?" I asked.

He stared dully at his own lawn for a time.

"I'm thanking of leavin'," he said. "Me and Boss don't get along like we used to."

"You got along last week," I pointed out.

"Yeah, but this week we don't," he said. "I thank I'll go to the Little Bomber's 'n get the whole line of specials, one after another. If that don't lift my spirits nothing will. Have you really got a Henry rifle in this car?"

I got it out and showed it to him. "Fourteen thousand to you," I said.

"Why not?" Boog said. "Come to the Little Bomber's and I'll give you a check."

He walked up the driveway with the rifle in his hand, looking utterly sad.

Chapter XII _____

Twenty minutes later I was in Wheaton. When Jean Arber, in her blue bathrobe, stepped out on her porch to get her morning paper I was sitting in the car in front of her house. The fifty pairs of Twine boots were lined up along her curb, waiting.

Jean saw me just as she picked up the paper. Then she saw the boots. After a moment, she went back inside. I waited. Almost immediately she came back out, a little girl on each hand. They were in bathrobes and slippers, their hair seemingly curlier than ever. They all looked at me, the car, and the fifty pairs of boots.

Belinda immediately broke ranks and came out to look the boots over. She squatted down in front of them.

"Where's any for me?" she asked. "Don't ya got *little* boots?"

"This man wasn't put on earth to bring you things," Jean remarked.

Belinda shrugged. "He could, though," she said.

"Where did you spend the night?" Jean asked.

"Baltimore," I said. "You'll never guess what I bought."

"You probably bought some stupid trunk, thinking you could bribe your way back into my good graces," Jean said, finishing her inspection of the boots.

"It's in the back seat."

Belinda began to hop up and down, trying to see. Jean went over and looked, but didn't pick her up.

"I'm the trunk person," she said. "You don't need to see."

She didn't change her expression, when she saw the trunk.

She was not wearing a particularly friendly expression, either. Still, she looked at the trunk for quite a while.

"You can get in the car and look," I said.

Jean reached down and picked up Belinda. "Nope," she said. "I'm not amenable to bribes. Belinda is but Beverly and I aren't. Beverly and I have better values."

"Yeah, Belinda's greedy," Beverly agreed.

Jean gave me a cool, critical look. If she liked the trunk, she wasn't going to say so. If she liked me, she wasn't going to say so, either. She kissed Belinda's neck a few times, savoring the smell of her daughter.

"Do you think we ought to cook him breakfast?" she asked, looking at Beverly.

"Sure," Beverly said.

"You're a pushover, Beverly," Jean said. "I'm surprised at you."

"We could go out for breakfast," I said. "There's a Waffle House up the road."

"Yeah, Waffle House," both girls said, in unison.

"No," Jean said.

"Why not?" Beverly asked. "We never go out for breakfast."

"Forget it," Jean said. "I'm not ready for society and I don't want to get ready for a while yet."

"I think you're being selfish," Beverly said, taking her mother's free hand. "Everybody wants to go out to breakfast but you. We have to put on our clothes anyway, don't we?"

"Yeah, but we don't have to get syrup all over us," Jean said. "That's what happens at the Waffle House. Belinda gets syrup all over us."

"Not over me," Beverly said. "I keep away from her."

"Somebody has to sit next to her," Jean said.

"Jack could," Beverly pointed out. "He *likes* her."

"Hey, you're right," Jean said. "He goes for the selfish ones, doesn't he. Let's give her away while we have the chance."

She handed me her daughter, who immediately began to feel around in my pockets.

"But you're selfish, too," Beverly said. "You won't let us do what we wanta do. You almost never do, you know."

"All right, all right, Beverly," Jean said. "I can't bear your accusations. We'll go to the Waffle House and Belinda can get syrup all over Jack."

We went, and Belinda did display an amazing talent for recklessness with syrup. She insisted on a full waffle all her own and then did everything to it but eat it. Jean and Beverly watched from the safety of the other side of the booth. Belinda strolled around between bites, sampled my French toast, and generally indulged herself.

"Eat your waffle," I said several times, to Jean's amusement. Each time I said it Belinda poured more syrup on the waffle.

"Too dry," she said. She filled each of the little squares on the waffle with syrup. When the plate ran over she stuck her elbow in the puddle. On the way home she insisted on helping me drive, which resulted in a very sticky steering wheel.

Jean didn't say much, the whole time. Her attitude was rather spectatorial. When we got back to her house we dawdled in my car for a while, the girls trying out different tapes on my tape deck. Belinda discovered a pen in my pocket and badgered Jean until she produced a small pad from her purse. Then the girls drew pictures. Beverly drew neat representational pictures of animals, chiefly pigs and cows, while Belinda drew swirls that bore a vague resemblance to people.

After a while I borrowed the pen and wrote Jean a note asking her if I could take her out that night. I folded the note into a little square and handed it to her.

"What does *it* say?" Belinda asked.

"I can't tell you," Jean said. "It's top secret information."

"It is not," Belinda said, trying to snatch it.

To thwart her, Jean ate the note.

"Did you *eat* it?" Belinda asked, rather impressed.

Jean chewed it up and when it was hopelessly chewed she took it out of her mouth and handed it to Belinda.

"Have some chewing gum," she said.

"I bet he asked you for a date," Beverly said.

342

"There's such a thing as being too smart for your own good, Beverly," Jean said. "Try and remember that."

"Are you going to go?" Beverly asked.

Both girls seemed to think the question of some importance. They looked studiously at Jean.

"Don't look at me that way," Jean said. "It's none of your business, what I do. Besides, it's no big deal. Lots of men ask me for dates."

"Who else?" Beverly asked.

"What's a date?" Belinda inquired.

"You know, like going to a movie," Beverly said.

"Oh, *Star Wars*," Belinda said.

"Beverly's right, I'm out of practice," Jean said. "The truth is nobody asks me for dates."

"Who's the babysitter?" Belinda asked. "Not Linda?"

"Why not Linda?"

"Not Linda," Belinda repeated.

"Okay," Jean said, opening the door. "You can take me out, but only because I need the practice. Get out, girls."

Belinda gave me a sticky kiss before departing.

They ran up the steps to their house, eager to get on with other things.

Jean walked around to my side of the car.

"Out where?" she asked.

"I haven't decided," I said.

"Since it's a practice date, take me to a fancy restaurant," Jean said. "Then I can spend the whole day deciding what to wear."

"Okay," I said.

"I don't think Belinda's ever seen me dressed up," she said. "I don't even know if I'm still capable of it. I'll probably go buy a new dress."

She was silent for a moment.

"You're causing me a lot of trouble," she said. "It's nerve-racking, knowing I have a date. I'll probably worry about it all day. Who knows what you might try?"

"It's a first date, sort of," I said. "I might not try too much."

"Anything's too much if it makes me nervous," Jean said.

"My gosh, relax," I said. "We are not quite total strangers, you know."

"Yes we are," Jean said. "I'm not counting that time you're counting. I was just holding my own with Belinda, that time. Besides, you lied to me since. This is a new ball game, understand?"

"Okay," I said.

"I don't even know why I consented," Jean said, and went in her house.

Chapter XIII _____

I drove around Wheaton until I found a decent street with big trees, parked at the curb in the shade of the big trees, and made my car seat recline so I could take a nap. My car seats are more comfortable than most beds. It was not a pleasant sleep, though, because I had a vivid dream of Coffee, sitting on the steps of our house in Houston and sobbing because she couldn't get her hippopotamus chair in her car. It was practically the one time she had cried, during our marriage, and I dreamed about it often. It seemed to symbolize all failure, but particularly mine. If only I had behaved better and been less obsessed with antiques and more tolerant of Coffee's bad taste in modern furniture I might never have brought her to that pass.

It hadn't been, in the end, such an awful pass. I borrowed a pickup from a junk dealer I knew and hauled the chair to Austin for her. Even that hadn't cheered Coffee up: she had wanted to make a clean break, and what was clean about my hauling her chair to Austin? She may have been right, too. If I hadn't done that maybe we *would* have made a clean break. Instead we had spent several years talking on the phone twenty hours a week.

The dream was so vivid that it woke me up. Naturally I called Coffee.

"Hello," she said, not very happily. She had a little gulp in her voice when she said it, as if she had not really wanted to speak but was compelled to by politeness.

"Are you okay?" I asked. "I just dreamed about you and the chair."

"Well," Coffee said, "it's awfully early for you to call. I just got to the office."

"I keep forgetting there's a time difference," I said.

"I wish you'd stop dreaming about me," Coffee said. "It's not very nice of you."

"What do you mean?" I said. "I can't help what I dream about. Nobody can. Don't you ever dream about me?"

"I don't have dreams," Coffee said. "I just sleep."

"That's nonsense. Everybody dreams. You have to. You'd get sick if you didn't."

"Well, I'm not sick and I don't," Coffee said. She was as dogmatic as Belinda.

"I guess you just don't remember them," I said, which was a mistake. Coffee's terrible memory had been a source of trouble ever since I'd known her. She really had almost no memory at all. Once she forgot what butter was, for example. Naturally she was extremely sensitive about her memory, and denied that it was bad.

"I want you to stop dreaming about me," she said.

"But Coffee," I said. "You can't control dreams. They just happen."

"Am I naked or what?" she asked, surprising me.

"No," I said. "You were just trying to get the hippo chair in the car."

"Well, am I ever naked?" she asked. "That's what worries me."

"Worries you how? It's *my* dream, not yours."

"Yeah, but I'm involved with Emilio now," she said. "If he knew you were dreaming about me naked, he'd have a fit. I told you how jealous he is."

"Coffee, would you be sensible?" I said. "Emilio can't possibly know what I dream unless you tell him, and there's no reason why you should tell him."

"He knows we talk," Coffee said. "He's always asking what we talk about."

That was interesting.

"What do you tell him?"

"Well, I sure don't tell him you dream about me naked," Coffee said.

"I don't dream about you naked," I said.

"You used to," she said. "You mentioned it once."

"When?"

"Once," she said.

It had begun to seem that if any woman made two remarks to me the second remark would be a complete non sequitur, bearing no relation to what we had been talking about, or to whatever might be happening in their lives. Often enough, nothing was happening in our lives anyway.

"Why did you gulp when you said hello?" I asked.

"Don't change the subject," Coffee said. "Just cut out dreaming about me naked. That way I won't have to tell Emilio."

"Fine," I said. "Why did you gulp?"

"I don't know," she said. "Where are you?"

"Maryland," I said, secure in the knowledge that her grasp of geography was so bad that she would take that to mean I was still in her part of the world. Coffee clung to the strange theory that the states were somehow arranged alphabetically. In her mind Maryland lay next to Louisiana, which was not too far from Austin.

"If you'll come we could eat some Mexican food," she said. "That's one of my problems with Emilio. He hates Mexican food."

"I'll come, and we'll eat some," I said.

There was a pause.

"Do you think we'll ever get married again?" she asked.

"I don't know," I said. "You didn't like it much the first time, remember."

"Yeah, but maybe I was too young," Coffee said. "That's what Momma thinks."

She was silent for a moment.

"If you keep dreaming about me you must want something," she said. "Anyway, I don't want to talk anymore. Now every time I talk to you I want to cry."

"I don't see why," I said.

"You don't want me enough, that's why," Coffee said wanly. "I always thought you'd be the one person who always did want me enough. Only now you don't."

It was sort of a terrible accusation. One reason it was terrible was because it was unanswerable. I was very fond of her, but I probably didn't want her enough—particularly since I was not the one who got to measure enoughness, the most elusive of all qualities. If one's wanting fell one degree short of enoughness the whole tenor of the relationship was spoiled, it seemed. Enoughness admits of no subtraction: either one's desire is enough, or it's a failure.

At that point, Coffee hung up. Though it was 1,700 miles to Austin I could feel her crying as I started the car and drove out of Wheaton.

I drove to Georgetown, where, as if by a miracle, the parking place in front of Cindy's shop that I had got the day I met her was empty again. I parked and went up to the gallery, to see if anyone there knew anything about the boot exhibit. The only person there was a thin young woman dressed in black. She was beautiful but quite severe-looking. My mere presence in the gallery seemed to affront her slightly. When I stopped in front of her she glanced at me over her glasses, but didn't speak.

"I'm Jack," I said. "Were you expecting some boots?"

"We were expecting them yesterday," she said, rather cuttingly.

"I don't know why," I said, stung by her tone.

"You did agree to bring them yesterday, didn't you?" she said.

"Look, I didn't agree to bring them at all," I said. "Nothing was said about yesterday, or about any particular day."

"That's not the impression I was left with," she said, with a trace of uncertainty in her voice.

"Listen," I said. "The boots are mine. I haven't spoken

to Cindy in three days. She never said for sure that she wanted them, much less what day she wanted them. There are plenty of other places I can sell them if she doesn't want them."

She was surprised, but not yet in a yielding mood.

"Couldn't you just tell me your name?" I asked.

"Amanda Harisse," she said. She seemed a little grateful that I had changed the subject.

"Harris' sister?" I asked.

"Oh no," she said. "Just a poor cousin."

"Is Cindy really going to have this exhibit?" I asked.

"The invitations went out yesterday," Amanda said. "That's why I had hoped to have the boots. It's dangerous to invite important people to an opening until you're sure you have something to show them."

"I'm surprised you work here," I said, smiling at her.

Amanda sighed. "That was Harris' idea," she said. "The only one he's had in ten years."

"Is Harris pretty broken up about being jilted?" I asked.

Amanda sighed again. I think she found talking to me a little trying.

"It takes Harris some time to realize things," she said. "I'm not sure he's figured it out yet."

"Does Cindy ever show up around here?" I asked.

"Could you just bring in the boots?" Amanda said.

I decided to be cooperative. I brought in the boots. Lined up against the bare white walls of the gallery, so far from cowboys, ranches, Texas, they looked pretty silly. Amanda obviously thought so, too.

"Well, they're no worse than bread sculpture," I said.

Amanda sighed again. I was beginning to like her a little. She looked tired, probably from the exercise of so much severity.

"I bet you think this exhibit is a terrible idea," I said.

"What I think has no bearing on the question," Amanda said.

"Does it have any bearing on any question?"

Amanda looked disgusted. "Don't ask me questions like that," she said. "I don't even know you."

348

"It's because you're not trying," I said. "I'm very easy to know."

"I don't think I want to know you," she said. "You're making my morning a lot more difficult."

"Well, I still own the boots," I said. "If you don't want to be bothered with the exhibition I could help out by just taking them away."

"I have instructions to buy them," she said. "Firm instructions."

"Then I could set a ridiculous price," I said.

Amanda shrugged. "We pay ridiculous prices for everything we buy," she said.

"Well, I want twenty thousand," I said. Actually it wasn't a ridiculous price, considering that there were fifty pair of vintage boots.

"Twenty thousand dollars?" Amanda said. "For *these?*"

"That's only four hundred dollars a pair," I said. "Some of these boots are worth four times that.

"I wish you'd smile," I added.

"Offer me a reason," Amanda said, looking at me gravely. She picked up the phone and dialed. Cindy must have been sleeping with her head on it, she answered so quickly.

"The gentleman is here with the boots," Amanda said, in a voice considerably more nervous than the one she had been using with me. "However, he wants quite a lot of money for them."

There was a pause.

"Twenty thousand," Amanda said.

I was expecting to be handed the phone, to explain myself to an irate Cindy. Of course, I might change my mind and just give them to her, for old times' sake—although there hadn't been that much in the way of old times.

Just as I started to reach out for the phone, Amanda said, "All right," and hung up.

It took me aback. I had been primed to hear Cindy's healthy Santa Barbara voice and felt quite disappointed that I wasn't going to.

Amanda then disappeared into a little office. In about a minute she reappeared and handed me a check.

"Didn't she say anything?" I asked.

"She said 'Give him a check,' " Amanda said.

"I guess it's worth twenty thousand dollars to her not to have to hear my voice again," I said. It was a depressing thought.

Amanda looked at me with what I felt was a hint of sympathy. Not much, just a hint.

"Do you want to go to lunch?" I asked.

"No," Amanda said.

"I wish you'd smiled, at some point," I said, folding the check. There was a pad on the desk. I picked it up and wrote Josie Twine's name and Boog's phone number on it.

"This is the name of a woman who can give you some background information on the boot collection," I said. "She knows the provenance, if that becomes a factor."

Then I also wrote the name and phone number of Bobby Secundy, my boot scout friend in the Texas valley.

"This man is an *expert*, in the French sense," I said. "He knows more about boots than anybody alive. If you send him Polaroids he'll give you full details on the makers of each pair."

Amanda read the names and phone numbers.

"Thank you," she said. "I can't believe we're really doing this show."

"I couldn't believe you were doing the bread sculpture, either," I said. "*Bread* sculpture?"

"Listen, that exhibit was really well received," Amanda said. "It did far better than the ice art we had just before it."

"Well, good luck with Uncle Ike," I said. "I expect he'll be calling pretty soon."

"He's called six times, collect," she said. "Is he really that old?"

"Yep," I said. "I imagine he just wants to make sure about the color TV."

"We've put him at the Hays–Adams," Amanda said. "I think Miss Sanders was hoping you'd be around to help us with him."

"If she was thinking that, why didn't she ask me?"

Amanda shrugged. "I just work here," she said.

I didn't really want to leave. There was no place I felt like going. It seemed to me Amanda would soften up, eventually, if I could just think of a pretext to stay around.

"If you're Harris' cousin how come you're poor?" I asked.

"I'm not exactly poor," Amanda said. "I'm just shabby genteel.

"I guess I always will be," she added thoughtfully. "Actually I would probably do better if I were poorer, rather than richer. If I got poorer I could just give up. I wouldn't have to buy respectable clothes, or look respectable, or be respectable."

"You don't like being respectable?"

"Well, it's very wearing," she said. "At least it is the way we do it in my family."

"Would you like to go to Texas?" I asked. "There's a lot of galleries down there—the art scene is booming. You could probably get a great job."

If the invitation startled her, she didn't show it. She walked over to the window and looked out. I thought perhaps she was contemplating my car, which was parked just beneath the window.

"You shouldn't be so whimsical," she said.

"Why not?"

"Because life can't be based on whimsy," she said.

"That's the respectable view, all right," I said.

"It's the mature view," Amanda said. "You just made more money than I made in a year. You did that whimsically, too. I don't think you're very mature."

I didn't say anything. I didn't feel up to mounting a defense of my maturity. Basically I agreed with Amanda. I wasn't mature, nor had I ever been able to decide what maturity involved.

"If I went to Texas with you I would probably permit nothing," Amanda said. Then, to my delight she grinned.

"I normally permit very little," she said.

"If you'd just smile once in a while it might be enough," I said.

For a moment I felt like laughing, at the absurd twists life could take. Little Joe's wife might take up a happy existence in Washington, while Harris' cousin took the Texas art world by storm.

Amanda toyed with her hair for a moment, half distracted, half coquettish. Then the fancy that she had been contemplating slipped past, as fancies will. The quiet merriment went out of her eyes. It was too bad: amusement had transformed her into an appealing young woman.

"It's not easy to stop being mature, once you're mature," she said. "I would probably enjoy stopping, but I can't."

"I guess that means you won't come," I said.

Amanda nodded. At that point the phone rang and she went off to answer it.

"How amazing," she said, when she came back. "That was John C. V. Ponsonby. He wants *you!* He won't even speak to my family, he considers us so *nouveau*. Well, actually he does speak to one of my great-aunts, once in a while. But why would he even think of speaking to you?"

"Because I have a truncheon he wants," I said. "I offered it to him a week ago when he was drunk. It's taken him a week to remember it."

"I hate him for not speaking to us," Amanda said. "Now I hate him more, since I know he speaks to you."

"Collectors can't afford these niceties," I said.

"He could have approached you through an agent," she pointed out.

"But while the agent was tracking me down he might lose the truncheon. It's taken him a week to get desperate. Now that he has he'll stoop to anything to get the truncheon."

"How much will you charge him for it?"

"I think I'll ask twenty thousand dollars," I said. "I only paid six thousand dollars but this is a day when I feel like asking twenty thousand dollars for everything I sell."

Amanda smiled again. She had a very winning smile, possibly the more winning because it was so rare.

"You are *very* whimsical," she said.

"Sometimes it works, to an extent," I said.

352

"Not if one has had a proper upbringing," Amanda said.

"It was nice to meet you," I said. "I'd like to leave you with one thought."

"Which is?"

"Maturity isn't necessarily progressive. You might lose it, at some point."

"People tell me I've had it since I was nine," Amanda said.

"All the more reason you might finally get bored with it," I said. "Maybe I'll just come by, when I'm in town. Check out your maturity level, once in a while. Anything might happen."

Amanda smiled again, a smile with a touch of resignation in it.

"Anything might, but so far not much has," she said.

Chapter XIV _____

Ponsonby lived in a classic Georgian house, on a block in Georgetown which was entirely occupied by houses exactly like his. Architecturally it was probably the most consistent block in America. In that block, the Federal period lived again, in more ways than one. The housemaid who asked for my hat—I had taken to wearing my hat almost constantly, when in Washington—asked for it so quietly that I didn't hear her. She left me in a small room, in which there was no object that had been made after 1806, except the lightbulbs. Before I could properly assess that fact an equally soft-spoken young secretary appeared. She was dressed in a variant of a middy blouse, a dark skirt, and sensible shoes. The secretary led me upstairs to a large sitting room, where, besides the lightbulbs, the only objects made after 1806 were several hundred truncheons, in polished walnut racks along the walls.

Ponsonby was clearly a perfectionist. His truncheons didn't dangle. Each rested horizontally, in a grooved rack. Space had

353

been left for a couple of rather smoky portraits of eighteenth-century Ponsonbys, but otherwise the wall space was totally filled with truncheons.

While I was glancing over some of the lesser truncheons, Ponsonby lumbered in. Although not particularly large, he seemed to lumber.

"Good morning," I said. You certainly have some wonderful truncheons."

"It is no longer morning and these truncheons are of no consequence whatever," Ponsonby said. "My better truncheons are in the study, where we will now proceed."

He was right, too. In the study, in equally well-polished racks, were more than a thousand truncheons. Even knowing nothing about truncheons, I could tell that these were superior.

"I shall come immediately to the point," Ponsonby said, lighting a cigarette with a somewhat shaky hand. "Do you still possess the Luddite truncheon?"

"Yes I do," I said.

Ponsonby was silent for a bit. He was not exactly in a trance, but neither did he seem in a happy or a communicative mood. The news that I still had the truncheon, far from cheering him up, seemed to have made him feel even more bleak.

"It's rather depressing," he said finally. "*I* was meant to have that truncheon. Woodrow Eberstadt had no business keeping it all his life, and Lou Lou most emphatically had no business selling it to anyone but me."

"May I make a point?" I said.

Ponsonby merely looked at me.

"Lou Lou hates your guts," I said. "That's the point. You were the *last* person she would have offered the truncheon to."

It was true. Lou Lou Eberstadt was a little Boston lady with a face like a dried-up apple, but that had not kept her from expostulating at great length on her dislike of Jake Ponsonby.

"Lou Lou was never stable," Ponsonby replied, his ego having automatically deflected the criticism.

"The truncheon's in my car," I said. "I'll bring it in and show it to you if you like."

I brought it in and laid it on a rather wobbly Colonial side table. I had it wrapped in felt, and I unfolded the felt carefully, as if I were about to display the Hope diamond.

As truncheons go, the Luddite truncheon was a crude piece of work. All it had to recommend it was extreme rarity. There were only two like it in America, and half a dozen in England.

Ponsonby didn't touch it, but as he looked at it he began to shake. There was a little silver bell on the side table and he seized it and rang it violently. Almost immediately the soft-spoken maid appeared with a glass of whiskey on a silver tray. Evidently she had been standing in the next room, waiting for Ponsonby to ring the bell that meant whiskey.

"It's rather sad," Ponsonby said. "Woodrow had only a common intelligence. He was wrong repeatedly, throughout his life, and he would never accept correction. Now it has come to this."

Though I had not observed him drinking, the glass of whiskey was empty. He was still shaking, but more gently.

"I am prepared to offer five thousand dollars for the truncheon, as it sits," Ponsonby said.

"Come now, Mr. Ponsonby," I said.

He looked at me contemptuously.

"I do not need to come, now or at any time," he said. "I am at home, as it happens."

"I'm sorry I bothered to come by," I said. "I assumed you were a serious man."

I stopped, and we considered one another.

"The price is twenty thousand dollars," I said.

Ponsonby immediately turned red—almost purple, in fact.

"Quite impertinent," he said. "I made you a fair offer. I want that truncheon."

"I *paid* Mrs. Eberstadt more than you offered," I said. "I think you're living in the past. Who knows what this truncheon would fetch if I sent it to auction. You do have rivals, you know."

Ponsonby sniffed. "None who can be taken seriously," he said. "I have over seventeen hundred truncheons. My rivals, as you flatteringly call them, mainly have only a few hundred."

"What about the Australian?" I said. "He may not have as many truncheons as you do yet, but I imagine he has more money. I have a feeling he wouldn't quibble over twenty thousand if I offered him the Luddite truncheon."

The blood that had just rushed to Ponsonby's head rapidly drained out, leaving him white and shaky again. He rang the whiskey bell and the maid immediately stepped through the door with another glass of whiskey.

Ponsonby looked at me again, not with renewed respect— he had never had any respect—but with a new wariness. The fact that I knew about Captain Kimbell, the fabulously wealthy Australian who was currently tearing up the truncheon market, clearly shocked him.

"The man is a vulgarian," he said.

"I know, but he's very rich."

"I will raise my offer to six thousand dollars," Ponsonby said, "though to do so violates principles that have guided me through a long and distinguished career as a collector. As a rule, I never haggle."

I began to wrap the truncheon with the felt.

"I never haggle either," I said. "I own the truncheon, and I didn't invite an offer. I set the prices on the pieces I sell. If you want it for twenty thousand dollars, fine. If not, I'll check out Captain Kimbell."

A look not unlike panic appeared on his face. He knew quite well that he would probably never see a Luddite truncheon again, if he let this one get away. He turned away from me and walked over to the window, as if to compose himself.

I waited, and was sorry I did. When Ponsonby turned again his manner had changed completely. He smiled, a terrible smile. After watching him flush and grow pale, this sudden baring of teeth was so unexpected that the hairs stood up on the back of my neck.

Obviously, he had thought his way through the dilemma. I had been ahead of him, now he was ahead of me.

He picked up the phone and in a voice full of the old contempt asked his secretary to bring up a check made out for twenty thousand dollars.

"No thank you," I said, immediately. "No check."

Ponsonby was still smiling his horrible smile. He turned it on me, not much affected by my remark.

I picked up the truncheon, which caused him to stop smiling at once.

"What are you doing?" he asked loudly.

"I'm taking my truncheon," I said, "unless you're prepared to pay me in cash."

Ponsonby glared, and he was clearly not a man who was used to having his glares ignored.

"Are you questioning my check?" he asked.

"I think you're good for twenty thousand dollars, all right," I said. "But if I took your check you'd stop payment on it before I got around the block. Then I'd have to sue you to get my truncheon back. I'd prefer to be paid in cash."

At that moment the young secretary walked in with the check on a silver tray. She sat the tray down and left the room.

I tucked the truncheon under my arm, ignoring the check. I felt just slightly apprehensive. For all I knew Ponsonby, like Cyrus Folmsbee, kept a neat Korean assassin in his employ for just such occasions. I took one of my cards out of my shirt pocket—it had a nice little cut of a 1906 Cadillac on it, plus my name and phone numbers and my address in Houston. On the back I wrote the name of my Houston bank, and my account number. I laid the card on the tray beside the check.

"If you object to cash you can make a wire transfer directly to this account," I said. "Then I'll deliver the truncheon."

"Do you think I'm a fool?" he said. "You would have my money but I would not have the truncheon."

"Oh, don't worry," I said. "I'll be glad to get rid of this truncheon. I've owned it long enough. Once I know the money's in my bank I'll ring your doorbell and hand it to your secretary."

Ponsonby continued to glare, but I didn't stay to be glared

at. Three minutes later I was across the Key Bridge and on my way out Wilson Boulevard toward the Little Bomber's.

Fortunately Boog's dirty black Lincoln was sitting there, in front of the Double Bubble. He if anyone would know what Ponsonby's sharklike smile had meant.

I found Boog in a hot tub with Lolly, Janie Lee, and a skinny brunette I didn't know. Although Boog had probably contracted for all the specials of the day, none of the girls were paying him the slightest attention. Lolly was practicing her shorthand in a little shorthand notebook, Janie Lee was watching a soap on the huge TV, and the brunette was reading a book about running.

"Look, Janie Lee, Jack's back," Lolly said, looking up from her shorthand practice.

"This is B.J.," she added, nodding toward the brunette.

" 'lo," the brunette said.

Boog had been taking a nap, but he groaned and opened his eyes.

"I thought somebody was gonna go get some barbecue," he said.

"Not right now," Janie Lee said, her eyes glued to the TV screen.

Boog looked at me unhappily. The moodiness which had suddenly seized him still had him in its grip.

"Get in here and help me with this orgy I'm havin'," he said. "We can split the cost of watching these girls do their own thangs. Ain't none of them doing much for my thangs."

"Oh, Boog, hush," Lolly said. "We're all real busy."

Boog suddenly slid downward, immersing himself in hot water. He stayed under for quite a while.

"I don't know what's happened to that man," B.J. said. "He used to be real jolly."

"It's a midlife crisis," Janie Lee said. "It's just like the one Richard's having."

"Who's Richard?" I asked.

"On *General Hospital*," the girls said, in chorus.

Boog surfaced. "What'd you do all morning, try to fuck my wife?" he asked.

"I had a little run-in with Mr. Ponsonby," I said. "Is he dangerous or just obnoxious?" I told him about the deal.

"Better men than you have runt from him," Boog said. "Whoever heard of charging twenty thousand dollars for a billy club? I imagine he would have just stopped payment on the check. Wonder what he does with all them billy clubs?"

There was a green lawn chair nearby. I pulled it up and sat in it.

"Lolly's gettin' real good at shorthand," Boog said. "Teddy Kennedy's gonna hire her to run his office any day now."

"Shoot, I may not even live here much longer," Lolly said. "Me and Janie Lee may move to California."

"Eviste moved in," Boog said. "Boss is gonna train him to mow the lawn or something, so he can pay his keep. He's gonna give the kids lessons in conversational Franch, so they can be worse snobs than they are already."

"Boog, you oughta take up running," B.J. said. "It's real good for depression and thangs."

"Depression ain't my problem," Boog said. "Thangs is my problem."

"Well, jogging's good for a wide range of problems," B.J. assured him.

"I ain't about to run up and down the sidewalk," Boog said. He climbed out of the hot tub and walked off to get dressed.

"My dad was real grouchy which is why Momma left him," Lolly said. "She took it for twenty years and then she couldn't take it no more."

Boog reappeared, still moody, in a bright green suit.

"You girls is all wastin' your lives," he remarked as we left.

"Yeah, but so what?" B.J. said. She had an argumentative look about her.

"What's wrong with you?" I asked, as we headed for the Cover-Up.

"Shut up and drive," he said. "You ain't no psychoanalyst, why should I tell you?"

He looked blankly out the window as Arlington merged imperceptibly into Falls Church.

"I been thanking about goin' back to Winkler County," he said.

"What could you do there?"

"I could thank about my roots," Boog said.

I snorted. The notion of Boog brooding about his roots was ludicrous.

"Laugh all you want to," he said. "Yore young. You ain't ground to a halt in the pit of pointlessness yet."

"The pit of what?"

"Pointlessness. The point at which all that was at one time more has become less."

"The girls are right," I said. "You're having a midlife crisis."

"It's a rest-of-my-life crisis," Boog said. "Them girls is sweet but they barely got brains enough between them to focus a TV set."

"I just mostly wanta go home and sit on the porch," he said, a moment later. "Watch the sun come up and the sun go down. Coexist in harmony with the possums and the skunks. At night I could listen to the sounds of the oil patch. Motors chuggin'. Might grow a tomato once in a while, or raise ocelots or something."

"You?" I said. I could hardly believe I was hearing this fantasy of the rural life from Boog Miller, one of the most compulsively urban people I had ever known.

Boog shrugged. "There is a great tendency to return unto the first place," he said. "The home of one's youth. The scene of the first humiliations. Winkler County, in other words."

"You wouldn't last a week," I said. "What would you do without massage parlors? Flea markets? Auctions? Politics?"

"I could read Spinoza," he said. "Might write my memoirs."

"You'd miss Boss a lot," I said. "Boss isn't going to Winkler County."

"No, she's got to stay here and teach that little Frenchman how to mow the grass," Boog said. "Boss and me been married thirty-two years. We couldn't miss one another if we tried."

360

It was strange to think that the Miller marriage was only one year younger than I was. When they had gone to the altar I had been tottling around the trailer house in Solino.

"She makes the best biscuits I ever tasted," Boog said. "I thank that's what kept us together. I appreciate good biscuits, a rare trait in modern man."

I parked at the Cover-Up, amid a few hundred Datsuns and Toyotas. Boog, who had been starving, didn't seem in any hurry to get out and go in.

"You want to go in the antique business with me?" I asked, thinking he might really like a change of profession, though at the moment the nature of his profession was rather vague. "We could still probably get one or two of the Smithsonian warehouses."

"Nope," Boog said. "Ain't interested. I thank I'd rather just go back to Winkler County and read Spinoza."

Chapter XV

The Cover-Up, as usual, was full of people with little plastic-sheathed security cards clipped to their lapels. Behind the counter, Freddy Fu was taking money and dispensing Princetonian suavity. There was no sign of Mrs. Lump. We had our usual order of goat and Tasmanian beer, and when we finished I asked Boog if he would make a reservation for two at the best restaurant in town.

"I'd like to meet this woman," he said.

"You might, someday."

"I doubt it," he said. "You're stingy with your women."

"I brought you Josie, didn't I?"

"Yeah, but she ain't yours," he said. "She's married to some little third-generation fuckup down in Henrietta. If it hadn't been for you, me an' Coffee would have been true sweethearts long ago."

"Coffee's got enough problems as it is," I said. "Do you know about the dope dealer?"

"Yeah, he's a midget I-talian who wears bracelets," Boog said. "That girl ain't leading a wholesome life."

On the way out he stopped at a pay phone and spoke in French to someone. I was surprised.

"I didn't know you spoke French," I said.

"Some polish is gaint with one's ruint, said she," he said. "That was your maître d'. You got your reservation. Just try not to disgrace me by orderin' the wrong wine or something."

In the afternoon I felt like an auction. I needed something to get my adrenalin pumping, so I wouldn't get sleepy and take a nap.

Unfortunately the only auction scheduled in the D.C. area that day was a mixed auction of Oriental rugs and estate glassware, at a gallery I was unfamiliar with. I seldom handle rugs, for the simple reason that most of them won't fit in my car, and what's called "estate" glassware by two-bit auctioneers is usually just ornate junk.

But an auction is an auction. I got out my map and managed to locate the gallery, which was one of a row of cinderblock warehouses in a warehouse area not far from the Pentagon. To my surprise, the place was packed, mostly with depressed-looking men in cheap suits. At any auction where there is glassware there will usually be a lot of women, but in this case there were only a handful, three or four hard-bitten ladies with silver hair who were obviously dealers, and a couple of young mothers who had thought to relieve the boredom of young motherhood by bringing their babies out to an auction. The babies were strapped in strollers and had their own boredom to contend with. They dealt with it mainly by trying to wriggle out of the strollers.

The auctioneer, a thin, nervous little fellow, was trying to teach a couple of surly Cubans how to hook the rugs to a pulley arrangement so they could be hauled up briefly for display.

The men in the cheap suits all looked pallid, as if, collectively, they had been raised under artificial light. The warehouse was dusty and the free coffee which was being served tasted like it had been brewed the week before. There was not one single piece of glassware that was even decent. One Chinese lacquer-ware dish might have been described as half-decent. The rugs were no better than the glass. The old ones were ragged and much repaired, and there were only a few of them. Most of the rugs had been manufactured since 1940.

Though there was no point at all in staying, I stayed, sitting in a hard little bridge chair and watching the terrible auction-eer auction the worthless rugs and terrible glass. The two Cubans were totally without interest in the proceedings and half the rugs slipped loose from the pulleys and flopped on the floor. Once a large one fell on the auctioneer, who was having a terrible day. He tried to laugh it off, but the rug that fell on him was big and dusty and from then on he was prone to fits of coughing. Every wretched little Canton plate he held up he described as being a "real early piece," his phrase for anything between the dawn of time and 1975. One of the young mothers worked up her nerve and bought a set of glasses which the auctioneer described as "real early crystal," when in fact they had been made in Minnesota within the decade.

It was such a disgracefully amateurish auction that I spent most of my time wondering why I wasn't leaving. I tried to tell myself it was discipline: after all, the principle that any-thing can be anywhere still held true.

Back there somewhere could be a rug that Genghis Khan had sat on, as he trekked eastward in his years of conquest. It could happen. The odds were scarcely longer than the odds on a great Sung vase turning up in De Queen, Arkansas.

At the same time, I knew it wasn't going to happen. For one thing, apart from two silver-haired ladies who undoubt-edly had an antique store somewhere nearby, I was the only professional there. Blink Schedel wasn't there, nor were any of Brisling Bowker's many runners. Of course, none of them had been in De Queen, either, but De Queen was out of their territory and south Arlington wasn't. If there had been some-thing great in the auction one of them would have sniffed it out and been there.

For the last forty lots of the sale I amused myself by winding up a windup plastic duck for the fat little child of the nearest mother. The duck was meant for a bathtub, and didn't perform well on the concrete floor of the warehouse. Its little plastic propeller kept tipping it over on its nose. This amused the child, a little girl with a few wisps of orangish hair. When the duck tipped over I picked it up, let its propeller spin down, and then wound it up again. In this harmless fashion the auction finally passed.

I had bought nothing, and what was worse, no adrenalin had pumped, as it would have at a good auction. I left feeling as flat as I had felt when I entered, went to the nearest phone booth, and called my banker in Houston, to see if twenty thousand dollars had materialized in my account.

It hadn't. John C. V. Ponsonby was losing his chance at the Luddite truncheon. Or maybe he wasn't. Perhaps a well-trained agent had already been dispatched, to deal with me. He might follow me to a swap-meet and steal the truncheon out of my car. He could slip a tranquilizing drug into my hotdog or something. Most swap-meets have a hot-dog stand nearby, a perfect cover for a well-trained agent.

I felt a little nervous, but since there was no way to anticipate the agent's moves I drove to Wheaton, checked into a motel, and lay in a bathtub until it was time to pick up Jean.

Soaking in water was more refreshing than taking a useless nap.

While I soaked I thought of women. My moods were flickering, like a radio with a loose wire. At moments it would occur to me that if I just continued to be a scout I could lead a consistent and interesting life. I didn't really *have* to have women. They were not a necessity of nature. In fact, they were a lot of trouble, disrupters of the peace, almost all of them.

For moments, as I lay in the tub, I thought how nice it would be just to drive around America buying things, not having one's own peace disrupted. America itself was very beautiful, very various. There was plenty to see. The skies over the west were so lovely that they alone should have been enough to sustain me.

When I looked at it that way I felt light for a few seconds —I felt like an escapee—from tantrums, confusion, fucking, and a million needs, stated and unstated.

Then, only a few seconds later, I would remember that I liked fucking, and was interested in needs, stated and unstated. Even America could get boring. I wouldn't really escape women. As soon as I got over one, another one would pop up. Things would repeat themselves, some of them nice things, some of them not. After all I had a date with a very appealing woman. We had even made love once, although so briefly that I couldn't really remember it. When I tried to remember it I got an erection, and soon after went to sleep in the bathtub.

At Jean's, Beverly let me in, edging out Belinda by a step.

"Mom's getting ready," she said.

"*I* was gonna get it," Belinda said, annoyed to have been edged out. Her hair was impossibly curly. The girls were both looking fresh and mischievous.

I sat on the couch and Belinda climbed into my lap.

"I thought you said you were bringing some presents," she said. She felt in my shirt pocket, to make sure no small presents were hidden there.

Then Jean came downstairs, looking a little discontent. She looked lovely, but she was not elaborately dressed. Often, in dressing up, a woman will make herself into a person that doesn't look like the self you know, but Jean hadn't succeeded in doing this at all.

"I failed," she said, anticipating my comment. At that moment the doorbell rang, and both girls flew to get it. Since Belinda was in my lap she was in a poor takeoff position. She tripped over my boot and fell sprawling. Once again, Beverly got to get the door. Belinda burst into tears at this double defeat. The babysitter was a thin teenage girl with lots of braces.

"He tripped me," Belinda said, sitting on the floor with a tear-streaked face.

"So?" Jean said. "Who told you to run?" She introduced the babysitter, whose name was Debbie.

"Nobody cares," Belinda remarked, still crying.

"That's right," Jean said. "You've exhausted all sympathies. You're going to have to go the whole rest of your life without any, because you're so greedy."

"What's sympathy?" Belinda asked.

Jean helped her up, wiped her face, kissed them both, grabbed a coat, and went to the door.

"Let's go," she said. "All this is Debbie's problem now."

"Have a good time, Mom," Beverly said.

"Oh, Beverly, you're so generous," Jean said.

Belinda gave us both a cool look and marched out of the room.

"She hates being omitted from the honors list," Jean said.

"You look awfully nice," I said.

"I hate talking about how I look," she said. "I hate thinking about it. I hate trying to change it. I spent all afternoon trying, but it didn't work. This is how I look."

"Why shouldn't it be?" I said. "You look fine."

"I meant to at least look sophisticated," she said. "But I can't. I'm too ordinary. I just have to come to terms with that fact."

When she said it she looked so appealing that I leaned over and tried to kiss her. She jerked back against the car door.

"I may get out," she said, "if you're gonna do that."

"Okay, okay," I said.

"Why'd you try to kiss me?" she asked, as we drove off. "You're supposed to take me out to dinner."

"You just looked kissable," I said. "One kiss wouldn't have limited your ability to eat."

"Yes it would," she said. "I'm scared of you and I can't eat a bit when I'm scared. Now you've already made me miss my one chance to enjoy a meal at the best restaurant in town."

"Don't be silly," I said. "You don't have to be scared of me."

"I told you I'm out of practice at dates," she said.

To complicate things, we were stuck in a traffic jam, four blocks from her house.

"I wasn't meant to eat in fancy restaurants," Jean said. "That's why this traffic jam is here. We'll never get there."

Just as she said it the traffic jam began to break up. I took a shortcut I had noticed and circumvented what was left of it.

"It's interesting you figured out that shortcut," Jean said.

"Anyone could figure it out," I said.

"I live here and I never did," Jean said. "I'm a very passive driver. I just endure whatever traffic I encounter, and I encounter a lot."

She had a lovely voice. Instead of rising when she was depressed or nervous, it sank and became more throaty.

Jean sat way over against the door. Although the door was locked, that made *me* nervous. I had a fantasy of having a car wreck in which she popped out and was killed. Though ridiculous, it was a powerful fantasy.

"I wish you wouldn't sit so close to the door," I said.

"Leave me alone," she said. "I'm having a lot of regrets about this date as it is."

We were silent all the way to the restaurant, which was very fancy. I had put on a tie, but still neither Jean nor I looked anything like the other people eating at the restaurant. They all looked more elegant than us, and more at home in fancy restaurants.

Jean was brooding over the menu. It was such a huge menu that it made her seem smaller than it was. Also, it was very elaborate and required a lot of thought. She was frowning as she gave it the thought.

"Why are you frowning?" I asked.

"Are you going to ask me why I frown every time I frown?" she inquired, peeping around the menu.

I shut up.

"It's because it makes me realize what a limited life I've led," she said, answering the question she had just objected to.

"We eat pizza, cheeseburgers, or carry-out Chinese," she said. "That's stupid, isn't it? But they're all in the neighborhood and I don't have the energy to change my habits. My girls won't know what to do in a restaurant like this because they'll never see one. I haven't seen one in years myself."

"Don't your folks ever take you out?" I asked.

"My folks don't eat out," she said. "They're worse than me. What are you gonna eat?"

I ate veal niçoise, and Jean ate a flounder stuffed with crab-meat. Then she had an endive salad. For dessert I had profiteroles, after having failed to persuade her to have some, too. They came in a rich chocolate sauce.

"I'd gain a lot of pounds if I ate that," she said.

"Well, you're small," I said. "A few pounds wouldn't hurt you."

"You don't know what you're talking about," she said. "I get lumpy very easily. Two or three extra pounds makes me lumpy. Then I feel even more discontent than I usually feel."

Then she stole several bites of my profiteroles anyway.

I had an irrational urge to propose to her, but managed to choke it down. It's an urge that strikes me often, whenever I'm truly charmed by a woman. I was charmed by Jean, although I knew I hadn't known her long enough to have made contact with her true character; however, lack of contact with her true character didn't keep me from being charmed enough to want to marry her.

"What are you thinking?" she said shrewdly. Her cheeks were glowing, probably from the wine.

"I was thinking it would be nice if we got married," I said.

"Probably would be," Jean said, wiping a speck of chocolate sauce off her chin. "I guess this sauce overcame my resistance. I could eat chocolate sauce all day if I let myself. Since I wasn't responsible for ordering it, anything it does to me is your fault."

"It won't do anything to you."

"Well, it might give me a pimple," she said. "Good chocolate sometimes has that effect. I'm glad we came to this restaurant. It's working. I'm beginning to feel slightly sophisticated. That's a treat for a full-time mom."

"Let's have some brandy," I said. "It might make you look even more sophisticated."

We had some brandy. Jean was looking quite happy.

"I guess you think it's utterly ridiculous, that I said that about marriage," I said.

"I hope you aren't going to start apologizing for yourself," she said.

"No," I said.

"You would have, given time," she said. "You should learn to stick to your guns. I don't see anything wrong with your wanting to marry me. I'm a good prospect. I know how to do marriage. It says a lot for your judgment that you said that."

"I just didn't want you to reject the idea too quickly," I said.

"Ha," Jean said. "I'm an experienced woman even if I'm not exotic. I don't reject ideas too quickly. Proposals don't grow on trees, if that was a proposal. Although actually I had another one last week, from a guy I haven't even gone out with."

"You did?"

"Yeah," she said. "He's always admired me from afar. We grew up on the same block, so I guess he feels he knows me. He just called up and proposed."

She looked a little depressed, just for a moment.

"Shows you what an abstraction marriage is, to some people," she said.

"Actually, it *can* be kind of abstract," she added.

"Was yours and Jimmy's abstract?" I asked.

"Not at first," Jean said. "It was very tangible, at first. Very much a realistic experience. Then the tangibility kind of drained out of it and it became sort of minimal. That was before he was angry. Then I decided to leave and he didn't like that. He got angry and it became sort of expressionistic. Very black blacks, and very white whites. Sort of Franz Kline. He still has the anger. He'll never forgive me for being able to leave him. All I'll ever get from that man now is big black swipes of anger."

Then she giggled. "For a relatively dull marriage it approximated quite a few modes of modern art," she said. "I hadn't thought of it that way. It makes it seem more interesting than it actually was."

Jean looked around the restaurant, which was beautifully

decorated and arranged, and still full of people who looked far dressier and more important than us.

"It's sort of magic," she said.

"What is?"

"The feeling you get, coming here," she said. "It's so elegant and the food is so good it convinces you you're living on a far higher plane than you're actually living on. But then you sink so quick, once you leave. It's why I'm not in a hurry to leave. I've been sunk for a long time. I wish I didn't have to sink again, quite so soon."

"Sink to what?"

Jean shrugged. "Oatmeal for Beverly and bacon fried absolutely crisp for Belinda," she said. "If there's one particle of unfried fat on a piece of bacon the little bitch won't eat it. I don't know how I could have had such a picky child. But that's what awaits me, at seven o'clock in the morning. Then I'll have to wash the saucepan I made the oatmeal in. Beverly only likes old-fashioned oatmeal, which is a lot of trouble. By the time all that's done there won't be a cell in my body that feels glamorous."

"It's a long time until seven A.M.," I said. "We could try and find a glamorous place and go dancing."

Jean shook her head. "Not necessary," she said. "This is all the illusion I require. Let's have one more brandy.

"Why do you think you want to marry me?" she asked, as we were driving home.

"I can't say I'd thought it through," I said. "We could go in the antique business together. Pool our talents."

"Pool *your* talents, you mean," she said. "I wouldn't mind being in business with you but it's certainly no reason to marry you."

"It might be an extra asset," I suggested.

"We have to get the real assets first," Jean said, looking out the window.

"Which are they?"

She didn't answer. When we got to her house she told me to wait in the car and take Debbie home. She didn't have quite enough babysitter money so I loaned her a dollar. The money she fished out of her purse was all crinkled up, whereas my dollar was absolutely crisp and new. The contrast amused her.

"I'm not sure your money would want to live in the same house with my money," she said, before going in.

When I returned the front door was unlocked, so I went in. Jean was nowhere around, but while I was inspecting various small objects I sensed a presence and turned to see Belinda, standing at the bottom of the stairs.

"What are you *doing* here?" she asked in a distinct, unsleepy voice.

"Just looking around," I said.

"Belinda?" Jean said, from somewhere upstairs.

Belinda marched over to the stereo and turned it on, though she made no move to play a record. She seemed mesmerized by the little green light that indicated the stereo was on.

Jean came hurrying downstairs. "How come you're not asleep?" she asked Belinda.

"I woked," Belinda said. "Wanta play Pat Benatar?"

Jean swooped her up and gave her a kiss. "I want you to unwoke," she said.

I followed them up and watched Jean put an uncomplaining Belinda back in her bed. As we were going out of her room Jean took my hand and led me a few steps down the hall, into her bedroom.

"I was gonna hide all my treasures but I didn't get time," she said. "It's simpler just to turn off the light. That way you won't know you're surrounded by treasures until morning."

The only light in the bedroom came from a streetlight a block away. I felt nervous. I hadn't allowed myself to assume I would be spending the night. I could see various dark shapes in the room that could have been chests or trunks but I couldn't tell a thing about them.

"You don't have to worry so much," I said. "I'm not going to try and buy your favorite objects."

"No, but you're gonna wanta look at *them*—as opposed to me," she said. She had her head tilted—she was taking off her earrings. I heard her put them on top of the TV at the end of the bed. I put my hands on her shoulders and encountered one of her small hands. She had been about to take off a small gold necklace she wore. I helped her.

"Belinda spoiled my elaborate seduction," she said. "It's stupid to plan anything with kids around."

"Why did you want to plan an elaborate seduction?"

"Because I never get to. Are you nervous?"

"Yeah," I admitted.

"I figured you for a shy one," she said. "It goes with your lying."

She bent and shucked her dress off over her head. "If the light were on you could see my whole wardrobe," she said, "It's scattered around here. If you could see it you'd realize how hard I tried before I gave up and decided to look like myself."

I sat down on the bed and began to take off my boots.

"I wondered about that," Jean said, coming to stand in front of me. She rubbed my hair a little.

"About what?"

"Whether you had to sit down to take your boots off," she said. "I've never seduced anyone in boots. It's an important question. If you could have done it standing up I would have been *really* impressed."

"Have you been fantasizing about me taking my boots off?"

"Ever since I met you," Jean said.

"I thought you were contemptuous of boots?"

She turned the covers back and hopped up on the bed.

"So I'm a little inconsistent," she said. "Hurry up. It's cold in here."

Chapter XVI _____

When I woke up the next morning very bright sun was shining in the window of the bedroom and Beverly and Belinda, in their red bathrobes, were sitting on the bed. Belinda held a huge pair of scissors and was cutting little pieces out of a section of morning paper, whereas Beverly, more serious, was reading a book.

"Good morning," I said.

"Hi," Beverly said. "Would you like me to read to you?"

She wiggled a little closer.

"Don't, Beverly," Belinda said, throwing her sister a dark look. "I'm *cutting!*"

"So what, I can't sit still forever," Beverly said. "Besides, you aren't cutting anything out. You're just making a mess."

"Still *cutting!*" Belinda insisted, as Jean came through the door. She too was in a red bathrobe, and she held two mugs of coffee.

"I hope you like company in the morning," she said. "Around here you get it whether you like it or not."

"He likes *it*," Belinda said.

Jean sat one mug on the bedside table and carefully climbed on the bed, holding the other.

I felt vaguely troubled about the night, since I found I had no memory of having made love. The bed was very comfortable, and I had been very tired. I had a vague sense that something might have happened, later in the night, but I couldn't be sure. Perhaps I had just gone to sleep and slept all night.

Still, if I had been a big disappointment, Jean seemed to be weathering it nicely. She looked quite happy, sitting on the bed with her girls. They formed a bright ensemble in their red bathrobes. Belinda sat across my feet, so that it was not easy for me to sit up and drink my coffee. There was a nice smell in the bed, namely the smell of young females and one woman, mixing with the smell of the hot coffee.

Jean and the girls were exchanging merry, conspiratorial looks, as if they were in on some secret that I didn't know.

"What's going on?" I asked.

Then I happened to glance at the room and saw that all the furniture was covered with sheets or bedspreads. None of the primary antiques were visible at all.

I must have looked surprised, because Jean and Beverly laughed and Belinda went into a paroxysm of giggles. She giggled so hard that the others began to laugh at her.

"It certainly is cheerful around here in the morning," I said.

Belinda lay across my legs, gasping for breath and waving the scissors around.

"Be careful with those scissors, Belinda," Jean said. "Don't you think it's time you girls got cracking?"

"I do," Beverly said. She left. Belinda continued to loll across my legs.

"Get going, Belinda. Play school," Jean said.

"Sleepy," Belinda said. "*He's* still in bed."

"Yeah, but he isn't being picked up in ten minutes."

"He could take us in the soft car," Belinda suggested.

"Nope, get going," Jean said in firm tones.

Belinda yawned. "Got up too early," she said.

Seeing that her words had no effect, Jean picked her up and carried her off. As she was being carried Belinda fixed me with an upside-down look.

"Come and get us in the soft car," she said.

"Don't make her any promises," Jean said.

In a few minutes I heard a honk and raised up to look out the window. The girls, dressed now, were being picked up by a woman in a station wagon. Beverly was going willingly, Belinda dawdling across the yard, urged on by Jean, who was still in her bathrobe. Belinda's movements were so slow as to be imperceptible. Finally, with several people yelling at her, she gave up and went on to the car, which immediately left.

A minute later Jean came back to the room and hopped on the bed.

"I've never known a child who could dawdle like that," she said. "She's always up to a contest of wills, whereas I'm not, always. Sometimes I win, sometimes she wins."

"It must make life interesting."

"It makes it exhausting," Jean said.

But she didn't look exhausted. She looked out the window for a moment, as if trying to remember something. She appeared to be extremely fresh and alert. I had no idea what thought or thoughts she might be busy with.

"It's very interesting, that you're never quite free of kids," she said, slipping out of her bathrobe. She got back under the covers with me. "What's gonna happen now is that Belinda's gonna fake being sick. She hates school because she can't dominate it, plus she doesn't want to miss whatever might happen with you here. I know her so well I can imagine every move she makes. Today she's gonna fake a stomachache, vaguest of all ills. Who can disprove a stomachache?"

"How long do we have before this happens?" I asked.

Jean looked at the bedside clock.

"A couple of hours, if we're lucky," she said.

I was still feeling guilty because I couldn't remember the night.

"Did anything at all happen last night?" I asked.

Jean looked amused. "Nothing appropriate to such a grand evening," she said. "How many hours had you been awake before you hit this bed?"

I tried to count up, mentally.

"Never mind," Jean said. "It doesn't matter. I got to watch you at a time when you were totally defenseless, which was interesting."

"Did you reach any conclusions?" I asked.

Jean rolled on top of me, looking me in the eye from very close range. She ran a finger across my lips. Her eyes were green flecked with brown. She didn't weigh much and she seemed to be in an awfully good humor. Looking at her alert face an inch away I felt myself sliding quickly down into love. The feeling was exactly analogous to one of the first feelings I could remember, that of sliding down the big slide on the school playground in Solino, Texas, when I was a young boy. It was a very slick slide. Once you climbed to the top all you had to do was lift your hands and whoosh, you were gone so rapidly that it created a funny sensation in the stomach and the groin. Looking into Jean's eyes, I felt the same sensation. I had lifted my hands—now I was gone.

"I love you," I said.

"Ha," she said. "You better do something about it before Belinda persuades them she's got cancer."

"You could take the phone off the hook," I suggested.

"No, because you never know," she said. "She might really get sick. A swing might hit her in the head and give her a concussion. A lot of things can happen to tiny kids. It worries me to have it off the hook."

"Forget it," I said.

Fortunately the morning passed without the phone having rung a single time. We talked several times about getting up but we didn't get up. Finally we both noticed that we were so hungry we felt hollow, so Jean went downstairs and made two enormous tuna fish sandwiches, and brought them back to the bedroom. We wolfed them down, and drank some milk.

"It's amazing how good tuna fish can taste when you're really hungry," Jean said. "It's almost better than sex."

"Last night you said it would probably be nice if we got married," I reminded her.

She shrugged. "That was last night," she said. "What makes you think it would work? It practically never does."

"I think I'm ready for it," I said. "I don't think I was before."

"Bullshit," she said. "How can you ever know if you're ready for a marriage when you're not in it? All you do is fantasize about the nice parts. Then you actually get in it and lose track of the nice parts. Or else what was once nice stops seeming nice."

"I think you're being deliberately pessimistic," I said.

Jean rubbed my hair again, as if I were a dog.

"Well, you're sweet but it's no deal," she said, grinning. "I think I'd rather hold you in reserve, for the occasional orgy."

"Why?"

"I don't want to get bored with you," she said. "Nor do I want you to get bored with me. I'd rather marry someone I was already a little bored with. Then there'd be no decline."

"You wouldn't really marry someone you were bored with, though," I said. "That would be insanity."

"That would be practicality," she said. "But you're right. I'm not capable of it. Still, it doesn't affect my position vis-à-vis you."

I was beginning to feel a little sad, suddenly. Jean seemed awfully clearheaded. I knew it was simplistic to think that love always followed sex, but I couldn't stop myself from thinking that way. We had had a fairly passionate morning, but the passion hadn't wrought any great changes, as it was supposed to. It had made us fonder and closer, but apparently it had not been all-consuming. Jean was cheerful, but she was far from consumed. I was getting depressed at the thought that I might not get to live with her.

I guess my worry showed. Jean sat her plate on the TV and came back into my arms. I couldn't think of what to say next. We held hands for a while.

"I like the thought of you being out there, you know," she said. "Off in odd states, where I've never been, finding things at flea markets. I think that's your life. I know it's charming to wake up in this lovely bedroom, with my delightful daughters piled on top of you. No doubt the three of us could keep you amused by one means or another for quite a while. But I just don't think it's your life. You're just getting scared of being lonely or something, so you think you want it to be."

"But my life is such a peculiar life," I said. "All I do is buy things. I spend all my time at flea markets or in junk shops or at auctions. Don't you think I'm capable of a more normal existence?"

"I think you're just getting lonely," she said. "You're leading a more interesting life than you think. You just don't realize it's interesting."

She gave me a quick kiss.

"I think you're romanticizing all this middle-class domesticity we've got around here," she said.

"But I don't even know if I still like scouting," I said. "The part that's beginning to depress me is seeing all the hope people invest in those objects."

Jean grew a little somber. "That's true," she said. "It's mainly all those women, hoping it'll be better if they can just find the right thing to buy. I used to do that myself."

"Such as the day I took the icon away from you?" I asked. "You must have been pinning a lot of hopes on that icon."

Jean nodded. "I did," she said. "I thought about it for a whole week. It took my mind off everything else. But it's good that you got it. The thrill would only have lasted a day or so and then I would have felt guilty about spending the money. My life wouldn't really have become any different."

"Although"—she paused—"this bedroom would be different. I was gonna put it on that wall, over my dower chest."

She jumped out of bed and whipped a sheet off the dower chest. It was indeed a wonderful chest. German rococo, decorated with nymphs and cherubs and still with its original paint, which was cracking, but cracking nicely.

Jean jumped back in bed. "Isn't it great?" she said. "God I love that chest."

She had a fine eye. The chest and the icon were nothing alike, but on her wall they would combine beautifully.

"I'm giving you the icon now," I said. "It belongs on that wall."

She looked me over for a moment. "Okay," she said.

Then she grinned. "I knew right away I'd get it from you," she said.

She looked out the window.

"Being a scout was sort of my dream once, before I got these girls," she said. "But I would never have been as good at it as you are. I'm too half-assed, plus I don't have any money and I'm not brave enough to drive all over America by myself. Besides, I was just basically lookin' to have myself a couple of girls."

"Okay," I said. "What I've got is the opportunity to drive about one hundred thousand miles a year in order to buy forty or fifty really nice things. Who are you to tell me that should be my life?"

"The woman who's not going to marry you," she said. "You really find wonderful things. It's a kind of art. You shouldn't give that up just because you've met a woman with a couple of cute kids."

"That's exactly what Beulah told me I ought to do," I said.

I told Jean about Beulah and the Valentino hubcaps, about her increasingly miserable yard sales, about the vodka and Kool-Aid, about the phone-book table. The story about the phone-book table touched Jean so that she couldn't speak. Tears came into her eyes, she fell into my arms, and we made love again.

"That's a terrible story," she said later, rubbing my shoulder. "That's probably how I'll end up."

"No it isn't," I said. "You'll end up with lots of nice grandkids."

Jean sighed. "Well, it's how I would have ended up if I had been true to my vision of my calling. You better see it's how you end up. I should really admire you if you ended up that way."

"Why are we talking about ending up?"

She shrugged. "We're not kids," she said. "The years will pass, and both of us will end up. I think it's an important thing to think about."

I thought of Goat Goslin, a man who had certainly been true to his vision of his calling to the end.

Jean suddenly looked decisive. She got up and began to dress. I sat up, too, but I had no sense of what to do next.

"Get out of here," Jean said. "Hit the road. Find me something wonderful. You can't come back till you do."

I couldn't think of anything to say. It seemed like a pointless order. Jean was standing by her dresser, sort of listlessly brushing her hair. She didn't have a great deal to brush. As I was putting my boots on she burst into tears. She didn't come over to me. She just stood there, crying.

"It's hard not to hope for things that can't really be," she said. "I wouldn't mind marrying you, to tell the truth."

"It *could* really be," I pointed out.

"Sure, and you'd end up a fat antique dealer with five or six fags working for you," she said. Then she went downstairs, leaving me to dress alone.

When I got downstairs she was standing in her kitchen, wiping her eyes and making tea.

"It seems a stern fate you've assigned me," I remarked.

"I didn't assign it," she said, with a flash of anger. "You chose it. Only now you want to wiggle out of it, when in fact the thought that it's fate is what tempts me about you."

"I wonder why Belinda didn't get a stomachache," she said a little later. "We better go pick them up."

When the girls came out of their nursery school and climbed in the car Belinda looked anything but sick.

"I hit a boy," she remarked.

"Why?" Jean asked.

"Didn't like *him*," Belinda said.

"I wish you'd make her behave," Beverly said. "Nobody in her class likes her."

"Un-uh, some do," Belinda said.

"I can't make her behave," Jean said, sniffing. She seemed to want to cry some more.

"I can't stop thinking about the woman with the phone books," she admitted.

On the way back we passed a yard sale, or the tag end of one. The sale had been going on all day and only dregs were left. Nonetheless we stopped and looked. The girls contemplated a broken doll and Jean and I poked through a couple of cardboard boxes filled with battered kitchen utensils.

"I could use a new blender," Jean said, though there were no blenders in the boxes. However, I did find a nice rolling pin, twenties vintage, for 75 cents. There was a woman in Vashti, Texas, who collected them. I could probably get twenty bucks for it if she didn't have one like it.

"You see," Jean said. "You can't help yourself. I didn't find anything and you found an appealing rolling pin."

"We found a doll," Belinda pointed out.

"Forget it," Jean said. "Let's go to Baskin–Robbins."

"What?" Beverly said. "Before supper?"

"I know, Beverly," Jean said. "It's a complete breakdown of discipline. However, it's what I feel like."

We ate ice cream cones, all except Belinda, who insisted on what she called a banana splut.

"Split, split, split," Beverly said. "You always use the wrong vowel." Belinda ignored her.

When we got back to the house the girls spotted a couple of chums sitting on the sidewalk a few houses away. They immediately ran off to join them, leaving Jean and me in the car. We sat and looked at one another.

"I think you're being too rigid," I said. "We might get along fine. There's nothing so great about driving around finding things."

"Listen, we're not talking about it," she said. "I don't think I'm planning to marry anyway. I'll just stay the way I am only I'll receive occasional visitors."

"Jimmy's detective is probably taking pictures of us right now," I said.

Jean made a face. "Who cares?" she said. "Jimmy's a jerk."

"I don't know what my role is supposed to be now," I said. "Can I at least bring you good antiques to sell?"

"Yeah, you can do that," Jean said. "Would you like to take the three of us to Disney World?"

"Of course I would. When?"

"Maybe in about a month," Jean said. "I've been promising them for about a year, but I don't ever seem to get the energy. I hear it's awfully crowded. I'd probably just lose one of them. Belinda runs on her own track, as you know."

"Sure," I said. "About a month would be fine."

"That would be nice, if we did that," Jean said. "Then I could stop feeling guilty for not taking them."

She opened the door and got out. I felt that things were not happening right but I also felt sort of paralyzed. I couldn't think of how to make them happen any other way.

Jean walked around the car and stood on the curb, looking worried, or maybe just perplexed. Down the sidewalk the four children were conferring. Belinda was looking out our way, watching her mother. Jean came over to my window, her hands in the pockets of her bulgy blue coat.

"I still think that coat's too big for you," I said.

She leaned in the window and gave me a quick kiss. For all her defiance I think mention of the detective made her nervous. After all, it was something she had to deal with.

"Go away and stop tempting me," she said. "This really isn't your life. But you better be back here in a month. I don't want to let these girls down."

She turned and went in the house. I thought of following and trying to make one more attempt to sweep her off her feet, but I knew it wasn't the kind of gesture she would appreciate. As I was easing away from the curb Belinda came skipping down the sidewalk. The wind, blowing from behind her, blew her curls into a kind of golden hood around her face.

"Where you *going?*" she asked cheerfully.

"I don't know, Belinda," I said.

"I don't *either*," she said. "Jist bring some presents when you come back."

Chapter XVII _____

I drove out of Wheaton and got on the Washington Beltway, headed more or less toward Texas. I had been given a sort of mandate, but the mandate had not contained any directions as to where I should go.

Clouds were gathering—it was the time of early darkness, gloomy dusks that would have been midafternoon had it been July. I didn't really want to go to Texas, where I had just been. I decided I might just as well aim for the far corner of the country—Seattle, maybe. There were some interesting junk shops in Seattle and several more in Portland and Spokane. I could angle up to Minneapolis and shoot right across the top of the great plains.

Nonetheless, I didn't really want to start. I kept thinking the car phone would ring. It would be Jean, changing her mind in the nick of time.

In order to give her a little more time I slipped off the Beltway and drove down to Cleveland Park, for a last check on the Millers.

When I came in Boss was sitting alone in the kitchen, drying her long raven hair with a blow-dryer and drinking coffee. She glanced at me but she did not look welcoming. She looked as if she preferred to sit and dry her hair and think her own thoughts. When I asked where everyone was she merely nodded toward the den.

I went in and found Micah, Josie, and Eviste sitting on the floor in front of the big TV set, like three small children. Dusk had fallen—it was almost dark in the room. Micah's little TV set sat on top of the Millers' big TV set. The little one was tuned to a Mary Tyler Moore rerun, so that Micah and Josie could play electronic basketball on the big TV set. It took only a glance to determine that Josie was winning.

"Howdy, wanta play a game?" she asked. "I got Micah whipped and Eviste can't understand the rules."

She was wearing a yellow T-shirt, yellow silk running pants, and yellow Adidas. All in all she was easily the most cheerful person in the house.

"This game has serious flaws," Micah said. "The refereeing sucks. I should have had about a hundred free throws by now."

Eviste was smoking pot and following the basketball in a rather dreamy way.

"Anyone want to go to Seattle?" I asked, not sure that I felt like taking such a long trip alone.

"Shoot, I'm staying right here," Josie said. "Boss is paying me twice as much as I could get in Henrietta and I'm learning the real estate business besides. If she opens up an office in Midland I might even get to run it."

"Theodore Roethke lived in Seattle," Micah observed.

"Hey if you see Little Joe will you explain the situation to him?" Josie asked. "He don't seem to be getting it too well, over the phone."

"Sometimes I feel like Ted," Micah said. At first I thought he meant Theodore Roethke, but then I realized he meant Ted on the *Mary Tyler Moore Show*. Josie, not steeped in Roethke, realized this right away.

"Sometimes you act like him, too," Josie said. "You spend

too much time making up poems. Why don't you ask Boss for a job?"

"But she's mad at me now," Micah said. "She *hates* me now."

The Miller household had always been strange, but somehow there had always been intimations of normalcy underneath the craziness. These seemed to have died or disappeared, gone wherever intimations go. The craziness had won.

The *Mary Tyler Moore Show* was approaching its climax and everyone turned to watch it, as if responding to subtle cues that I had missed.

"*Merde!*" Eviste said, evidently annoyed by some twist the plot had taken.

"I know," Micah said. "I hate it that Ted's always the scapegoat. I don't see what's so great about Georgette, personally."

In the kitchen Boss was still sitting. I stood beside her for a moment, and rested a hand on her shoulder.

"Want to go to Seattle with me?" I asked.

Boss shrugged my hand away.

"No," she said.

I didn't say anything. Boss looked up at me.

"I'm tired of men standing in my kitchen looking helpless," she said. "What do you want?"

I was immediately tongue-tied. I hardly knew what I wanted. Certainly a coherent summary would have been beyond me. I didn't even know how to ask what had happened within the Miller household. From what I could see the collective momentum had been lost. Boss still had her individual momentum, and Boog might recover his, but the momentum that had once attracted everyone in Washington to them had simply disappeared.

I decided I might as well just leave.

"Check on Coffee, this time," she said, as I was at the door. She went to the sink, rinsed out her coffee cup, and left the room without looking at me again.

Still, I had trouble turning toward Seattle. I hit the Beltway, but just before I got to I–66, the real start of the journey, I pulled over, stopped, and called Jean. I got Belinda.

"Where's your mother?"

"Upstairs," Belinda said.

A moment later Jean picked up the other phone.

"Hi," I said.

Jean was silent a moment.

"Get off, Belinda," she said. "The call's for me."

"*And* me, maybe," Belinda said.

"Hang up!" Jean shouted.

Belinda slammed down her receiver.

"Why are you calling?" Jean asked. "I just washed my hair."

"Oh, sorry," I said.

"What, precisely, are you apologizing for?" she asked. "There's nothing to apologize for. You've got to stop that."

I tried to think of a justification for the call—something I had forgotten, maybe—but I hadn't forgotten a thing and nothing came to mind.

"Listen," Jean said. "I'm not going to save you. Men always want women to save them from being what they really and truly want to be. I've been suckered that way before and I may be suckered that way again, but not right now, okay? I know you think you can wear me down, but you're wrong."

"Well, okay," I said. "I guess I'll probably go to Seattle, then."

Jean was silent a moment. "Drive carefully," she said as she hung up.

I drove carefully back down to Wytheville, passing within two miles of Mead manor, where, for all I knew, Mead Mead IV was dining by the pure light of a nineteenth-century light-bulb.

As usual, once definitely on the road, I felt a little better.

I soon went back in my mind to a conversation I had had with Jean, in bed in Wheaton that morning. She had made a lighthearted attempt to get to the bottom of me.

"What are you really looking for, in all this looking?" she

asked. "The perfect cunt? The perfect fried egg? The perfect little girl?"

"I don't think I expect perfection in any of those spheres," I said.

"Then how come everything you buy has to be beautiful and perfect?"

"It's just practical," I said. "It's easy to sell fine objects if they're perfect. You don't have to apologize for them."

Jean had been rubbing my stomach. She looked out the window and didn't say anything.

"It's hard to sell something if you have to start off listing its defects," I said. "That's all."

"Make a list of my defects," she said, looking me in the eye.

"No," I said.

"I dare you," she said. "I want to know how you'll go about disposing of me, when the time comes, defective as I am."

"I don't even know if you have defects," I said.

She chuckled. "You have a tendency to dishonesty," she said. "My defects are obvious. Skinny. No tits to speak of. Picky. Quarrelsome. I have a bossy daughter. No skills to speak of, except a few modest ones in the domestic areas. Plus I tend to get crazy unless someone loves me a lot."

"None of those would keep me from loving you a lot," I said.

Jean looked reflective.

"What might keep you from loving me a lot is that you don't want to love anyone a lot, I don't think," she said. "It's tiresome work. Means holding still and being bored half the time. I think you'd just rather move around collecting little loves. Affections. Little light ones that you can put in your car for a while and then get rid of."

"I don't think that's fair," I said.

"I didn't say it was bad," Jean said. "It's okay. You're not ungenerous. In fact you're rather giving."

Then she dropped the conversation, lay down with me again, and we cuddled for a while before making love again.

It had just been a little bit of bed talk, but it came back to me and stayed in my mind all the way across West Virginia,

Indiana, and Illinois. I should have been more conclusive, then, it seemed to me. If I had just said the right words, or if Jean had, we might have dispelled all the vagueness that afflicted our relationship—vagueness about what we both wanted, apart or with one another.

But we had started to touch one another again and had failed to reach any conclusion, leaving me to finish the conversation in my head as I glided across the Midwest.

For a while I felt as if I were actually about to reach a conclusion, after which I would understand everything I needed to know about myself, about my experience, and about my relations with beautiful objects and beautiful women. I felt heavy, and waited for the conclusion as one waits for a belch. Any moment, the belch in my head would come, and the first thing I would do was call Jean, wake her up, and explain to her that I finally knew exactly what was going on.

But if the conclusion was to come like a belch, driving proved to be my Alka–Seltzer. I slowly fizzed back into a blank, relaxed state, and instead of waiting for the conclusion I began to wait for St. Louis. The sun was well up before I crossed the river and passed beside the Gateway Arch. By the time I got tired enough to sleep I was in Nebraska.

Chapter XVIII _____

In the Northwest I had an extraordinary run of luck. For three weeks, every time I turned around I found something unusual, and unusually splendid.

The run started modestly at a garage sale in Vancouver, where I bought a New Guinea dagger made of cassowary leg bone. A spry, elderly, blue-eyed Britisher was holding the garage sale. When I bought the dagger he asked if I had an interest in a really unusual weapon.

"Sure," I said.

"What would you give for the club that killed Captain Cook?" he asked.

"I didn't even know a club killed him," I said, feeling that I was probably dealing with a nut, albeit a sprightly nut.

"Oh yes," he said. "It's a Tongan club. I have the full provenance, if you're doubtful. I am descended on my mother's side from Admiral Sir John Hunter, who was a very competent artist, if I do say so. He made excellent drawings of Hawaiian fauna. I've got the club just in here."

It was a wonderful club, whether or not it had killed Captain Cook. It was made of ironwood, had a little wrist loop, and was incised with genealogical ornaments of some kind, showing a bird, the sun, and the moon.

Amazingly, the old gentleman, whose name was Legh, did have a more or less believable provenance for it. Though it had once been in his family, it had somehow slipped out and had had to be bought back at auction, in the early seventies. I read the catalog description, which did make it seem likely that the club had been used to give Captain Cook a whack or two, although not until he had already been stabbed.

Mr. Legh's house was full of interesting weapons. He loved scimitars and had two hundred or so, some of them in splendid jeweled scabbards.

"I was posted in the Middle East for forty-eight years," he said. "Diplomat, you know. That's where I got the scimitars."

"Did you know Sir Cripps Crisp?" I asked, just curious.

"Oh yes, Jim, quite," he said, with a frown. Clearly they were not friends.

After a little negotiation I bought the club for $8,000.

"Why are you selling it?" I asked.

"The wife's had an operation, that's why she isn't here to serve us tea," he said, not at all depressed that the family heirloom was leaving the family once again. For good measure he threw in a couple more cassowary leg-bone daggers. He had a bushel basket full of those.

In Seattle the next day, in a junk shop, I found a Navaho double-saddle blanket, very old, with a pattern I had never seen. It was a wonderful saddle blanket. I bought it for a few hundred dollars and later sold it to Boog for $5,000. The same day I bought a Paduan lamp in the shape of a pelican. I knew I was having a run and ran it for all it was worth. I kept moving south, buying wonderful things everywhere I went. I bought a Victorian cannonball, a Ming jarlet with a wonderful blackberry and lily underglaze, a lizard-skin drum, an amazing Inro compartment with a swooping crane design, a lacquered rosewood tobacco boon, a Lalique *plique-à-jour* gold enamel necklace, a Fabergé carving of a mandrill, in jasper, and an extraordinary gold saddle-frame that was probably late seventeenth century.

The run ended at a flea market on the south side of Portland, in a delicate Oregon mist. As I wandered around, waiting for the mist to lighten just a little, I spotted an old couple sitting in green lawn chairs beside what was probably the rustiest pickup I had ever seen. It was a '48 Chevy without a speck of the original paint, or any paint, on it. It belonged in a Rust Museum, if there was such a thing, and I stopped for a moment, mainly to admire the pickup. The old man and the old woman were just sitting there in the mist, working their gums. They had laid out a miserable little display on the tailgate of the pickup and were apparently content with it. Their stock consisted of six or eight insulators, a few old tools, some fifties Coke bottles, and a little pottery. What wouldn't fit on the tailgate was on a rickety card table set between them.

"Howdy," I said. "I like your pickup."

"Yes sir," the old man said. "We like her too."

"I don't," the old woman said. "I been tryin' to get him to trade it in, but he won't. If we run it much longer we won't get no trade-in at all."

"She wants one of them with that power steering," the old man said, spitting a squirt of tobacco juice into the wet grass.

"Got anything good you're hiding?" I asked.

They studied me for a moment, trying to decide if I could be trusted to handle the good stuff.

"Got a box of Depression glass in the front seat," the old man said finally. "You can look if you'll be careful."

I had been neglecting my commission to buy Depression

glass for Momma Cullen, so I walked around and opened the pickup door. On top of the box of junky glass lay a dusty manila folder with a corner of something that looked like vellum sticking out. Just the sight of the vellum gave me a tingle of anticipation.

The folder contained a large leaf from a Moghul manuscript —a beautiful, delicate miniature showed a battle scene involving elephants. The elephants were surrounded by an army of small, stylized, but perfectly drawn people, their faces all calm despite the passion of the fight.

Some finds produce a stillness in you. Still, very still, was how I felt as I looked at the wonderful leaf, with its thin, elegant goldwork and its two tiny armies. After looking at it for several minutes I put it back in its folder and carried it and the box of glass back around to where the old couple were sitting.

"Nice glass," I said. "How much will you take for the whole box?"

"Three hunnert," the old woman said, without hesitation.

"How about this thing?" I asked, holding up the folder.

"Found that yesterday, down at Pleasant Hill," the old man said. "Hadn't priced it yet."

"We was thinking of giving it to our little granddaughter," the old woman said. "She likes elephants."

"I'd sure like to buy it," I said quietly. "That is unless you really have your heart set on giving it to her."

"Aw well," the old man said. "We could buy her some coloring books with elephants in them, couldn't we, Momma?"

"I guess so, Daddy," the old woman said. "That thing's got gold on it though. Must be worth something."

"Would you pay thirty-five dollars?" the old man asked.

I paid them the $35, plus $300 for the Depression glass. In the process I learned their names: they were the Haskells. The old lady told me all about her grandchildren as she carefully wrapped each piece of worthless glass in two layers of newspaper. She and the old man were wildly excited—this was their biggest day as flea marketers, ever.

I walked away feeling sad. The run was over. I didn't know what the Moghul leaf was worth, but it was worth a lot. In a way I had cheated the Haskells. I should have bought them a pickup with power steering.

But if I had, what balance would have been disturbed? The thrill of selling $335 worth in one day was in itself a thrill that would sustain them for years, that they could talk about, probably, for the rest of their lives. Paying them a fair price for the leaf might just as easily have destroyed them. They would never again have had a nice time, sitting in the mist in their lawn chairs, waiting for a sucker who might give $300 for a box of Depression glass. They had invited me to come by their home, next time I was in Oregon, and I said I would.

"If you're down in New Mexico, buy us some arty-facts," the old woman said. "Arty-facts still sell real good, up here."

A few months later I sold the Moghul leaf to a dealer in Memphis for $115,000. But that part of it seemed commonplace, not really exciting, either to me or to him.

When I left the flea market I drove all the way from Portland across to Montrose, Colorado—it was a Sunday night when I pulled off the road and hit a motel, in the shadows cast by the cold Rockies. Most of the drive I spent on the phone with Coffee, discussing various of her problems and trying to decide if we were up to a meeting. I had let Coffee's husky childish voice, talking endlessly, pull me slowly south and I was seriously thinking of paying her a quick visit before going back east to take the Arbers to Disney World.

As I was undressing to take a bath, I flipped on the television and was startled to see the freckled face of Uncle Ike Spettle fill the whole screen. Uncle Ike was working his gums, much as had old man Haskell back in Portland.

He was dressed in a clean white shirt and a $5 imitation-rawhide string tie. When the cameras rolled back a little I saw that he was in Cindy's gallery in Georgetown, being interviewed by Dan Rather.

Beside Uncle Ike, on a little pedestal, sat the boots of Billy

391

the Kid. They were under glass, or maybe under plexiglass, with a solid security guard with a pistol on his hip standing nearby.

I could hardly believe my good timing. The boot exhibition was happening, right before my eyes. Cowboy culture had come to the capital of the land and Dan Rather was there to tell us about it.

"Uncle Ike, how does it feel to be here in historic Georgetown?" he asked.

Uncle Ike worked his gums for a bit, eyeing the security guard skeptically.

"You reckon that boy can shoot?" he asked.

The cameras swung to the fat guard, who flinched visibly. He looked as if he would rather run than fight.

"And you're how old, sir?" Rather asked, struggling hard to get Uncle Ike to bring the past alive.

"I thought the President was comin'," Uncle Ike said. "If he is he's late, and if he ain't then he ain't gettin' my vote, the next time around."

"Heh, heh, the Democratic party will be glad to hear that, sir," Rather said. "We've been assured that the President *is* coming. However, this is quite a crowd, even without the President."

It was a clear signal for the crew to tour the crowd and get him away from the baleful old man.

After a second the crew got the message and the camera began to pan slowly around the crowd, pausing for a moment at Lesley Stahl, who was trying to get Yves St. Laurent and Ralph Lauren to comment on the many pairs of Twine boots spaced tastefully around the room, each in its own plexiglass cube. But the two designers didn't want to be caught using the same mike and slipped adroitly from pedestal to pedestal, boot to boot, smiling constantly but saying nothing.

It was obvious that Cindy had done a beautiful job of getting out the A-list, most of whom had donned Western garb for the occasion. Senator Penrose and his wife Pencil were there, both of them looking ridiculous in white chaps and big Stetsons. Lilah Landry had come as a Navaho and was wearing half her weight in squash-blossom jewelry. She stood in a corner talking to Ponsonby, who was in pinstripes. He stared with evident puzzlement at a pair of Mexican boots which stood on a pedestal beside him. All the boots had been highly polished for the occasion.

Oblivia Brown had come with Halston; he was in a tuxedo, while she wore designer denims. As they were chatting, George Psalmanazar wandered by wearing a corduroy suit and loafers.

A moment later I spotted Eviste, looking dapper in a red satin rodeo shirt; he was stalking a waiter who carried around a plate of pâté.

Old Cotswinkle, also in pinstripes, was glaring at Khaki Descartes, who had dressed Western even to wearing a brace of cap pistols. Cotswinkle glared into the camera a moment and then the camera wisely moved on and picked up his wife Cunny, who was chatting with Bill Blass.

Andy Warhol wandered up and stopped in front of the enigmatic Sir Cripps Crisp—Andy looked like himself and Sir Cripps was in white tie. As a waiter passed he adroitly snagged a fresh glass of champagne. Except for that one movement Sir Cripps was still as a statue.

Nearby, John Kenneth Galbraith was beaming serenely down at Arthur Schlesinger, Jr. Boog, Spud, and Freddy Fu were within eavesdropping distance, but weren't eavesdropping. Boog was done up in full Texas regalia—he looked like an overweight hillbilly singer.

Amanda Harisse, dressed severely in black, stood near one of the pillars, close enough that she could keep an eye on Uncle Ike. Amanda looked depressed.

Then, suddenly, heads began to turn, the camera turning with them. The President and the First Lady were coming through the door, surrounded by Secret Service men. They were in their best Santa Barbara Western-wear, they were smiling, they looked happy.

And there to greet them was Cindy, their sometime neighbor.

I had been waiting, expecting to see her, and still her

beauty caught me unprepared. Instead of dressing Western she had dressed Spanish, in the white dress that bared one shoulder. She wore a silver necklace, an antique concho belt, and a look of complete satisfaction. Her hair shone, her eyes were bright—in her freshness, youth, and health she made the President look suddenly leathery, the First Lady distinctly frail.

Indeed, she was so beautiful I felt the tears start: I didn't really see the President and First Lady greet Uncle Ike, or hear what they said to one another. Cindy stood to one side, serene in her moment, the summit finally won. For a moment it didn't matter that Jean was good, that Josie was generous, that Tanya Todd had a brain that worked at the speed of light. I knew Cindy's beauty was unearned, responsible to nothing, unaware. It didn't matter. I began to fantasize things that might happen—things that might bring her back. Then, not wanting to see her anymore if I couldn't have her, I clicked the TV off, only to click it back on a few seconds later, hoping to see her some more.

But Cindy was no longer in the picture. Josie Twine was in the picture, speaking to Dan Rather. She was decked out in a yellow cowgirl suit and new Tony Lamas, and looked right in them. She had dyed her hair a nice red and looked a lot more sophisticated than she had when I left, only three weeks before.

"Why yes," she said, "every one of these boots was used right there on the Twine ranch in Wichita County, Texas. Some was Big Joe's and some was his daddy's before him.

"Ain't you from Texas?" she asked, glancing at Dan's feet, which were in shoes.

"Yes indeed, Houston," Dan said quickly, turning back to Uncle Ike, who was still keeping an eye on the nervous security guard.

"It's a good thing the P.L.O. never tried nothing," Uncle Ike said. "I doubt that fat boy could hit the side of a barn with that hog-leg."

"Well, I don't think we need to worry about the P.L.O.," Dan said. The crush in the gallery had gotten worse, but the

President was gone and it was plain Dan felt it was time to wind things up.

"You must be pretty excited, Uncle Ike," he said. "Coming all this way at your age, and getting to meet the President."

Uncle Ike did not look excited.

"Well, he ain't no John 'Duke' Wayne," Uncle Ike said. "I knew the Duke. Me and him did a talk show in Albuquerque once. Nice fellow. Didn't know much about the Kid, though."

Then—one media legend to another—he reached up a freckled old hand and caught Dan's sleeve.

"Dan, see if you can catch that boy that's carrying around the goose-liver," he said. "See if you can get him over here. They run a little light on the vittles, up here in Washington, D.C."